LAWLESS HEARTS

BOOK 5, STEAM! ROMANCE & RAILS

E.E. BURKE

Cover Design by Erin Dameron-Hill

Train photography by Matthew Malkiewicz

Published by E.E. Burke

ebook ISBN: 978-1-956023-06-0

Paperback ISBN 978-1-956023-07-7

www.eeburke.com

CHAPTER 1

June 1, 1874, Parsons, Kansas

The tin roof on the saloon across from the sheriff's office caught a sunbeam and sent its glare into Jasper's eyes. He squinted, unable to shield his face, being handcuffed and chained.

"Look! It's Byrne!" someone yelled. "Filthy outlaw!"

A chunk of mud or manure struck Jasper's cheek. He didn't see who, among the crowd gathered in the street, hurled the clod or the insult, but he would give them no satisfaction.

"Thank you, folks, for coming out to see me off. Sure didn't expect a parade. You outdid yourselves."

The lawman at the other end of the chain gave a hard yank on the manacles. "Shut up and get in the cart."

U.S. Deputy Marshal Stokes put on a good show, too. He'd been sent to transport *a vile and dangerous outlaw* to the federal court in Arkansas to stand trial for robbing a train, and, by God, he'd show everyone how brave he could be against a man whose wrists and ankles were shackled.

Jasper did his damnedest to maintain his dignity while he used his elbows to pull himself onto the open bed of a horse-drawn cart. A

1

rock struck wood an inch from his face. He jerked, losing what little leverage he'd gained, and slid off the back.

The crowd roared with laughter.

Several railroad workers pressed so close Jasper could smell the smoke and oil on their clothes. One of them called for a rope. Someone grasped the shackles around his ankles.

Panicked, he kicked out.

A soft "ow" in a decidedly feminine voice made him pause. Whoever was behind him tried again, this time lifting his legs. *Helping* him.

Jasper heaved himself into the back of the cart and twisted to see who'd done him the kindness.

A woman. Youngish, gray dress, spectacles. Why had a schoolmarm waded into the middle of this bloodthirsty crowd to aid him?

The marshal blocked Jasper's view. "Get back, lady! Are you crazy?"

"Not at all, sir. I am a reporter, Alice Robb, from the *New York Daily Graph.*"

"I don't care if you're the Virgin Mary. Get away from my prisoner." Stokes bellowed.

After the marshal moved to climb into the driver's seat, Jasper searched for the red-headed woman. She'd been swallowed up in the crowd. God forbid that one of these men harm her for doing nothing more than a good deed.

Stokes cracked a whip and the cart lurched forward. The motion threw Jasper against one side. A sharp pain made him catch his breath. The guards who'd retrieved him from a bare cell behind the sheriff's office had knocked him down and kicked him in the ribs. They wouldn't have gotten away with the abuse had the previous sheriff, Frank Garrity, been in charge. Things had changed since the day he'd turned in his badge over a month ago. None for the better.

Jasper warily surveyed the crowd that followed the slow-moving cart. Ogling open-mouthed curiosity-seekers. Sneering self-righteous settlers. Resentful railroad workers. He didn't see a single soul who cared about him.

He'd half-expected that rascal Billy to show up and make good on his boast to attempt a rescue. Thankfully, the boy's new folks had the good sense to keep him away. Jasper felt nothing but relief. His first mistake had been getting involved in an orphan's problems, followed by his second mistake, giving a damn. He wouldn't have been captured if he hadn't saved Billy from a bullet. For that singular act, he wasn't sorry. He reserved his regrets for the things he'd done wrong.

His stomach lurched when Stokes brought the horse to a stop in front of the railroad depot where more angry townspeople had gathered.

From out of the crowd popped the reporter, Miss Robb. She pulled a pencil from a frizzy bun that tilted to one side of her head. "Marshal Stokes, I am here to do a profile on—"

"No comment," Stokes snapped. He thrust the woman out of his way before he used the chain to drag Jasper out of the cart, dumping him into the muddy street. On purpose, no doubt.

"Here, we'll help you," one of the observers offered with a smirk.

"*Help*, my ass," Jasper said under his breath.

More men, a few women, and even a couple of kids gathered around. They grabbed at him and snatched at his clothes. One of them tore his coat. Another yanked out some of his hair. Were they collecting souvenirs to show their friends?

"All right. Back off!" Stokes boomed. "Let me do my job."

What was that? Pulling on a chain?

Jasper struggled to his feet. He clanked behind the marshal, as fast as the shackles allowed, toward the arched doors leading into the railroad station. If he didn't keep moving, this rabid pack would tear him apart. They might intend to sell him in pieces to the circus.

These same good folks had paid for tickets to view the severed head of an infamous *bandito* when it had traveled through town, displayed inside a jar filled with formaldehyde.

Inside the depot, more jeering townspeople and railroad

employees waited. The marble floors and tall ceilings made their voices swell into an eerie echo.

"Give him to us! We'll hang him from a telegraph pole. Save you the cost of transport!"

"The accused has the right to a trial!" shouted the lady reporter.

"Not a thieving half-breed!" another man hollered.

Rights were reserved for white men, Jasper would inform Miss Robb if he could find her in this crowd. He'd also tell her his Cherokee grandfather was the most honest man he'd ever known, and his mother was the kindest woman. His white father had told him to be proud of his heritage. He was proud. Proud of half of it.

Stokes yanked on the chain again.

"Malicious sonofabitch," Jasper grumbled.

By the time Jasper exited the back of the building, his clothes were damp with sweat. At the edge of the platform, a waiting locomotive sent lazy puffs into the air. Engine Number 4 happened to be the same engine that had pulled the last train he'd robbed. The same engine would take him to face the consequences of his actions. Under other circumstances, he'd find the irony amusing.

The crowd along the tracks, only slightly better behaved than the previous mob, made way for the armed lawman when he headed in the direction of the freight cars.

The reporter appeared in Jasper's peripheral vision. "Excuse me, sir. May I ask you some questions?"

"You're more determined than a hound dog," Jasper said, with utmost sincerity.

"Thank you." She smiled, revealing long front teeth, which protruded over her lower lip.

"Lady, I said get back!" Stokes hollered, giving another hard yank on the chain. "This here's a dangerous outlaw. He'd as soon cut your throat as answer your questions."

"I haven't cut anyone's throat," Jasper told the startled woman, then cast a meaningful look in the direction of his tormenter. "Yet."

Stokes made a growling sound. If he pulled on that chain one more time, they'd go down together. Jasper narrowed his eyes in a silent dare.

"If he's so dangerous, how did you catch him?" The lady reporter's question broke the tense silence.

The marshal huffed a disdainful laugh. "Didn't have to. A twelve-year-old boy nabbed him."

Jasper corrected the mistake. "A deputy arrested me after I led the sheriff on a chase through town. The boy got in the way. If you want details, you can read about it."

Local newspapers had covered the fiasco with multiple stories, in which he'd gone from villain to hero then back to villain. To be fair, he'd only partly earned his fierce reputation. Much of the credit went to the reporters, who routinely exaggerated his *violent past, heathen proclivities,* and *pygmy stature.* That last label, in particular, was patently false, as well as infuriating.

"Here's the deal, lady. I'll give you an interview if you fix a mistake," he told her.

"What mistake?" Her wide-eyed curiosity tugged at his own.

Was she interested in the truth? He doubted it, but why not test her to find out?

"My stature." Jasper straightened. "As you can see, I'm as tall as the marshal, and no one calls him a *pygmy.*"

The woman nudged her spectacles upward. "I do believe you may be taller—"

"That's all." Stokes thundered. "Now leave."

Jasper followed the marshal rather than tolerate being pulled along. The reporter fell behind or gave up. He could no longer see her by the time he reached a line of cattle cars, most of which were empty for the trip south to Texas.

Stokes stopped in front of an open car. "Get in."

Jasper grudgingly shuffled up the ramp. No good could come from tangling with this lawman. He'd take his chance with a marshal rather than a mob.

The freight car had recently held chickens, based on the sharp odor and bird droppings. Dirty straw had been pushed into a pile in front of a stack of empty crates. It would be a perfect place to hide.

Was escape possible? Jasper considered it. He'd have to get his hands and feet free and slip away from the lawman. He couldn't accomplish either without help. Thus far, no one had shown up. It might be because he'd instructed the only people who might try to save him to stay away.

The marshal dragged Jasper over to the wall and chained him to a reinforced iron ring meant for animals. After securing a padlock, Stokes put the key into his coat pocket. He stepped back and pinched his nose. "Whew. You're lucky there were only chickens in here. Your kind belongs with the *pigs*."

Fat-ass Stokes had no cause to brag. The full mustache he was so fond of stroking didn't hide enough of his ugly face, and he stunk worse than sour mash.

One of the railroad workers outside lifted a chair into the car.

"Looks like I'll be riding with a pig after all," Jasper muttered.

"What did you say?" Stokes demanded.

"Nothing worth repeating." Jasper reminded himself to watch his tongue or he might not arrive in Fort Smith with his teeth intact.

For a decade, he'd evaded the U.S. deputy marshals, who had chased him from one end of Indian Territory to the other. This one appeared to have taken it personally.

The door to the car closed with a bang. Stokes lowered a bar to lock it from the inside, which would keep out anyone who might try to break in when the train made stops.

Jasper's hope for escape dwindled.

He put his nose close to an opening between the slats, which let in daylight and fresher air. Once the train started moving, the wind would blow inside and relieve the heat.

The lawman grumbled some more about *the stink* while he situated his bulk onto the spindly-legged chair. He withdrew a flask, uncorked it, then slipped it beneath his full mustache to take a drink.

Jasper licked his cracked lips. They hadn't even given him water for the better part of the day.

Stokes waggled the flask. "Want some whiskey?"

"Sure."

He turned it upside down. "Empty. Too bad." The cruel bastard laughed as he returned the flask to his coat pocket.

Moments later, a whistle sounded.

Slowly the train pulled out, then with increasing speed. The town of Parsons slid past. A short time later, they passed a field with rows of budding green stalks. After a bit, the prairie took over. The scent of buffalo grass heated by the sun stirred a deep longing as Jasper watched freedom pass him by.

He had planned every single job he'd done down to the last detail. He'd even planned how his final trip to Parsons would've gone —if Billy hadn't come after him. But his strategy to escape the consequences of his actions had failed because no one believed an outlaw over a rich railroad executive. Now, ready or not, the day of reckoning had come.

JASPER GREW drowsy from the heat and steady rumbling of the train.

The rhythmic noise and warmth, and the whiskey, had already put the marshal to sleep. His chin rested on his chest as he dozed. Why should he worry? His prisoner couldn't go anywhere.

A soft scrape arrested Jasper's attention. It sounded like it came from behind the crates where the straw had been piled up. Could be rats. He held still, listening for sounds other than the clacking of the wheels on the tracks.

After a moment, another rustle. Then, a loud sneeze.

Stokes jerked awake. He frowned at Jasper, apparently mistaking where the sound had come from and assuming his prisoner had woken him.

Jasper rubbed his nose on his sleeve. He wouldn't give away whoever had taken refuge in the car. It was probably just a bum, not one of his men. Even slow-thinking Candy would know better than to give away his hiding place.

A bump came from behind the crates, followed by a soft "darn it," in a vaguely familiar feminine voice.

The marshal scrambled to his feet and drew his gun. "Make yourself known. Fast."

"Don't shoot!" The crates shifted. From behind them emerged a skinny woman in a gray dress. Bits of straw clung to her hair, which stuck out in red corkscrews.

Jasper released a soft laugh of pure amazement. It was that lady reporter! She had been behind them earlier, yet she'd somehow managed to slip past and board without being seen.

"You!" Stokes bellowed.

"Yes...it's me, Miss Robb." Her round spectacles slid to the end of her nose. "I'm sorry if I startled you." She shifted the crates with her hip while holding her hands high, clutching a notebook in one and a tapestry purse in the other. "As you intended to ignore my request, I was forced to take extreme measures."

Jasper couldn't decide whether she was brave or crazy...or both. "You must really want that interview."

The marshal's face turned blotchy. His black mustache worked up and down like he was chewing or getting ready to spit. "Lady, you are under arrest."

"Why?" She lowered her hands, taking a moment to nudge her spectacles into place. "I paid the fare."

"Was it for passage in a freight car?" Jasper inquired.

"*You*, shut up. And you, lady, get over here." Stokes brought his arm down without removing his finger from the trigger.

He might be considering shooting one of them and hadn't decided which one yet.

"She doesn't look very dangerous," Jasper pointed out.

Miss Robb inched closer to the lawman, darting Jasper a curious look, which he met with equal curiosity. "If I might be allowed to speak—"

"You aren't allowed anything, except a one-way ticket to jail after this train stops." Stokes holstered his gun. He snatched the reporter's notebook away from her. "Sit down."

After adjusting his gun belt, he plopped his ass onto the only chair instead of offering it to her. "I've got nothing to say to you."

"That's fine. I don't want to interview *you*," she replied pertly.

Jasper fought a smile. Damn, but she had grit, even for a reporter. He'd never met a female in the profession. Maybe they were plentiful in New York. Wasn't that where she'd said she was from? Her clipped accent had a distinctly Northern tone.

He gestured with his chin to the dirty floor. "You can sit next to me, Miss Robb."

"Not too close," Stokes warned.

When Jasper shifted his position, the chain holding his arms clinked. "He must be worried that you know how to pick a lock."

Miss Robb frowned at him.

Well, all right. It was a bad joke under the circumstances. Stokes was already annoyed with her. "I'm kidding, of course."

"Of course." She swept her skirt to one side and sat down. When she curled her legs beneath her, it gave him a glimpse of red lace. A whore's undergarments beneath a spinster's dress.

Jasper found her whimsy amusing and a little intriguing. Her figure wasn't bad, if somewhat scrawny. Sadly, Miss Robb would never win a beauty contest. His mother would've called her looks *unfortunate.* Her best features were her smooth skin and golden-brown eyes, which sparkled with curiosity and mischief. Maybe that was it. He liked her personality.

Since when had he cared about a woman's *personality*? He steered clear of relationships that lasted longer than it took to get in and out of bed.

"I have so many questions, I hardly know where to start." She pulled her purse into her lap, keeping her hand over it.

The marshal noticed her furtive movement. She'd made it too obvious.

"How long have you been robbing trains?" she asked Jasper.

He gave her the easy answer, and a correct one, for the most part. "Ever since a Katy railroad executive hired me to do the jobs. His name's William Bond. Called himself Mr. Smith when I met him."

9

Stokes guffawed. "Don't pay Byrne any mind. He's been stealing ever since his mama weaned him off the tit."

Jasper simmered. It was men like Stokes who'd put him on this path in the first place. Men in authority who'd been only too happy to act on their prejudices. "Why don't you interview the marshal about his activities during the war? Ask him how many women he raped."

"Why you..." Stokes came off the chair, red-faced, and nearly tripped over the reporter. When she ducked to avoid being stomped on, he took hold of her arm and dragged her a few feet. "Byrne's a liar and a thief. Why do you want to print anything he has to say?"

She jerked her arm free in a surprising show of strength for someone who looked like a stiff wind might blow her away. "I'd be happy to hear about your exploits, Marshal. After I'm done with Mr. Byrne's interview."

"You're done now." Stokes confiscated her purse. "What are you hiding?"

He dug through the little bag and laughed as he withdrew a silver flask. "Well, now. What have we got here?" After he unscrewed the top, he smelled it. "Whiskey?"

Her cheeks turned a shade closer to the color of her hair. "It's for medicinal purposes. When my head hurts."

She reached out, but Stokes withheld the flask from her.

"Oh dear, I feel a headache coming on." He took a long swig, then wiped the back of his hand across his mustache. "It's got a kick."

"Don't drink it all," she complained.

The marshal finished the contents. He burped—more for effect, it seemed—before dropping the empty flask into her purse and offering it to her like he'd done her a favor.

"My notebook?" she asked in a frosty tone.

He tossed the last item at her, then he leaned back in the chair with his arms crossed. "Your medicine must be working. I'm feeling less aggravated already."

Jasper clenched his fists. If it spoke in her defense, it would only encourage the marshal's cruelty.

Miss Robb tucked the flask into her bag and turned her attention to Jasper. Whatever annoyance she felt at the marshal's rudeness didn't show on her face. "We have a lot to discuss, Mr. Byrne."

"Do we?" He prepared himself for the usual questions. How many men had he murdered? *None.* He'd only killed men in battle, and that was years ago. Since then, his name had been brought up in connection with numerous killings. He hadn't bothered to correct the misperceptions. Being feared had its benefits. It also had disadvantages. "Whatever I say won't matter anyway."

She lifted her pencil and balanced the notebook on her thigh. "Why do you think that?"

Only a few people had believed his sworn statement to be the truth. None of them had the power to grant him his freedom or to make sure justice was done. And his experience with other reporters hadn't been helpful. "Your sort writes whatever you want to. Generally peppered with words like *bloodthirsty* and *savage.*"

"Are you saying you don't deserve either of those adjectives?"

What he deserved had nothing to do with it. His foray into crime had started from necessity. Most of what he'd taken had gone to people who needed the resources more than those who had them. He could tell her this, but it wasn't what she wanted to hear.

Jasper shrugged. "The truth doesn't sell papers."

"We'll be pulling into Chetopa soon," The marshal slurred the name of the town. "You might get a good story there. The railroad boys are keen to give our train robber a proper send-off."

He gave a low chuckle that sent a quiver of alarm through Jasper. Was it the whiskey talking or did Stokes know something was about to happen?

Jasper peered between the slats. If a lynch mob wanted to nab him, Chetopa would be the place to do it. Once the train crossed the border, they would be passing through Cherokee land. The inhabitants there didn't like the railroad and liked white lynch mobs even less. If he could escape into the territory...

Miss Robb tapped her pencil on her notebook. "I am curious about something. How well do you know your way around Indian Territory?"

Had she read his mind?

"Well enough," he answered, acting disinterested. "I grew up there."

"True." She seemed pleased he'd passed her quiz. "And you've hidden out there for the past ten years."

The lady reporter had done her research. To what end, he couldn't guess. "So?"

"Why would a Cherokee citizen wanted for train robbery leave the relative safety of his tribal lands to come north into Kansas to a railroad headquarters town? Why risk it?"

He shifted to find a more comfortable position to ease the pressure on his aching side. His discomfort wasn't only physical. Her prying made him uneasy. "If you want to know what happened, read the sheriff's report."

"Yes. I did read it. The newspaper reports state that you abducted a twelve-year-old runaway after you found him hiding on a train you'd robbed. The boy escaped and you followed him."

Jasper huffed. "See what I mean? Why bother to tell the truth when no one believes it?"

"I didn't say I wouldn't believe the truth."

The truth wasn't important to most folks. They wanted to read something exciting or scary, especially if it supported judgments they'd already made.

On the other hand, Miss Robb had shown compassion. Maybe she'd be open-minded. He would offer her the truth and see what she did with it.

"I didn't abduct Billy," Jasper started with the most important part. "He'd run away from home. It was pretty clear he was lost, scared and hungry. I invited him to stay with me and he did. And he reported those same facts. The newspaper accounts spiced it up."

Miss Robb held Jasper's gaze with disconcerting directness. "You sympathized with Billy Frye because you know how it feels to be maligned and misunderstood. Alone."

Even if that was *the truth*, he'd never admit to being a tenderhearted sap. That was worse than folks thinking he was a cold-blooded killer.

"You've got a good imagination. I found out his guardians had offered a reward. Four hundred dollars. Good money for *my kind*," he said, with the same tone of derision he'd heard all his life. "I figured I could arrange the exchange in Parsons."

Surprisingly, Stokes hadn't chimed in with a snide remark. It appeared he'd dozed off again.

Miss Robb didn't spare the marshal a second glance. "I see..." She jotted something in her notebook. "The child was worth four hundred dollars, which explains why you threw yourself on top of him when you thought he might be hit by a bullet intended for you. To preserve your reward money."

Put that way, it sounded mercenary. An improvement over mushy.

Jasper acknowledged to himself that he had a soft spot when it came to Billy. After taking the boy in, something in his soul had shifted. He wasn't sure exactly why his conscience reawakened, but it was a hell of an inconvenience.

"Mr. Byrne, if you could start over, would you do things differently?"

Jasper released a pent-up breath. The lady reporter wasn't interested in his opinions. She wanted to write one of those *moralistic* stories. It should come as no surprise. Woeful tales sold like hotcakes. He didn't care what she wrote. At this point, he just wanted to end this uncomfortable interview.

"If I got a second chance? Sure, I'd try to do the right thing. You want to help me?" He was only half-joking. If vigilantes showed up, he'd need all the help he could get.

"Are you a man of your word?"

He couldn't fathom what had prompted that question. "I don't break my promises if that's what you mean."

"I'm glad to hear it." She threw a glance over her shoulder at the dozing marshal. "We may need to trust one another very soon."

The chair scraped as it turned over, dumping Stokes onto the floor of the railcar with a heavy thump. The big idiot had fallen asleep and toppled over.

Jasper held his breath. In a second, the lawman would jump up and start cussing him out for giving such a boring interview. But Stokes remained sprawled on his back. After a moment, he snored.

What the hell? He hadn't downed enough liquor to render him senseless.

Incredulous, Jasper turned to the woman sitting in front of him, who calmly put her pencil and notebook back into her bag. "What was in that flask?"

"It cured his headache," Miss Robb said dryly. "Where does he keep his keys?"

Outrageous as it seemed, the reporter had planned this. What Jasper couldn't figure out was why. "Look in his pocket," he directed her.

She scrambled to her feet and retrieved the marshal's key ring, then she proceeded to unlock the shackles around Jasper's ankles and remove the padlock from the chain that held him. "We have to make haste. As soon as the train stops, I'll open the door."

Jasper heaved a huge sigh of relief. His old friends hadn't abandoned him. They'd hired help. "Who sent you after me?"

A whistle sounded, signaling the locomotive's arrival at the station.

"I'll explain when we have more time."

"Right." Jasper extended his manacled wrists for her to unlock. The tortuous cuffs dropped with a clank to the floor. Before he could get to the unconscious marshal to disarm him, she'd retrieved the lawman's revolver.

"I'll keep this." She gripped the handle and pointed the gun at Jasper.

Confusion rendered him speechless. He might've misread this situation. What if she wasn't aiding his escape? What if she was part of the plan to lynch him? That would certainly sell newspapers.

A loud squeal sounded and the train began to slow. "When the train stops, do exactly as I say."

He could wrestle the gun away from her. She might get hurt. Maybe he'd just run. Or was that what she wanted him to do, then she'd shoot him in the back?

"How do I know you aren't leading me into a trap?"

"Remember what I said? You'll have to trust me."

If he'd given his trust to everyone who'd asked for it, he wouldn't have lived this long.

"Put that gun down first."

Miss Robb tucked the revolver into her bag. "Don't disappoint me."

He'd disappointed most of the people in his life. Why should she be any different?

As the train came to a stop, she lifted the bar and slid the door open. "Jump. I'll be right behind you."

He didn't need instruction to get off the train. Or to remain quiet when he dropped into a squat next to the tracks.

Down on the platform near the locomotive, a large group of men had gathered. One of them carried a wound length of rope over his shoulder.

A lynch mob.

Jasper's blood froze. The men hadn't looked this way yet, but it wouldn't be long before they noticed him. If he ran, it would draw their attention and they'd start shooting and might hit the lady reporter by mistake.

She knelt down next to him. "I put handcuffs on the marshal," she said in a low voice. "That'll keep them busy for a while. Come with me." She motioned for Jasper to follow before she ducked underneath the stationary train.

Generally, *he* was the one who made plans and gave orders. He wasn't used to following instructions blindly. Still, it made sense to escape beneath the waiting train rather than stay in clear view of those men waiting to hang him.

Underneath the train he went, crawling over the track and in between the ties. Gravel dug into his palms and the drifting smoke stung his eyes. When he came out on the other side, he spotted a horse grazing in a field not far from the tracks.

The lady reporter grabbed his sleeve as if she'd read his mind. "No! Don't try it. Come with me. I have a plan."

Of course she did. She had more tricks up her sleeve than a magician.

"Does it involve doctored whiskey?" he asked.

She pulled him along to an adjacent box car. "Quick. Open the door and get inside."

Back on the train? *Uh, nope.* Those vigilantes would soon find the sheriff passed out and his prisoner missing, and they'd fan out in a search, including the train.

Miss Robb moved behind him as if she expected him to bolt. "Those men will kill you before you cross the border. I know how to get us out of here without a lot of fuss. But you must trust me."

"Trust you?" he said over his shoulder. "Why should I?"

"I'm a friend."

"I don't have friends."

"Well, I'm not an enemy. Now hurry, unless you want those men to find us."

Miss Robb had broken the law by aiding his escape, which meant she was at risk, too.

He climbed up the side of the freight car and unlatched the door, pushing it open. Once inside the car, he stared in confusion at a plain pine coffin. What kind of plan was this?

"I need a hand into the car," she called in a loud whisper.

Jasper squatted to grasp her arms. Her weight, more than he thought it would be, triggered painful spasms in his side. He gritted his teeth rather than groan out loud.

"I think stealing a horse is a better idea," he told her after he'd gotten her inside.

"Until they see you and shoot you." She pulled the door closed.

Enough light filtered through the boards for him to be able to see. She opened the coffin lid and withdrew a black dress, bonnet, and veil. Nothing of much use. Like another gun.

"What's that for?" he asked.

"It's mourning attire." Without further explanation, she stripped out of her jacket and dropped her skirt.

Miss Robb wasn't scrawny. Her lithe form fueled Jasper's imagination about what her body might look like beneath the lacy underclothes. She'd be sleek as a thoroughbred.

She jerked the black gown up and drew it over her head. "Stop gawking," she scolded. "Have you never seen a woman get dressed?"

"Not exactly like this," he confessed. "Mostly they *un*dressed. I wasn't as interested in what they did with their clothes later."

She rolled the gray dress and stuffed it into the coffin. Afterward, she put on her bonnet and then lowered the veil.

"Get in," she ordered.

"In the coffin?" His heart kicked against his chest. "Is your plan to bury me?"

His half-hearted joke elicited a grim smile. "Not unless you get caught and hanged. The freight handlers will be here soon."

"What about you? Where are you going?"

"I'll be close. Stay quiet until I open the lid."

Whatever her goal, she had come up with an elaborate ruse to help him escape. Having no better plan, he'd put his faith in hers. For the moment.

Jasper stretched out inside the coffin. It smelled like freshly cut pine. "Did you buy this or steal it?"

Rather than answer, she closed the lid, casting him into darkness. "There are two small holes in the side. You won't suffocate."

He turned his head and located the holes and sucked in air.

A rumbling sound...the door, closing. Had she locked him in?

Jasper fought an urge to throw open the lid and take his chances alone. Every nerve in his body screamed, *get out!*

Stay calm. Think.

Those vigilantes would be looking for him. Open fields offered no cover. They would have a clear shot before he could get away. No one would know yet that a woman had aided his escape. They wouldn't be looking for Miss Robb. Even if the sheriff had come to his senses enough to describe her, the red-headed reporter in a gray dress had transformed into a grieving widow covered from head to toe in black.

Doubt infested his mind. Why would a reporter help him escape? Had someone bribed her? Candy didn't have the brains to conceive a scheme this elaborate. No, it seemed more like something Tom Bluejacket might've come up with...if he stayed sober long enough to plan it. The last event Tom had planned was a trip to Arkansas to purchase moonshine.

Jasper shifted to find a more comfortable position. There wasn't one. Coffins weren't made for comfort.

He froze at the muted voices coming from outside. The door rumbled open. Light shone through the holes drilled in the side of the coffin.

"Yes, that's it..."

Miss Robb's voice, though it sounded different. Not Northern.

"That coffin holds the earthly remains of my blessed Horace," she wailed. "Be careful when y'all move him."

A Southern twang, and a good one at that. Stokes would remember a woman who talked like a Yankee. These men would recall a Southern gal. Miss Robb was talented and quick-witted. Most men weren't half as clever.

As the coffin lifted, Jasper jerked. He tried to keep from rolling while the box was transferred. Thank God they hadn't taken him out head first or dropped him.

The movers slid the coffin across a surface. The jangle of a harness told Jasper where he'd been placed. The bed of a wagon. His rescuer must've arranged to have one rented and ready to go. No one in his gang, including him, would've come up with this crazy scheme.

"What's in there?" a male voice shouted.

"My darlin' Horace. He perished from *typhoid*. I'm bringing him home to bury him."

She sounded weepy, convincing. Fear of catching typhoid ought to keep anyone from opening the lid. If they did, he'd come out fighting. Deny he knew her.

Jasper tensed.

"Condolences, ma'am," came the gruff reply. "Be careful. A dangerous outlaw escaped off the train. He's a mean devil."

"Thank you." She sniffed, then blew her nose, loudly. "You don't think he'd steal my husband's remains, do you?"

"No ma'am. Far as we know, he's not one of them body-snatchers."

"I hope you find the scoundrel," she replied in a blithe tone.

"Oh, we will," the man replied. "And when we do, we'll hang him. If you see anything, let us know. There'll be a reward in it for you."

Sweat trickled into Jasper's eyes, stinging. The temptation of money might change her mind about giving him up. One thing he knew for certain. Everyone had their price.

CHAPTER 2

*B*rigit Stevens clucked to the mules pulling the wagon and directed them to a dirt road alongside the tracks. A glance over her shoulder revealed the vigilantes had moved on to check inside the freight car she'd just abandoned. Her heart beat a wild staccato.

She'd made a timely escape with her outlaw. Those men might've decided to check inside the coffin, had they not encountered a weeping widow.

Singing would calm her nerves, as well as throw off anyone who might think twice about her. Sacred songs or ballads would be appropriate in this instance. Other situations called for bawdy tunes. She recalled a nice hymn that would reinforce her pretense while giving Mr. Byrne some reassurance.

"Shall we gather at the river where bright angel feet have trod? With its crystal tide forever flowing by the throne of God..." Brigit sang out while she set a brisk pace south on the road leading south, past carts and loaded wagons, men on horseback, and local settlers.

Every time the wheels struck a rut, the coffin behind her bumped. She didn't stop to retrieve a handkerchief to wipe away the sweat on her face, and prayed Mr. Byrne wasn't suffering too much with the heat and bumpy ride. He needed to remain in the coffin until they were safely away.

By the time she finished the third verse of the hymn, she noticed fewer wagons and men on horseback.

Thus far, everything had gone according to plan. The ruse had worked. Her sister, Hannah, had ridden the train to Chetopa as a grieving widow accompanying her husband's body. Donning widow's weeds, Brigit had collected the coffin. Hannah would return to Parsons disguised as Miss Robb. It wasn't the first time the two of them had worked together to fool observers. Their mentor, Kate Warne, had recognized the benefit of recruiting identical twins as undercover agents for the Pinkerton Agency.

Unfortunately, Mrs. Warne had died a few years after hiring them. Mr. Pinkerton's sons, who weren't nearly as forward-thinking as their father or as smart, had taken over day-to-day management. They had assigned the female detectives to desk jobs. Women who had once protected the President doing *desk jobs!* Those men would soon change their tune when two women cracked a case no one else had been able to solve.

At length, Brigit passed a railroad shack with a sign staked next to it, marking the Kansas border with lands assigned to the Indian nations. Nothing about the topography looked different. It was still prairie dotted with clusters of trees huddled around water sources. But here across the border, lawlessness reigned.

A fissure of fear sent a wave of chills over her damp skin.

She started humming. If she had let fear overcome her in the past, she wouldn't have made it six months, much less ten years, as a Pinkerton detective.

Brigit glanced at the sun directly overhead. In a few hours, that arrogant U.S. Deputy Marshal would awaken with a raging headache, thanks to the chloral hydrate he'd consumed, along with the *medicinal* whiskey. Stokes would be in no condition to launch a search before tomorrow, which gave her at least a day's head start.

The outlaw she'd stolen had, thus far, cooperated. But he wouldn't remain in that pine box much longer. He'd be hot, thirsty, and impatient for answers. He believed her to be a reporter. She would continue the charade, which served her purposes and wouldn't scare him off. She'd used the role in the past, although she usually posed as a columnist for women's magazines and cozied up to suspects' wives rather than outlaws.

Near a forested glade, Brigit veered off the road. The land dipped then sloped down to a clear stream, one of the countless spring-fed creeks that flowed through Cherokee land. Other than birds and a babbling brook, she didn't hear or see anything. This was as safe a place as any to stop for rest and water. She drew the team to a halt at a spot where the mules could get a drink then lifted the black veil over her bonnet for much-needed fresh air.

Brigit tucked the marshal's revolver under the seat where it would be within easy reach. She climbed into the wagon bed and heaved the heavy coffin lid to one side. "All right. You can get out now."

The prone man blinked in the sunlight filtering through the leafy canopy overhead. His eyes went from black to the color of mature pine needles. Not brown, as she'd originally thought. The black bristle on his lean cheeks glistened with sweat. He moved as if his muscles and joints objected.

"Where are we?" His voice sounded raspier than before. It could be from a lack of water, or he might be suffering from some ailment.

God forbid. She needed a healthy man, not an invalid.

"We are at the river." She smiled at her cleverness. "Technically, this is a creek, but if the railroad map is correct, it flows into the Grand. Were you not paying attention to the hymn I sang? *Shall We Gather At The River?* I thought you might figure out where I was taking you."

He crawled out of the coffin. "Is that why you kept on with that infernal tune?"

Rather an ungrateful reaction after being snatched from the jaws of death.

"You didn't like my singing? Most people compliment it." She hopped down to the grass, undaunted. "It doesn't bother me if you don't appreciate my voice. However, I don't think it's too much to ask for a word of thanks."

"For a song?"

"For being rescued would suffice. You might remark on the brilliance of my plan."

He responded with a grunt. His expression remained taut as he lowered himself out of the wagon and walked stiffly to the creek.

Ah, now she understood. "Are you in pain?"

He sank to his knees and scooped a handful of cold water to drink. After he'd quenched his thirst, perhaps he would answer.

Brigit removed her hat and veil and left them on the seat before she made her way down the bank. She crouched close enough to the edge of the water to cup a handful to drink.

Her scalp itched, but she couldn't risk scratching it. Hot as the wig was, these false teeth were worse. They made her gums hurt. Still, this was one of her best disguises. An ugly woman didn't draw unwanted attention.

The outlaw peeled off a filthy coat and an equally dirty shirt. He then proceeded to dunk his head in the water and splash it on his chest. His skin was the color of tanned leather and looked just as smooth and supple.

He had a young man's body. His eyes, however, reflected an old soul. Cynical. Distrustful. Solitary. The condition of his soul wasn't pertinent to her investigation, but having an understanding of what made him tick would be crucial for her survival.

She tried to prompt a conversation. "The breeze feels good."

His response was to nod. After peppering her with questions *while* they were trying to escape, now, when it was safe, he'd gone mute.

He removed a dirty bandana from around his neck and rinsed it in the creek. Using his shirt, he dried his torso. Lean muscle, without an ounce of fat.

The observation in her head translated to shivers over her skin. It didn't feel like a reaction to danger. Those shivers felt cold. These were warm, strangely exhilarating...and very disturbing. The sooner he got dressed, the better.

"Don't bother putting on those filthy rags." She retreated to the wagon, where she retrieved the suitcase Hannah had packed with men's underclothing, a black suit, a white shirt, complete with collar and cuffs, and a thin tie. Her sister had even thrown in a flat-topped preacher's hat with a wide brim. "Here..." Brigit stacked the clothing and offered it to him. "Change into something clean."

His hands went to his waistband where he loosened the first button.

Startled, she threw the clothes on the ground and whirled around. "Warn me the next time you intend to drop your trousers."

"What's wrong, Miss Robb? You've never seen a man undressed?" His low rasp sent another warm shiver up her arms.

"Only a dead one." She regretted the retort the moment it was out of her mouth. If he waited for her to explain, they'd be there an eternity. It was a memory she'd rather not dwell on, much less share with a stranger.

Mr. Byrne had thought he was being clever when he'd paraphrased her tart remark from earlier when he'd gawked at her while she changed dresses. It wasn't the same. She'd worn several layers of underclothes. No, she wasn't a loose woman, as he assumed. But why should one have to defend her honor to an outlaw?

Brigit kept her back to him while he finished getting dressed.

"You can turn around now."

She wasn't sure she wanted to turn around. Her face still felt flushed, on account of surprise and annoyance, but he would think she was blushing. When she finally faced him, his steady regard unnerved her. He was an outlaw. That's why he made her nervous. Nothing more.

He settled the hat on his head and smoothed his fingers across the flat brim. "Am I supposed to be dressed for a funeral?"

"Precisely. I thought it would be less obvious. We're transporting a coffin. People won't pay us any mind. They'll be less likely to approach us if they assume we're both in mourning." She had thought this plan out to the last detail.

Brigit eyed her companion with satisfaction. Her guess at his size had paid off. Hannah had begged for clothing from her lawyer friend under the pretense of charity. Mr. Moore's suit was a good fit on Mr. Byrne if a tad tight across the shoulders. Jasper had attached the collar but hadn't finished knotting the tie. Probably because he couldn't see what he was doing.

"Let me help you with that." She reached up and made a quick knot in the string tie, then turned down his collar, which exposed faded scars around his neck. Her stomach knotted.

Could those marks have been made by a rope? Damage to his throat caused by an attempted hanging might explain his rasping voice.

She gently touched the old injury. "What happened?"

He grasped her wrists and flung her hands away. "Leave it."

Brigit moved back without another word. Whatever had happened, it had no relevance to this case, which meant she didn't need to know the details. The less personally connected they became, the better. If she allowed softer emotions to creep in, it could risk the investigation.

He flipped up the collar and adjusted the tie to cover the marks. "Who sent you after me?"

A logical question, and one that was easily answered.

"No one sent me. It was my idea."

"You?" A flicker of confusion crossed his face before it settled into the hard mask. "Why would you want to risk your life to free me?"

He'd finally acknowledged her actions on his behalf, even if it sounded like someone had pulled the words out of him. His tone had another quality that might be called disappointment. He'd expected someone else to be behind his rescue.

No one she'd spoken with had offered much information about the men who followed him. The stories made it sound as though Jasper Byrne single-handedly directed nameless armies. Whoever those men were, they weren't as loyal as he thought. In a way, it was sad, even if it made her job easier. At the moment, it didn't matter why his friends hadn't shown up. She needed him to accept *her* reasons for getting him off that train.

"I found out those vigilantes planned to force the marshal to hand you over so they could hang you. As it appears, he wouldn't have required a great deal of persuasion."

He narrowed his eyes. "And you decided to save a stranger. An outlaw."

Suspicious and unappreciative. Not surprising, given what she'd learned about him.

"A few days ago, I overheard the marshal tell one of the locomotive engineers that he would need to extend the stop in Chetopa for a necktie party. I knew I had to act fast. You wouldn't have made it to Fort Smith to stand trial."

His arched eyebrow told her she hadn't convinced him. "Why do *you* care if they hang me now or later?"

A fair question.

Brigit removed a handkerchief from under her sleeve and dipped it into the water. She used the damp cloth to cool her face and neck. Mr. Byrne might be less suspicious if she simply told him the truth and didn't bother to express her concern for him.

"Yours is the only testimony that implicates the current president of the Katy Railroad in a criminal act while he served as general manager. If I can find evidence that Mr. Bond was behind those train robberies, it will also bring down a more powerful man who is pulling his strings."

"My God." Byrne laughed and flung his arms outward. "You did all this because you want a *newspaper* story?"

She wanted much more than that, but couldn't trust him with quite so much truth.

Brigit shrugged. "It's a big story. *The New York Times* broke the Tweed Ring. If we can bring down a rich investor through his connection to a crooked railroad executive—"

"You're wasting your time, Miss Robb," Byrne said flatly. "I don't have anything more to give you on Bond than what I told the sheriff."

"I understand you may not, but someone else will. A man named Lester Kinkaid." She couldn't reveal her fellow agent's true identity without risking his life. "He came down here last month to snoop around and report on what he found. He's gone missing."

"Never heard of him."

Byrne could be telling the truth, although he'd adopted a defensive stance. The agent's last report had been from Parsons, and he'd mentioned Byrne's capture, among other things.

"Mr. Kinkaid has blonde hair, a light complexion, and blue eyes."

Byrne's stony demeanor didn't soften. "That describes more than a few men. Why didn't you ask the marshal for his help?"

"You've touched on the crux of the matter, sir. And frankly, one of the reasons I decided to recruit your help. Certain men in positions of trust can't be trusted." The last message from Mr. Kinkaid had said as much, without naming names.

Byrne gave her another long look. His expression shifted from hardened disbelief to wariness. "But you trust *me*?"

"Not entirely," she answered honestly. "Not yet. From what I've learned, though, you may be the only person who can help me. You were willing to cooperate with the authorities."

"Yeah, for all the good it did." Byrne gathered his old clothing with slow, careful movements that indicated fatigue, possibly pain. "I gave a sworn statement to the former sheriff. Garrity."

Frank Garrity, her brother-in-law. A fact she chose not to share at the moment. Instead, she maintained a curious expression. "I spoke with him."

"Then he would've told you, the federal judge released Bond anyway. Guess they didn't believe me. Shocking, I know."

"It is unfortunate," she conceded, with true empathy. Frank had been furious, too. "But I would think you would welcome the opportunity to prove you were telling the truth about Mr. Bond's involvement in the train robberies."

"How will finding a missing reporter prove Bond is a rat?"

It wouldn't. Finding a missing Pinkerton agent might.

"As I said, the corruption appears to be widespread. I believe Mr.

Kinkaid may have obtained critical information. If you help me find him and Bond's crimes are exposed, you will be exonerated, regain your honor, and possibly win your freedom. I would certainly write a glowing report about you."

The outlaw didn't appear grateful or even surprised by her offer. He also didn't seem inclined to accept it. If he decided it wasn't worth it, he could walk away. How would she stop him, short of shooting him?

Brigit squelched a flare of panic. She couldn't have been so wrong in her estimation. Her judgment regarding men's characters, while not flawless, was better than most. But if gratitude didn't prompt Byrne to help her, perhaps self-interest would. "There is something else you should know. Mr. Kinkaid was last seen in Parsons the same week you were arrested there."

Byrne's frown wasn't hard to read this time. "You think *I* murdered him?"

It was a possibility she'd explored when she and Hannah had first arrived. A two-week investigation and dozens of interviews had changed her mind.

"Based on what I've discovered about your whereabouts and activities that week, no, I don't believe you did. Still, others might see it that way. It is a very convenient story. Especially if someone needs a scapegoat."

A dark flush stained the outlaw's neck and face. "You should've led with that. It would've saved all that hot air you spewed about me being *exonerated* and regaining my *honor*."

Brigit snatched up his crushed hat from where it had fallen near the edge of the water. "You are entirely too distrustful of someone who just saved your life. I am not threatening you, Mr. Byrne. I'm pointing out what could happen if you refuse to help, and the men in power decide to let *you* take the blame for *their* misdeeds."

She thrust her fist into the hat and it came out the top. Rotten and useless. Like its owner? "If you help me, it will prove you had nothing to do with Mr. Kinkaid's disappearance."

Byrne muttered something foreign and guttural, a word she didn't have to understand to know it was a curse. "I *didn't* have anything to do with it. I've never met him."

Blast the aggravating, ungrateful man. "Didn't you say you wished for another chance? An opportunity to do the right thing? Well, now you have it."

He stalked off toward the wagon.

"Wait! Where are you going?" She'd known flight was a risk, but she'd relied on her instincts and what she'd learned about the complicated, admittedly fascinating, Mr. Byrne.

She had gotten on that train to free him, but she wouldn't have done it if she hadn't decided for herself that he was worth it. "Are you running away? I wouldn't have set you free if I'd known you were a coward."

He jerked to an abrupt halt next to the seat. When he turned his head slightly, she caught her breath. The way he stood there, poised, she knew he'd spotted the revolver beneath the seat. Her bonnet and veil, hanging from the seat, didn't hide it.

He could shoot her, steal her wagon, and abandon her miles from civilization.

Brigit's heart lodged in her throat. Hannah had warned her against recruiting an outlaw. It might turn out to be the worst error in judgment she'd ever made. Even more than a decision she'd made long ago to trust a man who had promised to protect her.

Byrne heaved his old clothes into the back of the wagon before he turned to her with a scowl. "Any more insults you want to hurl my way? If not, let's get the hell out of here."

CHAPTER 3

Simmering, Jasper took up the reins. He'd had enough of being bossed around, threatened, and abused by a slip of a woman, one who didn't have sense enough to know better than to abduct an outlaw. She was damn lucky he wasn't the worst of the bunch.

Bold as she was, Miss Robb wasn't prepared for the kind of men she would be going up against. The kind who'd made her friend Kinkaid disappear. She'd vanish, too, if she went after them alone. If she was foolish enough to do it.

"Wait!" She ran over and climbed up to the seat, moved her bonnet and the veil so it would cover something. He wouldn't need a gun to overpower her, and going after it might've caused her to panic and attempt to wrestle it away.

"I could've gotten the gun before now," he assured her.

"But you didn't. That speaks well of you."

"If you believed that, you wouldn't try to conceal it."

She retrieved the gun and put it on the seat. Her attempt at making a point came a little late. "Let's not leave yet. We need to stuff your old clothes and put them in the coffin. Just in case someone stops us and demands to take a peek inside."

He could admit to admiring this part of her plan. "Good idea."

She stared as if his remark had astonished her.

"What? You don't want a compliment? You begged for one earlier." Jasper conceded he was being an ass, but he couldn't seem to stop.

Jasper helped her out of the wagon. He picked up decaying leaves and jabbed them into his old shirt.

When she'd first opened that coffin, he'd been stunned, overheated, and one big bruise from all the bumps in the road she'd hit. Then she'd made that cute remark about her singing and brayed about her brilliant plan. Come to find out, she'd only saved him to get a juicy newspaper story. It might be the truth and might even make sense, but it stuck in his craw.

She stuffed debris into the trousers. "You're still angry with me, aren't you? Honestly, you should thank me."

He put a boulder in the place where a corpse's head would be. "What am I thanking you for?"

She released a short laugh. Incredulous or frustrated or both. "I risked my life, I even broke the law, to get you off that train and away from those vigilantes."

"Yep. But you didn't do it for me. You did it because you need me to help you. Since I'm doing that, it ought to be thanks enough." Jasper patted mud on the round stone so it somewhat resembled a face then plopped some wet moss on top. "Looks just like my grandpa."

When he walked down to the creek to wash his hands, she scampered along behind him.

She rubbed her hands beneath the running water. "Granted, we both stand to benefit. Still, my reasons for taking you off that train are more deserving than you give me credit for."

He didn't give a damn for her reasons. "You helped me escape. I owe you more than thanks. And maybe I'm a man who always pays my debts."

Jasper assisted her into the wagon. Her fingers were soft and slender, as well as damp. In his experience with gently raised women, they didn't undertake risky rescues or try to expose dirty coverups. They let their men take care of them. Had all the men in her life deserted her? If so, what did he care?

He climbed onto the driver's seat. At least she'd stopped talking.

She started whistling instead.

He guided the team back to the only road through the desolate area. The closest town was a day's ride. Every muscle in his body ached. His stomach felt emptier than a feed sack without grain. He needed food and rest, neither of which he'd get until they were in a safer location. It was going to be a long trip if he had to listen to her sing and whistle the whole way.

Should he agree to become her escort through the Territory? Not before he schooled her about what she was up against. Maybe he could convince her to change her mind about going after that missing reporter, who was probably coyote food by now.

"They'll send a posse after me. Men who aren't afraid to cross the border. Men who won't care if I'm traveling with a woman."

Had she caught his point? If so, she gave no indication it bothered her.

He tried a direct approach. "First rule when dealing with men who have no morals. Don't let down your guard. Not even for a minute."

"Are you warning me against you or someone else?"

"You really must not want my help," he grumbled.

"I was joking." She picked up the gun off the seat and tucked it into her lap between the folds of her skirts while she put on her bonnet and adjusted the veil over her face. "I'm glad we can trust each other."

"Is that another joke?" he asked.

"Why would I joke about that?" The heavy black netting made it difficult to see her expression. Some instinct told him she hid more than her face behind that veil. What did she not want him to see?

He shifted the reins to one hand so he could reach the netting to lift it over her head. "You might want to enjoy the breeze for a while."

She jerked away with a look of alarm then breathed out a soft laugh. "Oh...yes, thank you." A moment later, she scooted to the far side of the seat.

Was it how he smelled? She hadn't complained since he'd washed off. Maybe she was skittish around men. He recalled her odd remark about having seen only one man naked. A dead one. Had *she* killed him?

Jasper eyed the gun in her lap. He'd better clear things up before she overreacted. "Just so we understand each other. I don't take liberties with ladies. Unless I'm invited to do so."

"Then I shouldn't worry. I won't be giving you an invitation."

He found it hard not to laugh at her prim response. It wouldn't be funny if she shot him. "So, what's your plan for going after this Kinkaid fellow? I assume you have one."

"Yes, I'm working on it..." She readjusted her spectacles and blinked as if trying to bring his face into focus.

How blind was she? Her vision or otherwise. Either way, it didn't bode well.

"From what I've learned, Mr. Kinkaid had ingratiated himself with a gang of outlaws. They're hiding out in a place called Robber's Roost."

"Where did you hear that?"

"I can't reveal my sources."

Their temporary partnership, if it could be called that, wasn't off to a great start.

"For all that talk about trust, you aren't exhibiting much."

She dropped her gaze to her lap. Her reason for protecting her sources of information wasn't hard to guess, and he admired her for wanting to protect them.

"Let's say your sources are right. What do you know about Robber's Roost?

"It's a remote area in the southeast corner of the Territory. A sanctuary for thieves, rapists, and cut-throats. No lawmen will go there. Even the Indians won't police it."

"That should tell you something."

"What it tells me is that I need someone like *you*."

She didn't pull punches when it came to insults.

"Aw, and here I thought you stole me because I'm charming and irresistible. Would it make you feel better if I told you I'm ruthless and unprincipled?"

She smiled like he'd said something funny. "I heard from a reliable source that you are a gentleman, despite your rough exterior. You pretend to be mean but you aren't."

No wonder she wasn't afraid of him. He couldn't imagine where she'd picked up her information. Not from the Wanted poster that called him a *brutal savage*.

"Who have you been talking to?"

"I can't reveal—"

"You'd better, or we're stopping right here."

"Billy Frye insists you are honorable."

Jasper shook his head, astonished at her gullibility. "He's the *only* person who thinks that. And he's twelve. Keep that in mind."

"For a young man, he has a very mature view on life. I think his perspective is closer to the truth than you want to admit. Lucy Stevens also has a very high opinion of you."

Where had this reporter met Lucy? She and her husband had moved away from Parsons. Maybe they'd corresponded. Lucy Forbes —Stevens now—had promised not to tell anyone about what happened between them. And she'd broken her promise.

"She's just grateful I didn't kill her precious Henry after I caught him trespassing," Jasper grumbled.

"Mr. Stevens reported that he came to Lucy's rescue after you abducted her."

"Right," Jasper said dryly. "I have Indian blood. Therefore, I have an uncontrollable urge to abduct white women."

Miss Robb put her hand to her mouth, seemingly to cover her teeth when she smiled. "Why don't *you* tell me what happened?"

"All right. More truth. I found Lucy alone in the woods not far from the railroad stop at Vinita. She looked shocked and scared, and it was obvious she was running from somebody. I took her home to protect her."

"Sounds familiar. You took Billy home for the same reasons."

"Well, not the *same* reasons." He left it at that. She could figure it out.

"Let's just agree you have a history of taking in strays."

Jasper shook his head. "No. Let's not say that." Even if it was true. It made him sound pathetic. Bad enough she considered him about as dangerous as a toothless old hound. "It was all a misunderstanding. We got it cleared up. I didn't have to have to kill anybody."

He didn't go into the part where Lucy had offered herself to him to save her lover. He wouldn't have taken her up on it. Still, her courage had touched him. So much so, that he would've done just about anything she'd asked. All she'd asked for was her freedom—and Henry.

Jasper couldn't imagine a woman loving him that much. His mother perhaps, and look where that had gotten her. An awful thought struck. Billy had a habit of sticking his nose into places it didn't belong, and Lucy had a streak of recklessness. "Did Lucy or Billy encourage you to enlist my help?"

"Heavens, no. They don't have an inkling about my plan. They'll believe, along with everyone else, that you broke free and fled from vigilantes."

"Aren't you leaving out a few particulars?"

She smiled into her hand again. "The proud marshal won't admit to being tricked by a reporter, much less a woman. He'll find a way to publicly blame you."

Jasper could see how she might come to that conclusion. Nevertheless, he'd have to make sure Miss Robb was nowhere around when he confronted the enraged lawman. "You may be right. He won't forget you, though. Stokes is a dangerous man to have as an enemy."

"I don't doubt that," she said softly. "If you are trying to scare me off, it won't work. I am quite determined to go to Robber's Roost to find out what happened to Mr. Kinkaid."

And he was equally determined not to take her there.

35

For the moment, however, they had other things to worry about.

Ahead on the road, three men on horseback had appeared, seemingly out of nowhere. They'd probably been hiding behind those bushes around the slight curve ahead. They could be travelers or poor farmers. Except two of them had shotguns in their saddle holsters, revolvers in gun belts strapped to their waists, and ammunition belts across their chests.

"We've got trouble," Jasper stated.

His companion adjusted her skirts to hide the gun in her lap. Her cheeks looked to have gone a little pale, but other than that, he couldn't tell if she was alarmed. She might not fully appreciate the danger. "Act poor," she advised. "They might leave us alone."

"I *am* poor. They don't care. Give me the Colt."

She swiveled her head sharply to look at him. "They won't know we have it if *I* keep it. You disarm one of them, I can take care of the other two. I'm a crack shot."

Her vaunted trust only extended so far, though part of her reasoning made sense. Those men wouldn't anticipate an armed woman. Her plan might work *if* she was as good as she claimed. "You can see well enough to shoot?"

She blinked behind the thick lenses. "I can see just fine."

He could, too, and what he saw made him nervous.

Jasper pulled the brim of his hat lower to hide his face. "I recognize one of them," he said under his breath.

"Who?" she whispered.

"The old white beard in front. McKenzie. He's married to a Cherokee woman. They make moonshine. The other two white men, I don't know who they are but can guess what they are. They crossed the border to steal because they know the law won't come after them."

"How well do you know Mr. McKenzie?"

"Not well enough to ask for favors."

"Pretend you've given up your outlaw to become a preacher."

"He hates preachers." Jasper had no time to explain how he knew this. He and McKenzie had fought on opposite sides of a bloody, complicated war. But the old sergeant had made peace with his enemies after he'd married one of their women and took up moonshining. When had he become a thief?

McKenzie rode up in front of the team. He left his rifle in its saddle holster. But the other two pulled their revolvers and went to either side of the wagon.

Jasper assessed the situation. Miss Robb couldn't possibly get off two shots in opposite directions fast enough. He'd have to take care of the two white men *and* distract McKenzie. The old man might back down rather than cross him. "Mac?" he asked. "Is that you?"

McKenzie stroked his beard. A second later, his expression registered recognition. "I'll be danged! Raven! I thought they'd strung you up."

He'd used a nickname the other men didn't appear to recognize, which meant they hadn't spent much time in the Territory. Folks around these parts knew the name, as well as the reputation, of the man who owned it.

"Nah, I broke out." Jasper gestured to his companion. "This here's my sweetheart, Alice. We're taking her father home to bury him."

Miss Robb smiled shyly and kept her head down. She never brought her hands out of the folds in her lap. To an observer, she appeared bashful and unthreatening.

McKenzie's gaze shifted to the wagon bed and a look of consternation crossed his face. He took his hat off. "Condolences, miss—"

"Mac, we ain't makin' a social call," grumbled one of the other men. Greasy, straw-colored hair stuck out from beneath a slouch hat. He had his gun pointed at Jasper and held it steady.

The leader, Jasper decided, and the first person he would need to disable.

The third man had pale, watery eyes, which he kept blinking. The gun he held wavered too much for him to have a good aim, which didn't make him any less dangerous. "G-give us whatever money you got," he stammered. "We'll let you go on your way."

Jasper knew better. Robbers like these didn't leave behind victims who could talk. He watched the leader's trigger finger as he answered. "We aren't carrying gold or greenbacks."

"You got a wagon and two mules," the man pointed out. "Reckon if you're dead you won't need transportation."

"Wait." Jasper put his hands in the air to indicate surrender. "Her father's gold watch. It's in the coffin with him. It's worth more than those stringy mules."

Alice appeared appropriately horrified by his offer. She had some fine acting abilities.

"Open that coffin and get it," the leader demanded.

Jasper slanted a worried look behind him. "My people don't mess with dead bodies. I don't want to risk angering his spirit. If I open the lid, will you fetch it out?"

"Damn superstitious Injun." The leader rode toward the back of the wagon and motioned to the other man. "Go get it, Zeb."

The pale-eyed highwayman muttered while he dismounted. He handed his reins over to the leader, holstered his gun, and hoisted himself into the wagon bed.

Jasper climbed over the seat to join him. He pushed open the lid, releasing the smell of damp debris and river muck.

"Whew! That stinks," the outlaw exclaimed. He bent over to examine the *corpse.*

Jasper grabbed the man's neck and smacked him down, face first, into the boulder. Heard his nose break. He went limp without a sound.

A startled oath came from the leader.

Jasper hauled the dazed man in front of him, using him as a shield. The leader fired a shot. His companion jerked when the bullet found the wrong target. The gunman's horse did a nervous dance, which made the next shot go wild.

Had Alice ducked?

Jasper pushed the limp form of one robber off the back of the wagon. "Go to hell!" He flung himself at the leader's skittish horse with a high-pitched war-whoop.

The frightened animal reared, dumping its rider into the road.

Jasper hit the ground rolling to avoid the horse's flailing hooves. Dust filled his nose and mouth. In the chaos, as both riderless horses bolted, he pounced on the leader, wrestled away his revolver, then struck him on the head with it, knocking him senseless.

With a gun in his hand, Jasper jumped to his feet, fearing for Alice's safety.

He needn't worry. She had the marshal's big Colt aimed straight at McKenzie, whose face registered dread.

The old man had his hands up. "Wait! Raven! This weren't my idea. Them boys came by and told me if I didn't help 'em, they'd shoot me and my wife. I-I wouldn't a-killed you!"

"Sure you would have, to save your skin. If he moves, shoot him," Jasper told Alice.

He stripped the robbers of their revolvers and ammunition belts. The one who'd been shot might not make it. The other one, when he came to, could deal with his partner. Or Mac might take care of them. Permanently.

"Get down," Jasper instructed McKenzie. "Leave the Sharps in the saddle holster."

The old man complied.

Jasper buckled on one of the gun belts and stuffed the revolver that hadn't been fired into the holster. He secured the additional gun and belt to the saddle on McKenzie's horse. He had a decent mount, weapons, and ammunition. *Now* he was prepared for a trip through the Territory.

He mounted the roan and guided it beside the wagon where Alice sat. "We need to get off this road. We'll ditch the wagon and take a different route. Can you manage behind me astride?"

"I can manage." Alice handed him the gun she'd kept earlier. "Hold this for a moment."

She nabbed her gray dress from behind the wagon seat and rolled it up under her arm. With a little help, she got on the horse behind him, taking another minute to situate her skirts. It was only then, when she put her arms around him, that he felt her tremble.

Had she lost her nerve to continue this journey? If so, it was about time.

"I'll take my gun." She opened her palm.

That's all he needed, for her to fire a gun she held pointed at his crotch. He tucked the revolver under his belt and folded her hands over his stomach. "You can get to it when you need it. Hold on tight." The hot rush of energy had drained. His side hurt like the very devil, but he didn't want her falling off.

McKenzie's mouth hung open. Shocked, afraid, or just addled.

"I'll trade you the wagon and team for this horse," Jasper told the old soldier. "Don't care what you do with the contents of the coffin...or with them." He gestured to the unconscious men sprawled in the dirt. "But I'd appreciate it if you don't recall you saw me."

"Saw what?" The white-haired moonshiner climbed onto the seat with wide-eyed innocence. "I don't see nuthin' but two idiots."

CHAPTER 4

*B*rigit held onto Jasper's waist as he headed the horse at an angle through the tall grass. He appeared to be headed toward a line of trees where the robbers' two frightened mounts had disappeared. If she hadn't seen Jasper in action, she would find it hard to believe he could disable two armed men without firing a shot.

She hadn't anticipated how he'd use that boulder in the coffin. Then, when he'd thrown himself at the leader's horse with a blood-curdling scream, it had raised the hairs on the back of her neck. Even the mules had flicked their ears nervously.

He wasn't just fearless. He might be a little crazy.

"Where are we going?" She was curious more than concerned. Her level of trust had increased exponentially after he'd saved their skins.

"Eventually, we'll get to the farm where I was raised. We can stop there a few days and rest."

On second thought, his plan didn't sound like a good idea.

"Isn't that the first place the marshal will look for you?"

"Only a few people know where it is. He isn't one of them." Jasper shifted in the saddle, which made it harder to avoid pressing her chest against him. The close contact made her intensely aware of the hard muscles beneath his shirt and the heat his body exuded. The smell of his sweat disturbed her senses. And not in an offensive way, which made it worse.

When she tried to lean back while keeping her arms around him, it threw them both off balance. She let go of his waist and rested her hands on his hips.

"I said *hold on*."

Yes, she'd heard him the first time and had tried, but she wasn't going to admit to having the jitters from touching him. "You're hurt."

"You will be too if you fall off."

Brigit heaved a frustrated sigh. Her disguise as Alice Robb, ugly duckling reporter with a sharp tongue, had worked well enough to discourage his interest. He might be grumpy because he found the forced intimacy distasteful, but had decided to put up with it to avoid having to stop to retrieve her if she was unseated.

Once more, she put her arms around him. She searched her mind for a topic to distract her from his physical attributes. "Why did that man call you Raven?"

"It's a nickname my mother's people gave me. The name Byrne comes from an ancient Irish name that means Raven."

He had Irish roots, as well as Cherokee. She tucked the fact away. "Does Raven have a special meaning, other than its association with your surname?"

"Ravens are dark figures in Cherokee legends. They can be evil spirits and can change form. They're also considered tricksters."

His explanation left her feeling uneasy. Very possibly, the nickname suited him perfectly. He'd tricked that robber, hadn't he? Then he hadn't blinked at using his unconscious victim as a shield. Then again, what choice had he been given? Those men would've killed them.

"I can see why one might call you a trickster...as a compliment, of course. The way you out-witted those scoundrels was very clever."

"It could've gone the other way."

"But it didn't."

"We got lucky. If you insist on going to Robber's Roost, things will get worse."

She gave a soft laugh. "Are you always this pessimistic?"

"I'm practical. The men who hide out there are smarter and more dangerous than the ones we just encountered."

"Then it's a good thing *you're* the robber who's taking me there."

He let out a breath that conveyed either fatigue or disgust. She couldn't see his face, so it was hard to tell.

Before long, they'd reached another creek, which meandered in a southerly direction.

On the opposite bank, one of the horses that had run away earlier had stopped for a drink, still wearing its saddle and the owner's belongings. Sweat darkened the horse's white flanks. It lifted its head to look at them. Twitched its ears, one forward, one back. Indecisive, perhaps.

"Do you think we can catch him?" she whispered in Jasper's ear.

He reined in the roan. "We can if we don't spook him. I'll help you down, then I'll dismount. Don't make any sudden moves."

As she slid to the ground, Jasper maintained a grip on her arm, which helped soften her landing. He slowly swung his leg over the horse's back, but as he hit the ground with a soft thud his knees buckled.

She caught him under his arms.

The roan didn't stir. But the horse across the creek shied and blew out a nervous snort.

"Damn it, I said no quick moves," Jasper rasped.

Would it be best to let him fall on his face or push him into the creek? Either choice had its merits, although both would result in scaring away the white horse.

"Let go," he ordered.

"I'll let go if you agree to be nicer."

He stiffened.

Pure stubbornness compelled her to hold onto him. She held his hooded gaze until her attention drifted to his firm lips, pressed tight in irritation and mere inches from hers. If she leaned in, she could brush a kiss on them.

A fluttering in her chest preceded the hot flush in her cheeks. Why would she even *consider* kissing a man whose dark side was bigger than the moon's?

As ugly as she looked, her forwardness would repulse him, and his startled reaction would scare the horse they needed to catch.

She released him and picked up the roan's reins. "Go on," she said softly. "I'm tired of holding you up."

Jasper remained statue-still for another second before he sat down. Had he intended to land on his backside in the first place? She didn't think so.

While he wasn't looking, she checked her bonnet. Thank goodness she'd tied the ribbon tight beneath her chin or her wig might've slipped at some point.

He jerked off his boots and rolled up the black trousers, exposing tanned calves as muscular as the rest of him. Next, off came the coat and vest, and up went the white sleeves.

Perhaps undressing was part of his strategy to put the white horse at ease. It didn't work that way with her, based on the speed with which her heart accelerated. She couldn't stop staring at his golden skin, wondering if he was that color all over.

At last, he got up and made his way to the creek and waded through knee-deep water to the other side. His movements were slow, deliberate. The very opposite of those instinctive, lightning-fast actions he'd taken with the robbers. Whether moving fast or slow, he demonstrated a fluid grace she'd never noticed in other men.

The white horse kept its attention fixed on Jasper with its ears laid back. It didn't appear nearly as impressed with his graceful form or his lovely brown skin.

After he'd reached the opposite bank, Jasper didn't approach the horse directly. Instead, he sat in a cross-legged position on a patch of grass. He faced the babbling creek, remaining a few feet away from the horse.

It was so quiet she could hear crickets.

The gelding flicked its ears forward. After another moment, it took a few steps closer to the man who sat there, seemingly ignoring it. The horse lowered its head and sniffed Jasper's shoulder. He tugged up a handful of long grass and lifted it.

Jasper maintained his patient watch, staring at the water, pretending to ignore the horse while it munched on the peace offering.

A bubble of excitement burst in Brigit's chest. The animal stood so close to him. He could reach out and take hold of the bridle. Why was he just sitting there?

The white horse nudged Jasper.

Finally, the man gave the horse his attention. He rubbed its velvety nose before he grasped the dangling reins and stood. Another moment was spent petting the horse and speaking to it with low, unintelligible words.

Brigit sucked in a shuddering breath. His lover-like touch and tone sent a burst of shivers across her skin as if *she* were one being stroked and wooed.

Good Lord. She'd better shake off this odd fascination for the scruffy outlaw. More than inconvenient and inappropriate, it was dangerous.

Jasper led the horse across the creek. He didn't even have to pull on the reins to get the placid creature to follow him. He made the conquest look easy.

Men, in general, were quick to take advantage of women who were easy conquests. All the more so when the man in question was a scoundrel.

Brigit swallowed to relieve the tightness gripping her throat. Her mind had taken a flight of fancy. Jasper had made no effort whatsoever to woo her. Just the opposite. He seemed determined to frighten her away. Oddly, his gruff annoyance had produced a very different response. She couldn't fathom why she found him compelling. Maybe he had the same effect on other women, especially when he looked at them with that intense gaze.

When Jasper stopped in front of her, a slight smile lifted the side of his mouth. "You ride the roan. He's calmer. I'll take this one."

Proud of himself, wasn't he? Or had he noticed her staring at him, and that's what his smile was about? Had he forgotten how she'd had to catch him when he almost collapsed?

"Do you need help to mount?" she inquired solicitously.

The smile fell away. He straightened his shoulders. "Do you?"

Drat. She hadn't thought that far ahead. Could she lift her foot high enough to reach the stirrup? She looked around for a log, but none were large enough to use as a stool.

"I do." She had to suffer accepting a leg up.

After she'd gotten situated, with her skirts hiked so high her lacy pantaloons were in full view, Jasper gave her knee a paternalistic pat. "Comfortable?"

She fought to contain the butterflies in her stomach then lashed out at him for turning them loose. "Much better, now that I'm no longer compelled to put my arms around you."

"For you and me both."

His sharp remark pricked her pride. She wasn't a beautiful woman, but she wasn't as ugly as she'd made herself up to be. Although, his reaction shouldn't matter. She didn't want to attract the rascal. Thinking about him all the time would only interfere with her mission. She would put the irrational attraction out of her head and focus on her goal—getting to Robber's Roost.

Jasper pulled on his boots and the vest and coat he'd discarded. He secured the flat-topped hat and adjusted the gun belt around his waist before he mounted the white horse and turned it southward, following the creek. If he was in pain, he didn't show it.

They rode until nightfall caught up. The two bedrolls strapped to the horses came in handy. They wouldn't have to share one.

BRIGIT AWOKE BEFORE DAWN. Jasper's bedding was already slung over his horse, which was hobbled nearby. She spotted him down by the

46

creek, crouched at the water's edge with his back to her. She adjusted the wig, which had shifted during the night, and surreptitiously inserted the dental device she'd removed so she could get some sleep.

Could she do without the black bonnet and veil? It was so hot. Perhaps she should dispense with the disguise and tell him the truth.

Jasper might consider yesterday's rescue enough to repay his debt to her. She didn't want to test his commitment. Besides, revealing her true identity would send him running.

By the time he returned, she had put her bonnet on, without the veil, and was packing her bedroll.

"Catch anything to eat?" she asked him.

"We don't want to light a fire or leave evidence we were here."

"No, of course not." She would've thought of it if her stomach weren't growling so loudly.

He led his horse next to hers and offered her a strip of dried meat. "Jerky. I found some in the saddlebag. Enough to share."

She had a hard time chewing without disturbing the false teeth and managed only a few bites. "Tough, but tasty."

"Want more?"

Removing the dentures to eat would ruin her cover. "No, thank you. One is sufficient. It might be the only food we have for a while."

He lifted the leather flap on the saddlebag and tucked in the remaining jerky.

She craned her neck to see what else might be packed inside. "I am curious about what else is in there. Is it more food?"

"Nope."

"Money?"

"Not that either."

What was he keeping from her?

"Something that implicates you in other robberies?"

He brought out a square envelope and handed it to her. "You know what they say about curiosity."

She ignored his sarcasm and slipped her fingers inside the envelope, withdrawing a thin, tube-shaped piece of animal skin. Or an intestine? And a string. It struck her where she'd seen something like it. A prostitute she'd befriended during a case had kept items like these handy, to use on her customers.

Brigit stuffed the disgusting item in the envelope and returned it to Jasper. "It doesn't appear to be anything useful."

"Not at the moment."

She spun away before he could see her blush. "Shouldn't we be going?"

"Yeah. Unless you'd like to search me for more surprises."

Determined not to give the aggravating man the satisfaction of knowing he'd rattled her, she busied herself with mounting her horse astride while wearing skirts. *Search him, indeed.* It would serve him right if she took him up on the offer.

Jasper pushed southward into lands that could be termed *difficult*, at best. High, craggy hills, rocky bluffs, and thick forests. At the end of a wearying day, they entered a narrow valley between two hills that appeared gray in the fading light.

In the middle of a clearing stood a cabin constructed from hewn logs. Its low-slung roof extended over the porch. No smoke curled out of the stone chimney. Behind the house, a smaller structure, also made from split logs, likely served to shelter animals, though there were no signs of any. It would be a stretch to call this a *farm*, as he'd referred to it.

"Does anyone live here?"

"I do. Sometimes."

They rode past a stone-ringed cooking pit that didn't look as if it had been used recently.

On the front porch were two rocking chairs constructed from sturdy branches. A raccoon had curled up in one of them. It hissed at being disturbed before it hopped down and waddled off, vanishing between the pier stones supporting the flooring.

"Is that your pet?" she asked Jasper.

"I don't have pets."

"Ah, and you don't have friends either," she reminded him. "Is there anyone you care about?"

His hardened expression put a knot in her chest.

She wished she could recall the needling remark. If she wanted him to dislike her, she was making fine progress.

He dismounted, this time holding onto the saddle until he'd secured his footing. "You go on inside. I'll take care of the horses."

She made a mental note to look for something to use as a bandage to wrap around his ribs, which would make him more comfortable. Tired as they both were, they couldn't dally here. After they rested overnight and found something to eat, they needed to move on. The sooner she found Kinkaid's trail, the sooner she could crack this case and be done with her need for Jasper's assistance. They'd both be happier.

Brigit stepped up to the porch, walking carefully in case she encountered loose or rotten boards. It appeared some of the old ones had been replaced recently. When had Jasper had time for home repairs whilst robbing trains?

The door was made from thick pieces of wood expertly fitted together. It didn't budge when she pushed on it. "The door is locked from the inside," she called after him.

He'd disappeared around back with the horses and hadn't heard her.

She knocked. Didn't hear anything. Jasper certainly wasn't expecting anyone to be at home. The door might be stuck.

An open window overlooked the porch. The breeze fluttered curtains made from what looked like old flour sacks. Nothing prevented her from entering that way, except perhaps finding a family of raccoons in residence inside. She should've brought along one of the revolvers Jasper had taken with him.

Brigit hiked up her skirts and lifted one leg through. As she raised her other foot and stepped inside, she pushed the curtains away from her face—and looked straight into the double barrels of a shotgun.

CHAPTER 5

*J*asper turned the horses loose in the pasture. He'd let them graze while he fetched water and looked for the fishing traps he'd left down by the creek. He could put them in and whatever he caught—sunfish or crayfish—they could cook up and eat. Later, he'd set snares for rabbits. If he felt up to it tomorrow, he'd do some hunting.

He would be of no use to anyone if he didn't take a few days to rest and recuperate. And if he could spend some time away from Miss Alice Robb, it would also help his state of mind.

It made no sense, this strange attraction, and to an ugly woman, of all things. Well, *ugly* might be harsh. If it weren't for that frizzy hair and those teeth that wouldn't stay behind her lips, she wouldn't be too hard on the eyes.

He hadn't been thinking about her face when she'd ridden behind him with her front pressed up against his back, her slender arms around his waist, her long fingers splayed across his stomach.

Then, he'd embarrassed himself when he'd nearly collapsed. Her quick move had saved him and he'd snapped at her. For an instant, he'd gotten the distinct impression she'd been about to kiss him. That was before she'd flayed him with that sharp tongue of hers.

Holy Hell. The odd woman was making him crazy.

He walked back to the house to tell Miss Robb he'd be gone awhile. Days, maybe.

Up the two stone steps, he tromped, across the porch, then pushed the door. For some fool reason, she'd latched it. Maybe she thought it would be funny.

He shifted one of the extra gun belts over his shoulder and banged. "Open up."

A moment later the door creaked open, and Miss Robb appeared. Behind the glasses, her brown eyes looked larger than usual. Shocked.

The hair on the back of his neck warned him something was amiss.

"It appears someone besides you lives here," she said softly.

Jasper tensed. He guessed that *someone* had to be behind her, probably holding a gun. He narrowed the likely possibilities down to two—his partners, Candy and Tom, neither of whom would hold a woman captive, or the marshal had somehow found this place. He had to get Alice out of the way before the inevitable eruption of gunfire, but without tipping off whoever stood behind her.

"Step outside," he said calmly, as he drew the revolver from its holster. "I'd like to meet whoever thinks they belong in my house."

"Jasper?" The feminine voice coming from behind Miss Robb was frighteningly familiar.

"Sally?" He stormed past the astonished Miss Robb while holstering his gun.

His sister set her shotgun on the kitchen table and ran into his arms. "You got away!"

As she hugged him tight, the pain in his side blossomed and he couldn't stop a groan.

Sally drew back and gazed up at him with concern brimming in her dark eyes. She looked so much like their mother that it turned his heart inside out every time he saw her. "What's wrong? Are you hurt?"

He pushed her away from him. "Just some bruises. Nothing serious."

"Who's that?" Sally frowned at Miss Robb, who'd remained near the open door.

If the reporter had considered fleeing, she wasn't thinking about it now. Her color had returned and her expression couldn't be confused for anything but anger.

"Sally, meet Alice Robb. We're traveling together."

"*Traveling* together?" Sally's tone held curiosity, maybe a little surprise, too. He'd never brought a woman home with him before.

"You might've asked before you pulled a gun on me," Alice shot back.

Jasper sighed. This wasn't going well. Sally knew better than to be rude, no matter what ideas she might've formed, and Alice needed to put that sharp tongue back where it belonged. "Miss Robb, Sally is my sister."

Alice appeared surprised, then she got red-faced. "I'm sorry, Miss Byrne. Your brother told me no one else lived here."

"No one else does," he said firmly. "Sally lives in Tahlequah. I have no idea why she's here, in a place she *isn't* supposed to be."

With downcast eyes, Sally nervously smoothed her hands over the front of the soiled apron protecting her plain, homespun dress. Unadorned moccasins peeked out from underneath the hem. She should've purchased nice clothes for herself and her daughter with the money he'd given her. What had she done with it?

"I wanted to help break you out," she said in a low whisper.

"Break me out? What the hell are you talking about?" Fear surged through him. He grasped his sister's upper arms and stared at the top of her bent head. "Where's Rachel?"

"She's with *Na*," Sally murmured.

Jasper heaved a sigh of relief. His friend's mother, the woman they all called *Aunt*, would take good care of Sally's little girl. But what had his sister been thinking to risk herself in some crazy rescue attempt? "I wrote to you. Told you not to get involved."

"I know, but..." She looked up, finally, and her anxious expression put a vise on his heart. "We couldn't let them hang you."

"We?"

His gaze stopped in the corner of the one-room cabin where a hump beneath the quilt on the bed gave away her accomplice. His anger ignited. Was it Tom? Candy? Which of those two idiots had dragged his sister into an insane scheme to free him?

He marched over. "Get up!" he said and yanked off the cover. "Candy! Stupid sonofabitch! I should've known."

The big man rolled from his side to his back and his expression went from sleepy to surprised. His eyes had a glassy sheen and his wheat-blonde hair was dark with sweat. "Jasper? I thought you were dead. Are you a ghost?" he asked in a hoarse whisper.

"No. I'm real." Jasper's horrified gaze moved to a bandage wrapped around the larger man's torso in between rolls of fat. The white cloth had the same brown stains as those splattered across Sally's apron. "How'd you get shot?"

"Welcoming committee." Candy's eyelids fluttered. "Glad we got you outta there."

A chill prickled Jasper's skin. Delusions often set in with fever, and fever could lead to death. Years ago, when he'd been young and stupid, he'd joked with his pal about meeting death in a glorious blaze. Since then, he had seen dozens of men die. Nothing about death was glorious.

Jasper cleared a lump in his throat as he pulled the quilt up and tucked it around the larger man's shoulders. "Get some rest. We'll talk later."

Candy gave a contented sigh and slipped into sleep.

Something hot and hard centered in Jasper's chest. When he turned to Sally, he could barely contain his fury. "What happened?"

"Why don't I make us all some tea?" She took a step back, then spun around.

Jasper caught her arm before she could get past him on her way outside or wherever she'd intended to go. "Forget the tea. We can drink water or that whiskey I left."

"Tom finished it off."

Their cousin. Of course, *he'd* have a hand in this. Liquor had pickled his brains.

"Is he around?" Jasper said through clenched teeth.

Sally shook her head.

"Where did he go?"

"I'm not sure. After he brought Candy here, he left to look for you."

Jasper swore. A gasp from Alice made him aware of how tightly he gripped his sister's arm. He let go. Tossed his hat onto the table and plunged his fingers through his hair, about ready to pull it out from frustration. He had to get himself under control. "Start from the beginning."

"How far back?" Sally asked.

"When you got the foolish idea to come after me."

"I'm sure you must be thirsty." Sally hurried to a bucket next to the door. Using a ladle, she dipped water into two tin cups, handed him one, then offered the other to Alice.

His sister had recalled her manners and had offered their guest a refreshment, but she was also delaying.

"Thank you," Jasper told her. "Now stop dilly-dallying."

"I'm trying to remember." Sally headed for the open crates where Jasper kept dishes and utensils. Nothing wrong with her memory when it came to setting the table. "A few days ago, J.D. came by my house. He said he knew when you would be transferred to Fort Smith, and he had an idea about where they could get you off the train. He wanted Tom and Candy to help."

Jasper went from mild irritation to fury in an instant. "J.D.? Why the hell is *he* involved?"

"Who is J.D.?" Alice asked.

"A sorry dirtbag," Jasper replied bitterly.

His sister flicked an aggrieved look in his direction. "J.D. used to be your friend."

Her terse reply put a fresh burn on Jasper's heart. If he hadn't introduced his *friend* to Sally, she wouldn't be raising a child alone.

She pulled out one of the chairs. "You look tired, brother. Why don't you sit down?"

"I'd rather stand."

"Until you fall on your face," Alice said under her breath.

Jasper curled his fingers into a fist. He sorely wanted to punch the wall. He might also be tempted to toss that reporter out the door if she didn't keep her nose out of his business.

Miss Robb gave him a frown before she took hold of the chair his sister had pulled out. "I'll sit with you, Sally."

Earlier, they'd bristled at each other like two cats. Now, they were snuggled up together while glaring at him. And he hadn't done a damn thing.

His sister rested her arms on the table with a weary sigh. "J.D. and the boys planned to break you out yesterday after the train made its stop in Vinita. Tom said you weren't on it."

Jasper shook his head. Vinita was further down the line from where he and Alice had slipped away. "We got away at Chetopa and stayed off from the main road. The train would've arrived there long before we got here. Was the marshal in the car?"

Sally shrugged. "Tom didn't say. One of the railroad guards shot Candy."

One of the least useful men in the gang, but also the most loyal. But without a leader who'd hold him back and tell him what to do, the big ox would've charged ahead. Probably caught the first bullet. And his sacrifice had been for nothing.

"Why did you come along?" Jasper asked his sister.

"If anything happened, I wanted to be here to help."

"By *anything*, you mean if one of us needed to be patched up," Jasper clarified.

"Yes," she said softly.

Pain ripped through Jasper's chest. Over the years, he had turned to his younger sister when he'd been wounded. It had happened a lot. Too much. He never should've involved her in his life after he'd become an outlaw. She deserved better.

"I reckoned I'd be safe enough here, as long as I didn't do

E . E . B U R K E

anything to attract attention." After Sally finished speaking, she put her face in her hands.

Alice reached over and patted his sister's shoulder. "You're a very kind and loyal sister. I know your brother appreciates all your efforts on his behalf, even if he doesn't show it."

"I'd appreciate it more if you'd stayed home and safe." Jasper paced the length of the room, needing to keep moving so he didn't start tearing the place apart.

At one time, he wouldn't have cared who he hurt. Maybe if he'd remained an unfeeling bastard, he wouldn't be in this situation. He sure as hell wasn't worth anyone's efforts on his behalf, least of all his younger sister.

He paused in front of the stone hearth. It looked as if a small fire had been set, perhaps the previous evening, then put out so no one could see smoke during the day.

Smart girl.

It might not help, though. Not if those vigilantes managed to track his men to this place. Had they taken care to go the way he'd shown them? Covered their tracks? Only if one of them thought about it.

"Tom can't stay sober long enough to pull off a rescue. And Candy..." Jasper glanced at the bed. He couldn't look at the motionless lump without fury knotting his stomach. "He followed a bigger fool than himself."

"J.D. isn't a fool," Sally replied, though without nearly as much conviction as she'd shown at one time. She had to realize by now what kind of man she'd fallen for.

Jasper walked over to the table. He crossed his arms and squinted to hide the watering in his eyes. "I warned that worthless coyote that if I ever saw him again, I'd shoot him. Ought to shoot all three of 'em."

"They just wanted to help," Sally said into her hands.

"What the *hell* made them think they could attack a well-guarded train and get away with it?" Jasper demanded.

Sally lifted her head. Tears filled her eyes. "You, Jasper. You're the one who made them believe they could."

BRIGIT HELD her breath when Jasper strode past. A deep flush darkened his face, his hands were clenched into fists. What would he do with all that anger?

"Going down to the creek," he announced. "To set the fish traps."

He stormed out the door and slammed it behind him.

It was almost dark. She didn't believe for a minute that fishing was on his mind. Although his sister jumped up and started stoking the fire, presumably to cook whatever Jasper brought back. If he came back.

Brigit pushed her chair out of the way as she stood. "I'll go see what I can do to help your brother."

"Will you fetch some fresh water?" Sally asked.

"Gladly." Brigit looked around. It didn't appear they had a pump or any type of indoor plumbing. "Do you have a well?"

"We get it from the spring down by the creek. There's a bucket by the door."

Brigit grasped the rope handle and paused. She glanced over the one-room cabin, having noticed before how little they had. A table fashioned from hewn logs and planks held together with wooden pegs. Crates for storage. The bed was made from sturdy branches. It was the home of a poor man.

Based on observation alone, one could assume Jasper had either hoarded the money he'd stolen from the railroad or wasted it. Perhaps he'd given it to Sally. What had she done with it?

"Here. Take this." Sally brought over a lit oil lamp. "At the edge of the woods, you'll see the trail. Follow it down to the creek. Jasper can show you the spring. Watch your step."

The lamp shed barely enough light to locate the path, which entered the woods on the west side of the property. Jasper had told her earlier that anyone who came into this valley would have to cross one of two creeks. If they didn't know the way, they'd get lost.

He might've gone to see whether his enemies were close. Or he'd left to go after them. Either way, it could end disastrously, and derail her mission in the process.

After she entered the woods, Brigit held the lamp aloft to light her way downhill. A narrow trail with twisted roots and jutting rocks would make a perfect hiding place for snakes. She also watched for spider webs attached to low-hanging branches.

She'd dealt with creepy crawlies in a fetid basement where she and Hannah had lived for a time, and would be ready if confronted with larger threats. Swing her bucket. Aim for the head. Set fire with the blazing oil lamp. As a last resort, she could go for the small pistol under her garter. It only had one shot, but up close she was deadly accurate.

A high screech from a tree on the right startled her. She lifted her lamp and its gleam reflected in a predator's round eyes.

Brigit heaved a sigh of relief. Once, a bat had found its way into their room. It had been lost and confused. Owls were smarter. This one had seen her long before she'd seen it. Fortunately, she wasn't a rodent of interest to a hungry bird.

Jasper, on the other hand, had become prey. Those hunters wouldn't stop until they found him. Her plan would work only if she and Jasper kept moving and didn't give their pursuers time to set up an ambush.

She made her way along a cut-back that descended to the bank. The tree frogs and insects raised such a ruckus she could barely hear the sound of the water running its courses. And she didn't see the creek until she stepped out of the darkness of the woods.

The moon's silvery light spilled over large flat rocks, which jutted into the creek's winding path, narrowing the water's flow. It was likely a natural phenomenon, but it appeared as if someone had fashioned it with that in mind.

Near the water's edge, she saw the dark form of a man, hunkered down on his haunches.

As she drew closer, the light from her lamp shone on a basket with a lid.

He had no fishing pole.

Jasper didn't even look at her when she set down the bucket and lamp. He acted like he hadn't noticed, but he must've been aware of her approach for some time. Like that owl, he had keen senses, as well as quick reflexes.

As she straightened, she pushed the spectacles to the bridge of her nose. Tiresome things, although not as uncomfortable as the fake teeth and hot wig. She longed to rip off the disguise and toss it all into the creek. He probably wouldn't notice if she stripped naked. However, she hadn't come down here to reveal herself any more than he'd come down here to fish.

"Any luck?" she asked.

"A few fish are caught in the trap." Jasper pointed toward the water.

Brigit inched close enough to see the top of a long contraption made from branches, which had been wedged in between stones on either side of the narrowed passage. Fish in the downstream current would swim into it and get caught.

She released a soft laugh, surprised. "That's a far more efficient way to fish than I learned."

"Efficient and effective," Jasper replied. "Like most things my grandfather taught me."

"Was he a fisherman?"

"He was Cherokee. All Cherokee know how to fish. It's like learning to walk." Jasper finally looked at her. "Do you need something to do? You can clean the fish."

"Did your grandfather also teach you how to get out of the messy part of the job?" she teased. "What will you do?"

"I'll be back up shortly."

His curt answer could be interpreted to mean he didn't want company. On the other hand, he hadn't outright told her to leave, which meant he would tolerate her for the time being.

"I think I'll wait on you if you don't mind." She sat down next to him.

He continued to stare silently at the water, which left the conversation up to her.

Fine. She would be straightforward about her concerns. "We need to be gone before a posse shows up."

"I know. But I can't leave Sally in harm's way.

"Is there somewhere your sister could go?"

"Back to her home."

Brigit nodded. "Yes, that's probably best, but I can predict she won't leave your wounded comrade behind."

"No, she won't."

"Perhaps he could be moved. How badly is he hurt?"

"Bad enough, based on what I saw. He may not make it." Jasper's voice came out flat and emotionless.

Brigit knew better than to think he felt nothing. She'd seen his face when he'd realized the other man had been shot. Shock, horror, and then, guilt. He'd masked it pretty quickly, but she'd noticed because she'd been watching him. "Shortly after I moved to Chicago, I witnessed the death of a friend whom I was powerless to help."

Jasper glanced in her direction. "Didn't you say you were from New York?"

She cursed her stumble. "Yes. I spent some time in Chicago in my youth." And now, she would stop talking about her past. The more she said, the more likely he'd catch her in a lie. "Are you angry because your friends tried to rescue you or because you weren't there to help?

Jasper picked up a smooth stone. He rubbed it between his finger and thumb. "As Sally said, I'm the one who taught them. I always plan everything and tell them what to do. Candy isn't smart enough. Tom doesn't stay sober long enough to work out the details. J.D. is…"

Brigit waited. When he didn't go on, she prodded. "Is what?"

Jasper drew back his hand, then sent the stone skimming across the water. "He's not welcome anywhere near my sister."

"Do you think he'll hurt Sally?"

"He put a babe in her belly then left."

Brigit huffed in disgust. No wonder Jasper hated him. "Did he know about the baby before he abandoned her?"

"When she told me she was pregnant, I found J.D. and thrashed him for disgracing her. He left after that."

The picture became clearer. Jasper had taken matters into his own hands. It seemed he had run off J.D., although from what Sally had implied, the two lovers might have stayed in touch.

Brigit could imagine her brother doing the same thing to a man who'd dared to take advantage of her. If Henry ever found out... She shook off the troubling thoughts. Some things were better left in the past.

At present, she needed to focus on Jasper. What he'd said and what he *hadn't* said. He claimed he didn't have friends. That wounded man considered himself Jasper's friend. What about the others? Why had they gotten involved in a dangerous rescue attempt?

"Tell me about Tom."

Jasper threaded his fingers through his hair and gave a sigh that wasn't hard to interpret. Irritation. "What do you want to know?"

"Who is he, other than a man who drinks too much?"

"A cousin on my mother's side."

Family loyalty might explain Tom's motives.

"Why would J.D. decide to rescue you?"

"He wouldn't."

"But Sally said he initiated the contact with Candy and Tom."

"I don't know what's he's up to."

Men did things to impress each other all the time. If J.D. was in love with Sally and she with him, he might have decided to prove himself.

"Perhaps he wants to renew a relationship with your sister and his child, and he wants to win your favor, so you won't harm him."

Jasper shook his head. "I shouldn't have introduced him to Sally. Don't intend to give him another chance."

"I assume both Sally and J.D. are grown. Aren't they responsible for their actions?"

"Sally is my responsibility. She has been ever since..." Jasper didn't finish the thought.

"Since when?"

"Since I was thirteen and she was ten."

His account stirred a deep pool of empathy. "I assume you lost your parents. Was it an illness that took them?"

The lonely call of a coyote filled a long silence.

He picked up a rock next to his boot. After a moment, he flung it with enough force to reach the opposite bank, where it clattered off into the rocks. "During the war, soldiers came out to the farm. The federal patrol killed my father, raped my mother, and tried to hang me.

Shock lodged in Brigit's chest. "Why would they do that?"

"Because they could."

His blunt answer was as horrifying as his revelation about the assault.

When she had been doing her research on him, she had read about his involvement in the war as a guerilla fighter. Until now, she hadn't learned what had sent him down such a violent path when he'd been little more than a boy. The unspeakable cruelty those soldiers had inflicted had left him scarred in body and mind.

He leaned back on his arms and peered up into the starlit sky. "After the war, we had nothing left. We were beggars. I tried to find honest work, but there was none to be had. It just seemed more...efficient...to take what we needed from those who had more than enough."

His explanation wasn't presented as an excuse. He was just being honest about their needs and what he'd done. She had also fended for herself and her twin to survive when they had been out on the streets for a time. In some ways, she and Jasper weren't so different.

She scooted closer so she could see his face and to let him know she understood. "My parents died when I was eight. My mother had smallpox. My father..." How could one put it delicately? One couldn't. "He took his own life. My brother was fourteen. He had to go to work. He tried to support his three younger sisters. Most of the money he sent went into our guardians' pockets."

"You didn't stay together?"

"No. We were split up among relatives. My youngest sister went to one place, and my twin sister and I went to another. Until we were thrown out." No need to go into the reason for being booted and the awful man who'd caused it. "We were out on the streets for a time. We picked pockets to survive." She plucked nervously at a loose thread on a seam in her skirt.

Jasper's hand closed over hers. Her heart raced at his unexpected touch, and her hand trembled. He gave it a gentle squeeze. "I won't hurt you, Alice."

For all the anger he must carry inside, he could be surprisingly tender.

Tears welled in her eyes. She released her breath slowly and withdrew her hand. She couldn't accept Jasper's tenderness or comfort or any kind of authentic relationship. Friendship. Whatever it was he wanted, she couldn't give him. She couldn't even offer him her real name.

"My sisters and I missed our brother. We longed to stay together, but we knew it wasn't possible. My point is, that we had to learn how to be independent. I think your sister is more capable than you realize. She might've decided to give J.D. another chance. You should consider it, as well. If he proves to be worthy of another chance."

Jasper released a sound, not a laugh, exactly. "Worthy? None of us is *worthy* of another chance. We're criminals. Society won't forgive our mistakes."

Somehow, her sins had been forgiven. Or overlooked because someone else had too much to lose by exposing them. Somehow, she would help Jasper find his way to a new start.

"You don't know that yet. Maybe there is a path, maybe not, but what about you? Are you willing to forgive others, and yourself, for those mistakes?"

He frowned at her. "Why should I? We made those choices. That's who we are."

A knot formed in her chest and another in her throat. "Is that what you believe? That you are nothing more than your mistakes?" She refused to accept his pessimism. "No," she said with force. "That's not true, it can't be. If it is, then I am damned too."

The lamp's light from behind them flickered across Jasper's features. His deep-set eyes remained shadows. She couldn't see whatever might be reflected in them. Perhaps wry amusement at her desperate desire to believe there was hope for him. And for her.

"You know what I'd like to do right now?" he said in a very low tone.

She shook her head.

"Kiss you."

Brigit slapped her hand over her false teeth. He had to be teasing her. She peered into the shadows concealing his expression.

"You're afraid of me." He said it as if it were a fact. "You know what kind of man I am."

Not the kind he wanted her to believe. She was beginning to think he was nothing like the man those *Wanted* posters described. His startling proclamation about wanting to kiss her had little to do with desire or making a bad joke. He had to be testing her. Maybe he wanted to instill fear to reinforce his poor opinion of himself.

"That's not why I'm afraid," she stated.

"Then tell me why."

How could she? She'd already told him too much. One thing was easy to admit. "I'm ugly."

He gave a soft laugh. "Does it matter?"

Of course, it mattered, or it should. She'd planned it that way.

Brigit touched the false teeth to make sure they were still in place. Her head itched beneath the wig, but she didn't dare scratch. In the dark, he must've forgotten what she looked like. "You've noticed, I'm sure, that my teeth protrude, I have frizzy red hair, and I wear spectacles."

"And you have soft, smooth skin, and lean, strong arms..." He ran a fingertip over her sleeve and a shiver followed. "I suspect your legs are just as nice."

"No!" Brigit scooted away, her entire body aflame with some terrifying combination of embarrassment and carnal attraction. "My-my limbs are not something you should be talking about. I do not want you to kiss me—nor do you want to."

"If you say so." Jasper rolled to his feet next to the creek. He pulled up the trap, retrieved four fish from inside, and tossed them into his basket. "Let's go clean these so Sally can cook them. I'm hungry enough to eat them raw, but I'd prefer fried."

Brigit scrambled to stand. Thank God he'd stopped talking about kissing. She grabbed the bucket. "I'm supposed to bring back fresh water."

"Get it from the spring." He directed her to a place close to the bluff behind them where water cascaded out of the rocky bank.

After she'd filled the bucket, she lifted the lamp and followed Jasper, who'd already started up the path, as if he knew the way in the dark. Instead of the raven, the Indians should've named him after the stealthy owl.

She still needed to resolve her earlier concerns. "What do you intend to do tomorrow?"

"Go find Tom and J.D. before a posse does."

"But, what about my search? I have to find Mr. Kinkaid."

"It'll take four days riding hard to get to Robber's Roost. I can't wait that long to find those two idiots who took off to look for me. We'll find your missing man after I get back."

"I'll come with you."

"One of us needs to stay here to help Sally until Candy improves, then she can go home."

Brigit trudged behind him, frustrated. He acted as if *he* were in charge. "How do I know you'll come back? You might decide you need to lead whoever is tracking them away from Sally and your wounded friend."

"I might, and then I'll come back. You'll have to trust me."

Putting her trust in him was akin to following the path with a lantern. She had faith only in what she could see ahead of her. Which was why she planned to keep Jasper within eyesight.

CHAPTER 6

*T*he morning after Jasper threatened to kiss her, Brigit woke from a deep sleep with someone tugging at her hair. In her dream, Jasper had been stroking her hair, not pulling it.

She shifted her cheek on her folded hands, blinking in confusion at the log wall in front of her. He wouldn't have come up to the loft where she'd been situated as a guest. It must be Sally. She'd pull the wig off if she kept tugging.

Brigit rolled over—and came nose-to-nose with a furry snout, black mask, and twitching whiskers. "Ahh!"

She dove for the pistol tucked beneath the mattress.

The raccoon reared on its hind legs with its front paws in the air. Showed its teeth, then waddled, seemingly unafraid, over to the opening in the floor and disappeared down the ladder.

Brigit leaned on one arm, trembling. "What next?"

"Is anything wrong?" Sally called out from below.

"No, of course not. I always awaken with a raccoon attempting to dress my hair."

Sally's laughter drifted up. "*Kuh-tlee* won't hurt you."

"Who?"

"Raccoon. The one who lives under our house must've gotten

66

inside when I went out to collect eggs. You have to watch out for him. He's determined to get what he wants, and he can be very clever about it."

"Do you mean the raccoon or Jasper?" Brigit listened for sounds that might indicate someone coming up the ladder before she removed her wig to examine it.

The creature had chewed on the hair! *Disgusting.* When she attempted to tuck the gnawed strands into the ratty bun, it didn't help. With luck, she'd only need to wear it a few more days. She worked the wig over the net covering her hair, muttering expletives under her breath.

After she'd returned from the creek last night, she had gained Jasper's agreement to wait until morning to discuss their next steps. Regardless of his decision, she intended to go with him. She would no more hang around here than she would kiss a raccoon. Or a Raven.

It was time to get moving.

Brigit washed her face over the wash basin tucked into a corner of the small space. She brushed her teeth—the fake ones and the real ones—with tooth powder she'd put in her handbag. They would need to travel light so she would leave the widow's weeds behind.

She tucked the Derringer beneath her garter before she donned her gray dress.

Watching carefully for the raccoon, she descended the rungs of the ladder and stepped off near the head of the bed.

The injured man had pulled the quilt over his head. His soft snores sounded natural, not labored. It was a good sign, surely.

Jasper's bedroll, which had been rolled out on the floor next to the bed, was gone.

Brigit tamped down her anxiety. He might be checking fish traps or making a false trail, as he'd said he intended to do.

Sally sat on the stool next to the fireplace stirring something in a skillet. She hummed a tune off-key, almost as if she were trying to appear at ease.

"Where is Jasper?" Brigit asked nicely. Jasper had given her his word he would not leave.

"I'm not sure. Haven't seen him for a while."

"Is he around the farm or did he go somewhere?" Brigit kept her tone polite.

"He got up before I did." Sally continued to stir. "Are you hungry? We have fresh eggs for breakfast. The hens have been laying them in the grass."

Either Sally had a woeful lack of curiosity or she was being purposely evasive.

Brigit crossed to the front door. It had been propped open, which explained the raccoon. Jasper didn't appear to be on the porch or out in the yard. She turned with her hands on her hips. "Answer me straight. *Where* is Jasper?"

Sally removed the skillet from the heat and set it on the table. Only then did she meet Brigit's gaze with a guarded expression. "He left before dawn. I'm sorry."

Brigit clamped down on the rush of anger. "Why are *you* apologizing? You didn't betray me. He did, the low-down weasel."

As she headed out the door, Sally called after her. "Wait!"

She'd waited too long already.

Neither horse was out in the pasture. *The fiend!* She couldn't follow him on foot.

Brigit picked up her skirts and ran to the stables. How stupid to believe him when he said he would wait and talk to her. Clever, a trickster...and a liar, as well.

Inside the stables, the roan greeted her with a nicker. He'd taken only one horse, thank God.

Brigit's relief lasted as long as it took to check the grain container, where they'd stashed the extra guns and ammunition.

Gone.

She slammed the lid. "Damn you!"

The noise made the horse jerk its head up, and its ears went back.

"Easy, boy. I'm not angry with you." She reached for the roan's bridle, which Jasper had looped over a nail on a support beam.

The sun hadn't been up for long. If she hurried, she could catch up with him, once she figured out which direction he'd gone.

Sally burst into the barn. She grabbed Brigit by the arm. "Jasper hasn't betrayed you. He promised he'd be back and he will. He honors his word."

"He didn't honor our agreement. I won't wait and see whether he'll honor anything else." Brigit resisted the smaller woman's surprisingly strong restraint.

"You can't go after him alone. It's too dangerous." Sally grasped the reins and stubbornly clung to them. "Why would you risk your life for a newspaper article?"

A hot flush flooded Brigit's face. "Is that what he told you?"

Her pretense had given Jasper reason to think her mission wasn't all that important, certainly not in light of his priorities.

"This isn't about a news article. It's about preserving lives." It was also about saving her career, although that seemed far less important at the moment.

"Where did he go?"

"To find Tom...and J.D." Sally's hesitance indicated she wasn't eager for Jasper to find the second man. She released the reins, but her dark gaze begged for understanding. "My brother can be stubborn and difficult, but he isn't a coward. He hasn't run away."

"I know he's not a coward. That's not the point. He agreed we'd talk this morning and set out together." Brigit shifted the bridle over one arm and went to enter the stall, but then Sally moved in front of her.

"Yes, I told him he shouldn't leave. That he should wait and talk to you. Maybe take you along. He doesn't show it, but he's afraid for me, and you. He's just trying to protect us the only way he knows how."

By making himself the target.

He'd not only gone to find those men, Jasper intended to leave a false trail away from the farm. Sally understood this, and she hadn't been able to stop him either. Even if he intended to return, he wouldn't make it back if the men hunting him caught up.

Brigit considered physically removing the obstacle in her way. It wasn't just anger motivating her. She feared for Jasper and had become attached to the rascal. She had to remind herself about why Jasper was important and not allow emotions to get in the way. If she didn't go after him, she could fail in her mission. It was as simple as that.

It wasn't so simple to Sally, whose youthful features were twisted with anxiety. Did she fear her brother's wrath because she couldn't prevent their guest from following?

Brigit pulled the poor girl into her arms. "Don't worry. I won't let him hurt you."

"He wouldn't," Sally said into her shoulder. "He won't hurt you, either."

"Perhaps not. But I may punch *him* in the nose for leaving without me."

A distant pounding signaled the arrival of a rider. Brigit's hope and kind feelings toward Jasper rekindled.

"Could that be your brother?"

Sally broke away, wide-eyed. "No. I should've brought the shotgun."

"Stay behind me. I'll protect you." Brigit retrieved the Derringer from beneath her skirt.

"Hello?" A man called from the yard. "Anybody home? Sally?"

"I know that voice." Sally darted to the open door and peered around the edge. "Thank God. It's only Tom."

"Tom?" Brigit kept her pistol handy. "The one-who-can't-stay-sober, Tom?"

"Our cousin, Tom Bluejacket." Sally cast her reply over her shoulder and then ran across the yard toward her cousin to greet him.

Tom tied his spotted horse to the hitching post. In height, build, and coloring, he looked similar to Jasper, but Tom's black hair hung in long braids. One straight feather adorned his wide-brimmed hat. He wore a chambray shirt like a tunic over his denim trousers. Whatever his lineage, his mode of dress reflected pride in his Indian ancestry. The whiskey bottle in his hand, not so much.

Brigit put her pistol away and then went to meet Mr. Bluejacket with the best smile she could manage around the protruding teeth. If Jasper had found his cousin and sent him back with instructions, it wasn't what they'd agreed, but it was better than leaving her with no information.

Tom met Sally in front of the house. "How's Candy getting along? I brought some whiskey to cheer him up."

"He's sleeping. Better this morning, I think." She took the bottle from her cousin and held it up to peer through the amber glass. "It's almost empty."

"Had to make sure it wasn't tainted." Tom turned a penetrating gaze on Brigit, who returned the perusal. He had mastered the technique of what gamblers called a poker face. "Who is this?"

"She came here with Jasper," Sally explained.

"Is she Jasper's lady friend?"

Brigit couldn't control the blush. *Lady friend*, as in consort? "Why would you think that?"

"Tom, Miss Robb is a reporter." Sally's tone held a hint of rebuke. "Jasper told me she stole him off the train after she tricked the marshal."

Brigit nodded rather than curtsy. She smoothed stray frizz that had escaped the bun, strands chewed by that masked fiend.

Tom's almond-shaped eyes narrowed in disbelief. "This uh...white woman?"

He'd been about to say, *ugly* white woman.

"All it took was a flask of *tainted* whiskey," Brigit remarked dryly.

"She drugged him," Sally added. "It was very clever. I'm surprised Jasper didn't tell you about it. Where is he?"

It took Tom another moment to shift his attention to Sally. "He isn't here?"

His question erased Brigit's patience and good humor. "Wasn't he with you?"

"What made you think that?"

God help her. They were talking in circles.

Sally chewed her lower lip. "Jasper left at dawn to go search for you and J.D."

A small detail she'd forgotten to mention.

Brigit resisted the urge to clench her teeth, which would dislodge the false ones.

Tom removed his hat. He wiped away a ring of sweat with the back of his sleeve. "I rode like hell to get here. Maybe I missed him."

Something didn't make sense.

"Where did you hear about me, if you didn't see Jasper?" Brigit asked.

"I ran into old man McKenzie at a trading post," Tom explained. "He tried to sell me a coffin. Said he'd seen Jasper on the Texas road, going south, and he had a woman with him. A lady friend."

Well, that explained it, in part. The old codger had rid himself of those two outlaws but wasn't willing to waste a coffin.

"We did encounter Mr. McKenzie. Jasper told him we were on our way to be married."

"Married?" Tom and Sally spoke in unison with twin expressions reflecting their shock.

Brigit folded her arms over her chest. If they couldn't figure out it was a ruse, she wasn't going to explain it. "Mr. McKenzie promised he wouldn't tell anyone that he'd seen Jasper. I wonder, can any of the men in the Territory be trusted to keep their word?"

Tom stared at her with incomprehension.

Sally gave her chiding glance before speaking to Tom. "Where did J.D. go?"

"We split up to lose the men who were chasing us. Agreed to meet at the usual place in *Mus-co-gee* Station. I decided to come here first, to check on you and Candy."

Brigit wondered whether it was the town Claire had told her about. Her youngest sister pronounced it differently. "Do you mean the stop along the Katy line, the one they call Muskogee? I hear it's a lawless place with nothing but brothels and saloons."

"We have friends there," Tom said.

His factual reply reminded Brigit about the kind of men she was dealing with.

"Ah, yes. Of course, you do. Why wouldn't you? Does Jasper have friends there?"

Tom looked off in the direction of the woods. Then he turned to Sally. "You got any food? I'm starved."

He either didn't know where Jasper had gone or he wasn't telling.

Brigit went in the direction Tom had looked, down the trail through the forest that led to the creek. The rocky, root-gnarled path had been cleared of any tracks, including their footprints from the night before. Even the fish trap was gone.

Jasper had come this way at some point, but she couldn't determine where he'd gone from here, much less how to find her way through these woods. As much as she hated to admit it, she had to wait until he came back for her or risk getting lost.

By the time she returned to the cabin, discouraged and frustrated, the eggs left for her were cold. Sally kindly offered to warm them and served one of the thin cornmeal pancakes she'd made the night before.

The man in the bed struggled into a sitting position with a great deal of moaning and groaning. Sally took him a plate and sat at the bedside, coaxing him with small bites interspersed with encouragement. Her nurturing instincts were on full display.

Brigit looked away, vaguely uncomfortable. Not every woman had such tendencies, despite society's general opinion. Nothing was wrong because she didn't possess a keen desire to settle down and become a homemaker. Hannah felt the same. They had interesting, well-paying jobs so neither was compelled to marry simply to survive. It was up to them to make sure things stayed that way, and this case was key to their success.

Jasper had better return within the hour.

After finishing her breakfast, Brigit cleaned her dishes, using water from a bucket set inside a trough that served as a dry sink. She could take care of her mess and refused to be waited upon.

Tom watched her every move. It was difficult to tell from the stoic expression whether his interest stemmed from suspicion or curiosity, but it made her uneasy.

She faced him with her hands on her hips. "Is there some reason you're staring at me?"

"I don't have anything else interesting to look at."

"What about them?" She pointed at Sally and the man they called Candy.

Tom didn't spare the two a glance. "I've seen them before. You're new. Different."

"Different?" Brigit shook her head. Had he intentionally avoided a more precise word, such as *unattractive*? "What is that supposed to mean?"

"I've never met a woman reporter. Or one who stole an outlaw off a train."

"Is it the fact that I'm a *woman* you find surprising or that I pulled off the heist without getting anyone shot?"

"Both."

God help her.

She would lose her mind if she had to hang around here all day, waiting for a man whose return wouldn't be timely or even guaranteed. From what Tom had said, it sounded as if the men had a regular meeting place in Muskogee. Jasper might've gone there. It was even possible that some of his so-called friends there had at one time met Lester Kinkaid. They might even know of the missing agent's whereabouts.

"How long will it take Jasper to reach Muskogee?" she asked Tom.

"On horseback, a day. By train from Vinita, a couple of hours. He won't take the train."

An assumption that would be obvious to even the dullest person. And Tom had unwittingly played his hand. He'd confirmed Jasper's likely destination.

"How often do southbound trains leave Vinita?"

"Once in the morning, once in the afternoon."

"What time?"

"Depends on the day of the week, and the weather, and whether or not the train gets stopped or held up."

Brigit gave an exasperated laugh. "How do you know when to be there to meet the train?"

"I don't know when. I just show up and wait." Tom tipped the bottle toward her. "Want a drink?"

"No, thank you. Save it for your friend."

"Jasper will come back," Sally repeated her mantra as if by saying it over and over, her prediction would come true.

"Your faith is stronger than mine," Brigit said.

Jasper tricked her into thinking he felt obligated to her and she had let down her guard. He had asked her to trust him and she had, only to have another man disappoint her. Experience should've warned her. But last night, when Jasper had given her a glimpse into his tortured soul, he'd touched her heart, stirring up feelings she hadn't believed could be revived.

Maybe that's why she was so angry and hurt. Wounded pride. She would be better prepared when she caught up with him. He would not so easily dupe her again.

Brigit cleaned the remainder of the dishes while Sally changed the dressing on the injured man's wound. Tom sat at the table with his hand curled lovingly around the bottle. Could he stay sober enough to be of assistance?

Brigit approached the man lazing at the table. "Mr. Bluejacket. Would you please make yourself useful?"

"How?"

"Guide me to Vinita."

Sally twisted around from her bedside perch. "Why are you going there?"

"I intend to catch the afternoon train to Muskogee. I need Jasper's assistance to complete my assignment."

"You want to go to *Mus-co-gee* Station?" Tom's question implied his hearing wasn't good. Or it could be that he didn't want her to go after Jasper for some reason.

"Yes," Brigit said firmly. "Why shouldn't I?"

"The only women who get off the train at that stop are working girls."

Prostitutes. Which she most certainly was *not*, and pretending to be one seemed a bad idea.

"Don't worry about me," she said, although she sensed he hadn't remarked out of concern. "I'll be sure to keep my visit brief."

CHAPTER 7

*J*asper tied the white horse to a hitching rail outside the biggest, most popular watering hole in *Mus-co-gee* Station. The road behind him teemed with patrons of numerous saloons, gambling houses, and brothels, which lined the only street.

The town had sprung up about a year ago when the railroad had established a post office. Since then, the Katy had gone broke, along with the rest of the country, and outlaws had swarmed the Territory. They gathered here like flies at a picnic.

Jasper knew most of the Creek families who lived around the town, some of the outlaws who visited, and a few of the whores. In the past, he might've lingered for a drink or a card game, occasionally, a woman's company. Tonight, he didn't plan to stay any longer than necessary to locate two men.

A warm light emanating from the saloon's windows and open door cast shadows of couples engaged in banter or business. Some of them didn't bother with beds.

One of the unoccupied women approached Jasper. She drew her long black hair over a bare, bony shoulder exposed by the low-cut, ill-fitting dress. "I like you. You like me?"

Even the low light couldn't disguise how worn out she looked or how young. Younger even than his nineteen-year-old sister.

Jasper held up his hand to indicate he wasn't interested. He'd dug up his savings to buy information, not women. As she reached for his coat sleeve, he caught her wrist. "Not tonight."

Her hollow-eyed gaze filled with desperation and triggered his pity.

He pressed a coin into her hand. "Go, get yourself something to eat. Come back and watch my horse, and I'll give you another dollar."

She looked up with surprise, then a tremulous smile. "*Muh-doe.*" She thanked him in the Creek language before she spun around and ran off down the street.

Jasper watched until she vanished into the darkness. Would she do as he asked? She might instead purchase drinks or laudanum or something else that would help her forget the cruelty of the life she'd been subjected to. Young women like her hadn't chosen their profession. Choices were for the rich, not girls like her.

Even if he robbed every train that passed through the Territory, he couldn't vanquish the inequities that smacked him in the face everywhere he turned. At one time, he'd foolishly imagined he could tip the scales. He knew better now. He'd be lucky if he could take one rich bastard to hell with him. First, though, he had to find a traitor.

With a tired sigh, he adjusted his coat over the handle of his revolver and entered the brightly lit saloon.

The original structure had burned down a few months ago. This version, aptly named The Phoenix, had a painting over the bar of the legendary bird emerging from the flames. In rebuilding, the industrious owner had used what was at hand. Railroad ties and rails for the bar. Other paintings featuring naked nymphs hung on uneven lengths of boards reinforced with metal siding, which might've come from a scrap heap.

Jasper rubbed his thumb over the lapel of the black suit that made him look like a preacher. New clothes couldn't transform an outlaw into a godly man. Not any more than a rescue plan would make J.D. Liddle a hero.

It was risky as hell to attempt to take a bound man out of a rail car at a station teeming with guards. Only the bravest or luckiest could manage to free anyone under those conditions. Unlike Miss Robb, J.D. was a stupid coward. It sure looked as though someone else had planned the scheme and then paid J.D. to lure Tom and Candy into an ambush.

The Phoenix was packed with the usual assortment of blood, breeds, and white trash. Up in Kansas or down in Texas, these men wouldn't have associated with each other. They didn't like each other any better here, yet they were drawn together for one reason. The local tribe wouldn't police the railroad town.

One of the toughs, Brad Collins, stood at the bar, deep into his cups. Jasper had nothing against him. They were both outlaws and considered breeds. But that's where the similarity ended. Collins took offense easily and was quick to kill, particularly when he was drunk. He wouldn't have any useful information. Tom and J.D. were afraid of him and stayed out of his way.

Jasper spotted Tom's favorite fancy girl, a Seneca woman who'd named herself *Truly*. She had on her customary skimpy costume and heavy make-up and was laughing over something her customer was saying.

The white peddler bought up Indian medicine and sold it for more money than he paid. Greedy, but not stupid. It was unlikely he'd have anything to do with the ambush.

Jasper made his way through the crowded room toward the couple. He passed behind Collins without saying anything.

Outlaws didn't greet each other unless they wanted to instigate trouble. For the most part, Jasper kept to himself. If the trouble found him, however, he wouldn't run from it, which was why he couldn't have brought along that lady reporter. Miss Robb would attract trouble.

Jasper slapped the gabby peddler on the shoulder. "That's a funny story, mister. I need to borrow Truly for a minute, then you can tell her the rest of it."

The man appeared annoyed at first, then nervous. He scurried away like a mouse.

"I think he recognized me," Jasper said, mildly.

"That was rude," Truly scolded. "He's a customer."

"Yeah. You can go tickle his ear in a minute." Jasper led her to the back of the saloon where they were less likely to be overheard. "Have you seen Tom Bluejacket?"

She eyed him speculatively. "No. Not for a while."

"What about J.D. Liddle? Seen him around?"

Truly pursed her lips like she was thinking.

Jasper slipped her a dollar.

"He left this morning for Denison," she said promptly.

Denison was a few hundred miles south across the Red River in Texas. Two railroad lines converged there, along with scores of cattle and the drovers bringing them there to be slaughtered. A cattle town wasn't a place where J.D. would typically go, and it was in the opposite direction of the farm where he'd left Sally with a promise to return.

"Did he say why he was going to Denison?" Jasper asked.

Truly shook her head. "I don't know anything more."

The sounds of drunken laughter and sharp feminine objections caught Jasper's ear. A flicker of annoyance went through him. Even if the girls in here got paid, they didn't make enough to put up with abuse.

He glanced over his shoulder, then did a double-take, disbelieving what he'd seen.

Alice Robb shouldn't be here, but there she was. Dressed in gray, like a spinster, attempting to elbow her way past Brad Collins. The drunken lout had taken hold of her and was laughing his ass off while she wriggled in his arms. Her face was red as a berry.

It might've been funny, except Collins had a reputation for beating women when they made him angry. And Miss Robb had a sharp tongue without enough sense to go with it.

Truly slipped off before Jasper could stop her. He'd gotten all he could from her. Now he had to figure out a way to get Alice out of here unharmed without starting a brawl.

Impossible.

The outlaw stole Alice's bonnet and waved it in the air like a trophy.

She grabbed her bun like it might fly off. "Stop it! Return my bonnet at once!"

Collins laughed and jerked her up against him. "Come on, sweetheart. I've always wanted to poke an ugly woman. I hear they're good in bed."

The slap she gave him could be heard across the room.

Jasper jerked himself out of his shock and stormed to her rescue. He pushed men aside if they didn't give way, setting a straight path with the certain knowledge that he was about to ignite a keg of dynamite. He'd have one chance to catch Collins off guard and give Alice a chance to escape the inevitable explosion.

Collins didn't notice Jasper's approach. The oaf was too busy chasing Alice around a table.

She sidestepped another clumsy lunge.

Before the drunk could go after her again, Jasper grabbed him by the shoulder and spun him around with an angry command.

"Leave her alone!"

Miss Robb peeked around her attacker's shoulder. "Thank heavens. Jasper. We need to—

"Who's gonna make me?" Collins shoved Jasper's chest.

He flexed his fists. This was one fight he might enjoy. "I'd be delighted."

"No! Stop!" Alice stepped between them at the same time Collins threw a punch.

Jasper shoved her out of the way, but he wasn't quick enough. He watched in horror as her front teeth went flying across the room.

~

BRIGIT STAGGERED when Jasper pushed her. The other man's punch had glanced off her fake teeth and her spectacles had ended up under her chin. She pulled them off and put her other hand to her mouth. *Ow!* A split lip, and—

Oh no. The teeth were gone!

She stuffed the twisted spectacles into her bodice then dropped to her hands and knees and searched for the missing custom-made false teeth. Two men at a nearby table howled with delight. She'd become the new entertainment.

Jasper and the black-haired drunk landed on top of the table. It collapsed beneath them with a crash, sending cards spinning into the air. The men who'd been sitting there, laughing, toppled backward. She grimaced at the sound of breaking glass.

Cheers went up as the fighters grappled on the floor, snarling like animals.

Between the men's legs, Brigit could see her tormenter straddle Jasper and punch him in the face. The next moment, Jasper flipped his enemy and seized the upper hand. He hammered the man with a ferocity that both fascinated and terrified her.

No, no, no... She didn't want him to fight her battles.

The flash of a blade sent her heart into her throat.

Jasper grabbed his opponent's wrist and slammed it to the floor, loosening his grip on the knife. The other man used his free hand to land a solid punch that knocked Jasper sideways, then rolled and came to his feet with the knife in his hand and his back to her.

As Jasper scrambled to get up, he darted a look in her direction. Only for an instant but long enough that he didn't see the arcing slash. The knife sliced through his coat sleeve and drew blood.

She gasped. Why didn't he use his gun?

Because facing her as he did, she might be hit.

"Stop!" Brigit levered herself off the floor, lifting her skirt to retrieve the pistol. She was close enough to fire a shot at the scoundrel without hitting Jasper if she aimed at a part of his body where the bullet wouldn't pass through.

Suddenly, she couldn't move. Someone behind her had grabbed her hair.

The next instant, her wig popped off.

Brigit ignored the startled shout behind her and fired at the knife-wielding man's buttocks.

Collins jerked, then howled in pain, but didn't lose his footing. His enraged roar drowned out the jeers as he turned to face her.

Her heart lodged in her throat.

Before her attacker could reach her, Jasper's arm snaked around his neck, which gave her the opportunity she needed.

She delivered a hard kick to the man's genitals.

His knees buckled. Jasper released his hold as the other man toppled to the floor with his hands between his legs. His eyes bulged and his mouth moved, but the only sounds that came out were high-pitched grunts.

The room erupted with a mixture of groans and coarse laughter.

Jasper appeared dazed. Blood streamed from his nose and bright red spittle clung to his lips. One eye had started to swell.

She stepped over the prone man and grabbed Jasper's uninjured arm. "Come on. We have to go."

He peered at her as if he were having trouble seeing. "Did you find your teeth?"

"I don't need them."

"What happened to your hair?"

"Gone. It's not important." She hauled him toward the front door.

Someone handed Jasper his hat and patted him on the back. Another man glared at her. He made a crude remark about Mr. Collins using his knife to remove her breasts.

Jasper went for his revolver. "Sorry, son-of-a—"

"Oh no, you don't. We're leaving!" She jerked him out the door, trying hard to act brave, yet trembling inside. Who knew how many friends that awful man had, or how long it would take them to decide to come after her and exact revenge?

She drew Jasper's good arm across her shoulders to provide

support and to prevent him from engaging in a gunfight. "We have to get out of this town."

"I need to find Tom," he muttered.

"He's fine. He returned to the cabin. He's the one who let on you'd be here."

"Ought to strangle him." Jasper pulled her to a stop in front of the hitching rail. "Here's my horse."

An Indian girl, who'd been sitting on the side of a trough, stood up and smiled as if she'd been expecting him. A burst of jealousy surprised Brigit. Jasper's dalliances were the last thing she needed to be worried about.

"We won't get far before you fall off from exhaustion or loss of blood."

A whistle sounded.

She'd gotten off the train a short time ago, and had walked less than a block to the largest saloon to look for Jasper. In the meantime, the train had finished getting water for its tanks and would be leaving in five minutes. Would her luck hold out that long?

Brigit gripped the front of his shirt. "We can catch the train if we hurry."

Jasper hesitated only a moment before he handed the horse's reins to the girl. "Take him. He's yours."

She heard the Indian girl say something in her language as they hurried away.

They walked as fast as Jasper's condition allowed. He didn't seem to notice or care about the men who stared at them as they passed. No one offered to help.

By the time they reached the platform, the train had started to move.

"Run!" she yelled. "We can make it."

She sprang toward the steps leading up to the back door of a passenger car, then moved up to give Jasper room. He made it, but his injured arm struck the railing and he lost his balance. She grabbed his coat and hauled him against her, the force propelling them back onto the metal landing. He lay sprawled on top of her, breathing heavily.

"As lovely as this is," he gasped. "I think we could find a better seat."

A loud release of steam enveloped them in warm, moist clouds.

She released her tension in a laugh. "You do know how to woo a woman."

After he'd rolled away and she'd helped him to his feet, he peered at her with an expression that might've been confusion—or pain. Once they were inside the car, she slipped onto the first open seat. Jasper sat down and leaned heavily against her.

At the other end of the aisle, the conductor looked up, noticing them. He probably wouldn't recognize the train robber sitting next to her. But just in case...

Brigit embraced her companion and drew his face against her shoulder, using his hat to shield his features. "Don't look up," she whispered.

A moment later, the conductor stopped next to their seat and peered over his spectacles.

Brigit braced herself for an inquisition.

"Tickets?" he asked.

"Tickets...yes..." She hadn't planned that far ahead. "I'm sorry. We were late boarding and didn't get them. Can I pay you?

"What's your destination?"

"Um..." She had no idea.

"Denison," Jasper whispered. He moved his arm beneath him, reaching inside his coat, then handed her a wad of bills.

Where on earth had he gotten all this money? She'd ask him later.

"Denison," she announced.

The conductor referred to a card and quoted the fare.

Why Denison? Another question to add to her list.

She adjusted her hold on Jasper to count out the correct amount. His hat slid off and landed at the conductor's feet. Long dark hair hung across Jasper's face, shielding his eyes, but the swollen lip and the torn and bloody sleeve made it apparent he'd been in a fight.

The conductor bent to pick up the hat and handed it to her without comment.

He might report them to his superiors if he got suspicious. She needed to come up with a plausible excuse.

Brigit hugged Jasper and tried to look worried, which wasn't difficult because she *was* worried. She used her handkerchief to wipe the blood from beneath Jasper's nose. "My husband is a man of God. We stopped to preach the Word in that sinful place. It wasn't well received."

"No, I imagine not." The conductor walked away, shaking his head.

She put her lips close to Jasper's ear. "I'm fairly certain he bought the story and doesn't know who you are," she murmured.

Jasper stirred. He raised his head to look at her with the one eye that remained open. "I know who *I* am. Who the hell are you?"

CHAPTER 8

"*N*ext stop, Denison!" The conductor's shout brought Jasper back to awareness.

He'd fallen asleep with his head on Alice's shoulder, waiting for her to answer his question. If she had, he hadn't heard her, but he didn't think she'd spoken for the past few hours, which was the longest period the aggravating woman had remained silent since he'd met her.

He groaned as he sat up from his cramped position. At some point, she'd removed his tie and wrapped it around the cut on his arm. It wasn't bleeding. Or he couldn't feel it.

"Well?" he asked her. "Who are you, besides being more trouble than you're worth?"

She shifted on the bench away from him and kept her eyes trained straight at the back of another man's head. "I'll tell you, as soon as—"

The shrill squeal of the brakes drowned out whatever condition she'd put on her answer.

He'd wring the truth out of her when they didn't have a crowd around them.

As the train slowed to a stop, Jasper snatched up the black hat. He grabbed the back of the bench when his stiff muscles objected to standing. Alice came off the seat in a hurry to put her hand beneath his elbow, which he promptly jerked away. He wanted no more of her concern or sympathy, which he'd bet were as false as her teeth and hair.

Jasper waited while she exited the car then followed her down the steps. She had brown hair, at least what he could see of it, braided in tight rows beneath a hair net.

He caught up to her. The spectacles she'd worn were tucked between two buttons on her jacket. She didn't trip or run into anything, so he assumed she didn't need those either.

He reached out to pull up her lip and she bared her teeth. Straighter than his.

Although she looked a little roughed up, no one would call her *ugly*. He'd thought she had resisted his advances because she lacked confidence in her looks. The truth was probably less flattering to him.

When they were a few feet away from the cars and the smoke, she turned to face him with her hands planted on her hips. "Why did you want to come to Denison?"

She had some nerve, asking him a question before she'd answered his.

"Why did you pretend to be an ugly reporter?" he shot back.

After holding his gaze another moment, she sighed. "We'll talk about this later."

"You've put me off for hours. How much later?"

She turned her back on him and set off.

He would've grabbed her if some of the departing passengers weren't watching them. If they got to arguing, someone might intervene, or worse, send for the local lawman.

Jasper swallowed his anger and followed her at a short distance. When he'd finally put together the pieces, he'd realized that Alice probably wasn't a reporter. Or, if she was, she'd disguised herself so she could later shed her identity and claim to have nothing to do with his escape. As far as she was concerned, he was a useful tool in a scheme he didn't fully understand.

He'd stay with her long enough to get the truth. Then he'd take care of his business before deciding what to do about hers.

Rail cars stacked with bricks were parked outside the half-completed station. He'd heard that the original structure had burned to the ground under suspicious circumstances. Another thing the railroad had tried to pin on him. If he'd done half of what he'd been accused of, he would've needed a twin brother to help him. Hadn't she mentioned a twin sister? Just think of all the things she could've gotten away with.

Alice halted abruptly. The yellow glow from a mounted gas lamp in front of the new depot cast enough light to see the wide road in front of them, paved with mud and manure.

She wrinkled her nose. "What's that smell?"

"Cow shit. You ought to be familiar with it, considering how much you've been shoveling."

She jerked her attention to him with a frown. "And what about you?"

"What about me?"

"You've been doing everything in your power to avoid helping me find Mr. Kinkaid."

"Yeah, while you're at it, tell me about this missing reporter. Who is he really, and what is he to you?" Jasper clenched his fists. He didn't care, or if he did, it wasn't because he was jealous.

Alice stared across the street. Was she afraid to look at him and admit she'd lost her lover? "I'll tell you everything. After we find a place to stay. My brother and his wife recently relocated to Denison, but they travel a great deal. I don't know if they're at home."

More lies?

"Do you even have a brother?"

She glared at him. "Yes, I do, as I told you before. But I'd rather not involve him."

"Assuming you aren't just stalling, I can't suggest a place to stay. I've only been here once after the railroad arrived two years ago. Back then, it was mostly canvas tents with dance halls, saloons, and brothels."

"You must've felt right at home," she said under her breath.

Hell, he needed a shield against her sharp tongue. As it was, he had to rely on his wits, and those weren't nearly sharp enough. "Where do you feel at home, Alice?"

"At the moment, a hotel. That one looks like a possibility." She gestured to the largest building across the street. Warm lights gleamed from behind lace curtains in paned windows. "Let's try there. We need food, rest...and privacy."

Her choice of words conjured up an interesting image, and an opportunity for him to give as good as he got.

"I like the sound of that. Privacy." He offered her his arm.

She pointedly ignored his gallant gesture. "So we can talk freely, and we had better tend to your wound."

"Ah, and then you'll take advantage of me." He made sure his tone sounded crude, not hopeful.

She gave him an eye roll. It would've been amusing if he weren't so annoyed with her.

The noise warned him before he saw the source, coming at breakneck speed. He stopped Alice before she stepped into the street.

A half a dozen cowhands on horseback thundered past. Obviously, in a hurry to get to women, whiskey and cards. The type of places J.D. would frequent. Jasper noted the direction he'd need to go after he and his lovely companion had a talk.

Without as much as a thank-you, Alice was off, headed for a place where she'd feel *at home.* He couldn't say the same, but she didn't seem to realize this.

He caught up with her in the middle of the street. "I can't stay at that hotel,"

She gave him a speculative once over. "Why not? You look more white than Indian."

Well, damn. The color of his skin wasn't exactly what he'd been talking about, but she'd sure hit that nail on the head.

"You think so? I don't feel *more white,* but that's beside the point. Look at me." He gestured to the torn suit and beat-up face. "I look like I belong where those drovers are headed."

She slipped her arm through his, giving him the distinct impression that she was escorting him and not the other way around. "Come with me. I'll get us in there."

Having little experience with highbrow places, he sure as hell didn't possess her confidence, but he pulled a wad of cash from inside his coat pocket. "This might help."

Surprise flashed across her face before she waved her free hand at him. "Put your money away. Flashing it around is a sign you don't have much."

He released a disbelieving laugh. "Maybe where you come from."

"Trust me," she replied.

Jasper shook off her hold on his arm. "You think you're in a position to ask for my trust?"

She stepped up to the opposite sidewalk and then whirled around, barring his way onto the raised platform. The difference in inches brought them nose-to-nose. "You broke your promise after asking for my trust."

He wasn't about to carry on an argument while standing in cow shit.

Jasper moved to one side and stepped onto the boardwalk. "No, I didn't break my promise. I delayed the time frame for delivering on it."

"That's not how I see it." Beneath the street light, the hurt feelings were illuminated on her face.

He refused to feel bad about acting in what he considered her best interests. Besides, she'd done more than engage in rash behavior. "And your lies and duplicity? How am I supposed to see that?"

"You mean the lies and duplicity that saved your life?"

Jasper gripped the pole holding the street lamp and had to resist tearing the damn thing out of the ground. He didn't want to look into her challenging gaze and admit she was right. "Yeah, you saved my sorry hide. And I owe you thanks and a favor, as you keep reminding me."

"That's not what I meant. You've asked for my trust. At least give me a chance to earn back yours." Her plea drew some of the anger out of him.

"Why do you think I followed you over here?" he muttered.

"I'm glad we agree."

Her expression softened, which made her prettier. Noticing sent his mood south again.

If she thought she could sweet-talk him into helping her after this, she had another thing coming. "We don't agree on anything, including this hotel."

She directed his attention to a sign next to the front door. "*Stay here and feel at home. Clean beds a specialty.*"

"They'll throw me out before I can dirty them." He reached for the door to open it and then followed her inside.

Two well-dressed gentlemen seated on leather chairs in the lobby glanced up. One of them gave Jasper a discouraging look. Another sign he wouldn't be welcome. As if he needed another.

The standing clock chimed.

"It's half-past seven," he told Alice. "Whatever rooms they had are spoken for by now."

"It doesn't look like they have many guests." She held onto his arm and pulled him across the lobby.

Jasper straightened his coat. He couldn't do anything about his state other than look proud of his cuts and bruises. Her dress had stains from crawling around on a barroom floor and holding onto him.

"We need fresh bandages for that cut," she said in a low tone.

He glanced down at where she gingerly held his arm. "It's not bleeding anymore. The tie appears to be working."

"The wound could become infected. Then your arm will rot off."

He was in too much pain to find *her* sarcasm funny. "Too bad. Then I couldn't hold you."

Her silent response wasn't as blessed as he'd thought it might be.

Hell, he'd been hurt worse. A lot worse.

Behind the registration counter, a slight man with small eyes and a sharp nose stood stiff as his starched collar. He took one look at them and his nose twitched.

Alice stopped when they came to a plush sofa. "Sit here. Put your head in your hands. Act injured," she said in a low voice.

"I am injured."

"Then it shouldn't take a great deal of acting ability."

Jasper sank onto the sofa. He'd let her go embarrass herself. In a minute, the hotel staff would toss them out. Then she might stop acting like she was in control and allow him to help her navigate this rough cattle town. He held his head while keeping his good eye on her.

She approached the discerning mouse behind the counter and asked whether they might have rooms available.

The clerk shook his head.

Alice dug out a blood-stained hankie and burst into tears.

Jasper tensed. She'd lost her composure. Granted, it had been a hell of a day. But they could find somewhere else to hole up. It wasn't the end of the world.

"I'm so sorry," she blubbered to the clerk. "I can't help it. My poor husband. He's a man of God with a kind, compassionate heart. We were preaching the Word to a bunch of heathens when a drunken sinner assaulted me. Brave Mr. Johnson tried to protect me and he was sorely beaten..."

Jasper kept his head ducked while he surreptitiously watched her put on an act fit for the stage. One of the two guests stared at him with curiosity while the other made himself scarce, probably fearing she'd descend on him next with her pitiful story.

By this time, she'd worked up a fountain.

The clerk handed her a clean handkerchief and she eased off the tears but kept sniffling piteously. He spoke to her softly. Jasper couldn't make out the words or her reply, but after another minute or two, the clerk patted the back of her hand and handed her a key.

She hadn't even had to show him any money.

With her head humbly bowed, she returned to the sofa.

Jasper came to his feet, tempted to give her a standing ovation.

Instead, he allowed her to circle her arm around his waist. More play-acting. Nevertheless, he wouldn't lean on her like a weakling. After all, he was *brave Mr. Johnson*. Might as well act the part.

A man wearing a uniform asked if they had any bags. Then he led them upstairs and lit the lamps inside the room before he went to the door and waited.

"Tip him," Alice whispered to Jasper.

He gave the man a dollar, having no idea whether it was enough.

The bed was larger than the ones he typically slept on—when he slept on a bed. The washstand held a ceramic basin fancier than the bowls his family had used for soup. The wardrobe had doors, and the rug on the floor wasn't made from rags. His mother had come from this kind of wealth, but her family hadn't been able to bring it with them out west, and she had married a poor immigrant.

Jasper glanced around for a place to sit. He ached from head to toe, yet he was hesitant to dirty the furnishings. "I don't generally rent a room as fancy as this one. Unless someone comes with it."

Alice sat down on the bed with her brows knitted into a troubled frown. Maybe she felt out of place, too. "It was the only room available. Sit down and let me look at your arm."

His sarcasm hadn't amused her. Then again, she'd probably been *pretending* to like him. In her eyes, he was a low-life, dirty outlaw, and his only usefulness was in getting her to where she wanted to go. "My arm doesn't hurt."

Not much.

"Why are you so stubborn?"

"Why are you so false?"

With a sigh, she stripped the net off her head and unpinned the tight braids fastened close to her skull. After she'd freed her hair, she ran her fingers through chestnut waves, which reached her shoulders. She wore it shorter than was customary, yet the length made an attractive frame for her fine-boned face.

Jasper tore his attention away, cursing his stupidity for not seeing through her disguise sooner. He peeled his coat off slowly to avoid tearing open the cut on his arm. "A bath would be nice. I'd be willing to share it. And the bed."

Rather than acknowledge his crude remark, she made a slow perusal of the room, showing nothing more than thoughtful consideration. Was she embarrassed, excited, angry, or afraid? He couldn't trust himself to read her. She was an expert actress. "The bath may have to wait. I'm sure we'll manage with one bed. After we clean up and tend to your wound."

Her placid acceptance of his crude implication they'd sleep together startled the hell out of him. Or was she just saying that to remind him of his manners? He'd left those on the train.

"You take the bed," he grumbled. "I'll sleep on the floor."

"That's kind of you to offer, but there's no need for either of us to be uncomfortable. I trust you can behave like a gentleman."

For some reason, her show of trust annoyed him. Probably because of her earlier remarks.

"When did I go from being comfortable in brothels to being a gentleman?"

She wiped her hand over her face in a gesture of pure weariness. "Jasper, please. I'm not up to any more banter. We can start again in the morning when we're both refreshed. We have a room with a clean bed, and we both need to rest and recuperate."

Her reasoning, he couldn't argue. What he couldn't handle was the storm she stirred up inside him. It confused him, made him feel awkward, and he didn't like it one damn bit.

He stood there, planted, and tried not to sway.

She got up and walked over, held his uninjured arm, and cupped his cheek with her cool fingers, gazing at him with bewilderment. "Why is it so hard for you to accept my kindness?"

He wouldn't have any problem accepting her kindness or her soft touch or the warmth in her eyes, the concern in her voice—if it was *real*. What upset him most, even more than her deceit, was that he'd let down his guard and had started to care about her. Desire her. He wanted her more than ever while fully aware of being manipulated.

He clenched his jaw rather than give her the satisfaction of knowing she'd gotten past his defenses.

She made a sad face and let her hand drop to her side. "All right. We'll do this your way."

Jasper squelched the urge to pull her to him and ravish her mouth until she gave in and stopped trying to control him. But he'd never forced himself on a woman, and wouldn't start with this one. He'd remain in here with her for one reason. To find out who she was and what she wanted. "Is your name Alice?"

"No. My name is Brigit."

His heart lurched. Brigit, a variation on *Brigid*, his Irish grandmother's name. If he didn't know better, he'd think his Pa had played a trick on him. "I like Alice Robb better."

Her eyes glistened. "Truth be told, so do I. Alice was my mother's middle name. Robb was her maiden name. She was the strongest, most compassionate woman I've ever known."

Jasper resisted her attempt to play on his heartstrings. She'd drawn him in before when she'd told him about her dead parents, and being thrown out into the streets. If that was true. How would he know? She could be very convincing. "What do you want from me?"

"Exactly what I told you. I need your help to find Mr. Kinkaid, and to gather evidence against William Bond, and whoever else is involved in his conspiracy."

She might be a great actress, but she was deluded.

"You think an outlaw and a reporter can do all that?"

"No..." She looked in the direction of a glass window where their reflections wavered against the darkness. "But an outlaw and a Pinkerton agent can."

CHAPTER 9

A knock at the door interrupted the tense silence.

Brigit's heart constricted when Jasper drew his gun. She lifted her hand to stop him. "I asked the clerk for something to eat and bandages. That's probably someone bringing it now."

Jasper lowered the gun. His glower followed her to the door. She didn't have to see it. She could *feel* it on her back like the sun on a blistering hot day. Her heart withered beneath the heat of his disdain.

She was pretty sure he'd drawn his gun due to the unexpected knock and not because he wanted to shoot her after she'd told him the truth. Her heart didn't want to believe he'd kill her. More people would believe it than those who would defend his honor and decency. After seeing him in action, there was no question about how dangerous he could be.

When she answered the door, she could run. Run to what? Failure? Having come this far, she would continue to trust her instincts. Thus far, they hadn't misled her.

Brigit hastily pulled back her hair and tried to pin it up to make herself more presentable.

The distinguished gentleman in the hall wasn't a porter or

97

kitchen staff. He did, however, offer her a tray containing two sandwiches and coffees. "This was left next to your door."

"I am a doctor." He held a black bag, which made him appear legitimate. "I overheard your conversation downstairs with the clerk and thought your husband might need medical attention."

Jasper's arm did need looking at, but he hadn't allowed her to help him beyond a temporary bandage. Maybe he'd let the doctor do the honors. Rather than ask and risk his stubborn rejection, she opened the door. "Thank you, sir. We would welcome the efforts of a Good Samaritan."

Brigit ignored Jasper's scowls. She acted as if nothing were amiss and untied the bandage on his upper arm. Thankfully, he didn't shove her away. His antagonism toward her was understandable, but now wasn't the right moment to deal with it. "I'm sure the doctor will be happy to help you with removing your coat and shirt."

She brought over the washbasin and a clean rag. The kindly doctor aided Jasper with removing his clothing without worsening the injury. He cleaned and dressed the cut then wrapped the wound —not as deep as she'd feared—with a fresh bandage.

After taking a look at *her husband's* swollen eye, the doctor pronounced Jasper's vision to be *fine* and then gave him a vial of laudanum to help with sleep.

"Let me pay you," Jasper offered.

The older man closed his bag with a snap. "No, sir. I don't expect or require compensation. I am doing the Lord's work, just like you and your wife."

Brigit managed to hold a smile until she'd closed the door, then she turned and leaned against it, drained, and more than a little ashamed about the impact of her lies on yet another unsuspecting man. "It was very kind of the gentleman to stop by. I sometimes forget there are good people out there. Like the doctor...and you."

Jasper didn't spare her a glance or even act as if he'd heard what she said. At least his wound had been treated. And he'd finally sat down on the bed and was eating one of the sandwiches. He might be in a better mood when his stomach wasn't empty.

Brigit picked up his coat and shirt from the floor and hung both inside the wardrobe. "If I can locate some thread and a needle, I know how to repair clothes."

He drained one of the cups. "The rest is yours."

Neither polite nor rude, just chillingly indifferent, which was worse than his anger. She'd prepared herself for that.

She picked up the tray and sat beside him. If she was nearly faint with hunger, how must he feel? He'd been locked away for over a month. "Thank you for sharing."

"Don't thank me. I didn't order it." He removed his boots, stretched out on top of the covers, and rolled away from her, hugging his injured arm.

Brigit ate in silence. The beef sandwich was filling, if not flavorful. The coffee was lukewarm. Better than having nothing to drink.

The vial of laudanum remained on the tray, untouched. He might not trust her enough to take something that would help him sleep soundly.

How could she explain herself in a way that Jasper would understand and accept? She'd spent three hours on the train thinking about it and hadn't come up with a convincing speech.

Her gaze strayed to his bare back, the same lovely color as the rest of him—what she'd seen. Earlier, she had misunderstood his concerns about his heritage. No matter. Her remark had been insulting.

"Are you asleep?" she whispered.

"No."

"I am sorry I insulted you about being able to pass as white."

"Was that an insult? I am half white."

"Yes, I know, but...I didn't mean to imply there is anything wrong with being half Indian."

"There isn't anything wrong with it."

Brigit released a sigh. Her fumbling apology wasn't helping, and he wasn't in the mood to receive it. He had to be fuming over what she'd told him right before the doctor showed up. "Do you want to ask me anything about what I said...about being a Pinkerton agent?"

"No."

Perhaps she should've stuck with her story about being a reporter. No. She was sick of lying to him and pretending it didn't matter. He might not help her after she told him the full truth, but he had earned the right to hear it.

After setting the tray outside the door, she returned to the bed, sat down, and addressed Jasper's back. "Lester Kinkaid, the missing man, is a Pinkerton agent."

"I figured."

Indeed. Jasper wasn't stupid. He was very clever, as well as thoughtful and brave, and truthful. Most of the time. He'd been honest about who he was and what he'd done, which was more than she could say for herself.

She swallowed her regret and continued. "So is my sister, Hannah. She helped me to free you. You asked me how I knew Lucy. She is my sister-in-law. Henry Stevens is my brother, Claire is my youngest sister. She married Frank Garrity, the former sheriff. They have three adopted boys. You know one of them. Billy."

"Are they all Pinkertons?" Jasper's tone remained flat, so it was hard to tell without seeing his face whether he was being his usual sarcastic self, but she assumed as much.

"No, it isn't *our* family's business. Henry builds railroads and Lucy writes books. Frank and Claire have a farm where they raise corn— and children. As I understand it, both are very demanding jobs."

Jasper didn't shoot back with a remark or give any sign he'd picked up on her levity.

"If you have any questions, I'm ready to answer them."

He rolled to his back and rested his bandaged arm across his stomach, which looked to be as rock hard as his back. His expression revealed nothing. No anger. No curiosity. No emotions whatsoever. He'd retreated to a place she couldn't reach him—or hurt him.

Her vision blurred.

"Those tears aren't going work with me," he said flatly.

"It isn't intentional." Brigit quickly dried her eyes. "I understand why you think I'm being dishonest, as well as manipulative because I have been. It's what I have to do, as an undercover agent. Pretend to be someone else. Hopefully, someone more interesting than me," she added with a weak laugh.

Jasper didn't crack a smile.

"I know, it's not very funny." Brigit laced her fingers together so the trembling inside wouldn't work its way out. She resorted to wry remarks in the same way he used sarcasm, as a way to avoid honest confrontation. "What I'm trying to do, and doing poorly, is to say... I owe you an apology."

"You don't owe me anything. I'm an outlaw. You're a Pinkerton. Let's move on."

Did that mean he'd accepted this apology or was he simply stating facts? Either way, he no longer wanted to hear anything more about her choices or her regrets.

"Yes, you're right." She turned and drew her leg up onto the side of the bed, and readjusted her skirt to get comfortable. Or tried, anyway. In this position, she could face him squarely and he could see her sincerity. "I know you don't trust me. I'm not sure I can trust you either, now that I've told you who I am. But we need each other. We have to work together so we don't both end up in jail."

"Why would we both end up in jail? Aren't you here because somebody with authority hired you to take me off that train?"

"No. I made the decision myself, more or less."

"What does that mean?"

She shifted on the side of the bed and turned to face him. "Our supervisors know we're here. As for taking you off the train, they don't know about that. I devised the plan with Hannah's assistance."

A plan she still believed in, if she could keep Jasper with her.

As he continued to lay there, stretched out in a deceptive posture, his gaze strayed to the far wall. She had no idea what he might be thinking. Debating whether to toss her out the window, perhaps? At last, he returned his attention to her and his uninjured eye narrowed.

Good. Get mad. Irritation, anger, suspicion, *anything* was better than indifference.

"Why didn't you ask Frank Garrity for help? Or one of your many relatives? Why would you risk your life to take me off that train? And don't tell me it was because you wanted to save my skin."

She had wanted to prevent his lynching and couldn't think of a better way to intercede in time, but that wasn't the reason she'd initially decided on him. "I didn't want to bring too many people into the investigation. Not until we know more about the players involved. You admitted to working for Mr. Bond to rob trains. Agent Kinkaid was sent down here to investigate the former general manager's criminal connections, then the detective went missing. I believed you could lead me to him."

"And I'm expendable," Jasper added.

This time, his remark didn't carry the edge of sarcasm. It rang true, and it would be for most of her colleagues. Her heart ached because Jasper believed she shared that view.

"I suppose you have reason to believe that. It's not what I think or how I feel."

The mask he'd put in place to guard his reactions slipped. He searched her face, looking for something. No, *someone*. The real person behind the one she presented. What did she, Brigit, think? Did she give a damn about him?

Brigit rested her hand on the side of the bed with her fingertips almost touching his side. Becoming closer to this complex man would be dangerous. No more dangerous than letting him go and being on her own. She had to take the chance and see whether her intuition was right. If they were to go forward together, they had to trust each other. "Mostly, I chose you to help me because I believe you to be an honorable man."

Jasper reacted with the arch of an eyebrow. "What gave you that idea?"

"The opinions of several people I know and trust, and my observations. You've tried to convince me otherwise, but the man you are, the one you deny, he keeps showing up."

He'd laced his fingers across his middle. She scooted closer and reached out to touch his forearm. Perhaps a physical connection would help to convince him.

"If you think I'm some kind of hero, you are sorely deluded," he said dryly.

She smiled at his choice of words. "I didn't say that, and I don't believe in heroes, except for in legends. Real people are more complicated. With varying degrees of goodness, some more than others. You, Mr. Byrne, possess an honorable soul. Deny it all you want, but that's the man I've seen. The person I've come to know."

His frown this time appeared to be a thoughtful one. Good, she had gotten him thinking. Or he might be wondering why she cared about his honor, outside of his usefulness for her mission. She gathered her courage to forge ahead with a confession.

"As for the truth about how I feel, I..." She removed her hand from his arm. Suddenly, the gesture seemed *too* intimate. And she couldn't find words for how she felt. It was a jumble of emotions that were hard to sort. She could express her thoughts. "I value your life. I care about you, more than I thought I would, and don't want to lose you. That's why I followed you to Muskogee. I wasn't certain you would make it back because you were on your own."

His expression flattened. "You followed me because you thought I couldn't take care of myself?"

"No. That's not what I meant."

Infuriating man. His shell was harder than a turtle's. Or her confession made him uncomfortable because he didn't share those same feelings. If so, it would be more awkward for her, not him.

It wasn't awkwardness or embarrassment she felt. Oddly enough, it could be called an ache. Or more precisely, a physical longing. She yearned for something she'd never thought she wanted before she met Jasper. Sentimental declarations were too simple to contain the whole of what she felt. There just simply wasn't a word for it.

He lay there half-naked, a wounded warrior, studying her with such intensity it made her skin grow warm and tingly. She wasn't sure what his motive had been when he'd made that remark about wanting to kiss her. Correction, he'd wanted to kiss *Alice*, not Brigit. Still, she couldn't forget about it.

Even now, she couldn't stop looking at his lips, wondering how it would feel if she pressed her mouth against his.

CHAPTER 10

*B*rigit's heart jumped to her throat when Jasper took her arm and drew her to him. Had he read her mind? She had another thought, a brief one, that she ought to resist. When he burrowed his fingers into her hair, curiosity born from an inexplicable yearning overcame her reticence.

He brought their lips together, barely touching. The most pleasurable river of sensations coursed through her and her fears dissolved. She sighed against his mouth. His fingers tightened on her hair as he deepened the kiss.

She whimpered when the kiss stung. Before she could pull away, he'd already loosened his hold, allowing her to draw back.

He gently touched his forefinger just above her upper lip and frowned. "You have a small cut."

"I forgot all about it." She hadn't even thought about the injury since it had happened. She reached up to find the tender spot.

Jasper captured her hand before she could touch it and kissed her fingers. "I should've noticed."

Did he blame himself? He hadn't delivered the punch, couldn't have anticipated she would step in the way of that clumsy drunk's fist. The man in her past who had truly hurt her had blamed her for igniting his lust and then punished her for it. Jasper hadn't even been aware he would hurt her, then he'd immediately given her freedom to get away from him.

Even now, he kept his touch light and unrestrictive, as if to communicate his intention not to force her to anything she wouldn't concede.

"Do you want to stop?" He offered her the choice.

Brigit shook her head. *No.* She wanted him to finish what he'd started, though she was too tongue-tied to tell him. Instead, she tried to show him. She propped herself across his chest, using her arm to hold her weight and protect his battered ribs.

With a frown, he knocked away her support and caught her in his arms.

"I don't want to hurt you," she said breathlessly.

"I'm not breakable." He caressed her lower lip with the side of his thumb, and the pleasurable river became a flood.

She sighed and closed her eyes.

He slid his hand behind her head and his whisper warmed her lips. "Let's try that kiss again. This time, I'll be careful."

Careful. The word he'd used described perfectly the way he held her. As if he knew she was the breakable one. Encased in a shell as fragile as glass. Fear ensured she kept her distance from anyone who could break it and hurt her again. But Jasper wasn't trying to break anything, and what he was doing was nowhere near hurtful, though it did make her ache. Her breasts. Her private places. Even her heart.

He replaced his thumb with his lips. Touching, nibbling, suckling her lower lip, while avoiding the injured one. His kisses were better than she'd imagined.

Brigit rested her arms on either side of his head and combed her fingers through his thick hair while she mimicked his actions. She had no earthly idea how to kiss properly. The only other kisses she'd experienced had been forced on her. If she liked what Jasper was doing to her, she figured he might enjoy the same.

His fingers left a shivering trail down her neck before he splayed his hand over her breastbone.

Her breathing staggered and her heart pounded harder. She fisted his hair, a reaction more to a rush of excitement than fear. Was this passion? A feeling she'd heard about but had never understood, much less experienced. She would find out if she let Jasper continue to work wonders with his kisses.

His fingers moved again, and now he stroked the base of her throat. Her bare skin. He'd unbuttoned her collar.

Inside a dark place in her mind, the old fears stirred. They pressed against a door she'd closed and locked a long time ago. She grasped Jasper's hand, stopping his progress and ending the magical kiss. "What-what are you doing?"

"Unbuttoning your jacket." After stating the obvious, a tiny smile curled the side of his mouth and a dimple appeared. She hadn't noticed it before because of the bristle.

She stared in fascination while struggling to reframe her question, though it was hard to string together words when her mind kept wandering back to that dimple and his moist lips. "*Why* are you unbuttoning my jacket?"

"To make you more comfortable." He tucked a strand of loose hair behind her ear. "If you keep looking at me like that, I'll have to kiss you again."

A rush of heat swept through her. *Passion. Desire. Lust.* She didn't know precisely what to name it, only that she was certain it would carry her away if she didn't let go of him. Strangely enough, she felt safer holding on.

"Or you can kiss me," he said. "Either way."

She couldn't help returning his wry smile. His gentle teasing eased the tightness in her chest. He hadn't forced her to do anything. He hadn't railed at her for tempting him beyond endurance. He hadn't torn her garments or threatened her with reprisal if she didn't let him have his way.

Brigit leaned down for another kiss. He started with soft, delicate pressure, as though her lips were made of spun sugar. When he kissed her with more hunger and urgency, it released her desperate yearnings. Breathing became more difficult.

"We should remove the rest of our dirty clothes," he murmured between kisses. "Or these bedsheets won't be clean for long."

True... On the other hand, she wasn't so naive she didn't realize what a temptation being unclothed would present. In this case, for both of them. Her desire to experience more of this newfound passion warred with her fears.

"I'm not sure...that's a good idea." Her voice came out breathy and labored, rather than firm, as she'd intended.

"You'd rather remain in your dirty clothes?" He whispered in her ear, producing more shivers.

She withdrew from the distraction his kisses created and looked down at him with a frown. "No. I'd rather be comfortable and sleep beneath clean sheets. But if I undress and get into bed with you, it's to go to sleep. Agreed?"

He gazed at her for another long moment. Each time she put a question to him, he seemed to mull it over, as if he were trying to figure out the right answer. Perhaps kissing had the same dissembling effect on his mind as it did hers.

"Whatever you want." He reached up and wound a strand of hair around his forefinger, then let it slide away, illustrating his willingness to give her complete freedom to decide for herself. She could stay or go. She could kiss him or not. She could sleep or they could—

No. They could not do *that.* Talk about mistakes.

She had to approach this logically. Having been a Pinkerton detective for nearly ten years, she'd learned to make do in all sorts of uncomfortable circumstances. None of those had included sharing a bed with a man. But she could manage sleeping next to Jasper for one night if he could manage to keep his word. His record on promises was somewhat spotty, but she conceded his good intentions. He'd shown her respect thus far and she would hold him to it.

"We have a deal."

He smiled again when she grasped his hand and shook it.

Brigit got off the bed. With her back to him, she removed her jacket, then shed her skirt and petticoat. Her hand stopped at the hooks holding her corset. Sleeping in it would be uncomfortable, but removing it would make her feel naked.

"Do you generally sleep in your corset?" Jasper's voice sounded casual.

She threw a wary look over her shoulder. "Not usually."

He rolled to his uninjured side and sat on the side of the bed, shirtless and barefooted, and far too tempting. "Turn around. I'll help you remove it."

She shivered just thinking about what having his hands on her would do to her senses—and her good sense. "Thank you, but no. I can unhook it from the front."

He shrugged, although his expression conveyed disappointment. "As you wish."

Twice now, he'd made that statement. Since when had he become so agreeable?

Since she'd let him kiss her. It seemed to have made him downright docile. Purring, like a cat. Perhaps she should've tried it earlier and would've avoided the need to chase him all over creation.

Brigit heard a sound from behind her and glanced around. While she'd stripped down to her shift and stockings, he had shucked off...everything!

The white bandage around his arm stood out in stark contrast to his dark skin. He was, in a word, *magnificent*. Lean and muscular, hard, not flabby like—

Don't think about it.

She jerked her head around and threw her corset into the wardrobe. "For heaven's sake, get under the covers."

Venturing a second glance, she noted with relief that he'd indulged her.

Thank goodness.

Brigit hesitated another moment before she slipped beneath the sheets. She might tell herself it made no difference whether he slept in the nude, but her racing pulse said differently.

After fussing with the pillow, which he'd kindly left for her to use, she laid down with her back to him. She heard him breathe out with what sounded like a chuckle.

What was he thinking? He might not believe she was untried. After all, she had declared having been in the company of prostitutes. If she traveled with a man and slept in the same bed with him, she knew what kind of signal that sent. Even so, she'd made her wishes known and they had shaken on it. They would sleep. Only that.

On the other hand, she had enjoyed his kisses and yearned for more. She was torn between hoping he'd kiss her again and fearing what might happen if he touched her. If she kept thinking about this, she'd never fall asleep.

She forced her breathing to slow and listened for his to fall into a measured rhythm.

A moment later, Jasper shifted closer and slipped an arm around her waist. He spooned her close against him. So close, she felt his arousal against her backside.

Shock slammed into her chest. Every muscle in her body froze.

"Does that mean you're impressed?" Jasper nuzzled her neck as he ran his hand over her hip and down to a garter holding up her stocking.

Prickles raced across her skin in response to his hot breath on her neck. When she felt his rough palm through the thin shift, she tried to speak, but what came out was a loud gasp. He squeezed her breast. Not hard and painful, like before. This touch was gentle and exploratory. Her body betrayed her when his thumb brushed the sensitive tip. "You want this?"

Memories exploded out of the cellar in her mind, sending a cold surge of fear racing through her veins. Her breath came out in spurts, her heart raced so fast it made her lightheaded.

Devlin held her breast in his hand. She could feel his hot breath on her neck.

"You want this."

But she didn't! God no! No, she didn't want it! She didn't want him to put that thing inside her again and hurt her.

"Please—" She tried to beg him to stop, but fear locked her throat.

He rolled her onto her back, draped his leg over hers, and pinned her arms over her head. In the darkness, she couldn't see his evil smile. "I like it when you say *please*," he rasped.

His voice sounded different.

"Say please," the devil ordered.

If she didn't, the belt would come down again across her raw buttocks.

With a broken cry, Brigit jerked her arms, yanking her wrists out of whatever cords he'd used to bind her. Before he could get to her again, she rolled away. Became entangled in the blanket, and it went with her, trapping her legs. She hit the floor with a thud.

The fall dislodged her mindless fear. Breathing heavily, she sat there a moment, struggling to think clearly. She wasn't in the room with her guardian. He was dead. Buried. She was safe.

No! Not safe. Jasper had attacked her!

"Brigit? Are you hurt?" His rasping voice sent shivers across her skin.

A moment later, a match flared. He lit the lamp, revealed his nakedness, and walked toward her. Coming after her...

She tore the blankets away and came to her feet with a curse, reached for where she always kept her pistol, and encountered only the garter. Her heart nearly burst in a blast of panic. "Where is it?" she demanded.

Jasper sat on the bed and reached behind him. He held up her pistol. "You mean this?"

The blood drained from her head. She felt dizzy, sick. "How did you—?"

"Disarm you?" A look of uncertainty flashed across his face, but then he put on his cocky smile. "Sweet girl, there's a reason I'm still alive. I don't get into bed with a woman who brings a gun along."

Icy dread doused her. Then she broke out in a sweat. Her chest burned.

He'd lured her into trusting him, taken her weapon...and now he would exact payment for her deceit. He'd rape her.

She darted a furtive glance at the pair of revolvers hanging from the bedpost. Before she could grab one of them, he was off the bed and had clamped his arms around her from behind.

"Let me go! Get away from me!" She fought his hold.

"Brigit? Do you hear me? Calm down. I won't hurt you."

A sweating, florid face appeared in her mind. That's what *he'd* said, too. If she cooperated, he wouldn't hurt her. But he *had* hurt her. "Noooooo."

Jasper gripped her right wrist and pressed something into her palm.

Her fevered brain registered the shape. *Her pistol.* Her fingers snapped around it.

"That's right. You've got it," he said evenly. "Easy now. I'm letting go."

JASPER SNATCHED his trousers off the floor and put them on. The peashooter Brigit held pointed at him wasn't cocked, and, if he recalled correctly, she'd already fired the single shot into Brad Collins's buttocks. In the unlikely event that she had reloaded somewhere along the way, he didn't want to be carted off buck naked.

When he turned to face her, she backed away, still holding the pistol straight-armed. Her hand trembled so hard she would never hit whatever she meant to aim for. Likely, his balls.

Her lithe form was visible beneath the thin shift. If she hadn't been shaking like a leaf in a high wind, he couldn't have controlled his natural reaction to a beautiful, well-formed woman. But her wide-eyed, frozen gaze cooled his ardor.

Something stronger than pity squeezed his heart. His first inclination was to hold her, at least until she stopped shivering. Touching her at this point wouldn't make her feel safer. If that peashooter didn't fire, she might try again to use one of the other guns to kill him.

He could reach them before she did.

Jasper released a sigh. No, he wouldn't hold a gun on her or restrain her, which would only terrify her more. He couldn't bear to do that. Not even to a woman who appeared to have lost her reason. He left his revolvers hanging on the bedpost and sat down on the bed.

"I'm sorry I frightened you." He spoke in a low tone intended to soothe, although he wasn't sure it came out that way. Other women had told him his raspy whispers sounded scary.

Brigit hadn't acted scared of his voice. She'd been eager for him, right up to the moment he'd pushed his luck too far. What had she imagined he'd do to her?

Based on the fact that she still held a pistol pointed at him, it was pretty clear what she'd imagined. "I t-told you. Only sleep. Why-why did you...touch me?"

Her trembling question twisted a knife in his chest. He had no excuse, only an explanation. "I didn't think you wanted to sleep. I thought we were..." Trifling. Teasing. Dallying. None of those words was right. "Pretending."

She slowly lowered her arm and her eyes filled with despair. "P-pretending? Is-is that what you were doing when you kissed me?"

Her question jerked a knot in his heart. He'd picked the worst possible word.

"Hell, no, I wasn't pretending about that. I *wanted* to kiss you, and it seemed like you were up for it. Then I wanted to do a lot more. From what I could tell, you did too. Or so I thought."

She wrapped her arms around her slender body, clothed only in a thin shift. "That's what *he* said. He said I'd lured him to my bed. He said I wanted it. Then you...you said... It-it's my fault, isn't it?"

Jasper swore under his breath. How could he have been so *stupid* not to put the clues together? She'd been assaulted, probably raped. Worse, she blamed herself for what happened. Then, and now. "No! That's not how it is. My poor behavior is not your fault. I convinced myself you wanted to—" How could he put it delicately? "Lay with me. And I didn't honor our deal."

He hadn't meant to prove how dishonorable he could be, though he'd done just that. She had every reason to despise him, but he didn't want her to be afraid of him.

A flurry of emotions played across her face, stark and unvarnished. Fear, confusion, doubt, a poignant hope. It took every ounce of his willpower to remain seated. He longed to go to her, hold her, reassure her. But no, he'd keep his hands to himself, as he should've done before.

She took a few deep breaths, then looked down at the pistol in her hand, as if just noticing it. "My God." Her expression twisted into horror and she lowered the gun to her side. "What if I'd shot you in a fit of terror? I would never forgive myself."

"I'd forgive you," he said, with complete sincerity.

She started at him, still looking horrified.

Tension permeating the silence became so heavy, that he added a quip to lighten it. "That is, I'd forgive you if you accept my apology. If not, the deal's off."

Chagrin wasn't quite the reaction he was going for.

"You don't have to apologize, Jasper. I let you kiss me. I wasn't pretending."

He scrubbed his fingers through his hair. Her attempt to absolve him lashed his heart. "You aren't experienced. I sensed that, but didn't listen to my instincts..." Because he'd been damn near blind with lust.

Her sweet kisses had drained every drop of anger and resentment and had aroused him despite his injuries and fatigue. Maybe that explained why he'd been so slow to pick up on her cues. Still didn't excuse him.

He shifted over and put his hand on the edge of the bed. "Will you sit down? You can bring the pistol if it'll make you feel safer."

She shook her head. "I don't want to get anywhere near you with a gun."

He breathed easier when she placed the pistol inside the wardrobe. He considered putting his guns there, but she seemed over the worst part and back to herself. Mostly.

Brigit picked up the blanket she'd taken with her to the floor and wrapped it around her before she sat down, leaving several inches between them.

In hindsight, he should've realized she wasn't engaged in flirtation. Her preference for red petticoats didn't mean she was a loose woman. She hadn't been adept at kissing, though she'd picked up on it quick. He'd told himself she was like those women who preferred for men to put a little effort into seducing them. It was a game he knew and was comfortable with.

Except, Brigit was unlike any woman he'd met. She was a fascinating combination of innocence and worldliness, strength and weakness, cunning and compassion. He'd never wanted a woman as he wanted her, and he'd come up with all kinds of reasons to explain away the warning signs.

He gripped his knees and stared at his bare feet, feeling guilty as hell.

After a moment, she patted the back of his hand. "You didn't hurt me."

"A ringing endorsement." He regretted the remark the moment it left his mouth. When he couldn't find the right words, he'd resorted to sarcastic ones. "I wouldn't intentionally hurt you."

"I know that now."

He turned his hand over to grasp hers gently. It surprised him when her grip tightened.

"I did enjoy the kissing." Her softly spoken admission put a smile on his face.

"So did I." He could come up with something better than that. "You're a passionate woman."

"Really? I never thought so. Before you, I didn't know what passion felt like." Her wistful declaration twisted the hook deeper into his heart.

He squeezed her hand. She'd been holding him in a death grip. When she let go, he flexed his fingers.

She bit her lower lip. "I'm sorry, I didn't realize... Do you have any feeling left?"

Why did she assume she could hurt him? The only part of him she could damage was out of her reach.

"Squeeze my hand all you want. If I thought it would help, I'd hold you, and promise not to let anyone hurt you." Guilt niggled at his conscience. He knew better than to make that vow. "Except...that's a promise I can't keep. I wasn't even able to protect my mother."

She seemed surprised by his confession. "What could you have done, Jasper? You told me you were attacked, too. They put a rope around your neck. Whatever they did, it was so bad it damaged your voice and left scars. How could you possibly have protected her?"

He curled his hands into fists. Brigit didn't understand. "I should've found a way. After the attack, Ma wandered around the farm. She went back to the burned buildings, looking for Pa. Sudden noises, especially loud male voices, frightened her so bad it gave her the shakes. I should've gotten her help. Instead, I rode off to seek revenge."

"As I would have, had I been in your place." Brigit's voice became stronger and more forceful. When he didn't respond right away, she showed a flicker of uncertainty. "Do you regret seeking vengeance?"

He had regrets aplenty, but not for the reasons she thought. "Do you regret shooting that bastard who attacked you?"

Brigit looked away and her throat worked as if she were having trouble swallowing.

He'd guessed right. For all her grit, she had a tender side, too. She'd described her mother as strong and compassionate. The apple hadn't fallen far from the tree.

"No," she replied in a strained voice.

"Neither do I," he conceded. "Though I'd wager I can bear the weight on my conscience better than you can."

"Don't be so sure about that." She lowered her head, almost like she was about to say a prayer. "Part of me can't be sorry and can't forgive. It eats away at my soul. You feel it, too, don't you?"

"Yes." In the end, revenge hadn't solved anything. He still despised himself for being unable to protect his family. Too late, he'd veered

116

away from his vengeful quest. He wouldn't seek absolution. It was too late for that. He'd likely hang for his crimes.

Her head came up and she looked at him, somber and clear-eyed, almost as if he'd spoken his thoughts aloud. "I expected to hang for shooting my guardian."

"Your guardian?" Jasper was horrified. A man entrusted to protect her instead had abused her.

She closed her eyes. Her chest rose and fell. Deep breathing, perhaps to calm herself. "I was behind bars for a few days. Until his wife told the authorities the shooting had been an accident. She knew I wasn't his first victim, and didn't want it to be dragged out in a highly publicized trial."

Jasper rubbed his thumb over the back of Brigit's hand. He had no words of comfort. What the hell could he say? It was a miracle she'd escaped with her life. "How did you get the gun?"

"He brought it with him to threaten me into cooperating. When he was done, then bent to collect his clothing, I picked the gun up off the side table and shot him."

Her matter-of-fact delivery didn't mean she felt nothing. Just the opposite. She'd erected a wall around her heart to protect it. Jasper knew this because he'd done the same thing. The fact that she'd stayed in the same room with him demonstrated her courage. But taking him into her confidence showed a level of trust that humbled him.

He gave her hand another slight squeeze before letting go.

Her shoulders sagged. The sigh she heaved sounded a lot like relief. "Thank you for listening, Jasper."

He nodded. Again, he had nothing useful to offer, other than his willingness to listen and understand. She'd needed to unburden herself. He'd also told her things he hadn't told another soul. He didn't want to delve too deeply into what that meant. He couldn't allow himself to get too attached to someone who would leave as soon as she'd accomplished her task.

Brigit covered a yawn. "Pardon me. I'm getting tired."

"I got there ahead of you," Jasper said as he stood. He lifted her feet onto the bed. "Time for some shut-eye."

She scooted over and curled into a ball, hugging the blanket.

He went to turn down the light.

"Will you stay with me? Help me find Mr. Kinkaid?" Her voice conveyed cautious hope.

Had she thought he'd abandon her? Other men she'd trusted had left her, betrayed her. It made sense she'd be thinking, *why not him?*

"As I said before, I'll help you. But you need to be patient. I have a few things to do before we set off to find that Kinkaid fellow." Jasper stretched out on the rug next to the bed.

A moment later, a pillow dropped next to him.

"Is that all you require? For me to be patient?"

"Tomorrow, you can tell me everything you know about the case. And you'll start listening for a change, and let me be in charge of making the plans." He tucked the pillow under his head. Even if he issued a long list of instructions, she wouldn't follow most of them, and that's not what she'd meant. "And I won't demand special favors in return."

Her silence made him wonder whether she'd fallen asleep or hadn't decided whether he would honor his word.

He rolled on his side and heaved a long sigh. "That's a promise I can keep."

CHAPTER 11

*B*rigit pulled the sheet from over her head. Outside the open window, dawn had painted the sky a soft shade between purple and gray. After her emotional breakdown, she hadn't thought she would be able to close her eyes, but she'd slept the night through. Not only that, her heart felt lighter. Confession was indeed good for the soul. Even if she'd unburdened herself to an outlaw instead of a priest.

Faint footsteps came from overhead. Hotel guests were beginning to stir. She sat up and stretched before peeking over the side of the bed.

Jasper lay on his back with his head on the pillow she'd tossed to him. His chest rose and fell in a slow rhythm, lifting the arm resting across his midsection. His eyes were closed, jaw relaxed, lips parted. Sleeping, he appeared less dangerous, more vulnerable.

If the reports were correct, he'd recently reached his twenty-sixth year. Every one of them had been carved into his features. His harsh life had shaped him in more ways than what could be seen on the outside, and yet all the violence hadn't destroyed his soul. Some innate goodness, miraculously preserved, had prevented him from becoming a monster. He'd demonstrated as much last night.

She ought to be glad for his pledge not to ask for *special favors,* but couldn't deny a twinge of disappointment, knowing he wouldn't be kissing her again. Unless she asked for it.

No. Keep things light. Focus on the business at hand rather than dwell on their mutual attraction, which they couldn't afford to indulge. Fate had brought them together. Destiny would one day separate them, and it would be foolish to believe otherwise.

He opened his eyes and blinked sleepily. Shifting his arm to the floor, he levered up with a groan. "Is it morning already?"

"A rooster outside thinks it is."

"What rooster?"

She smiled at his sleepy reply. "Well, I didn't personally hear him, but there's bound to be one out there somewhere."

"You can take a census—after we have breakfast." Jasper came to his feet with a grimace.

The poor man had to be sore, considering what he'd gone through and sleeping on a hard floor. Despite his injury and the bruise beneath his eye, he didn't look half bad. In fact, he looked quite well without his shirt on. Impressive even. His smooth skin didn't sprout a forest, not like someone she'd rather not think about. A patch of black hair extended from Jasper's navel like an arrow downward, disappearing into his trousers, which were unbuttoned at the waistband and hung low on his hips.

Brigit jerked her attention to his face and hers grew warm.

He didn't seem to notice her flush. His gaze had moved downward.

She glanced at the thin shift. Horrified, she crossed her arms over her chest. He hadn't noticed her gawking at him because he'd been ogling her breasts.

He spun away, buttoning his trousers, then made for the wardrobe where he grabbed her clothes and flung them at her. "Get dressed. I need something to eat."

While she fumbled with her corset, Jasper pulled on his shirt. She huffed when the ties on her petticoat became knotted. If she stopped dwelling on his every move, she might manage to get dressed before next Sunday.

Noises drifted in through the open window, what sounded like animals bawling. An occasional curse punctuated the air. "What is that awful smell?" She shook out her skirt and noticed the mud on the hem. "Oh. Goodness. It could be me."

Jasper sat on the bed and pulled on his boots. His clothes had blood stains and the coat sleeve puckered open where it had been cut during the fight. He appeared unconcerned about his state, though he did raise his arm and sniff.

"I'd love a bath, wouldn't you?" she asked.

He straightened with his spine rigid. "Now?"

Oh no. She hadn't meant together, in here.

"After breakfast, we can find a place to purchase *separate* baths." Brigit finished buttoning her jacket. "And my hair needs washing."

Jasper remained seated at the end of the bed, silent as a mummy. While she'd been babbling, he hadn't said much. Perhaps he wasn't sure what to say or how to act. An honest acknowledgment of the situation might ease the tension.

"I suppose after what happened last night, it's natural to feel awkward," she ventured.

"If you have clothes on, it'll feel a lot less awkward,"

"I'm dressed." Brigit tucked her pistol beneath her garter about the time Jasper stood to face her. "Don't worry. I won't use it on you."

Her remark was meant to be lighthearted. Based on his expression, it landed flat. Was it too soon to joke about almost shooting him last night? Probably.

After breakfast, she would find her footing again. Things would be back to normal between them, or as close to normal as they could be, considering their unconventional—and temporary—relationship.

After they left the hotel and ventured outside, the source of the sounds and smells became obvious.

A herd of long-horned cattle filled the street, along with the cowboys driving them. Pedestrians scattered when one of the drovers charged onto the sidewalk to recover a stray.

Jasper grasped her elbow and steered her in front of a newsstand. Perhaps he thought it would provide them with some degree of protection.

"I wonder where all those cattle are headed?" she remarked.

"New York, ma'am." The operator of the newsstand offered her a folded paper. "The first shipment of beef in a cold railcar leaves Denison today. Newfangled *refrigeration*. Invented right here in Texas. Read all about it."

She liked to read about new inventions, but it was a column on the right side of the front page that caught her eye. It featured a stylized drawing of a steam locomotive above her sister-in-law's pseudonym. She held up the paper for Jasper to see. "Look at this! Another installment of *Lace and Steele* from L.M. Forbes. How exciting."

"Thrilling." Jasper paid for the newspaper before she could search for change. "Let's get going. I see a diner."

Brigit tucked the newspaper under her arm. He didn't appear to know, or care, what she was talking about, which might mean he hadn't read Lucy's stories. Could he read? Many poor men were illiterate. "Are you interested in reading the article or the series?"

"Neither. But you appear interested, and I didn't want to stand there while you read it."

"You'd be surprised at what one can learn from newspapers."

He gave a short laugh. "Yeah. Most of it made up."

"You don't put much faith in the honesty of the press?"

"Or the honesty of reporters."

Ouch. His barbs were getting sharper. Perhaps he hadn't felt the same sense of relief at unburdening his guilt last night.

He opened the door to the small cafe. "Good thing you aren't a reporter."

She breathed out a laugh. Ah, he was joking, a good sign. "Does that mean you trust me?"

"Not entirely."

"Mostly?"

"More than yesterday."

Which was his way of saying *yes* or he wouldn't be bantering with her about it.

Brigit entered the diner feeling hopeful for having gained a bit more trust, which she suspected was something Jasper rarely extended. She would need his trust when it came time to take him to court to face charges. If her mission ended in success, she could make a good case for a lighter sentence.

They found a seat at a booth away from the other diners. After they'd finished a big breakfast, Jasper enjoyed a cup of coffee while she scanned the front page.

"This is a very interesting story about that new refrigerated railway service. It's a venture involving several local businessmen. The MK&T is a primary investor." Brigit looked up in anticipation. "Do you find that suspicious?"

Jasper shrugged. "Makes sense the railroad would invest in something like that. Transporting beef will make them a lot of money."

"True. It may be perfectly legal, but I think we should check it out. You asked me to tell you everything I know. Frankly, it's not much more than what I've told you already. The Katy was in financial distress when Mr. Bond took over as general manager. Then, things got worse for the railroad while his finances improved. This was during the time you were robbing trains for him."

Jasper's lips tightened into a thin line.

"What are you thinking?" she asked.

"I'm thinking I could've made better decisions."

Couldn't everyone? Jasper's decisions just happened to be the kind that got men put in jail. Some men, anyway.

"Tell me about your agreement with Bond?" She was curious about details that weren't in official records.

"He offered to set things up. Told us which trains carried payrolls. Said he'd make sure it would be easy. It wasn't. But he still got his share. Fifty percent." Jasper stared into his coffee cup. "He couldn't have gotten rich off what we made. The reason he wanted us to rob trains was to ruin the railroad, so his buddy could buy it. Cheap. I can't prove it. It's my word against his."

She considered how much to tell Jasper about what the missing agent had uncovered. "We have reason to believe that Bond's schemes didn't end there, and you are not the only other person involved."

Jasper leaned on his arms, seeming more interested. "Who else?"

Brigit released a sigh. "I wish we had names, but we don't. My experience with high-class criminals is that you have to follow the money and see where it leads."

"So you think Bond is involved in something illegal with this new business?"

"I'd say the odds are good, wouldn't you?"

Jasper gazed out the picture window. "We'll check it out. After I'm done with the man I came here to find."

"Who are you looking for?"

"J.D. Liddle."

Brigit lowered the newspaper. Jasper harbored ill feelings toward his sister's lover. Earlier, he'd questioned the man's commitment. But would that send him chasing J.D. to Texas? She knew better than that. "You think he betrayed you."

Jasper's curled fist gave her the answer even before he spoke. "He's not smart, like you. He couldn't have come up with a plan to get me off that train in Vinita. But he knew Tom and Candy would fall for it. After I find him and he tells me who paid him to set up an ambush, we can do what you suggest. Follow the money."

His conclusion made sense, and it was nice to hear a rare compliment. "You think I'm smarter than J.D.?"

"My horse is smarter than J.D."

She fought a smile. "I'm as smart as your horse? My, I'm flattered."

"Bandit is *very* smart."

"Bandit?"

"The horse I trained from a colt. They confiscated him after I was arrested. I don't know who has him now." Jasper stared out the picture window at the busy street.

His sadness touched a place deep inside her. He'd only been half-joking about that smart horse. Another emotional investment he had made and then lost.

"If I could find Bandit, I'd buy him and return him to his rightful owner," she declared.

Jasper's wry smile returned. "The chances of that are about as slim as me avoiding a noose."

His remark dealt her heart another blow. He'd all but accepted his fate. How could she convince others to believe he could change if *he* didn't believe it? She had to find a way to open his eyes to his better qualities. Last night, she'd tried to tell him, but he'd forgotten or ignored it.

Brigit smoothed newspaper on the table and a brilliant idea came to her. If her opinion hadn't swayed him, maybe Lucy's would. "Does the name Forbes sound familiar?"

"I don't know. Maybe. Why?"

"The author of the *Lace and Steele* series is my sister-in-law, Lucy. She writes under her maiden name, L.M. Forbes. After she and Henry moved to Texas, she sold a syndicated series."

He eyed the newspaper with more interest. "What's it about?"

"Her adventures out West, and the people she's encountered. She gives the characters fictional names, but if you know her, you'll know who she's talking about. For instance, the railroad chief in her story is named Mr. Steele, but he's based on Henry. Lace is—"

"Lucy," Jasper finished. He shifted forward.

Good. She'd caught his interest. Rather, her sister-in-law had. Henry still swore the outlaw carried a flame for his wife. Lucy insisted that Jasper only feigned affection to aggravate Henry. Brigit suspected the truth was probably somewhere in between.

Did knowing this inspire a twinge of jealousy? Honestly, yes, but it didn't matter. She had no claim on Jasper. If Lucy's words could help him view himself through a kinder lens, it might change his perspective and put him on a new path. One that didn't lead to the end of a rope.

Brigit turned the newspaper around. "There is a train robber in the series. She calls him Bran. He and Mr. Steele are often at odds.

But they both care about the people who depend on them, and they give their money to folks who are less fortunate. Lucy told me the public loves Bran. She receives letters written to him. It makes Henry so jealous."

Jasper leaned back and folded his arms across his chest. His bristles couldn't conceal the blush on his lean cheeks. "Am I supposed to be flattered?"

Brigit restrained the urge to laugh. It would only make him more embarrassed. "You should read her stories. I think you'd find them interesting. And it might help you see things differently."

"See things differently? What's *that* supposed to mean?"

Did she have to spell this out?

"What do you think Bran would do if he suspected one of his old friends betrayed him? Would he kill the man without giving him a chance to explain?"

She waited for Jasper to conclude that Bran would show compassion, then she would point out that he—Jasper—would do the same. No matter how angry, he'd give J.D. a chance to explain, and, if possible, let him go. In her heart, she was certain of it.

Jasper's face darkened and his eyes narrowed. "Here's what I see *differently*. Bran would be a damn fool to give some Judas another chance to double-cross him."

JASPER COULDN'T DECIDE whether to laugh or cuss. Brigit thought he planned to murder J.D. Sure, he'd thought about it, and J.D. would fear it, which meant he wouldn't have to kill the worm. After the sniveling coward gave up his information, he'd be in a big hurry to leave the Territory and disappear before whoever else he betrayed caught up with him.

Had she asked, he would've told her that was what he, Jasper, planned to do. But she hadn't asked. She had assumed the worst and made a moral comparison with some character who wasn't even real.

Still, who could blame her? Thus far, he'd done his damnedest to make a bad impression, and last night hadn't helped. Even if they'd found some common ground, it hadn't changed her mind about him. She'd all but called him a cold-blooded killer.

She turned the page of the newspaper and heaved a sigh.

He lifted the cup of coffee to his lips just about the time she spoke.

"I thought we had become friends."

After he stopped coughing, he wiped his napkin over his mouth.

"Did I say something shocking?" Her innocent expression infuriated him.

Damn her for falling back into that acting routine.

"*Friends?*" He released an ugly laugh. "That's not what I expected you to call me after—"

"After you sat with me last night and held my hand, and listened compassionately while I poured out my soul? Is that what you were about to say?"

He opened his mouth to retort, but no suitable response came to him after her abrupt about-face. "Where are you going with this?"

She shook her head. "It's not a puzzle. Even Bandit could work it out."

He fumed while she drank her coffee and perused the open pages of the newspaper. "What could *Bandit* figure out?"

She stopped reading and looked him in the eye. "Mr. Byrne, I intend to keep you alive and help you avoid the noose. If you would cooperate, it would make things much easier."

Keep him alive? Save him from the noose? She was *using* him so she could solve her case. There wasn't a damn thing more to it.

"Since when did my future become your mission?" he demanded.

She gazed at him with those big brown eyes, which seemed to exert some kind of special power over him because he couldn't look away. "When I took you off that train, I not only took a risk. I accepted responsibility. I told you if you helped me, I'd help you. I meant it."

He laughed at his foolishness. The closeness he'd imagined last night had dissolved in the light of day or her concern had never been personal. "It's a deal, is that it?"

"No, that's not *it*." She turned her attention back to the paper while she kept talking. "We do have an agreement, yes. But, as I told you last night, I care about what happens to you. Because I do, I want to help you make a fresh start."

Despite the pretty words she'd put around it, he knew what she meant. She wanted to fix him. He'd become a project.

He threw his napkin on the table. "No thanks."

Her head jerked up. "What do mean?"

"After we're done, I'll shake your hand, you'll shake mine, and we'll go our separate ways. You, back to wherever you live. Me, somewhere out West where I can hide out. If I start over, it'll be on *my* terms."

"Do you wish to be a fugitive for the rest of your life?" Her disappointment in him was so obvious it landed another blow to his pride.

He scowled to avoid appearing hurt. "It's better than spending my life behind bars or ending it on the gallows."

"There could be another option, if—" Brigit stared at something in the paper that had disrupted her optimistic prediction. Whatever it was, she appeared alarmed.

"What's there? Another fascinating story about a good outlaw?" he quipped.

She didn't smile or even roll her eyes. Instead, she cast a worried glance around the diner and muttered under her breath. "Don't look now, but—"

"Don't look at what? Who?" He did exactly what she'd told him not to. He didn't see anyone suspicious. None of the four other diners appeared to be paying attention to them.

"I mean, act normal."

"Do I usually act abnormal?" He reached over and grabbed the newspaper, turning it so he could read whatever had spooked her.

The half-page advertisement had his name in the headline along with the biggest reward ever offered for his capture. A thousand dollars! Dead or alive. The stark headline shook him, but not half as much as the next lines. They'd upped the ante and included his supposed consort, Alice Robb, implying she was part of his gang.

A sense of inevitability stole over him. He had known for years what his end would look like, but he refused to take a woman to hell with him. Especially this woman.

Last night, he'd lain awake for hours, haunted by what she'd told him about that hellish attack. She hadn't let it defeat her or lead her into a miserable life like his. Despite her grit and ingenuity, or maybe because of it, she remained vulnerable. He had to convince her to give up this quest and go home.

"This is worse than I thought it would be," she said in a low voice. "Every bounty hunter in the region will be out there looking for us."

Jasper rested his arms on the table and reached for her hands. His had gotten warm or hers had gone cold. "No one is looking for *you*. They're after another woman. One with buck teeth and curly red hair. No one will suspect the two of you are the same person. Turn me in. Collect the money before somebody else does."

She stared at him with her mouth half-open.

He'd rendered her speechless. Quite an accomplishment.

Brigit jerked her hands away and then gathered up the newspaper. "Don't be ridiculous."

"How is it ridiculous? I'll even admit to doing away with that troublesome reporter. Everyone knows I'm not nearly as nice as Bran."

"Stop mocking me," she said in a rough whisper. "I will not let you throw your life away."

Her declaration tightened the snare around his heart. If it would do her any good, he'd give it to her, but he had only one thing worth something. "My life is my own. I can throw it away if I choose."

"Fine. Throw it away. That won't stop me."

He leaned back against the booth and tried his damnedest to appear indifferent. He had no other cards to play. Even if he turned himself in and diverted attention away from the fake reporter, Brigit would continue to put herself at risk to find that missing agent and solve this case. For reasons beyond what she'd told him, it was important to her. He knew better than to think he had the power to protect her. At the same time, he saw no option except to try.

"You don't like my plan. What's yours?"

Brigit tapped her fingers lightly on the table in a gesture that might indicate irritation or impatience. It seemed he inspired a fair amount of both. "You're right in saying no one will be looking for a woman who fits my description. Unless they talk to some of those men in the Phoenix where I lost my disguise. One of them may remember me."

He captured her nimble fingers and stroked them. Touching her hands to comfort her didn't count as *special favors*. "They'll recall a woman who got her teeth knocked out and her hair pulled off. If they recall anything else, they won't be giving that information to a lawman. But to be safe, you stay out of the way while I finish my business, then we can attend to yours."

Jasper let go before she got over her surprise and withdrew her hands. He pulled out his cash and peeled away a few bills, which he offered to her. "I'll go look for J.D. You get that bath you wanted, buy yourself some new clothes and meet me back at the hotel later."

She frowned at what he considered a generous offer. "No, thank you. If you find him, you won't come back. You'll go after whoever paid him to betray you."

A deep ache settled in the center of his chest. Despite last night, or perhaps because of it, she still didn't trust him. He didn't resent her opinion of him. He had no one to blame but himself. He shouldn't put his trust in her, either. Their relationship, like all the other ones he'd had with women not related to him, was primarily transactional. His heart wasn't worth much, but he probably ought to keep it for now. "I told you I'd help you," he reminded her.

"Yes, you did, and I'm holding you to it." With an air of determination, she folded the newspaper. "We'll both go find a place to get spruced up, and we'll purchase new disguises."

Jasper released a soft groan. "That's the best plan you can come up with? More disguises? You already dressed me up like a preacher. What now? A monk?"

"That's not a bad idea. Except a monk wouldn't be in the company of a woman."

A monk wouldn't be sleeping in the same room either, but when they shared quarters again, he'd have to act like one.

Come to think of it, maybe he'd already died and gone to Hell.

CHAPTER 12

*A*s they left the diner, Brigit took Jasper's arm. He wasn't getting away. Despite what he'd assured her, he might decide to go after J.D. on his own and leave her behind. They had to remain together to help each other.

She cast worried glances at passersby on the sidewalk. Businessmen, farmers, cowboys...men mostly. Some of them showed a passing interest. Would any of them recognize Jasper? Or guess her association with him? They would if she appeared scared.

"When in doubt, show confidence until you find it."

Yes, she would take her mentor's advice. Kate Warne had excelled at acting.

Jasper either had no fear or he was a good actor, as well.

Brigit pulled at his arm and directed his attention across the street to a business advertising hot baths and haircuts. "The Palace. Aptly named for those who wish to be treated like royalty. It's also the best place in town to gather information without being obvious."

He stopped her before she could step off the boardwalk. "The reward in the newspaper mentions the scars on my neck. If the barber sees them, he might put it together."

"Keep your collar on," she suggested. "Tell them you have a bad rash and prefer that they don't shave your neck."

"Or put a rope around it," he muttered. "I can find another place to get cleaned up. Where they won't ask questions."

He didn't say *brothel*, but she guessed that's what he meant. The image of Jasper being lathered by a prostitute didn't sit well. Jealousy wasn't the reason she advised against it. "Your favorite brothel is exactly where anyone searching for you would expect you to go. No one will be looking for you in a proper establishment."

Jasper touched the bruise below his eye. "I don't look like I belong in a proper establishment."

"The swelling has gone down. We can find something to put on it to cover the discoloring. In case you haven't noticed, it looks like a majority of the men around here get into fights. No one has paid us any mind. In my experience, hiding in plain sight can be one of the best deceptions."

"It's a risk."

"Every decision we make involves risks," she pointed out.

"Some more than others." As he gazed down at her, his gaze darkened with an undefinable emotion. He'd already demonstrated he could be fearless in the face of danger. What, other than capture, could be troubling him?

He unexpectedly cupped her cheek and stroked it with his thumb. Her skin heated and her heart raced. She had a fleeting thought that she ought to step away. Instead, she turned her face into his palm, wanting nothing more than to feel his touch.

Abruptly, he dropped his arm, breaking the spell.

Brigit rubbed her hand over the spot where he'd touched her. Why had he done it? He'd promised he wouldn't press his attentions on her, so it was just as well he'd ended it. Logically, she knew this, so she shouldn't be hurt or disappointed. "W-whether or not you like it, we can't afford to be separated. We need to stay together."

"I can't protect you and watch my back at the same time."

The age-old concern. Men believed women were weak in mind

and body and couldn't be counted on to take care of themselves. She was so tired of this myth, having disproved it time and again.

"I'll watch your back. You can watch mine."

He released a sigh. "Do you always have a counterpoint?"

"Most of the time it's a good one."

After a wagon had passed, she drew him into the street. "I know you like to be in charge, but will you trust me enough to follow my lead?"

"Where are you leading me?" His voice carried a hint of amusement.

"At the moment, to a barbershop."

Jasper moved up alongside her. Either he was being polite or demonstrating his unwillingness to be led. Regardless, he went along with her. For the time being.

Inside the shop, the smell of soap and cologne permeated the air, along with conversation and laughter. Four chairs, two of them occupied, were set up in a row in front of a mirror. Two men whose dark skin contrasted with their crisp white aprons tended to the customers. Based purely on observation, she'd guess they were a father and son.

"Welcome to The Palace," the older barber called out. "What can we do for you?"

"I would love to purchase a hot bath. And do you style women's hair?"

"Cut and style."

"Wonderful."

Jasper nudged her. "We shouldn't linger," he whispered.

"No. But at this rate, our scent alone will leave a trail," she replied in a low tone. Her next comment she directed at the barber. "My companion needs a haircut and a hot bath."

When Jasper frowned at her, she smiled sweetly. "Isn't that what most men want?"

"Shave?" the barber asked him.

"Shape it up," was his curt reply.

The barber eyed him doubtfully, and for good reason. The bristle on his face had no *shape* whatsoever. "Is there a particular style you got in mind?"

Jasper stood there, mute. It wasn't a far reach to assume he might be a stranger to fashion and wouldn't know what to ask for. The best disguise would be a look he would never choose for himself, and thus would make him less recognizable.

"A half-shingle haircut and burnsides would look nice," she suggested.

After she was done with him, he'd look the very opposite of an outlaw.

THE MAN who owned The Palace was a former slave named Gentry. He'd traveled from Georgia to Texas after the war, working as a barber and pulling teeth on the side. Jasper knew all this because the old man and Brigit had chatted nonstop.

By the time they got escorted to separate bathing areas, he'd learned the names of Gentry's children, as well as the names of the influential men who owned most of the real estate downtown, including a new refrigeration facility. It was hard to say what was more impressive—how many details Gentry retained or how much information Brigit managed to squeeze out of him in less than an hour.

After the clean-up, Jasper allowed her to drag him into a men's clothing store, then over to a dress shop. He used money he'd hoarded for himself to purchase her a new wardrobe, which included a matching bag and a little headpiece she wore tilted jauntily to the front. One couldn't call it a proper hat. Her pleasure at the results made his investment worth it.

If he had the wealth and the time, he'd be inclined to spoil her rotten.

Brigit paused outside the dress shop in front of the picture window and began to fidget with his tie. Her golden-brown eyes sparkled with deviltry as she smoothed the wide lapels on his new tweed coat. "How smart you look."

He'd hardly recognized his reflection in the glass. His hair was shorn so short that his ears showed beneath a new wide-brimmed hat called a Stetson. It was the only part of the outfit he liked. His facial hair extended from the front of his ears down along his jaw in a fashion she'd called *Burnsides*.

"I look like a dandy," he grumbled. "And smell like a two-bit whore."

"Nonsense. You're a daisy!" She patted his vest. "You look like a fine gentleman."

Clothes wouldn't make him a *gentleman*. She knew that of course. Now they were pretending. She just didn't have to stretch so far to pretend.

He admired her with his eyes and kept his hands at his sides. "You cut a fine figure in that green gown."

"The right term for this color is *chartreuse*." She touched the top of the bodice, bringing his attention to the wrong place.

"Sure it is..." He jerked at the vest for something to do with his hands. "And this ain't red. It's vermillion."

She gave him a saucy smile. "Cheer up. No one will recognize you. They'll think you're a businessman."

"Or a snake-oil salesman."

"One with extra money to invest." She rubbed his coat. If she kept that up, he might have to take her back to that hotel.

He captured her gloved fingers. "You done fussing over me?"

"For now."

Jasper slowly raised her hand to his lips, which made the color rise on her face. It was only fair, considering what she'd put him through.

She'd taken to heart this new project to fix him up. Too bad it wouldn't last very long.

That reward would unleash and hellacious manhunt. Plenty of folks would sell their grannies for a thousand dollars. He'd half expected the barber to nab him after he refused to expose his neck.

It was only a matter of time before he ended up in a bounty hunter's crosshairs. He had to get Brigit to safety before that happened.

Jasper tucked her hand over his arm as they headed toward the new station. "I'll go with you to check out those shady businesses. After that, you can wait for me at the hotel."

"We agreed to stay together." Brigit adjusted the small handbag on her wrist. She'd put her pistol in it, saying she'd need quicker access to it, in case they ran into trouble, which was precisely why he didn't want her to go with him.

"You don't expect me to take a lady across the tracks where she'd run into card sharps and calico queens. I won't be long. J.D. likes to show off when he's got money. I can easily follow it. The sooner I find him, the sooner we can get out of town."

"If someone has paid him to betray you, they may be setting a trap. I'll bet he expects you to show up alone. We'll go together, in disguise, and surprise him."

She was better at defending her position than a lawyer.

"We'll argue about this later," Jasper conceded.

"Fine. Let's visit the Crystal Ice Company first. It's there, next to the depot." She directed his attention to a large warehouse with a big sign attached to the roof. "The owner's name is Pat Tobias. He was quoted in a newspaper article about the refrigeration railcars. He should be able to tell us who else has invested in the company. We might turn over a rock and find another cockroach."

"That's a perfect description of Bond and his cronies."

Brigit's answering smile was fleeting. "I hope Mr. Tobias isn't one of them. Before he settled here and started the ice business, he was a locomotive engineer with the Katy."

"The name sounds familiar, but I doubt we've met. I didn't linger around locomotives. My men stopped the train while I went for the safe."

"So we needn't worry that Mr. Tobias will recognize you?"

"Not dolled up like this." Jasper didn't feel as confident as he sounded. He'd have to be careful not to give himself away. "What do you know about Tobias, other than what you read or what the barber told you?"

Brigit walked more slowly as they approached the warehouse. "Two years ago, when Henry was still general manager of the Katy, he gave Mr. Tobias an award for being a top-rate engineer and a fine, upstanding employee."

Her uncertain expression implied she had her doubts. About Tobias or her brother?

Henry Stevens had lost his job and his fortune after a scandal unrelated to his successor. Or was it? Did Brigit fear that Henry had gotten involved in one of Bond's schemes? It would be hard on her if her brother ended up in jail and she had a part in putting him there.

Jasper laid his hand over her gloved fingers to let her know he understood. "Your brother left his job under a cloud of suspicion, didn't he? Falsified records, as I recall."

Brigit slipped her hand from beneath his and gave him a stern once over. "Henry put his fortune and his life on the line trying to save the Katy. He's not a criminal."

Jasper stared at her, surprised both by her sharp response and her misunderstanding. He hadn't been throwing stones, but her assumption said a lot about what she thought. Just when he'd started to feel a connection growing between them. Maybe that was it. She didn't want to have feelings for an outlaw. Her hypocrisy angered him more than her rejection. "Is that how you see it? It's fine for Henry to break the law to save the railroad, but when I do it to save my family, it's wrong."

She gazed up at him and a small crease appeared between her brows. "Is that what you think I meant? That I hold you to a different standard or think less of you because of it?"

Her soft, apologetic tone caught him unprepared. She could be performing again. He didn't know what to believe, which was why he'd be a fool to bare his soul to her. She'd already pried open his heart. If he let her burrow any deeper, she would have the power to destroy him more thoroughly than his enemies.

"It doesn't matter," he lied. "I'm only pointing out that your brother might be mixed up in this. If you can't deal with that, we can call off the hunt."

"Henry is not involved. I'd stake my job on it. As for how much I stand to lose, I am well aware."

Jasper admired her faith and her confidence. At the moment, he'd possessed neither. "So, what's your plan when we get to the ice company?"

Brigit formed a shield over her eyes to look in the direction of the large warehouse. Sunlight gleamed on its tin roof. "I'll introduce myself as Henry's sister. That will loosen Mr. Tobias's tongue and speed up the process of getting information."

"Why would you take a risk like that?" Jasper stopped.

Brigit kept right on going, forcing him to keep up. "Mr. Tobias would never suspect Henry's social circles to include a train robber."

She couldn't have mistaken his meaning, but if she'd intended to wound him, her shot didn't even penetrate his tough hide.

"Outlaw is the part I play best. What else do you suggest?"

"I'll introduce you as a friend of the family. A wealthy investor." She slipped her hand through his arm again and her expression softened. "Will you accept my suggestion?"

Did she mean her peace offering?

He took it, not because he was a sucker but because he didn't wish to waste energy on feelings like anger. Or hurt. "I need a different name."

"Do you have a preference?"

Jasper thought about it. "A grandfather of mine was an O'Malley. He didn't have two pence to rub together."

Brigit smiled. "Very well, Mr. O'Malley it is."

She liked the name or appreciated his sense of humor. Either way, it helped restore his good mood.

Once they were inside the ice company, Jasper looked around while Brigit sought the owner.

The employees, who wore heavy coats and gloves, used large tongs to move blocks of ice into metal-lined boxes, which were then loaded into wagons waiting outside. On the other side of the warehouse, a larger dock opened up to railroad tracks. Two cars parked outside were painted with bold black lettering. *Texas & Atlantic Refrigeration Co.* The business Brigit wanted to investigate.

One of the men working inside the chilly warehouse waved at Jasper.

He tensed. Had he been recognized?

Another employee waved.

It struck Jasper then. The workers had offered him the customary greeting for a visitor who looked important. The transition Brigit had put him through was working.

Jasper acknowledged both men and tried to act like it was normal to be fawned over and given special privileges.

"Mr. O'Malley!" Brigit called out. She hurried across the warehouse, followed by a rotund man wearing a suit embarrassingly similar to Jasper's. "I'd like for you to meet Mr. Tobias. He owns this impressive establishment."

Jasper shook hands. The less he said, the less likely his rasp would become obvious.

"Mr. O'Malley, what a pleasure." Pat Tobias's smile emphasized the roundness of his pink cheeks. If the former locomotive engineer was one of the cockroaches, he appeared to be a harmless one. "Miss Stevens tells me you are a friend of the family."

"Yes, indeed."

Tobias launched into praises for Henry Stevens. How generous "the Chief" had been to the Katy workers. How difficult things had gotten under new management. "I left the railroad just in time. Some of my friends weren't so lucky," the former engineer bemoaned. "After the Katy declared bankruptcy, they lost their jobs."

"Unfortunate." Jasper folded his hands behind his back and maintained a sympathetic expression while he wrestled with his conscience.

When he'd started down the outlaw road in his youth, it had been the only way he could strike a blow against the rich and powerful. Some ten years later, around the time he'd met Billy, he had recognized his hypocrisy but had convinced himself it would ultimately serve his purpose if he could bring down a wealthy executive. He'd been sure that Bond's arrogance would be his undoing. It had turned out the other way around.

"You're just in time to see two of the new refrigeration cars." Tobias indicated the large dock.

"Oh! That's so exciting!" Brigit clapped her hands as if he'd performed a difficult magic trick. "Our friend, Mr. O'Malley, is on the lookout for good investments. As fortune would have it, I saw an article in today's paper about refrigerated rail cars. We're interested in finding out who else has invested."

"Did you read about its unique vapor compression system? Invented here in Texas." Tobias went on about the marvels of the steam-powered invention. "With the new operation, we will be able to send weekly shipments of beef from Denison to New York."

He'd need a lot of beef for such an operation. There were plenty of cattle in Texas, as well as ranchers who'd want top dollar for their beeves.

"You'd be hard-pressed to find a better investment for your money, Mr. O'Malley."

Jasper gave an agreeable nod. If it returned so handsomely, they had to be getting a deal.

"Do you have any observations about our operation?"

Only that he'd guess there were cattle rustlers involved somewhere along the line. Perhaps in business with the slaughterhouse.

"Very impressive," Jasper remarked.

"Is that all you have to say?" Tobias peered over his spectacles and his brows beetled. His tone begged for a longer reply.

"Mr. O'Malley is a man of few words," Brigit said lightly. "It is a good thing you aren't, Mr. Tobias."

The two of them enjoyed a good laugh.

Jasper released a relieved breath. Her quick thinking had averted an awkward moment and now she had the owner's undivided attention. When she turned on that warm, funny personality, his partner could charm a lizard off a rock.

What about a cockroach?

Thus far, no one in the warehouse, including Mr. Tobias, appeared nervous about the sudden appearance of nosy guests, which could imply they had no idea they were shipping stolen beeves. Or Brigit's name-dropping had put them at ease.

Something still didn't feel right. Jasper reached up to rub the back of his neck as he swept another look across the warehouse.

On the other side of a large ice-making machine, a heavyset man appeared to be hiding. Waiting. Or watching. It was difficult to see him clearly from this angle. He wasn't dressed in the workers' heavy coveralls. His hat brim was pulled low, shielding his features...except for a bushy mustache.

A spurt of fear shot through Jasper. *No.* Couldn't be. How would Stokes know they'd be here? If he'd come here for another reason, had he recognized them?

"Mr. O'Malley?"

Jasper jerked his attention to Tobias. "Sir?"

"I was telling Miss Stevens how our local slaughterhouse has benefited from a big increase in business due to the new refrigeration techniques. Another investment opportunity, perhaps?"

"Perhaps." Jasper adjusted the loose-fitting coat to cover the shape of his revolver beneath so it wouldn't give him away.

"Isn't the Katy a major investor in the slaughterhouse, too?" Brigit dangled the bait.

"Yes, I believe so. Come with me. I want to show you something." Tobias led the way.

Jasper cast a nervous glance over his shoulder as he trailed Brigit. The man lurking around the machinery wasn't there anymore. Stokes might be looking for someone else or something else. Stolen beef, perhaps.

"Mr. O'Malley? The real show is over here," Tobias called.

Brigit's frown indicated her concern with Jasper's distracted behavior. He couldn't alert her to the marshal's presence without drawing attention, but if he veered away to confirm his suspicions, it could result in a shoot-out.

Hopefully, the tour would end soon and they could leave.

Tobias stopped at the edge of the dock where a railcar had been parked. "You'll be amazed at how cold these new cars keep the meat. The beeves in this car were dressed and loaded at the slaughterhouse yesterday and brought here this morning. They'll leave our yard today, and within a few days, New York diners will be enjoying fresh steaks!"

The owner ended with a flourish, right as one of the workers slid the door to the rail car open. After providing a ramp, the worker stepped aside to allow Brigit to enter first.

Jasper broke into a sweat. He didn't want to get cornered in that refrigeration car. On the other hand, he wasn't leaving without Brigit and she'd forged ahead. He stayed close behind her to put himself between her and whoever might be after them.

The cold temperature inside the car turned his damp skin clammy. Huge sides of marbled beef hung suspended in neat rows. The air smelled sharp with blood.

Brigit jerked to a halt with a gasp.

Jasper put his hands on her shoulders to avoid a collision. Then he saw what had stopped her in her tracks, dangling from one of the big hooks. A man.

CHAPTER 13

"*J*.D.," Jasper whispered, unable to look away from the dead man's colorless features. Lank strands of blond hair clung to powder burns on his forehead where a bullet had been fired at close range. A pool of blood had congealed beneath the toes of his scuffed boots.

Who had done this? The only clue was a one-word note pinned to the dead man's coat.

Judas.

"Oh, dear..." Brigit lifted her hand to her forehead with a languid motion and swayed.

Jasper caught her before she collapsed. He scooped beneath her knees and lifted her into his arms as fear pumped heat into his cold muscles. "Brigit?" he whispered anxiously.

"Ohhh..." she moaned, then fluttered her eyes in a dramatic gesture that suggested acting rather than reacting.

Was her pretense meant to distract him or the men behind him? Regardless, it wrested his attention away from the gruesome sight. He snapped back into character.

With Brigit secure in his arms, Jasper did an about-face—nearly colliding with the man behind him whose ruddy face had gone as white as a bleached bone.

"That's not beef," Jasper growled.

Horror filled Tobias's wide-eyed gaze. "My God," he said in a strangled voice. He came to his senses enough to shout over his shoulder. "Rufus! Pete! Get in here! There's a dead man!"

Jasper pushed past the workers who'd bunched up to get a look inside the car. "Make way!" he shouted. "The lady has collapsed."

Men came running from all parts of the warehouse. The marshal didn't appear to be among them. But Jasper didn't intend to linger inside the warehouse, waiting to be recognized. Whoever had murdered J.D. wouldn't hesitate to kill a woman who got in the way.

"Mr. O'Malley!" Tobias called after them. "Take Miss Stevens to my office. I have a sofa in there. She can recover while we await the sheriff."

"We're not staying," Jasper said, more for Brigit's sake. The other man couldn't hear him over all the distressed shouts. He veered in the direction of a hallway that led to the door they'd entered.

Brigit made a distressed sound in the back of her throat. She put her lips close to Japer's ear. "We can't leave yet. What about J.D.?"

Jasper's surprise nearly tripped him. "How the hell did you know that was J.D.?"

"You whispered his name. That's why I pretended to faint. So no one would notice."

Brigit had kept her wits about her. Even when confronted with a violent spectacle. Her quick thinking had given him time to recover from his shock.

And he thought *he* had iron nerves. Well, he did have, before he met her. Before her reckless courage had given him a reason to panic.

Whatever the hell was going on—with J.D., the railroad, the marshal—it was too dangerous to investigate until Brigit was out of harm's way.

He set Brigit on her feet in a spot where no one else was around. "We can't stay. I saw Stokes," he said, breathing heavily.

She twisted to look. "Where?"

"I don't know anymore. He was behind some machinery."

Brigit appeared unconvinced. "He couldn't know we'd be here."

"Maybe he wasn't waiting for us." Jasper took her hand and hauled her through a door that led outside.

He blinked in the sunshine.

The yard next to the building was deserted. Everyone had probably gone inside to check on the ruckus, or they'd set off to find the sheriff. Next door, passengers were gathering outside the new station to board a waiting train.

Jasper made a decision. The risk was too great for them to remain together. If they hurried, she could make it onto the next train while he stayed behind to lead the marshal—or whoever else might be after them—away from her. "Over there. Let's go."

Passing through a cloud of steam drifting from the waiting locomotive, he directed Brigit around the passengers. He pressed a twenty-dollar gold piece into her palm. "Go buy a ticket to Parsons. I'll make sure no one follows you."

Brigit fisted the coin. "We should go see Henry. Warn him. I introduced myself as his sister. The authorities are bound to go to his house."

"All the more reason *not* to go there," Jasper pointed out. "If the marshal is after us, we'd lead him right to your brother."

"And your idea to run is better?"

"I'm not running. You are."

"Why are you so determined to get rid of me?" Brigit's belligerent expression softened into one of understanding. "I don't expect you to protect me, you know. And what about you? If I leave, who's going to protect you?"

Why the hell did she care about him? He wasn't worth as much as her little finger.

He forced his features into indifference. "I am not your responsibility."

"Yes, you are," she insisted.

"Why? Because you stole me?"

She narrowed her eyes, clearly irritated at him for paraphrasing her earlier explanation. "Because we're *partners*."

Partners. Like those men, she worked with. If that was all he meant to her, he ought to be glad. Or maybe not. She'd risked her life to find that missing agent.

"We have to stay together and figure out what's going on," she insisted. "Find out what J.D. was involved in, who would have reason to kill him, why the marshal was snooping around."

Jasper flexed his fingers at his sides and fought a ridiculous urge to kiss her to shut her up. "Your pigheadedness is going to get you killed," he said in a low growl.

She raised her chin. "Then I'll be in good company."

"For Pete's sake, stop stalling!" He was tempted to beat his head against that brick wall. "I'll catch up with you later."

She planted her hands on her hips. "Will you? I give it a fifty-fifty chance. I'm sure you saw that note pinned to J.D.'s vest."

Her suspicion caught Jasper by surprise. He might've threatened murder, but he wouldn't have killed his niece's father. The man Sally loved. A comrade he'd once considered a brother, though he'd never admit as much. "What's your point? Do you think I killed him? While you were sawing logs, I snuck out and found him. Murdered him and hung him on a hook—"

"Oh, stop it, please." Brigit snatched his lapels. "If *you* killed J.D., you wouldn't make a production out of it. Whoever did this wants to send a message."

Jasper peeled her fingers away from his coat. "Precisely. Which is why you're leaving, and I'm staying here to distract them."

Her shoulders slumped and defiance drained out of her. "I'll go purchase a ticket."

Finally, she'd come to her senses.

While she was gone, he kept a nervous watch across the tracks.

Several men on horseback had ridden up to the loading dock. The local sheriff, he'd guess. No sign of the marshal, but that didn't mean Stokes hadn't left the building from another exit. Jasper considered the possibility that Stokes had gone to Tobias's office to look for them.

The locomotive spewed a thick cloud of smoke, which obscured Jasper's view of the warehouse. He didn't have to wait long before Brigit returned.

"Last call!" the conductor shouted. "All aboard!"

"Time to go." Jasper took her arm and hauled her to the steps of a passenger car. They had to wait behind a woman with two fussy children and an old man wobbling on a cane.

Brigit sighed. "Since you won't come with me, I suppose I'll have to find Mr. Kinkaid on my own."

Her casual remark had a chilling effect. If she wandered around that no man's land where criminals gathered, she'd get lost or molested...or killed.

"Go to Parsons," he instructed. "Wait there until I send word."

Her gaze held a mixture of sadness and determination. "I won't go back until I've completed my investigation."

Jasper ground his teeth in frustration. "Last night, and again this morning, you agreed you'd listen to me."

"I am listening. I never agreed to do as you say."

The conductor cleared his throat. "Are you two getting on board?"

She handed the conductor two tickets.

Vixen. She'd planned this.

Brigit stopped with one foot on the step and a look of alarm crossed her face. So, she wasn't so certain he'd follow her. She held out her hand. "Come with me. Please."

She acted like he had a choice. Well, he did, but the lesser of two bad choices was to stay with her so she wouldn't get herself killed. At least she was getting on the train. With any luck, Stokes hadn't seen them and they could get away before he showed up.

Jasper took her hand.

Inside the car, he nudged her past a free seat near the front. He never sat somewhere he couldn't get away quickly. The only other seats available were on a bench across from the fussy children. He heaved a resigned sigh. Things could be worse.

The departure whistle sounded.

As they sat, the train began to move.

The next moment, a late-arriving passenger appeared in the doorway at the front of the car. He held his hat on his head with one hand, as if to prevent it from blowing off when he'd jumped onto the steps leading up to the car. A black, bushy mustache framed his downturned lips.

∾

BRIGIT'S HEART, already pounding, raced in fear. She slumped in the seat at the same time Jasper tugged at his hat brim to shield his face.

Had Stokes seen them board the train? He didn't appear to have noticed them yet, but it was only a matter of moments before he did.

She held her breath as he made his way down the aisle.

The train picked up speed.

Stokes moved unevenly, apparently having a hard time keeping his balance. Or he could be drunk. That would be a blessing. A man who was deep into his cups would have slower reflexes.

Jasper grabbed her hand. "Let's go. Now."

She wasn't about to argue. If they delayed, they'd be trapped.

Brigit cast one last glance over her shoulder. The marshal's eyes widened with surprise and then narrowed with fury. Had he not expected them to run? Maybe he hadn't recognized them earlier. He might've seen them, become suspicious, and boarded the train on a hunch.

Jasper pulled her through the rear door, then unlatched a chain blocking the steps. They weren't moving so fast they couldn't jump, but her feet didn't want to obey.

He tightened his grip on her hand. "No, not that way." He led her onto the adjacent car to a ladder next to the door. "Get on top. Quick!"

She gripped the cold metal and climbed as fast as she could.

Jasper came along right behind her, so close he pushed into her skirts. When she made it to the top of the train, the wind ripped off her teardrop hat. She flattened herself on the metal catwalk before it blew her off the train.

Jasper stretched half on top of her with his hand pressing on her shoulder, indicating that she should keep down, which she'd already figured out.

Would their feint fool the lawman?

She leaned over to peer off the side at the ground rushing past.

A moment later, the marshal jumped off the train. He rolled to the bottom of the grade, came to his feet with a gun in his hand, looked around, and then up.

Brigit jerked out of sight, breathing in ragged gasps. If Stokes had seen her and fired at them, the sound of the gunshot was drowned out in the roar of the train's departure.

Jasper tapped her shoulder. He motioned for her to follow him down the ladder. Once they'd reached the bottom, he held out her hat! "Lose something?"

His quick reflexes had saved more than her hat.

Brigit's hands shook so badly that she had trouble tying the ribbon beneath her chin. She followed Jasper into the next passenger car where they found an open seat. Other than a few curious glances, no one paid them any mind.

Jasper waited for her to slide across the bench seat before he sat next to her. He rubbed his arm—the one that was injured. It had to be hurting after the calisthenics. No blood appeared on his sleeve. Still, she'd keep an eye on him. They'd need to change the dressing at some point.

Out the window, the ground became a blur.

Her heightened energy drained and a chilling reality set in. Any suspicions the marshal might've had upon spotting them at the ice company were now confirmed. He could obtain her name. Drag her family into a murder investigation.

She put her hand to her face and squeezed her eyes shut to hold back the tears. If she could sing a song to keep her thoughts from spiraling into a pit of fear, it might help. Except singing would attract too much attention. She tried to hum, a few notes from a happy tune, but she couldn't remember the rest or even the name of the song.

Her plan to disguise them and use her family name to gain information hadn't worked as well as expected. Nothing, thus far, had gone as she'd expected. Least of all, Jasper's stubborn determination to sacrifice himself for her sake.

He brushed his fingers over the side of her face, tucking a stray lock of hair behind her ear.

The tender gesture undid her. She twisted around and buried her face against his shoulder. He smelled of sandalwood. It was a fairly common fragrance that barbers used, but from now on, she would always associate it with Jasper.

He held her as he might hold a tearful child—gently, gingerly, with an awkwardness that was heartbreaking and touching at the same time. The last of the edifice she'd built around her heart crumbled beneath a force too powerful to resist.

Was this what love felt like? She wouldn't know because she'd never been in love before. From the time she'd been thrust from a loving home into an uncaring world, she had guarded her heart. Only her twin had been allowed inside the inner realms. Somehow, Jasper had breached those walls. If he'd meant to steal her heart, he didn't act as though he wanted it. He seemed determined to get rid of her. Still, she couldn't help but wonder about his true feelings.

He put his hand on her head and patted as he might do with a puppy.

Her laugh came out in a snort.

"Does that mean you feel better?" he asked.

Foolish might be a better word to describe it. If she confessed her love, it would only embarrass them both and add to his burdens. She'd already done enough to make his life difficult. Brigit sat up and located her handkerchief.

He eyed her warily. Did he fear she might dissolve into a messy, feminine heap?

She dabbed her eyes and regained control of her emotions.

"Never fear, I shan't lose my composure again and fall into your arms."

"I don't mind...the part about you falling into my arms."

Neither did she, but for different reasons.

Brigit squelched the unproductive thoughts. She had more important things to focus on besides her unrequited affections for an outlaw.

"I've been thinking..." Brigit shifted on the seat to remain close enough to converse without being overheard. "What if J.D. was killed at the slaughterhouse late last night or very early this morning. The murderer sent his body in the car over to the ice house to divert attention there, and then waited to make sure things worked out as he planned."

Jasper bent his head next to hers. "Stokes?"

"The coincidences point that direction. Perhaps J.D. was involved in more than setting up an ambush for your men, something the marshal didn't want anyone to find out about. What do you think the marshal is protecting?"

"Follow the money," Jasper whispered. "All that beef being shipped north."

The pieces fell into place. "A cattle-rustling operation."

"Probably operating out of Indian Territory. J.D. must've gotten involved. Whoever's running it could be bribing the marshal to keep the law away." Jasper released a soft huff. "All theories. No evidence."

Brigit fisted her hands. Whatever Stokes's shady purpose for being at the ice house, he would now have a scapegoat for J.D.'s brutal death if he could place Jasper at the scene. "I won't let him get away with this."

"You need to stay the hell out of his way!" Jasper's heated breath warmed her ear. "After he tells the sheriff you're helping me, they'll put out a warrant for your arrest. You won't be safe anywhere."

He confirmed what she already knew, but the implications reverberated through her and sent her anxiety soaring. She had no way to warn her family. If the agency learned of her involvement before she could produce evidence, she'd be considered a rogue, and so would Hannah, by association. To make matters worse, she had unwittingly led Jasper to the very place where J.D.'s body was found, and Stokes would use it to his advantage.

"Having second thoughts about bringing me along?" Jasper asked in a whisper.

"No." She would never regret a minute spent in Jasper's company. She would regret it for the rest of her life if he paid the price for a wrong decision. "It's not too late."

"For you, no. For me..."

His unfinished remark pierced her heart.

"Hey..." He gathered her hand in his and squeezed. "I'm watching out for you. And we're partners, right? We'll find that missing agent and figure this out."

His gaze held an apology he didn't owe her. He'd done nothing except try to protect her the only way he knew how.

She placed her other hand over the two of theirs to signal her commitment. "Yes, *partners*."

For now, even if it wasn't forever. Their lives were on different trajectories and wouldn't land in the same spot. Not unless the quest they were on ended in tragedy, which it would if she lost sight of her goals and let her heart confuse her mind.

She began to hum to soothe her nerves. No particular tune, just fragments of songs as they came to her. As she hummed, she rubbed her thumb along the side of Jasper's forefinger. Another scar marred his smooth skin. How had he gotten this one?

Lifting his hand, she kissed the side of his finger, then realized what she'd done and dropped his hand. "We must find Mr. Kinkaid. Quickly."

CHAPTER 14

Finding the missing Pinkerton agent wasn't the only thing on Jasper's mind when they got off the train at the first stop in Indian Territory. He could still feel the imprint of Brigit's kiss on his finger and the weight of what it meant on his heart.

Had she made the terrible mistake of allowing herself to care too much about him? He hoped not. He had a long history of ruining people's lives when they became too entangled with his. That was why he'd sent his sister away to live with their mother's clan and maintained infrequent contact. He had few friends, mostly outlaws. None he would introduce to Brigit's law-abiding family.

As Brigit stepped to the ground, her buttoned boots sent up a little puff of dirt. He held her hand to assist her and felt her fingers tremble. She cast her eyes downward and her face turned pink, which was very unlike her.

She could be suffering from embarrassment. That kiss she'd bestowed on his finger might be nothing more than a show of gratitude after their hair-raising escape.

He could handle grateful.

Jasper looked around. They were the only passengers who'd disembarked at this desolate stop with a single bench and overhead shelter. Nearby was a trading post, but no boarding houses or other lodgings. "We're on Choctaw land."

She held her fancy hat as the wind tried to snatch it again and looked up at him. "What does that mean?"

"If you're not Choctaw, it means you're not welcome."

"They aren't friendly to visitors?"

"Depends on the visitor. But it's not members of the tribe we need to be worried about." Jasper offered her his arm. "You're my wife if anyone asks. Out here, women don't travel along with men who aren't their husbands.

"Am I to be Mrs. O'Malley...or Mrs. Byrne?" she asked.

Her question caught him off guard. For a moment. *Idiot.* She was joking. Smart, practical Brigit, even if she had a soft spot in her heart, she wouldn't suggest a permanent arrangement. With him? It was laughable.

Except, she wasn't laughing...not even a smile.

Even if she was half-serious about a longer-term relationship, it was only because she'd fooled herself into thinking he was more like the fictional gentlemen she'd turned him into.

Well, if she wanted to pretend, so could he.

Jasper tucked her gloved hand over the sleeve of the fancy coat she'd selected for his disguise. "Shall we, Mrs. O'Malley?"

"Lead on, Mr. O'Malley. Where do we go from here?"

Nowhere. His usefulness to her would be short-lived. Only long enough to help her find that missing agent. Then, she would discard him. And he didn't give a damn. Or shouldn't.

He gestured eastward with a sweep of his arm at a place where the high prairie rolled up to an ancient mountain range. "Out there, that's where we're going. On a map, it's Choctaw territory all the way to the border with Arkansas. In reality, that's no man's land. Unless you happen to be an outlaw. Which I am, so it's your lucky day."

Brigit looked askance. "Do we have to walk?"

"I see a possible solution." He pointed it out to her.

Behind the trading post, two horses paced in a small corral while a dog kept guard.

"Are you suggesting we steal those horses?"

All the newspapers made him out to be a scalawag with no morals whatsoever. He could simply reinforce the image so she wouldn't get too attached.

"It might be the easiest thing," he teased.

She gave him a disappointed frown.

"All, right. We won't do the easy thing. Let's head over to *Wiley's Trading Post* and see if we can strike a deal."

Brigit seemed up for that, which suggested she didn't fully understand what horse-trading meant in these parts.

She hugged his arm as they walked. "Do you know Mr. Wiley?"

"We haven't exchanged introductions if that's what you mean. He's white, which is why the railroad lets him use their right-of-way. He married a Choctaw woman, which is why her people tolerate him. And they say he's a sharp trader."

"He'd have to be with a name like that."

Inside the trading post, blackened haunches of venison hung from hooks attached to a ceiling support beam, and the smell of smoked meat mingled with scents of tobacco and gunpowder.

Jasper's empty stomach turned. Hungry as he was, he might never be able to eat meat again. Not any that came off a hook.

A short woman with braided black hair maneuvered a broom around a barrel. She wore a man's shirt over a wrapped skirt with a woven sash tied around her waist. Likely, she was the owner's wife.

Jasper tipped his hat. Normally, he'd speak a greeting in her language, but it might be best to continue the charade of being an ignorant dandy. "Good afternoon, ma'am."

She peered around him at Brigit, who offered her a friendly smile, which was not returned.

"Howdy, folks!" The proprietor called from behind the counter. Mr. Wiley had to be twenty years older than the woman, and she hadn't married him for his looks. "What brings you here?"

What he meant by the question wasn't how Jasper chose to answer it. Feeding the old man's curiosity wasn't necessary to do business, and the less he knew the better.

"We need supplies." Jasper surveyed a stack of open crates that served as shelves for canned foods, tools, blankets, and other goods.

Prices were inflated all over, especially in remote places like this one. What little money he had left wouldn't go far, and he didn't have enough to outright buy a horse. What could they barter?

The man's wife continued to eye Brigit, sizing her up. Or was she comparing their sizes? The fine attire might appeal to a woman who wished for nicer things but didn't have them.

Jasper latched onto the idea. He *did* have something to trade. Would Brigit go along with it? She'd have to if she didn't want to walk to Robber's Roost.

He placed several tins of canned food on the counter, along with a blanket, pocket knife, rope, and extra ammunition. "Do you own those horses in the corral?"

"I might." Mr. Wiley had the look of a man who saw easy money coming his way. "You want to buy one, along with those goods?"

"Let's make a trade," Jasper suggested.

"What d'you got?"

The storekeeper's wife continued to sweep and each step brought her closer to the counter. Good, she needed to hear this.

Jasper reckoned the old man wouldn't immediately pounce on the idea of rewarding his wife with fancy clothes without getting something for himself. And his woman would be keen to dress him up, as befitting a store owner, which would give her more bragging rights.

"I can see you are a man of good taste." Jasper took hold of his coat lapels and opened them. "You'd recognize the value of these fine clothes."

The old man squinted. "How valuable?"

"How valuable, you ask?" Jasper peeled off his coat and removed the red vest. He wouldn't make the mistake of putting a dollar value on it. They were trading. "Why, it's pure wool, the latest fashion. From, uh, New York."

"France," Brigit said at the same time.

"France, New York." Jasper didn't know if there was such a place, but he made it sound like he visited there frequently. "All the successful men wear these. I daresay, every chief in the territory will want to own one of these vests. They might offer you a pony in exchange."

Mr. Wiley's wife sidled over. She picked up the vest, rubbed her fingers over it, smelled it, examined the seams, then sent her husband a signal with her eyes. She gestured to Jasper's coat. "That too, and the shirt."

Jasper stripped off the articles and laid them on the counter.

Brigit's soft gasp came from behind. Did she not think he was making a good deal? Just wait until they got to *her* clothes.

He would need something to wear. That deerskin tunic hanging on the wall looked to be just the thing. Soft, yet durable, decorated with stitched arrows and other Choctaw markings, which would be a plus in this region. "Throw that in, as part of the deal."

Wiley hesitated. The shirt probably belonged to him.

"I can make another," his wife said.

The woman picked up Jasper's coat and insisted her husband try it on. It was made for a man who was taller and with broader shoulders and a flat stomach, but it was a fair enough fit to satisfy her. She spoke to him in her language.

Jasper knew enough to understand that she'd instructed her man to take the vest and coat but to ask for more. Mr. Wiley might pose as the sharp trader, but it was his wife who drove the bartering.

"That's still not enough for a horse," the trader told Jasper.

He knew this, of course, which was why he had to push back. To make sure he got a deal and they believed they'd gotten one too. "Those two nags out there are skinny and sway-backed."

Wiley crossed his arms over his chest. "Go find others, if you like."

Jasper held up his hands in mock surrender. "You drive a hard bargain, mister. We have more to offer." He drew Brigit in front of him so the Choctaw woman could see her. "What do you think?"

The old trader's grizzled eyebrows shot upward. "How much do you want for her?"

"Her dress is what I'm offering."

Brigit's back went straight as an iron rail. "Just a moment. I need a word with my *husband*." She twisted around and used her hands to push him. He took a few steps backward.

"You should've warned me," she whispered.

"I know." He kissed her on the cheek like he was making peace with her, then whispered in her ear. "We need them to think you don't want to get rid of your pretty things. It'll make them more eager to deal."

Her frown conveyed disbelief. "What do they want with our clothes?"

"What all people want. Respect. Trust me on this."

By the time he was done, he'd have the supplies and horse they needed, and she would retain no illusions about him whatsoever. She'd probably turn him in herself.

Brigit gave him a searching look. "I do trust you. Just don't leave me in my underclothes."

He patted her shoulder. "Don't worry, dear. They'll want those too."

CHAPTER 15

The rangy horse Jasper had obtained for them cantered across a prairie that had appeared flat. Deceptively so. It was some of the roughest terrain Brigit had ever experienced. Her backside, in particular.

She clung to Jasper's waist and gritted her teeth. They had to ride hard, he'd said, to reach Robber's Roost by the end of the day. A long, torturous day, on this bony beast.

Why couldn't he have bartered for *two* horses? That might've left her entirely naked. Was this his revenge for tricking him into getting onto the train with her? He demanded that she pretend to be his wife, then he'd let that odious man think he might trade *her*. She hadn't found that joke the least bit funny.

"I don't believe we came out ahead in the deal you negotiated." She shifted to find a more comfortable position behind the saddle, which he'd gotten in exchange for her lace undergarments.

Jasper shifted back, then, as soon she leaned against him, he moved forward again. "What do you mean? We have a horse, supplies, clothes—"

"Yes, you have a lovely deerskin tunic. I am attired in a man's shirt and a wrap skirt without proper undergarments."

"Perfect for out here."

Granted, her beautiful dress wouldn't have been useful, but that wasn't the point. Jasper had helped her select it and had purchased it with his savings. His admiration for her when she wore it made her feel beautiful and desirable—and he'd bartered it away like it meant nothing. "I wouldn't have minded giving up my gown if you'd asked me first."

"Don't you switch disguises all the time? I didn't think you'd mind all that much. Your new hat is more useful than that little doily you were wearing."

"It wasn't a doily. It's called a teardrop."

And he'd traded it for a slouch hat meant for a man. Then had told her she ought to be pleased with the effect.

His silence indicated this conversation was over, as far as he was concerned. She couldn't say more without revealing too much about why it mattered, and there was no point in getting emotional about it. He was focused on survival and she ought to be as well.

She adjusted the skirt's extra length beneath her to soften the ride. The *skirt* was essentially a long section of fabric that could be turned into just about anything. Highly practical.

Being careful not to lose her seat, Brigit twisted to take another look behind them and judge the distance they'd traveled. The trading post had vanished, but the shapes of two horses and riders appeared on the plain they'd just crossed.

Alarmed, she squeezed Jasper's waist to get his attention. "I see two riders in the distance who appear to be following us. I can't tell how far away they are, but they weren't there before."

Jasper glanced over his shoulder and frowned. "Only the trader and his wife know the direction we're headed."

"Which means they told someone else. What if it's the marshal?"

"He wouldn't have caught up this quick. I'll bet that old fox sent a couple of thieves after us to retrieve the horse." Jasper handed Brigit his revolver. "Here. I've got to pay attention to where we're going. If they get too close, shoot them."

His frank instruction sent a shiver down her spine. "I can't shoot someone without knowing who they are or what they want."

"You won't get the chance to find out if you wait for an introduction." Jasper turned back to guide the horse.

Brigit tucked the revolver beneath the woven belt around her waist. Shoot first and then ask questions? That wasn't how she preferred to handle things. Still, he could be right.

At the moment, she prayed he knew precisely what to do when they reached those dark green hills, which would usher them into a rugged mountain range filled with uncharted canyons and caves. Robber's Roost was up there somewhere.

"We'll lose them soon." Jasper urged the horse to continue its pace as they ascended. He appeared to be headed toward a forested ridge.

She clung to him, every so often casting nervous glances over her shoulder. He kept the horse at a brisk clip, dodging boulders and bushes, riding back and forth, up one side of a hill and down the other, with no apparent path. Yet, his guidance seemed intentional, as if he followed a map in his head.

When they'd reached a higher altitude, he slowed their mount to a trot and entered a stand of trees where the air smelled of pine. Layers of brown needles cushioned the sound of the horse's rhythmic gait.

"I think we've lost them."

"Or they decided not to follow us after they figured out where we're going." Jasper eased the horse into a comfortable walk.

He, too, believed they'd escaped, which made her more confident. He had a predator's cunning and the survival instincts of prey, which explained why he'd been able to evade the authorities for so many years. But up here, it wasn't lawmen one worried about encountering.

"Do you think they're afraid of the outlaws?"

"Outlaws...or spirits."

"Spirits?"

"You'd call them ghosts?"

She would've laughed, except she could tell from Jasper's tone he was serious. "Who are they, these spirits? Rather, who *were* they?"

"Souls that can't rest."

Brigit started at a fluttering sound, which turned out to be a robin. She loosened her tight grip on Jasper and laughed nervously. "We investigated a medium who claimed to speak to spirits. Her tricks had more to do with the living than the dead. Why aren't the outlaws who live out here afraid of ghosts?"

"Getting hanged is a lot scarier."

She couldn't argue that. "Do *you* believe these hills are inhabited by spirits?"

"No. But it's a good story. It keeps superstitious people away."

"Agent Kinkaid isn't superstitious. He discovered something important. I think he may have come out here to find answers. Whoever waylaid him isn't among the dead."

"If he was looking for cattle rustlers working for crooked railroad executives, he'd find plenty of enemies who'd want *him* dead."

If what Jasper suspected was true, it would also give powerful men a good reason to hunt them.

Brigit's heart beat faster. What if they couldn't find Kinkaid or the evidence he'd uncovered, where did that leave her and Jasper? Running for their lives until the authorities or the criminals caught up with them.

She clamped down a rush of anxiety. "We need to conduct a thorough search in places where Agent Kinkaid might've gone."

"Out here?" Jasper laughed without sounding amused. "The only way we'll find your man is if we can get help."

She found his choice of words odd. "Mr. Kinkaid isn't *my* man. He has a wife and family."

"Then he should've stayed with them."

She wasn't arguing career choices with an outlaw.

The horse slowed to a walk. Brigit adjusted her hold on Jasper's waist, no longer needing to cling so tightly, but he held onto her hands. Was he aware of it?

She ventured to rest her cheek against his shoulder. The deerskin shirt he'd obtained felt supple, as did the warm, solid muscles beneath.

He leaned forward suddenly. She lost her balance and slid to the right. Catching her by the arm, he steadied her.

"Careful," he warned.

"Then stop pulling me against you," she grumbled, tired of the mixed signals. "Where will we find help?"

"A friend of mine." He guided their mount alongside a gurgling stream.

The large boulders in this mountainous region were half-buried with smooth, rounded surfaces. Perhaps the shells of primeval turtles rising from the forest floor. A fanciful notion, like those spirits.

"You have friends out here? One of the ghosts?" she teased.

"Worse. A Cherokee train robber."

"What is he doing down here?"

"Hiding. Charley and his cousin took a white woman hostage four years ago. White folks don't forgive Indians for that."

"Did they return her?"

Jasper's pause seemed long. "She married his cousin."

"What is your point?" It couldn't have possibly anything to do with marriage. "You didn't take me hostage. It was the other way around."

"The point is, you recruited me to escort you safely through the Territory, and that's what I'm doing. Your job is to cooperate."

"My *job* is to find our missing agent and then make sure you get rewarded for your help."

The sound Jasper made this time wasn't a laugh, more like a grunt. "Stop worrying about my reward. Focus on your safety."

His retort stung. It implied she wasn't being smart or sincere or both. "I promised I would do everything within my power to gain your freedom. I intend to keep that vow."

Her arms began to ache and she loosened her grip around Jasper's waist. He would probably be delighted for her to stop hugging him.

"Don't let go yet," he warned her.

Her heart constricted with yearning. She didn't want to let go, and at this point, she couldn't, even though her meddling in his affairs had done neither of them much good. Still, she didn't want him to think she was losing hope. "We'll find Mr. Kinkaid and the evidence that will exonerate you."

Jasper's chest swelled as he took a deep breath before he exhaled. "You didn't set out to exonerate me. You set out to find dirt on a railroad baron. If you don't find it here, look elsewhere."

"You make it sound easy. Have you forgotten about the reward or that persistent marshal?"

"Hardly. I've had a price on my head for years. You can't do anything about that." Jasper squeezed her hands. "But if you break away from me, you can continue your work. The way I see it, you've got to go back to Parsons. Tell them I abducted you and forced you to help me escape before you got away."

Brigit recoiled at his suggestion. She'd never been comfortable with such underhanded tactics, and feeling as she did about him, she would rather die than send him off under false charges to save herself. "No. We're partners. We have to stay together and solve this. We agreed. Remember?"

The horse stopped at the edge of a stream where Jasper let the thirsty animal take a drink. He dismounted and helped Brigit. Her legs felt permanently bowed and her muscles trembled from being tense for so long. He had to be sore, too.

She held onto him for another moment. "You didn't answer me. We're partners, right?"

He gazed down at her with a troubled expression. "For now. Get some water. We can rest for a few minutes."

A few minutes? She was desperate to rest for hours.

She wobbled to the edge of the water and knelt to take a drink from the clear stream. His confirmation, with its implied limits, made sense, but it also saddened her.

Jasper went down on one knee and scooped water with his hand. He drank without making a sound. For that matter, he walked silently, as well. He had the adeptness of a wild creature, likely a skill developed after having lived like one for so long. She, on the other hand, was out of her element and had been from the moment she'd released him from that coffin.

At the time, she'd imagined she could bring him into the light and give him another chance at a better life. As it turned out, he'd been the one who had dispelled the darkness enveloping her heart. In a sense, Jasper had freed her, not the other way around.

If he didn't wish to remain with her, she could hardly fault him. Things had gotten too complicated. In particular, their relationship and how she felt about it. How *he* felt about it was less clear to her. But he'd agreed to a temporary partnership and she would hold him to it.

When she tried to stand, her legs refused to cooperate. "How do you do it?"

"Do what?"

"Remain upright."

He helped her to her feet. Her heart raced when he removed her hat and tenderly brushed aside the damp strands of hair clinging to her face. His fierce expression seemed incompatible with the tender gesture. "I'm not, you know."

She licked the excess water from her lips, trying to make sense of what he said, and finding it difficult to think about anything except how her skin tingled when he touched it. "You're not what?"

"Upright." He dragged her against him and kissed her.

The abruptness should've startled her, but it didn't. A different instinct thrust fears aside and awakened desire. It thrummed through her veins and made her heart pound.

This time, she was ready for it.

She brought her arms around his neck and returned his kiss with the same ferocity. If he wasn't *upright*, neither was she. He'd turned her life upside down. She didn't want this wild ride to end. She wanted it to go on, forever.

An owl hooted from the branches above them.

Jasper ended the kiss as abruptly as he'd started it.

She clung to him. "Why did you stop?"

"The owl."

What did a bird have to do with anything? Unless... She darted a cautious look around. "Do you think someone's out there? Is it a signal?"

He pulled her arms from around his neck. "No. It's an owl. But owls are a sign."

"What kind of sign?"

"Death."

⁓

BRIGIT'S golden-brown eyes reflected confusion. A moment later, her lips quivered. Was she about to burst into tears? Jasper wished she would slap him or kick him. Do something, anything but cry.

She emitted a soft snort before doubling over with laughter.

The sound sent prickles over his flesh. Just like before, his thoughtless actions had sent her over the edge of reason. He'd known she was vulnerable, but she had beguiled him. No, that wasn't fair. Her innocent eagerness didn't excuse him. It condemned him. And her continued giggles were unnerving him.

He grabbed her arms and pulled her up. "Stop laughing!"

Brigit gazed at him with tears rimming her lower eyelids. "You don't think it's funny?" She sniffed and chuckled again. "Oh, God, Jasper, laugh. You just gave me the most incredible, life-affirming kiss...and then...then you compared it to the kiss of death. I don't think I've ever been so thoroughly insulted."

Insulted? The owl's call had jerked him back into their reality. He'd meant to share a dose of it with her. Not to offend her.

"We're out here in a wild place, being chased, riding into worse danger..." He heaved a sigh as he let his hands drift down her arms until he reached her hands and clasped them. "That's all I meant by it."

Her smile faded into a bemused expression. "You didn't mean to kiss me?"

He couldn't very well say *no*. It was intentional. But if he said *yes*, she might presume he'd done it because he had feelings for her, and he wasn't about to admit to such a thing. He tried for a cold, indifferent tone. "You had it coming."

She stared at him for so long that it seemed as if she were reading his mind. Whatever she surmised made her smile again. "Ah, and you are angry with me because you were trying to teach me a lesson but I kissed you back? Is that it?"

"No, I'm not angry, and I wasn't—"

"You didn't like it?"

"I didn't say that—"

"You *did* like it." Brigit hugged his waist and laid her head on his shoulder. "I like the way you kiss, too." She stroked the back of his neck and tickled the short hair above his collar, beneath which he'd started to sweat.

Pretending disinterest wasn't working. She wouldn't accept it. Nor did she seem willing to consider that he might be a low-down snake. What should he do? Hold her? Shake some sense into her? Lay her down on the blanket and make love to her? The third option held the most appeal, though it wouldn't improve her fragile state of mind, which was the only explanation for her erratic behavior.

He released a harsh breath. "Miss Stevens, you aren't thinking straight."

"I've never had better clarity of thought." She nuzzled his neck, which obliterated every clear thought in his head. "Don't you think it's time we stop fighting?"

"Fighting? We're not..." He cupped his hands on her shoulders. It took every ounce of willpower not to bring her to him for another kiss and prove how far his thoughts were from *fighting*. "We have to leave. Now."

She gave him a dewy smile.

"Don't look at me like that."

"Whatever you say."

Since when had she agreed with him without an argument or a smart remark?

Yep. She'd gone loco.

Worry nibbled at him while he adjusted the saddle blanket to make the ride as comfortable for her as possible. He mounted, then helped her up behind him.

"It's a good thing I'm skinny," she remarked.

"You aren't skinny." Her lean, sleek form might not appeal to some men, but he wasn't one of them.

"What a flatterer, you are." She laughed as she wound her arms around his midsection and pressed her front against his back.

He couldn't fault her breasts for being in the way. She had nowhere else to put them. He'd brought this misery on himself when he'd traded away her undergarments, and the ache in his groin was just punishment.

He kept his thoughts to himself and rode on.

Brigit wasn't cut out to be an outlaw's consort. For all her unconventional ways, she was a well-bred lady who deserved a hell of a lot more than he could ever offer her—no matter how much she *liked* kissing him.

The sun had slipped behind the trees by the time they'd climbed high into the foothills. By dusk, he spotted the massive stones that shielded the hideout. "There it is."

"It looks like a pile of rocks," Brigit said from over his shoulder.

"That may be what it looks like, but there's a cave back there. These types of peculiar formations are all over these mountains. The elders tell a story about how our mother, the Earth, made shelters like these for her children. To protect them."

"Her *unruly* children?" Brigit gave him a quick kiss on the neck, which set off the ache again and spoiled his attempt to educate her.

"Pay attention. If Charley is here, he's already aware of our presence."

"I am paying attention. I've been watching behind us and listening. For owls."

Maybe she thought joking would ease the tension. Generally, it did. In this case, flirting didn't cure the kind of tension he was experiencing.

Jasper brought the horse close to a creek and dismounted to refill their canteen. Beneath the surface, several trout used their wavering tails to fight the current, pausing in one spot before darting to another. He could fish here later. If necessary, he could also take a dip in the cold water.

"Jasper, I can't get off this horse without collapsing in a heap."

He helped Brigit dismount but then let her go the instant her feet touched the ground. She held onto his arm and groaned.

"I am certain I have blisters where I've never had them before."

Well, that inspired an interesting image. He had to ask. "Where might those be?"

"Not in a place I'd show *you*."

Jasper released a relieved breath. She'd recovered from her strangely agreeable state and was back to being sassy. Perhaps her odd behavior earlier could be explained by too much riding and a lack of water. Fortunately, they were surrounded by streams and waterfalls.

"I'll hobble the horse. We have to walk from here." He hefted the tack and a rolled-up blanket. His injured arm ached, but he wasn't about to admit it and have her start fussing over him.

Brigit carried the bag containing their supplies. She followed along behind him as they climbed the rocks. Some were slick. It was a good thing she'd traded those fancy shoes for soft leather moccasins.

He jerked his gaze away from her slender ankle. It was an *ankle*, for Pete's sake! He'd seen one before. Several.

Jasper halted next to a dead tree where a spotted hawk perched on a branch took flight. Other than the hawk, he discerned no other activity.

Behind the rocks, the earth had thrust two slabs of stone upward. The formation created a narrow passage, which led to a cave. It was wide enough for one person, but anyone proceeding down that way could easily be stopped and identified—or killed—before they reached the hideout.

No sounds came from the passageway. Not even the telltale *click* of a hammer being drawn back.

Jasper motioned for Brigit to hand him the revolver he'd given to her earlier. "Wait here," he instructed her.

He crept along the passage until he came to the cave's entrance. The inside wasn't completely dark, thanks to a circular opening Nature had formed in the ceiling. Directly beneath it was a firepit.

Jasper rubbed cold ashes between his fingers. It had been at least a few days since anyone had set a fire. The only sign of a recent occupant was a frayed bedroll with a faded quilt thrown over it.

Next to the bedding, a brown jug lay on its side.

He sniffed the empty jug. The smell of liquor suggested the owner had been here fairly recently, although strong odors could linger for weeks.

If Charley had moved, he would've taken his bedding and his jug. As it was, it almost appeared that he'd gotten up, walked outside, and hadn't returned.

"Do you suppose anyone's home?" Brigit whispered next to Jasper's ear.

He shot up and spun around, instinctively bringing the revolver up. "Are you trying to get shot? I told you to wait."

She eyed the gun with less worry than might be prudent upon approaching an armed man from behind. "I'm impatient. Besides, it seemed safer to come in here with you."

Jasper holstered the revolver. A lecture about minding him wouldn't do any good. Neither would one about the consequences of blowing into his ear.

Brigit knelt next to the fire pit and tested the ashes as he'd done. "Are you sure this is the right place?"

"It's where Charley was holed up when I saw him last."

"Who is he to you, besides a friend?"

"You remember Sally mentioning *Na*? She's Charley's ma. We're distant relations through my mother's clan. During the war..." Jasper considered how much he ought to reveal. Some of it wasn't his story to tell. "Let's just say, Charley and I had good reasons to hate soldiers who wore a blue uniform. After the war, we found a new enemy and robbed trains together."

Brigit gave Charley's belongings a sideways glance. "Does he stay out here alone?"

"Most of the time. When he gets bored, he goes out to a ridge that overlooks the railroad line and shoots at trains as they pass by." Jasper set the jug upright. He didn't add that Charley had become a pathetic shadow of his former self, which just proved there was a worse fate than one found at the end of a rope.

"Maybe that's where he went."

It would explain a few things. Such as why he'd left these belongings and taken others.

"It's not safe to go looking for him at night."

"What should we do while we wait?" Brigit stood and reached for Jasper's hand. Her touch distracted him and her question took his mind in a different direction.

"Make use of the bedroll?" He spoke his thought but then took his hand away from her. Bedding her would introduce a whole new set of complications he wasn't ready to face, that's what his mind told him. His body had other ideas. "Forget I said that."

Brigit arched a sable eyebrow in a slight gesture more tempting than if she'd pushed him to the ground. "Why should I forget? It's an interesting idea."

She'd become incorrigible. And damn near irresistible.

Jasper looked away. Hell, was he blushing? "We'll get a fire going. Catch some fish. Eat. Wait for Charley. He'll be back soon, I suspect."

"How long, do you think?" she asked.

"I wasn't blessed with the Knowing, but I'd say a few hours. Overnight, maybe." If the Fates intended to prolong this delicious torture. "A few days."

She cast a worried glance at the cave entrance. "We don't have days. Whoever followed us may catch up when they have light tomorrow. Or Marshal Stokes..." She hugged her arms as if she'd gotten cold suddenly. "Will he come out here, do you think?"

"He might try. It's not as easy as it seemed to get here. Stokes won't know the fastest way. We'll be gone by the time he arrives."

"And if Charley doesn't come back?"

Jasper couldn't offer a more optimistic prediction. Charley might not show up for weeks. He wasn't exactly dependable. And Brigit was right about one thing. They were running out of time. "We'll come up with another plan."

He lifted off the ammunition belt he'd worn over his shoulder and across his chest. It wasn't the weight of bullets that felt so heavy. The end of their time together was getting a lot closer than he wanted to admit. Without help, they had no hope of finding that missing man.

He'd already told her what she ought to do, but she'd flat-out rejected his idea. If he couldn't convince her to make up a story to save herself, he would have to do it.

Come morning, if *Tsa-li* didn't return, he would make up some reason to take Brigit back to his cabin. Once there, he would tie her up, then go find her brother-in-law, Frank Garrity.

Surely, the former Labette County sheriff would accept an outlaw's surrender. He'd swear that he had been the one to arrange his escape and had used Brigit. But then he'd fallen for her and couldn't let her take the blame for his misdeeds. It was sappy, as far as excuses go, but it came close enough to the truth to be believable.

He'd also claim that Brigit would lie to try to save him.

CHAPTER 16

*W*hile they waited for Charley to return, Brigit helped Jasper gather wood for a fire. He shaved off thin strips of bark, then used his knife and a piece of flint to set sparks to kindling.

"Stay in the cave," he instructed. "I'll go take care of the horse, and see if there's any fish in the creek that want to be our dinner."

She found his choice of words amusing. "If I were the fish, I think I'd refuse the offer."

"Sacrifice can be an honor," he answered without smiling.

Were they still talking about fish?

Jasper returned the knife to his pocket and the flint to a small, leather pouch he'd produced. She hadn't seen it before. He could've gotten it in his deal with the trader, as he had the knife, or maybe he'd had it all along, tucked away somewhere, like the secrets he kept.

He'd gone quiet, which could signal a desire to be left alone. Or he might be thinking about doing something he ought not to do. For instance, leaving her here while he went off to search for Charley.

Brigit stopped him before he left the cave. "You aren't venturing far?"

"Only far enough for food. I'm hungry. Aren't you?"

"Yes, I am. Very hungry," she whispered.

Hannah's laughter erupted in her mind. *Oh, Brigit. That was awful.*

Jasper stared at her hand, still clutched on his arm. Did *he* think her innuendo was awful?

Before meeting him, she wouldn't have dreamt of flirting with a man, much less being intimate with one. But almost from the start, she'd been comfortable enough around Jasper to be herself. And now, she felt safe enough to explore these new yearnings.

If he would take the hint.

"I'd best leave if you want something to eat." He put his hand over hers and gave it a reassuring squeeze, but still didn't meet her steady gaze. His lean cheeks darkened above the soft black hair that had been shaped into burnsides along his strong jaw.

He wasn't *dis*interested. Perhaps he was trying to be a gentleman. Another reason she loved him. Despite all its lawlessness, his heart had remained honorable. She sensed his need for love was even greater than hers, even if he hadn't yet realized it.

"I can go with you," she suggested. "Help you."

"Someone needs to tend the fire."

Brigit sighed with frustration. "That's what I'm *trying* to do."

He looked away, which confirmed he'd gotten her meaning but was choosing to ignore it.

A wave of longing swept through her. This could be their last night together. Charley might not return or have any idea where to find Kinkaid. The agent could be dead and buried in an unmarked grave. The authorities would eventually catch up. Jasper would try to protect her, she wouldn't leave him to fend for himself, and they would be caught in a descending spiral.

"If we are killed, what would you regret?" she asked.

"The dead don't have regrets," he said bluntly.

"Don't they? What about the souls that can't rest?" She harnessed the courage to put her arms around his neck. "I know what *I* would regret. Never having known what lovemaking feels like."

"Here. I'll show you." He grasped her buttocks and pressed her against him. Bending down, he licked her cheek and whispered in her ear. "Does that make you want to scream?"

A shiver raced across her skin. *Fear?* No. She wasn't afraid of him. Not anymore. She'd seen his truest self, which he protected fiercely, yet hadn't been able to hide from her.

"Are you trying to scare me?" She drew him into a breath-taking kiss. What she couldn't put into words, she tried to show him with her lips.

He cupped her face between his palms, softening the kiss before he ended it. "I'll come back. You don't have to bribe me."

As a jest, it would've stung, but the roughness in his voice and the gentleness in his touch made it an endearment. She put on her most confident smile. "That's not a bribe. It's a promise."

~

WHILE JASPER WAS GONE, Brigit fed fuel to the fire. She would rather nurture a different kind of blaze, but Jasper seemed to prefer to let that one die.

She stood and paced restlessly. The flames gave off enough light to see as far as the back of the cave where it narrowed to a crevice barely large enough for a child to fit through. Did it lead to another way out or deeper into the cave?

Curious, she explored as far as the light illuminated but found nothing more than a stirring of dust and sand. It appeared Charley had left without leaving many clues behind.

Brigit picked up the faded quilt. A talented seamstress had stitched together pieces of her life into a visual story. A green satin square, perhaps a beloved wedding gown, a bit of calico from a favorite dress, white linen from her husband's worn-out shirt, soft flannel—a baby blanket? Was the woman who made this coverlet Charley's wife? Jasper hadn't mentioned her.

A deep sadness came over Brigit. It wasn't anchored to any particular thought. The feeling seemed to come from the quilt. It felt saturated with sorrow. She dropped it with a shiver.

Too much talk about ghosts, that's what it was.

Brigit shook out the blanket Jasper had obtained from the trader. Nothing frightening about it. Red with white stripes, and soft, and soon to be imbued with wonderful memories. She hoped.

The fire eventually burned to embers. Tendrils of smoke curled through the darkened hole in the ceiling, taking with it some of her confidence in Jasper's promised return.

He appeared at the cave's entrance as quietly as he'd left. With a laugh, she jumped to her feet and met him. He dodged her kiss and it landed on his cheek.

He'd fashioned a stick into a spear, upon which he had two fish already cleaned and dressed. "Let's cook these and eat."

They wasted no time, both being hungry.

After dinner, Jasper burned the bones and used the stick to stir the fire. He hadn't said much. She wasn't sure what to say. Flirtation didn't come naturally to her.

Brigit knelt beside him and put her hand on his shoulder. "If you'd like, I can take a look at your arm. Change the dressing. Make sure the cut is healing."

"It's healing on its own. I washed it at the creek."

What else had he washed?

Darn. She should've gone with him. Although, it felt safer in here where they could hear whatever might sneak up on them.

In the dark, it would likely be a snake.

Jasper continued to stare at the glowing embers in what seemed an effort not to look at her.

Should she tell him about the quilt and the odd feeling it inspired? Heavens, no. That wouldn't put him in a romantic mood. He would think her mind had snapped and he'd blame the kiss he'd given her earlier.

Maybe he was afraid she would lose her reason again and shoot him. It was different this time. She knew he wouldn't hurt her, and she wasn't afraid.

He stabbed the stick into the fire and it broke. The pieces became more firewood. Another attempt to fuel his resistance?

Brigit let her fingers drift down his arm. "You aren't saying much."

"Don't have much to say."

If she waited on him to talk or act, they could be here all night, exchanging awkward glances. She got up and went over to the bed she'd prepared for them.

"It's more comfortable over here."

"I'm comfortable."

"Squatted next to a fire with your face screwed up? You don't look comfortable."

He appeared to be determined to keep his word and not press his advantage. While she appreciated his chivalry, she'd made no such promise. He needed her as much as she needed him, even if he wouldn't admit it.

How did one begin a seduction? She supposed it must start with one of them lying down.

Brigit stretched out on top of the blanket and patted it. "Come over, beside me."

Jasper glanced in her direction. "Do you intend to sleep?"

"No."

"Then I'd better stay here."

She stifled a laugh. This was a new, and somewhat amusing, tactic. "Why, Jasper. You are behaving like a coy virgin."

"Enough!" He shot to his feet. A second later he stood next to her. Her heart beat faster when he dropped to his knees on the blanket and hauled her up against him. "Are you in your right mind?"

"Yes, I am..." Be honest. "Saner than most people would be, under the circumstances."

Beneath a deep frown, his eyes had gone nearly black, reflecting anguish, and another, darker emotion. "Good. Because I'm not. You've stolen the last of my reason."

Brigit released a nervous laugh. "Really? That's not exactly the kind of praise a lady wants to hear, but it'll do for—"

He sealed his lips over hers before she finished.

She'd pushed him into reacting, and great heavens, he certainly had. He didn't kiss her like a man who had surrendered. More like one who was leading the charge.

Brigit put her arms around his neck. What had she unleashed?

As if he'd read her mind, Jasper eased up on his assault. His ravenous kisses became a delicate exploration of her lips, her face, her nose, and even her eyelids.

Her heart raced in response and her breathing grew more ragged. Now, before he pulled away again, she would offer him more than a kiss. She reached for the buttons on her oversized shirt and fumbled with the first two.

Jasper tipped her chin. Tension had pulled his face into tight, harsh lines, but his eyes were deep pools that reflected her desire. "Tell me what you want."

Wasn't it obvious?

"I want you to undress me."

"And then we screw, is that what you want?"

She felt a hot blush. "A rather blatant term, but yes."

He smoothed a strand of hair away from her eyes. "You need to be certain it's what you want. There's nothing more I can give you."

Her heart constricted at the harsh statement. He hadn't meant to hurt her. He was only warning her. If she said *yes*, there were no guarantees. She might never have his love. But if she stopped, she would lose her chance—likely, her only chance—to give him love.

Brigit took his hand, kissed his rough knuckles, then brought his fingers to the buttons on her shirt. She couldn't be more direct. If he balked, she'd lose her courage.

He took over on the third button, and a moment later the shirt was gone. The skirt went next, unwound before she could catch her breath. The only piece of clothing remaining on her body was a thin undergarment made of handwoven flax. In no time, he'd dispensed with that, too.

She crossed her arms to cover herself, couldn't help it. But before she could change her mind or even think about changing her mind, he eased her back onto the blanket.

"Don't be afraid," he whispered, right before his lips touched hers.

His kiss made her heart race, but fear wasn't driving it. Excitement. Anticipation. She put her arms around him and gave him access to her body to show him she trusted him.

He took his time, kissing her, petting her, allowing her to get used to his touch before he moved his hand lower. When she tensed, he started the whole process over again, never pressuring or insisting.

After several starts, she was able to relax into the pleasure his touch brought her. She pulled his head to her chest and then gasped when he mouthed her breast. The tips stiffened and tingled and the place between her legs throbbed and grew damp.

Jasper proceeded to worship her body. She could think of no other word for what he did to her with his hands and his lips, even his tongue. He didn't miss an inch of her exposed skin, which prickled at first, then warmed beneath his expert stroking. He fueled the fire until it became an inferno.

She needed...something. Something just out of reach. Something only he could give her. With his hand, he was doing marvelous things, but there had to be more.

"Jasper, please," she moaned. "I need..."

"Baby, I know what you need. I need it too." He placed another kiss on her lips before he sat up and pulled off his boots.

Without a word, he got to his feet and shucked his trousers. She held her breath while he drew the deerskin shirt over his head. Naked skin stretched tight over lean muscle gleamed golden in the firelight.

She gazed at him with a sense of wonder. His powerful, lithe body didn't frighten her. It inspired awe and a longing to touch.

He knelt and guided her hand to his thigh, waiting patiently while she explored, moving higher, eager to learn his body as well as he knew hers.

It wasn't long before he rolled her to her back and lowered himself over her. His heavy breathing triggered a flickering memory and a shimmer of fear. But then desire washed over her and swept her into deeper water.

So deep she might drown.

Jasper wouldn't let her become lost. Hadn't he brought her safely this far? He would guide her home.

She reached for him, releasing her pent breath in a shuddering sigh. "Love me."

~

JASPER'S BLOOD roared in his ears, so loud he wasn't sure what he'd heard. He held himself up on his arms, trembling, poised at the entry to her body. A thread of restraint held his raging need in check. "What?" he gasped.

"Love me," she repeated.

Did she have any idea what she asked for? His love would ruin her life. Endanger her. How could he give her love when he knew it to be a curse?

He hung his head until his lips were next to her heart. "I told you, I-I can't promise."

"Then don't." Brigit continued to cling to him, welcoming him into the cradle of her hips, not withholding anything.

God, he burned for her. If he let go, gave in, he'd go up in flames, and he'd take her with him. Without promises. She'd sacrifice her heart without getting what she wanted. She deserved better.

He groaned.

"Jasper?" Her sultry voice flowed over him. "What's wrong?"

"Nothing."

Everything, damn it.

"I don't want to hurt you."

"You won't," she said with more confidence than he possessed. Her fingers moved over the back of his head. She read him as a blind person might, as if by touch she could know him.

She couldn't know how badly he would hurt her. If by some

miracle, they made out of this place alive, one day soon they would be parted. He could make no promise he'd be able to stay with her.

She hadn't asked him to stay with her. She'd asked him to love her. Couldn't he do that?

He'd gladly give her his belongings, slim as they were. She could have his beat-up flesh, his worthless life, even his deformed heart. Who was he kidding? She'd already taken that.

If he spoke the words, he couldn't take them back. Hell, it was too late anyway. He loved her, whether or not he said it. She'd baited a lure with something he couldn't resist.

Brigit had given him a chance to become the kind of man he'd always longed to be. He had to be that man for her now. He had to give her not only what she wanted, but what she needed. Patience. Tenderness. Fulfillment.

She hugged him in a tight grip with her arms and legs and with the muscles guarding the entrance to her body. When she shifted her hips, her movement allowed him to delve deeper.

The throbbing need demanded he sink into her and lose himself, think of nothing else.

She gasped before she started shaking.

As desperately as he wanted to plunge inside her, to show her how good passion could be, if he wasn't careful, their joining might set off an explosion of bad memories.

"We'll take it slow," he whispered, easing up on the pressure. "I won't force you."

"I know," she said, trustingly.

His heart hammered louder. He was surprised she hadn't commented on it. He tried to slow his breathing, but it was no use. He heaved like the bellows on a steam engine.

She passed her hand over his hip. "Are you...in pain?"

Agony.

"Nope. Not a bit. We got all night." He kissed her and stroked her, murmured encouragements in English and love words in Cherokee.

As he worked over her with a slow but steady pace, a rising tide flowed between them. Their joining made him feel powerful, and, at the same time, helpless. He couldn't resist and didn't want to.

He sank willingly into the current, letting it pull him under, sensing it could quench his thirst. Or it might make it worse. She'd become as important to him as water and air.

Brigit's eager kisses and soft mews of pleasure assured him they had passed through her dark valley of fear. He released his hold on the reins restraining him and his hips bucked as his body's needs took over.

Her release came in waves that crashed against his soul and sent him hurtling into shattering completion.

After a moment, Jasper became aware he'd collapsed on top of her. He couldn't move. He could hardly think. As his heartbeat slowed, a bewildering sense of peace came over him.

He was no stranger to sex, but this? He couldn't relate what he'd experienced with Brigit to anything he'd done before. It was entirely new. She'd teased him about acting like a virgin. Damned if he didn't feel like one.

She stroked his hair and hummed in his ear. A wartime love song. *Aura Lea.*

Brigit had sang and hummed the day she'd stuffed him into a coffin and they had made their escape. She'd hummed again on the train when they'd been fleeing from the marshal. Was it to distract herself from frightening thoughts?

He couldn't blame her. Love was scary as hell.

CHAPTER 17

"*R*aven."

Jasper blinked, disoriented by the darkness and the name he'd heard someone call. When he'd last opened his eyes, the embers had still been glowing.

Brigit remained curled up at his side with her head on his shoulder, her breathing soft and even. If she'd spoken aloud, it was in a dream.

"*Go-lah'-nuh.*"

The disembodied voice whispering his nickname in Cherokee sent shivers across Jasper's bare skin.

From the fire pit, a flame sputtered to life and its light revealed a man's face. A jagged scar extended from his eyebrow to the side of his mouth, pulling his lips into a grimace. Twin braids dangled an inch above Jasper's face.

His heart started up again, and with it, a hot rush of anger.

"*Tsa-li.* What the hell? Jasper breathed out the words so he wouldn't startle Brigit awake. The sight of a scarred warrior crouched over them would frighten her to death.

"Meet me outside," Charley said in the same creepy whisper he'd used earlier.

Jasper cursed himself for not remaining awake and alert. What if the intruder had been an enemy? He carefully extracted himself from Brigit's embrace and picked up the quilt nearby to cover her nudity.

She lay curled up with her hair all mused and a slight smile still on her lips. Why disturb her sweet dreams? Neither of them had slept much over the past week. She could get a little extra shut-eye while he talked to Charley.

Jasper pulled on his clothes in a hurry. He left his gun behind so she'd know he was near, should she happen to wake up. As soundly as she slept, he'd be back before then and could tell her what was going on. And, he'd speak the words she wanted to hear.

He would tell her he loved her, for what it was worth. Frankly, his love wasn't worth much, but it was important to her. Therefore, it was important to him to assure her she had it.

Charley had gotten a head start. He'd gone down to the creek and had climbed onto a flat boulder. He didn't move from his squatted position with his arms crossed over his knees, not even when greeted. He had never been talkative, but he generally had more to say.

Jasper crouched down next to his old mentor. He tried to not feel disappointed by the aloof reception. He wouldn't be thrilled either if someone showed up and moved into *his* living quarters. "Sorry we didn't let you know you'd have visitors," he quipped to break the silence.

"Only a fool would send word," Charley replied in Cherokee.

Jasper hadn't meant for the remark to be taken literally. "I know that."

"Who is the white woman?"

The question triggered Jasper's protective instincts. "A friend."

He didn't elaborate. Brigit's identity, and their relationship, weren't Charley's business. Not unless she decided she wanted to make it his business. In the meantime, he would get right to the point. "We're looking for someone.

"Is that what you were doing in there?" Charley replied in the same flat tone.

Jasper's face grew warm. How long had Charley been in the cave, watching them? It unnerved him that someone had managed to sneak up on them. "You might've given us a warning."

"I did."

"What? I didn't see anything except your bedding. And a jug."

"You seek a missing man. A Pinkerton agent." Charley's abrupt pivot made it clear he knew what their visit was about. And more importantly, he had encountered Kinkaid.

Jasper tensed. "You met him? Where is he?"

Charley continued to stare straight ahead. "He showed up here with a gunshot wound. I tried to save him. It was too late."

Why would Charley want to save a Pinkerton—or any stranger, for that matter? Had he known Kinkaid?

Jasper shook his head. Ah well, it didn't matter. Not anymore. And he refused to be disappointed. He hadn't been nearly as optimistic as Brigit about the outcome of this mission. "Who shot him?"

"A deputy marshal—is what he told me."

That snake kept showing up in all the wrong places.

"Stokes? Why was he after Kinkaid?"

Charley still didn't look at him. "I do not have all the answers."

Someone did.

"Where's the body? Did you bury him?"

"Next to a bluff, beneath a ledge. Not far. I will show you."

Jasper came to his feet. "Let me wake Brigit."

"Leave the white woman."

"I can't do that."

"She is not in danger."

Jasper scanned the still, dark forest around them. He didn't see Charley's horse or any sign of another person guarding the cave. "Did anyone else come with you?"

"There is no one near this place except us."

He'd checked it out. Good.

"It won't take long. I'll go wake her. You'd like her if you got to know her."

"She would not like me."

Charley's disrespect was wearing thin.

"Brigit won't care if you're an outlaw or an Indian or a surly bear. She isn't like any woman I've ever known—"

Charley hopped down and walked off.

He'd judged Brigit without giving her a chance. Just like he'd despised the railroad heiress who'd married his cousin, Jake. Even after Kate had done many good things for the tribe. But there was no changing Charley's mind once it was made up.

Jasper cursed as he slid off the boulder. He had to run to catch up. He'd find out where Kinkaid was buried and what the agent might've told Charley then get back to the cave and wake up Brigit. "Did Kinkaid tell you anything before he died?"

"He gave me a journal that he stole."

"A stolen journal?" This was a new development. "Who did it belong to? Where is it?"

"In a safe place."

Jasper trudged along behind the taciturn man in front of him. Charley had likely stashed the stolen journal with the body or somewhere close. The timing couldn't be more perfect.

They walked along the creek for what seemed like a mile. The craggy outline of a bluff appeared black against a sky lightened to gunmetal gray, which dawn would soon turn dusky blue. When daylight shone into the cave, Brigit would wake up. He would be back by then.

Charley halted at a clearing where a limestone shelf jutted out, forming a ledge at about ten feet. On the ground, rocks had been piled up, enough to cover a body.

Jasper stood over the makeshift grave in the pre-dawn stillness. He'd seen so much death he didn't think it could move him. Maybe he felt something because Brigit had talked about the agent and knew him, and this death would hit her hard. He heaved a heavy sigh and looked up.

Charley was gone. He'd been standing there a second ago, then *poof*.

Hell, he hadn't just vanished. For some reason, he'd slipped away as silently as he'd arrived. Those bushes along the creek would make a good hiding spot if he thought to play a trick.

When had the dour old warrior ever played a practical joke? He must intend to sell the journal for whiskey money. Why hadn't he stayed around to discuss the terms?

"Raven."

Charley's voice came from above Jasper's head, raising the hair on the back of his neck. He peered at the ledge where the voice seemed to come from. No one was up there. He reached for the knife in his boot.

"Behind you, look sharp."

WHEN JASPER CAME to his senses, he was lying on his side on a bed of gravel and his head ached like the very devil. *"Tsa-li?"* he groaned.

He shifted to get to his feet, but couldn't move his arms or legs. His wrists and ankles were bound. Was Charley crazy? Where was Brigit? Had he gone back? Hurt her?

Jasper fought his bonds while he blinked to clear his blurred vision. A tree trunk came into view. He faced the creek and forest, which meant the bluff was behind him.

He thrashed, cursing.

"Flop around all you want. You won't get free."

Terror clogged Jasper's throat. He craned his neck to see the man who'd knelt at his back, although he'd already recognized the voice.

Stokes.

Jasper released a harsh breath. Was it a setup? No way Charley would've betrayed him. Not to a marshal. The old trader must've pointed Stokes in the right direction and he'd gotten lucky.

From where Jasper lay, he couldn't see anyone else around. Why would a U.S. deputy marshal come out here, of all places, without a posse or anyone to watch his back? And where was Charley? He must've seen the marshal and hidden—or run off.

Tsa-li had never been a coward.

People could change.

Jasper's heart lurched. *He* had changed. Thanks to Brigit and her determined belief that he *could* change. Only, his transformation might've come too late. Worse, he'd underestimated his enemy.

"*Tsi-s-dv-na a-da-tsv-i-s-gi,*" he whispered under his breath.

"What did you just call me?" Stokes demanded.

"Fucking scorpion." Jasper jerked at his bonds, furious.

"Say it again and I'll rip your tongue out." The marshal worked a noose over Japer's head and tightened it around his neck, sending another surge of panic through him. Did Stokes intend to kill him here? Now?

He had to stall for time until he figured a way out of this mess. Before Brigit showed up on the scene. She would think he'd left her to go search for Charley on his own, which would infuriate her and guarantee she'd come after him.

"You didn't kill me right off," Jasper said more calmly. "Must be a reason."

"Aren't you clever?" Stokes casually tossed the remaining length of rope over a sturdy tree limb above Jasper's head. He attached the other end to a saddle on a paint pony.

Recognition slammed into Jasper. "Bandit!"

The horse turned its head and flicked its ears forward.

No wonder Stokes had found his way up here so fast. Jasper had taken his horse over various routes many times. Being smart, Bandit would remember the way. Probably thought he was coming to see old friends.

"I see you two know each other." Stokes pushed the horse's head to make it look away. "Got him in an auction. Thought I recognized the markings." The chuckle made it clear Stokes knew exactly who the horse had belonged to. "Your horse helped you commit crimes, and now he'll help me hang you. I'd say that's poetic justice."

The fury coiled inside Jasper sprang loose. He jerked at the bonds on his wrists and ankles, cursing himself six ways from Sunday for not paying better attention. No one had been able to ambush him since the day he'd turned thirteen. When a dozen soldiers had ridden up to the farm.

Stokes took up the reins. "Calm down. You and I are going to have a little talk. Cooperate, I might let you live. Where's your lady friend?"

Jasper struggled until he'd achieved a sitting position. It was more dignified than lying there, flopping like a fish. For Brigit's sake, he had to reinforce the perception that he was a lone wolf. "I don't keep ladies around past their usefulness. Especially not her kind."

"Sure, you don't. That's why you took *Miss Stevens* with you."

Stokes hadn't had the time to confirm Brigit's identity. He must've overheard someone talking about her. It had to be a guess.

"Why do you care?"

Stokes narrowed his eyes. "Your little actress and me, we've got a score to settle."

Over my dead body. Nope, take it back. Over your dead body.

Jasper gave a huff like it didn't matter whether Stokes found her or not. "She is a good actress. Goes by lots of different names. And she charges a steep price, in case you're wondering."

"An actress and a high-priced whore. You make interesting friends."

"I don't have friends."

"There aren't many left, that's true." Stokes seemed to think this was funny. "One of your former friends thought you might know where to find something that belongs to me."

Jasper's stomach took a sick fall. What had Charley done? Sold him out for liquor? "What are you talking about?"

The marshal indicated with a nod of his head in the direction of the bluff.

Jasper twisted to look. The pile of rocks had been taken apart, tossed every which way. Next to the grave, a corpse lay sprawled, partly unclothed, as if someone had picked through its pockets.

The stolen journal. That had to be what Stokes was looking for. Charley still had it. Had he gone after it? Did he plan to bargain with it?

Jasper stalled for time. "I don't know who that is. He's not one of my friends."

The black mustache twitched above Stokes's sneer. "Is that how you want to do this? Act ignorant? Well, all right..." The marshal led Bandit forward, which pulled the rope tight around Jasper's neck.

Panic spurred Jasper into action. He managed to stand to relieve the pressure, but with his ankles bound it was hard to keep his balance. The tug on the noose had helped him get to his feet. In another second, it would choke him.

Stokes brought the horse to a stop. His gaze reflected satisfaction...and pleasure. He enjoyed inflicting pain and terror. He would drag it out, and make it last as long as possible.

Jasper had a hard time swallowing. The rope rubbed against scars from another rope. During the war, he'd met men like Stokes. One of them had killed his father and tortured him as a boy. He'd tried to rid the world of them, but they kept crawling out from under rocks like scorpions, or, as Brigit had rightly called them, *cockroaches*.

"I can't help you if you won't tell me anything," Jasper rasped.

Stokes pointed at the desecrated corpse. "*That* is what is left of a thieving piece of filth called Kinkaid. He stole something out of my saddlebag that he shouldn't have. I want it back."

The journal belonged to Stokes? This shed a whole new light on his actions, and it explained why he hadn't rounded up a posse to come with him. He didn't want anyone else to know about it.

"What property?" Jasper pretended not to know to see what Stokes would say.

The marshal's florid face darkened. "By God, if you don't tell me where that journal is, I'll find your woman and I'll..." he narrowed his eyes. "I'll *enjoy* her before I kill her."

Jasper's frustration, his fear, and his fury coalesced into a single thought. He had to protect Brigit from this monster. "I told you, she's not here. If you want my help, I need more information..."

While he talked, he rotated his wrists. Sweat had dampened his skin, which made it possible to stretch the leather straps, but he needed more time, and that required a distraction. Something to spook Stokes and take his attention away. A silly, but useful trick.

Jasper cleared his throat.

Bandit threw his head up and whinnied, just like he'd been taught.

Stokes jerked on the reins. "Stop that." He bent to pick up a stick and struck the horse on the side of the head, making Bandit whinny with fright and confusion.

Jasper swore an oath. He'd kill the sonofabitch the minute he was free. "Don't beat him."

"What? You got a soft spot for this ornery pony?" Stokes wound the reins around his palm, still holding the stick in the other hand.

Jasper ground his teeth in frustration. This wasn't the intended distraction. "The horse senses someone nearby."

The marshal's smile faded, but not the calculating glint in his eyes. "Is that so? I didn't see anybody. I think this pony needs to know who's in charge." He wagged the stick, causing Bandit to shy away, then struck the horse again.

Jasper jerked at the blow. He had to get the marshal to focus on something else. "You saw the other person if you followed me."

Stokes shook his head, chuckling. "Damn, you are not nearly as smart as they say you are. I saw you walking by the creek alone. You were so engrossed in a conversation with yourself, you didn't notice you were being tracked."

It was a taunt. He had to have seen Charley at some point.

The damp leather bonds stung, but they were getting looser.

Keep talking.

"He led me here."

"Who?"

"You know who."

"Oh, we're playing a guessing game. One of your friends? Another crazy Indian? Did he happen to tell you where he hid my journal?"

"No. Charley went for help—"

"Charley?" Stokes let out an ugly laugh. "No, *he* wouldn't tell. He won't be going for help, either. I killed him."

A cold sweat drenched Jasper's skin. This would explain why Charley hadn't come back. Or it was another means of torture. When would Stokes have had the time to track Charley while he was tying up a prisoner? "When did you kill him? Where is his body?"

Stokes dropped the reins to the ground.

Jasper couldn't give Bandit a command to come or go. If the horse responded, it would pull the rope and unintentionally hang him.

The marshal approached with the stick. "Let me see if I can recall the details. About a month ago, I caught up with your drunk friend on a ridge overlooking the railroad line. I knew Kinkaid had come down here to get help from his outlaw friends. But that damn savage wouldn't tell me anything. He just smiled. I hit him and I cut him. He kept smiling at me." Stokes smacked the stick against his palm. "I left his body at the bottom of a ravine."

Charley, dead for a month? No, it wasn't possible. He'd come into the cave. They had talked. Had it been some strange vision?

Jasper fought a wave of dizziness. He didn't have visions. He wasn't crazy either. He'd seen Charley and talked to him. "If Charley's dead, how did you find me?"

"You're smart enough to figure that out."

It didn't take a great deal of intelligence. He and Brigit had guessed the connection already.

"J.D." Jasper continued to stretch the bindings against his blistered skin. The pain was excruciating, but he turned it into anger. "That traitor was working for you, wasn't he? That's why he met you in Denison."

Stokes snorted. "Yeah, he did. Turns out, he was double-timing me worse than a cheating wife. He thought I meant to pay him. And I did."

And had enjoyed the kill after torturing J.D. for information. The thought sickened Jasper.

"J.D. told you where to find your journal?"

"He swore he didn't know a thing about it. But he thought you might."

Jasper hadn't known about it until this morning when Charley had visited him. If his friend's spirit had taken on his old form, it would've been nice if he'd stuck around a little longer to scare this sadistic sonofabitch.

"Stop mumbling. Speak up!" Stokes struck low with the stick.

Searing pain knifed through Jasper's groin, weakening his knees. The noose tightened around his neck. He struggled to remain standing while Stokes smiled.

"We can have more fun, or you can start talking."

First, he had to catch his breath. "How do you suppose...I found out where it is? I was in jail for the past month."

"I did wonder about that..." The marshal appeared to ponder the question, which occupied him for a moment. "J.D. might've lied."

Jasper pulled at the bonds. His wrists were on fire. His balls ached. As long as he remained alive, pain could be conquered.

Stokes shook his head. "He admitted he introduced Kinkaid to your friend Charley, who didn't know Kinkaid was a Pinkerton. When I first met the agent, he told me he planned to cozy up to your gang and learn their secrets. He'd recruited J.D."

Kinkaid had also two-timed the marshal. Jasper refrained from pointing this out.

Stokes jabbed him in the stomach. "You were part of it, too, weren't you? They recruited you and you turned on your old railroad friend, Bond. Then, when it didn't work out the way they planned, the Pinkertons sent in one of their females to rescue you."

It wasn't quite like that, but what he said made a sickening sort of sense.

"You got a good imagination."

Stokes tapped Jasper's cheek with the stick almost like a woman might if she were teasing him. "Mm. Took me a while to put it all together, but I'm not as dull as you think I am. You're right, though, that skinny gal is a good actress."

Jasper's head spun with the implications. Had Brigit known about Kinkaid's connection to J.D.? If so, she hadn't revealed that specific bit of knowledge. She would've told him if she'd known. She wouldn't have come this far without arming him with all the facts.

He narrowed his hands to free them from the loosened straps.

He had seconds, not minutes.

"Time's up, outlaw." The marshal walked back to where the horse had obediently remained after the reins were dropped. Something else Bandit had been taught.

The horse knew other tricks, too.

CHAPTER 18

$\mathcal{B}$rigit shivered. The fire must've died out. She tugged the cover as she rolled over, reaching out. Her hand landed on an empty blanket and her heart stopped.

Where had Jasper gone?

Tossing the quilt aside, she sat up. Breathed a sigh of relief when she spotted his gun belt and revolver in the same spot where he'd left them last night. Jasper wouldn't venture far unarmed. He'd probably gone to check on the horse.

Charley might've arrived.

She pulled on the thin undergarment, tied on the skirt, buttoned the shirt, then knotted the woven belt. Running her fingers through her hair, she decided to leave it loose. Jasper had remarked on its silkiness. He'd used his hands and lips to tell her what he thought about the rest of her.

Last night, she'd begged him to love her, and Lord had he ever, and she had given herself to him, body and soul.

This morning, the world seemed to have changed. Everything was brighter. That might have something to do with the daylight shining through the hole at the top of the cave.

Brigit laughed at her giddy musings as she bent to pick up the cover she'd discarded. The quilt had lost its power, or her heart was so full there was no room for sadness.

She frowned. What was this mark on one corner? Faint rust-colored stains. From blood? If so, someone had tried to wash it out. Could this have something to do with what happened to Charley...or Kinkaid? She would show this to Jasper and ask him what he thought. He had a quick mind and sound instincts. They made a good team in more ways than one.

On a whim, she buckled the gun belt around her hips. Jasper would find it amusing when she showed up looking like a gunslinger.

As she descended the hill to the creek, she looked around. The white horse they'd ridden stood near the edge of the water, still hobbled. Jasper wasn't anywhere she could see him.

He wouldn't up and leave without a word. Certainly not after last night. He'd fought their mutual attraction longer than she had, but when he'd raised the white flag, they had both willingly surrendered. This morning, she had no regrets. Did he?

Brigit knelt in front of a boulder near the bank to examine indentions in the soft soil. Jasper's boots would've made these. They appeared again, leading away from the cave alongside the creek. He'd walked off without being concerned that someone might follow. She didn't see any other footprints. He'd gone this way alone.

Unease intruded on her good mood. Neither of them had spoken of love. She'd been waiting for him to speak first, but he wasn't one to talk about his feelings. He was a man of actions and deeds. But he had shown her how much he cared for her. He wouldn't desert her without a word.

She stood, taking a deep breath. For all she knew, he'd wandered downstream to where he thought the fish would be. He wouldn't want her to call out. Voices could alert those they might not want to attract. She would follow his trail.

Near a bend in the stream, another set of footprints appeared. These weren't alongside Jasper's. The other person was tracking him. Her heart beat faster as she put her finger into a deep mark made by a man's booted heel. He was heavier than Jasper.

Worry quivered through her. Was it one of their pursuers? What if Jasper had been captured? Or... *God forbid.*

A horse's whinny arrested her attention. That hadn't come from their horse. It seemed to echo off the bluff ahead.

She hurried, following the two sets of footprints. Perspiration beaded on her upper lip. Where the creek made a V, the ground became rockier and the tracks were harder to follow.

Brigit stopped at a growth of bushes when she heard voices coming from the other side. Low. Male. It was hard to make out what they were saying.

She pulled the revolver from its holster and crept in her moccasins until she came to a spot where she could see through the leafy branches into a clearing.

A horse, white with patches of black and brown, jerked its head, attempting to move away from a husky man who held the reins. He had his back to the bushes, but his shape and a rush of dread confirmed her fears. It had to be Stokes.

Beyond him and the horse, under a tree— Jasper! With a noose around his neck! His ankles were bound and his hands appeared to be tied behind his back. The rope went up over a thick limb and across to the horse's saddle.

Brigit's breath came out in short, frantic bursts. Stokes was about to hang Jasper! She had to stop him without getting herself shot or spooking the horse.

She inched closer, being careful where she put her feet. She'd sneak up and hit Stokes on the head. Or surprise him and disarm him. He'd surrender if he saw he had no choice.

A shrill whistle split the air.

The horse reared and kicked out, knocking Stokes to the ground. *Now!*

Brigit charged between the two bushes with Jasper's gun raised. "Put your hands up!"

The marshal rolled to one knee and pointed his revolver...not at her, but Jasper.

She pulled the trigger. The gun roared and kicked.

As Stokes pitched forward, another blast filled the air, then the hand clutching his gun dropped to his side. He didn't move after that.

Her nose and eyes stung from the stench of gunpowder. Had Jasper been hit? Through a faint haze, she spotted him, dangling in midair with a tight grip on the rope above his head. He strained to lift his weight, but the noose was choking him.

She holstered the revolver and lunged for the dangling reins.

The horse shied away from her.

Jasper croaked a word that sounded like *banded*.

No, not *banded*. *Bandit!* His horse?

"Shh, Bandit," she crooned. "Easy now."

The horse perked its ears forward. It remained still when she reached out to take the reins.

"Back," she commanded, patting the horse when it obeyed.

The tension on the rope eased. Jasper's feet touched the ground. As the rope went slack, he dropped to his knees, clawing at the noose.

Brigit untied the rope from the horse's saddle before she rushed over to help Jasper. "Can you breathe?"

His gasps reassured her.

He pulled the noose over his head. She untied the straps around his ankles. His wrists were raw and bleeding, and the bindings lay on the ground. By some miracle, he'd been able to free his arms just in time.

"Is Stokes dead?" he rasped.

"I think so." She ought to make sure.

Brigit crossed the creek to where the marshal lay sprawled, partly on his side. Beneath the black mustache, his lips were parted. His eyes remained open in a sightless stare.

She broke out in a cold sweat and her stomach turned. "He's dead."

"Get the gun," Jasper ordered.

"Yes, of course." She knelt and pulled the revolver out of the marshal's death grip, focusing on the task rather than her churning stomach.

By the time she turned around, Jasper had moved to the edge of the creek. He knelt on one knee and scooped a handful of water, spilling more than he drank.

He'd come so close to dying. If she'd been a moment later it would've been too late.

She crossed over to him and touched his shoulder to reassure herself.

He took deep breaths. "How did you find me?"

"I followed your tracks, and heard Bandit's whinny."

The horse had remained in the same spot she'd left it with the reins resting on the ground. Only excellent training would produce such obedience amid chaos.

She stared at Jasper in surprise. "The whistle. That was you. That's why Bandit kicked."

"Yeah. It was all I could think to do. Wouldn't have mattered, if you hadn't shown up." Jasper got to his feet slowly. He drew her into his arms.

She hugged his waist while holding Stokes's gun in her other hand. Pent-up fear pressed against the inside of her chest. Her eyes burned. She couldn't let go. Not yet.

Jasper retrieved the marshal's revolver. "I'll take this one."

He could have it.

"How are you doing?" he asked. It seemed he had recovered or the cold water had revived him.

"Me? I'm...fine." Two men's deaths were now on her conscience. Perhaps she ought to feel something more than numb relief.

Jasper tucked the marshal's gun into the waistband of his trousers before he cupped her shoulders. "I found Kinkaid."

His solemn tone warned her the news wasn't good.

She took a breath to calm her unsteady nerves. "Where?"

He turned her to face the bluff. "Over there."

In all the confusion she hadn't noticed a hollowed-out grave, scattered rocks, or the desecrated corpse.

"Oh, no." She closed her eyes, struggling not to break down. That poor soul could be someone else. Jasper hadn't met the agent. "I have to make sure."

Brigit drew numbness around her like a shield before she crossed the creek to get to the place where the makeshift grave had been unearthed. She'd encountered dead bodies before while working on murder cases, but she hadn't known the victims.

A distinct odor lingered near the disturbed body, which had already reached an advanced state of decomposition. The rocks had kept scavengers away, but not the warm weather and the insects. Even so, the fair hair that remained, the size of the corpse, and the location in the general area where he'd fled, left little doubt in her mind about who it was—or had been.

Lester Kinkaid.

A wave of cold sent a shudder through her. Her vision dimmed. As she whirled around to escape, Jasper caught her in his arms. While she gasped for breath, he stroked her hair and made soothing sounds.

"I know, I know...I'm so sorry," he murmured.

He was always thinking about her, worrying about her. He might've joined Kinkaid in a grave had she not gotten here in time. Why had he gone off alone?

She struck him on the shoulder. Anger made a comforting salve for fear. "You already owe me twice for saving you. Don't make it three."

He didn't flinch at the reprimand or defend his actions. Jasper wasn't careless or stupid. For some logical reason, he'd left her behind while he'd gone off on his own.

Brigit regained her composure enough to speak without bursting into tears. "Tell me what happened."

"Stokes tracked me here and ambushed me."

"How did he do that? You're too canny to get caught."

A flicker of annoyance flashed across Jasper's features. She would've sworn it was directed at himself, not her. "I got distracted. Stokes strung me up to torture answers out of me. He was looking for a journal Kinkaid stole from him."

"A journal?" Brigit hadn't considered that possibility. "It must contain the evidence Agent Kinkaid mentioned."

"I reckon. Stokes was dead-set on getting it back. He shot Kinkaid, and..." Jasper heaved a sad sigh, as his gaze shifted to a point over her shoulder. "Killed Charley."

She turned to follow Jasper's line of sight. Was there another body out there somewhere? He appeared to be contemplating the ledge. "Charley arrived?"

Jasper hesitated before answering. "He showed up before dawn and led me to the grave."

She shook her head in confusion. "I don't understand. Did he come to the cave right before he was killed? Where is he?"

"He isn't here, he's..." Jasper wiped his hand over his face. His swarthy complexion had taken on an ashen tone. "I don't know if I dreamed it or if he was a spirit...I can't explain it."

Jasper walked off, splashing to the other side of the creek.

Had his brush with death snapped his mind? She might be seeing things too, had someone nearly succeeded in hanging her.

She called after him. "Did you say, *spirit?*"

"I said I can't explain it." Jasper stepped over the marshal's body and then knelt behind it. His troubled expression turned grim. "We need to come up with a good story."

"What do you mean? Stokes tried to kill you and I stopped him. Isn't that good enough?"

"The bullet entered the back of his head."

Brigit licked her lips nervously. What Jasper meant, other than pointing out the fact, was how it might look during an inquest. "I fired in defense."

"My defense, not yours."

"Well, yes, but anyone would agree, it was justified."

The expression on Jasper's face said otherwise.

Behind him, Bandit snorted and tossed its head.

"Hands up!" The order came from a man who stepped out from behind the bushes armed with a shotgun.

Brigit immediately recognized the tall, lanky man with shaggy gray hair visible beneath his wide-brimmed hat. "Frank! Don't shoot!"

She didn't recall the hard look in his eyes. He'd never given her that before. It was directed at Jasper.

Jasper had frozen on his knees, gripping the handle of the revolver tucked into his waistband. With slow movements, he lifted both arms into the air. He'd recognized the former sheriff too and knew Frank wouldn't gun him down if he surrendered.

She released a long, relieved breath before her words spilled out. "Where did you come from? Did you hear the gunshots? Heavens, I wish you'd gotten here earlier."

"So do I." Her brother-in-law's solemn expression remained unchanged. He continued to hold his rifle aimed at Jasper. "Is Stokes dead?"

"As a doornail." Jasper kept his hands high.

"Hand me the gun, carefully," Frank told him.

As requested, Jasper turned over the marshal's revolver.

Frank didn't lower his weapon. Maybe he misunderstood the situation.

"I'm not in danger," she assured him.

More rustling came from the bushes on the other side of the clearing and another man emerged. White Stetson hat, coffee-dark skin...Frank's former deputy, and he held the largest revolver she'd ever seen.

Neither man understood the situation. She would relieve their concerns. "Mr. Branch, we're pleased to see you, too. Aren't we Jasper?"

Gideon Branch acknowledged her with a polite nod. "Pleasure's all mine, miss. You can put that Colt away now. You're safe."

Brigit stared at the gun in her hand. She didn't recall pulling it. Thank God, she hadn't fired it. She stuffed the heavy revolver into its holster. "Yes, of course, I'm safe. But I am not the one who was in danger. Did you notice the rope? The noose?" She gestured at the offensive items. "Marshal Stokes tried to hang Jasper. That's why—"

"I killed him."

CHAPTER 19

*J*asper lowered his hands after he confessed. Brigit might be a respected Pinkerton detective back East, but she'd become a fugitive out West. It didn't matter that Frank Garrity was her brother-in-law or that he and Gideon Branch were no longer certified lawmen. They were dyed-in-the-wool tin stars in their hearts. And no Western judge or jury would accept the shooting as justified. They'd see it one way—a cold-hearted woman had shot a U.S. deputy marshal in the back of the head to save her outlaw lover.

Brigit spun around with disbelief on her face. Her eyes glittered with anger. She seemed to think he'd confessed purely to annoy her. "Mr. Byrne did *not* kill the marshal. That would've been impossible. He was unarmed and hanging from the end of that rope." She indicated the noose on the ground. "His hands were occupied—holding himself up—to prevent being choked to death."

He hadn't been able to loosen the noose as it tightened. Had Brigit delayed, he would've lost consciousness. She'd saved his life. He wanted to kiss her. But to return the favor, he had to discredit her.

Jasper rose to his feet as she marched past. She stopped at a spot near the bushes a few feet away from where Stokes's body lay in its death pose.

"I was here when the horse reared and knocked the marshal to the ground." Brigit pulled her gun for the re-enactment. "I ordered him to put his hands up. Instead, he came to one knee and aimed at Jasper." She indicated in the direction of the hanging tree.

The two hardened lawmen who'd stumbled upon this fiasco appeared riveted by her story. They were buying it. A jury would too —until she got to the last part.

"The marshal didn't acknowledge me." The gun in her hand wobbled. How in God's name had she held the revolver straight enough to make that shot? "I didn't have time to negotiate a surrender. I had to act. Or—" her breath hitched. "Watch Jasper die."

Jasper blinked fast so no one would notice he'd teared up. She'd killed a lawman to save his worthless hide. That's what everybody else would think. And that hitch in her breath would be her undoing. A good prosecutor could make the case, especially if they figured out that Brigit was the same woman who'd helped the train robber escape.

It was time to put on a show, one that would hurt her but was necessary.

Jasper brought his hands together, clapping a few times. "Bravo. That's a fine story, Miss Stevens. A lie, but it's a good one."

"*Why* would I lie?" She held Jasper's gaze with defiance.

Standing there in that Choctaw garb with her hair loose and his gun hanging on her hip, she looked dangerous and determined. He had never been prouder of her or more committed to protecting her.

"Why? Because I showed you a little attention and you fell in love with me." He used a blunt, uncaring tone, adding an arrogant afterword. "It's understandable. I have that effect on women."

She drew back as if he'd slapped her. In a sense, he had. He'd falsely presented their relationship as lopsided, which meant she would be ridiculed when the story got out. She would also be alive.

"No!" She seemed to be aiming for a shout. Her voice cracked in the midst of it. "You can't do this...I won't let you."

His chest ached worse than it had when he couldn't draw his breath. He would rather rot in hell than hurt her. But she'd be hurting a lot worse if she ended up in jail. "Do what? Tell the truth about how you begged me to—"

"You!" Garrity hollered. "Get over there. Sit down and shut up."

Jasper, assuming the sheriff was talking to him, ambled over to a fallen tree, as directed. He wasn't ready to *shut up*. "Check the gun you took off me. There's a bullet missing."

He'd heard it go off. Stokes must've twitched his finger and fired wild when he was hit.

"Stokes heard something in the bushes. Brigit, I reckon. While he was distracted, I got my hands loose..." Jasper held up his wrists to show off the injuries that helped support his version. "I wrestled his gun away and killed him. Defended myself pure and simple."

"Was this before or after Brigit showed up?" Garrity's casual tone didn't fool Jasper. The former lawman was sifting through two versions of the story to get to the truth. His rumpled appearance concealed a methodical mind.

"Before."

Brigit's eyes got big. "That is the most unbelievable story I've ever heard. Frank, you don't believe it, do you?"

Garrity's expression softened. He wanted to believe it. "Give me your gun, Brigit."

She removed the belt and handed over the holstered gun. "Check it. There's a bullet missing." Her mimicking comment held a hint of sarcasm.

Garrity checked both revolvers without saying anything.

"Find a seat and rest," he told Brigit, without returning her gun.

As Jasper had anticipated, the former sheriff would be forced to resolve a conundrum. Both revolvers had an empty chamber.

Brigit marched straight over to where Jasper sat. Based on her tight-lipped expression, she wasn't about to *rest*. She looked angrier than a hornet whose nest had been knocked down.

Jasper scooted over to make room for her. She plopped down surprisingly close.

"Why are you doing this?" she asked in a harsh whisper.

"I almost got my neck stretched. Again. Why wouldn't I defend myself?"

She gave him an incredulous look. One that conveyed concern for his mental state.

The former deputy brought two horses into the clearing and proceeded to untie the bedrolls. He retrieved two oiled canvasses used to keep bedding dry. Smoothed one out near the marshal's body and laid the other beside the decomposing corpse of the Pinkerton agent.

Garrity's expression remained stoic as walked around the makeshift grave. "This fellow, what do you know about him?"

"That is—I mean, was—Lester Kinkaid. A Pinkerton agent." Grief flashed across Brigit's face before she schooled her features. "He was sent to investigate criminal activities involving the railroad. In his last message to the agency, he indicated he had obtained incriminating evidence, but he didn't trust the local authorities."

She gave Jasper a cautious look. "Tell them about the journal."

Would it matter if they couldn't produce it? It was an important fact, even if it wasn't something they could prove or likely ever find. Not unless Charley's ghost came back and told him where to look.

Jasper shared what he'd heard. "Kinkaid stole a journal out of the marshal's saddlebag. Stokes didn't say what was in it, but he wounded the agent, then tracked him here and found Charley. When Charley wouldn't turn over the journal, Stokes killed him."

Garrity removed a notebook from his pocket, along with a pencil. "Where did you hear that?"

A ghost.

Jasper had no believable answer so he kept silent.

Brigit spoke up. "We haven't found Charley's body yet. But I discovered a piece of evidence in the cave where we spent the night. A quilt with old blood stains on one corner. It looks to have been washed. I presume Charley tried to help Mr. Kinkaid, then after he died, Charley buried him."

Jasper couldn't believe she would've kept such an important fact from him. "When did you notice those stains?"

"This morning after you left. They were faint." Her voice lowered. "We wouldn't have seen it in the dark."

"You don't have to make excuses for not noticing earlier," he said in a low tone. "I should've been more alert." He knew the dangers. His instincts had tried to warn him, but he'd let himself get distracted.

Garrity cleared his throat, interrupting the intimate moment.

Jasper wiped the concern from his face. Her remarks about finding the quilt would help reinforce the nature of their relationship. It wouldn't help prove Stokes was a killer unless they could string together facts that showed he had gone on a murder spree.

Time to steer the conversation in a direction that might yield something useful, if investigated.

"While we were in Denison, we saw Stokes," Jasper told Garrity. "He was skulking around at the scene of a murder."

"Yes!" Brigit picked up the thread. "The killer left the man's body hanging in a refrigerated rail car. He'd been shot in the head. It was J.D. Liddle. Jasper recognized him—" She stopped, as if realizing she might have set her partner up for another murder charge, then added. "Mr. Liddle was an informant for Stokes."

Garrity stopped making notes and looked up. "How do you know that?"

Jasper took the question. "Stokes told me Liddle double-crossed him. But if J.D. knew where the journal was, he would've said so. Instead, he told the marshal where to find me."

"And why were you out here?" Garrity asked Brigit.

"I am a Pinkerton agent, Frank." As if that settled it.

Her brother-in-law returned the notebook to his coat pocket. "That much, I know. Your sister came out to the farm to recruit my help."

Brigit straightened with a look of alarm. "Hannah told you about our secret mission?"

Jasper shook his head. She'd honestly thought they could keep all this a secret?

"A couple of men showed up looking for Kinkaid after you left

208

town," Garrity said. "They identified themselves as Pinkertons. Hannah said she got worried because she'd never met them before. Instead of waiting for me, she went off to find you and Jasper. Billy decided she needed a guide through the Territory."

Jasper's stomach clenched. That kid was more prone to getting in trouble than any other person alive, with one exception. "You should've gone after them," he told the boy's adopted father.

"We did. And I sent Billy home." Garrity gave Jasper a quelling look that closed down further discussion.

The curt explanation didn't ease Jasper's concern, but Billy's antics were the least of his worries at the moment. He did wonder about something that neither Billy nor Hannah could've known. "How did you find us out here?"

"We stopped into a trading post yesterday," Garrity answered. "The old man and his wife described a couple who'd stolen one of their horses."

"We didn't steal anything!" Brigit retorted. "We bartered."

She was taking this too personally. Jasper wasn't a bit surprised by the trader's actions. White men who worked in the Territory weren't known for their integrity.

He shrugged. "Just goes to show, you can't trust someone named Wiley. I'll bet he made a deal with them if he thought they were bounty hunters."

"He sent you after us to kill us?" She sounded shocked. Had she not figured that out?

"We took his information. Not his offer," Garrity said dryly.

The former sheriff put his notebook away and helped his deputy wrap the agent's body for removal. Then they moved over to where the marshal lay.

Frank Garrity, in particular, appeared to be pondering something. Even a greenhorn could see how the scene would've played out the way Brigit had described it.

Jasper held his nerves in check. Did it matter who pulled the trigger? He was to blame either way, and these two lawmen ought to understand that. Things would go a lot easier if they would just accept his confession and be done with it.

Both men finished their examination of the scene before they wrapped the marshal's body in the second canvas. They'd known Stokes, would've worked with him, might even have considered him a friend, but their stoic expressions didn't give away what they thought or felt.

Lawmen generally stuck together. These two wouldn't be inclined to believe an outlaw's self-defense claim. Neither would a jury if it got that far.

Beads of sweat formed on Jasper's upper lip. He'd better prepare for the worst.

Garrity stood and wiped his forehead. He took out the notebook once again. "You mentioned seeing the marshal in Denison. What were you doing there?"

"Looking for Mr. Kinkaid," Brigit answered before Jasper could. She launched into a brief recounting of their trip to the ice house, leaving out small facts that would've cast him in a poor light, and finished by saying she hadn't left his side the entire time they'd been in town.

Her story, meant to help, would shred her reputation. How could she expect a jury to believe anything she said if they thought she was a woman with loose morals?

Jasper released a regretful sign. He'd have to use her defense of him to strengthen his argument and insist that she was naive, foolish even, for falling in love with him. God, she would despise him—and herself—before they got through this ordeal.

She sat with her spine rigid and her chin up. Did anyone else notice the slight quiver in her lower lip? Despite her tough act, she was scared. And her soft heart had to be hurting bad right about now. She'd lost a friend and thought her lover didn't give a damn.

With every fiber of his being, he longed to reach out, put his arm around her, and offer her comfort. He shifted closer at the same time she twisted around and threw herself into his arms.

He couldn't refuse to hold her if his life depended on it.

When she lifted her tear-streaked face, he brushed a kiss over her soft lips. That wasn't enough. If this would be the last kiss they shared, he'd make it a good one.

The crunch of gravel beneath boots penetrated Paradise.

Jasper's brain started working again.

He pulled back, caught his breath, then looked up at Frank Garrity and grinned. "See? What did I tell you? She can't keep her hands off me."

BRIGIT GASPED when Frank yanked Jasper to his feet and then plowed a fist into her lover's face. Jasper stumbled backward and landed on his rear end with his arms splayed behind him. His lower lip bled freely.

Her heart bled more.

"You foul skunk..." Frank pushed up his sleeve. He appeared ready to take Jasper apart piece by piece for insulting her.

And Jasper just sat there. He didn't move or lift a finger to fight back. He had the reflexes of a mountain lion, could catch Frank's fist, take his gun. Instead, Jasper let himself get pummeled.

Brigit broke free of dazed disbelief and shot to her feet. She blocked her brother-in-law before he could take another step. "No. That's what he wants."

Frank looked at her like she'd lost her mind.

Gideon had moved behind Jasper, sneaking up, silent as a cat.

"Don't!" Brigit cried. "He's not..."

The brawny bounty hunter twisted Jasper's arms behind him and locked a set of iron cuffs. With a grimace, Jasper leaned forward to make it easier for the other man to restrain him. Those manacles on his raw wrists would be agony.

She dashed away tears on her cheek. Weeping would help Jasper's mistaken cause not hers. "Can't you see what he's doing? He's harmless."

Gideon rose to his full height. He rubbed his chin. "Mm. 'Bout as a harmless as a rattlesnake."

Jasper put his head down. He wouldn't look up because his expression would give him away. It was all an act. Everything he'd said, all the hurtful jabs, his actions—all except for the kiss. That had been the most honest thing he'd done since Frank and Gideon had shown up.

"He's misbehaving on purpose."

"Why would he do that?" Frank asked.

"Because he loves me." Even if he hadn't said the words, his kiss had told her as much.

Jasper chuckled at the ground. "Sure, I do. I love all the women who want me to love them."

Frank met her steady gaze with pity in his eyes.

Men were so arrogant and thick-headed. They assumed only women lied for love.

"He wants you to think *he's* a callous killer because it would keep *me* out of jail," she explained to her brother-in-law. "Jasper has protected me all this time we've been together."

Her claim received a disdainful huff from her champion.

It was time to put an end to this charade and only one person could do that. The one with a bloody lip.

"Excuse me." Brigit went to the edge of the stream to wet the ends of her shirttail.

Behind her, Frank and Gideon conversed in low tones. She heard enough to conclude that Frank planned to take Jasper to the federal jail in Fort Smith, where he'd been headed in the first place. Disappointing, but not surprising. She had to convince them to search for the journal first, but she would need Jasper's cooperation.

While the two men secured the bodies over the back of Jasper's horse, she went to confront him. Using the wet shirttail, she dabbed the cut on his lip. "Where do you think that missing journal might be? In the cave somewhere. Perhaps the crevice in the back?"

"That's the first place anyone would search for it. Charley knew a thousand hiding places." Jasper's despair was evident in his gaze. He didn't think they had even a slim chance of finding the evidence they needed to back up their assertions. Without it, one of them would likely hang for the murder. He was making sure that would be him.

His selfless actions only proved what she had claimed and he'd denied.

She tenderly smoothed back a lock of his hair that had fallen into his eyes. "If you don't cooperate, I'll turn myself in and say I killed for love."

Jasper narrowed his eyes. "Don't you dare."

"Time to leave," Frank called.

Brigit stood up to face off with her by-the-book relative. "We can't leave until we've looked for that missing journal. It's safe to say the marshal was involved in unlawful activity, and that might prove it."

"You got any idea where to find it?"

"We can come up with several possibilities—"

"If you don't know where to look, we can't afford to take the time right now. I've got two dead bodies and an escaped outlaw to bring in, and I don't want to spend another night out here."

"Then leave me. I'll look for it."

"No!" Jasper's outburst drew Frank's attention. "I'll take you to a spot where Charley might've hidden the journal. Brigit and Mr. Branch can search the cave where she found that quilt. If we split up, we can get to the railway stop before sunset."

Frank's steady gaze remained on the bound man, perhaps assessing whether Jasper was trustworthy or leading him into a trap. "Brigit, you and Gideon go search the cave. I'll take Byrne and these bodies. We'll meet up and catch the last train."

Brigit considered Jasper's motivation. Keeping her safe. That's why he'd suggested it. And maybe he had also come up with an idea of a place to search. He wouldn't be able to ride handcuffed.

She went over to Gideon and put out her hand. "I need the key to those cuffs. Mr. Byrne is not going to flee, and his wrists are raw. There's no need to torture him."

"You care if she takes them cuffs off him, Sheriff?" Gideon waited for Frank's reply.

"Go ahead," came the reluctant answer.

After Brigit removed the cuffs, Jasper washed away the blood and dirt at the creek. Gideon offered her a tin of salve and a roll of fresh bandages. She took both and knelt next to Jasper. "Hold out your arms."

"Yes, ma'am." His mocking tone was meant to drive a wedge between them. Which only made her more determined not to allow him to succeed.

She dressed his wrists, trying to be tender. "Where will you take Frank?"

"It's another hideout. You focus on this one. If you don't find anything, don't risk going elsewhere. The men who hide out here are thieves, murderers, and rapists."

"I'll be careful." She put her arms around him and held him tight.

He pressed his face into her hair as if he were taking his last breath of her. "I mean it. Don't linger. Don't take chances. It's not worth your life."

"What about your life?"

He drew back, replacing the mask that had slipped for a moment. "I haven't made any promises."

Which meant he would sacrifice himself to keep her safe. How could she make sure he wouldn't do something rash before they met up again?

Brigit gripped his shirt in her fists. "You did promise something, you know. You promised to protect me. You can't do that if you're not alive."

CHAPTER 20

$\mathcal{J}$asper gave up trying to prove he was a varmint. The two lawmen already believed it. Brigit never would, and it was taking too much energy trying to convince her otherwise. He hugged her neck and left her in the care of the deputy. It was the hardest thing he'd ever done.

An hour later, he stood at the edge of a high ridge, which offered a panoramic view of the western plains and a railroad line that ran through it.

The noontime train would be coming soon. Car after car would be filled with cattle. Some of it was stolen if his suspicions turned out to be right. How much had the marshal known and what part had he played, if any? Were the answers in that journal? Probably. If it could be found.

Bandit nudged Jasper's arm to get a nose rub. The horse had balked when two dead men were slung over its back. Didn't like the smell or the dead weight.

Jasper had been forced to double up with the sheriff.

"Yeah, I'm not happy with the arrangement either." Jasper directed his next remark at Garrity. "This here is Charley's favorite spot for shooting at trains. If he had the journal when he came out here last, he would've stashed it in our old hideout. Below us, about halfway down."

Garrity remained mounted on his big bay. "Let's take a look."

"Hold on." Jasper lifted his hand. "The path isn't wide, and it's likely washed out. We can't risk taking the horses."

His warning was met with a look of doubt.

"Where did you put your horses before?"

That question implied he was lying. The only things Garrity hadn't questioned were the lies Jasper had told about using Brigit as a foil. Garrity hadn't commented at all. He didn't talk a lot at any rate, so it was hard to know whether he believed the story. There was no reason *not* to believe it.

"We built a small corral." Jasper directed the other man's attention toward a densely forested stretch of land. "Over there. If you don't want to take the time to find it, stay up here. I'll go take a look around."

Garrity made Jasper wait for a reply. Was he worried his prisoner might've led him into an ambush or had a gun hidden down there? What questions might be tumbling around inside the lawman's head was impossible to know. He wore the same, set expression, regardless. "Make it quick," he said, finally.

"I didn't plan on taking all day. Unlike you," Jasper muttered.

He moved as fast as he dared on the narrow path that wound down one side of the steep incline. Loose rocks rolled beneath his boots. The difficulty in getting to the cave had been what made it so attractive as a hideout, as well as its view of the railroad.

This was where he'd come to prepare his first heist after he'd decided to take William Bond up on his offer. That had been two years after Katy crews had laid tracks through Indian Territory, besieged by rain, mosquitos, and resentful tribes. The force behind all that construction—the previous general manager, Henry Stevens —would never have paid someone to rob his trains.

Jasper wished he'd taken more time to consider the consequences of his decisions. He wished he'd gotten wiser earlier about a lot of things. It now seemed somehow proper that his compensation for undermining the Katy—and all those people who'd poured their blood, sweat, and tears into it—would be to save the sister of the man who built it. Even if she didn't act like she believed she needed saving.

Why the hell had Brigit gone and fallen in love with him? She was smarter than that.

A little more than halfway down, he looked up. From this spot, bushes growing out of the rocky soil blocked his view. Garrity might get impatient if he lost sight of his prisoner. He had better not try to bring those horses down. They'd all end up at the bottom of a ravine.

As Jasper neared the entrance to the cave, he removed his hat and wiped the sweat off his forehead. It was hotter than hell out here in the sun. When a breath of cool air hit him, he stopped abruptly. That's when he noticed a sound coming from inside. Rhythmic. Sonorous.

Snoring.

He bit back a curse. Something—or someone—was holed up in there.

Jasper took a step back...and missed his footing. He grabbed an outcropping as he slipped. Stones went tumbling from beneath his feet as he tried to find a toehold, and his heart ricocheted inside his chest.

Above him, at the cave's entrance, two men appeared. They had the dazed look of those who'd been awakened from a deep sleep. Except, they'd been alert enough to draw their guns.

Jasper recognized one of them, the older one. A big man with deeply tanned skin and snow-white hair.

Tom Starr.

Jasper would've preferred meeting a bear.

Tom let loose a laugh. "I'll be damned! Jasper Byrne! You're lucky I didn't shoot you."

Lucky?

The vengeful old coot had killed Jasper's great uncle during a feud amongst the Cherokee years ago. Later, Jasper's father had inadvertently saved Tom's sorry hide when he'd tipped off a mutual acquaintance about the presence of Union soldiers. Which was partly why those same soldiers had sought out James Byrne and shot him. The Starrs were bad luck.

Jasper felt his precarious hold slipping. It would be a long, painful slide to the bottom. He would take his chances with old man Starr. "*O-si-yo,* Tom. Can you give me a hand?"

Tom reached down and grabbed Jasper's wrist with one paw. He pulled with so much strength it sent Jasper stumbling into the cave. An unsmiling man caught and righted him. One of Tom's many sons, based on size alone.

"Thanks," Jasper said, with a forced smile.

Father and son watched expectantly while he dusted off his trousers and searched his mind for a good excuse for being there. "That path is washed out since the last time I came down. Just thought I'd check things out. Didn't reckon on finding anyone."

The elder Starr peered over Jasper's shoulder. "Is Charley with you?"

Jasper couldn't mention the lawman who waited for him without risking Garrity's life. But there was no reason to lie about what had happened to Charley.

"He's dead." Jasper let the news sink in and watched their faces to see if they'd known and were testing him. Both men appeared surprised.

"How?" Tom asked.

"A dirty marshal shot him." Jasper hesitated to provide more information until he knew what these two were up to. "What brings you out here?"

"We agreed to meet Frank and Jesse. Ellis told them about this place. Good scouting location."

The James brothers were on their way?

Jasper glanced over his shoulder and tried not to appear nervous. "I haven't seen those two in a hog's age."

Encountering the James's would not be a pleasant surprise for the former sheriff, but there was no way to warn him without alerting the Starrs.

"How soon will they be here?"

"We thought they'd be here by now." Tom gave Jasper the once-over. "Where's your firearm, boy?"

Jasper acted surprised. "Must've lost it when I slipped."

"Give him one of yours, Ellis."

The son offered Jasper an old Navy service revolver.

Why so generous? It appeared he had better weapons to choose from. Near the back of the cave was an assortment of rifles, handguns, and ammunition belts, along with several small barrels. Dynamite? They might be planning a job.

"I heard you escaped from under a marshal's nose..." Tom let his sentence trail off and waited for what his smile implied would be an amusing story.

It was amusing in some places, terrifying in other parts. But Jasper wasn't keen to share it or bring Brigit into the picture. On the other hand, he might be able to prime the pump and find out what these two knew.

"Yeah. I skipped a necktie party arranged by a U.S. Marshal. Stokes. He didn't want me to tell anybody about the dirty work he's doing."

Tom and his son exchanged knowing glances before the older man spoke. "He's a dirty one, all right. He came by the house a few months back and offered to cut me in on a deal...with a slaughterhouse down in Texas. Me and my boys, we ain't cattle rustlers."

Ellis nodded gravely.

Tom and his *boys* had tracked down and killed upwards of thirty enemies. They drew a line somewhere.

"Stokes wanted to hire you?" Jasper clarified.

"He said he'd hook us up with the folks that needed hands," Tom explained. "We'd pay him a finder's fee or some such nonsense. I suspect he was squeezing them, too."

"Damn! I knew it!" Jasper wished he had a nickel for every time he got incriminating information and no one, except other outlaws, was around to hear it.

He risked sharing another nugget. If nothing else, it would keep the two men busy for a while. "Stokes told me Charley had taken something from him. That's why he killed him."

Tom's eyes widened with interest. "You came here to find it?"

"I already checked Charley's other hideout." Jasper didn't want them rushing to where they'd encounter Brigit and Gideon. "Have you found anything of value in here?"

"Oh, hell, yeah," Ellis piped up.

Jasper tried not to appear too excited. "What did you find?"

Tom stepped aside and gestured at the small barrels. "Best whiskey we've tasted in years. We figured Charley had stolen it off a train, not a marshal!" The big man hooted.

"That explains why you two were snoring when I got here." Jasper laughed along, despite the urge to cuss—or cry. Charley likely had stolen the liquor off a train. Where the hell had he put the journal?

Someplace safe. Not out here, Charley's voice seemed to echo.

The plaintive wail of a train broke the spell. Then another sound. Footsteps.

A moment later, a man stumbled inside. *Garrity.* Followed by two others. The taller one had the expression of a tired hound. The younger man had fiery blue eyes and a personality to match.

Frank and Jesse had arrived.

Jasper's hope for a safe exit flew out of the cave.

IF CHARLEY HAD HIDDEN the marshal's journal in this hideout, he hadn't left a single clue. Brigit had gone over every inch, including that crevice. Gideon had combed the tunnel outside the cave. An hour later, they met next to the firepit.

Last night, a warm blaze had kept her and Jasper warm. Sometime this morning, the embers had died. Brigit refused to consider it symbolic. Jasper's untimely demise at the end of a rope wasn't inevitable any more than hers. She just had to keep searching.

Gideon removed his hat and seemed to lapse into a reflective mood before he spoke up. "We best go, miss."

Thankfully, he didn't repeat Jasper's earlier warnings about the dangers. It was getting tiresome to be reminded of things she already knew. She was also painfully aware of the danger of showing up in court without enough evidence to prove the marshal had the motivation to go on a killing spree.

She gazed wistfully at the rumpled bedding where she had spent the night in Jasper's arms.

What about the quilt?

Brigit ran her hands over each square. Nothing felt like a book or papers hidden inside with the batting. She blinked back tears. Not because of the quilt, it seemed to have lost its strange power. If the journal couldn't be found soon, it might never be recovered. Then what did they have left? Only her word and Jasper's. It wouldn't be enough.

She folded the faded quilt over her arm. "Jasper's sister might be able to testify about what J.D. was up to. She knows both men well."

"You think the federal judge is gonna listen to her?" Gideon's tone was doubtful.

Brigit fumed as she rolled the quilt inside the blanket. "In other words, no one will believe a woman who might care about Jasper. Is that what you're saying?"

"You said that, miss, not me."

Brigit stood, angry, needing to strike out. Only, Gideon wasn't her enemy. He could be an ally if he'd just admit to what was obvious to even the least-trained professional. "Jasper did not kill the marshal. You know that as well as I do."

Gideon's implacable expression softened a little. "You might consider what *he* knows. He's facing robbery charges, likely a murder charge for killing his accomplice. I reckon he knows taking responsibility for one more crime ain't gonna make a noose hurt no worse."

Brigit clamped her teeth together to hold in a sob. She spun around with the bedroll clutched to her chest. It wasn't right or fair, the whole idea was unbearable. "No man should hang for murders he didn't commit. Regardless of his past."

"I agree. Don't mean it won't happen."

She shook her head. "It's not inevitable. I won't let Jasper give up."

"He's not giving up, miss. There's a big difference between that and choosing to sacrifice yourself for somebody else. One's the action of a coward. The other is a hero's deed."

Brigit spun around. "I don't need a *dead* hero. I need a man who will fight to stay alive."

The deputy secured his white hat. "If you insist you killed that marshal, we got no choice but to accept your confession. The federal authorities are sure to charge you with his murder unless you got evidence to prove he wasn't doing his job."

"He was acting in the role of an executioner!"

"You'll get the chance to tell your story on the witness stand."

But who would buy it? Wasn't that what Jasper had warned?

It didn't matter. She would not let him lay down his life for hers.

"You don't understand love, Mr. Branch."

A look of pain flickered across the former deputy's broad face before he straightened his shoulders. "That so?" He reached inside his coat to withdraw something then opened his hand for her to see what lay across the lighter skin of his palm. A plait of black hair tied with a thin ribbon, which might've been yellow at one time.

"This here is all I got left of my Sadie. I could've stayed with her. But she pushed me to escape and get to freedom." He closed his hand over the treasured relic. "When I went back for her after the war, I found out she'd died a couple of months after I left."

Brigit's heart had stopped midway through the story, then lurched into an anguished rhythm when he finished. "I'm so sorry."

"Didn't tell you that to make you sorry."

He'd told her to educate her on the true meaning of love.

Brigit tucked the bedding under her arm, more determined than ever to save the man who had taught her how to love. "Charley had to know what was in that journal. He would've hidden it somewhere close. We just need to keep looking."

Gideon Branch peered upward at the opening in the ceiling where the sun shone through, perhaps estimating the time remaining before they had to leave to catch a train. "If it was me, I wouldn't hide something that important close to where I stayed. Too chancy. I might get caught. Or killed. I'd give it to someone I trusted."

"Who would that be?"

The bounty hunter met her gaze. "Me? I'd give it to Frank Garrity. I don't got any other family."

Before she'd met Jasper, the only person she'd trusted unequivocally was her twin sister. Brigit smoothed her hand over the faded quilt. Whom would Charley have trusted? The person who'd likely made this, his wife, was dead.

Na.

Brigit caught a sharp breath. The word seemed to have been spoken, but she'd been staring right straight at Gideon and his lips hadn't moved.

"*Na*," she repeated, and her breath quickened. "Oh, heavenly stars! Gideon that's it!" She laughed, clutching the quilt to her chest. It wasn't sad anymore. Neither was she. "Charley must have given the journal to his mother for safekeeping! She's his closest family. Jasper knows her, he calls her *Na*. He'll know where to find her."

JASPER ESTIMATED his chances of saving Garrity's life at about a hundred-to-one, and the odds of his survival only slightly better, should any of the outlaws in this cave figure out he was traveling with a former sheriff, who had another strike against him for his wartime activity as a despised Jayhawker.

For the moment, it appeared no one knew Garrity or recognized his face, or maybe he'd just aged a lot in the last couple of minutes.

Jesse held the lawman's gun on him. "We caught this weasel on the path, sneaking up on y'all. Found two horses on the ridge and two corpses. But *he*..." Jesse motioned to the man on his knees. "Ain't talkin'."

This James brother wasn't long on patience. Like Jasper, he'd been a resentful kid when he'd first set out to fight a war. Unlike Jasper, he hadn't grown out of it. They both robbed trains. That was about all they had in common.

Or was it?

Hadn't Jesse and Frank recently married their sweethearts? They might have sympathy for another fugitive in their predicament.

"He's my new brother-in-law. Francesco." Jasper chose a name that sounded foreign to throw the men off track. No lawmen he could think of were named Francesco.

"Francesco?" Jesse gawked at the kneeling man. "What kind of name is that?"

Garrity held Jasper's gaze in a baleful stare. He didn't answer the question.

"A family name, I reckon." Jasper shrugged. "Can't say much for my sister-in-law's tastes. But you know how it goes. You can pick your wife, but you can't pick your relatives."

Four men nodded. A muscle beneath Garrity's eye twitched. Other than that, he remained motionless.

Jesse squinted. "You know, come to think of it, he looks like a—"

"Farmer," Jasper interjected, before Jesse's mind caught up to his mouth. "Funny, how they all look alike."

"What's a farmer doing with two corpses?"

Another hint as to Frank's identity. But it was also an opportunity for an outlaw to take credit and gain standing in the eyes of men who saw nothing wrong with eliminating their enemies.

"Oh, those belong to me. One's a marshal. He killed Charley—."

"Who killed Charley? Francesco?" Jesse motioned at Frank.

"No, the dead marshal."

"How did a dead marshal—?"

"Stokes was alive when he killed Charley," Jasper explained slowly.

"Why didn't Franceso tell us this?" Jesse's voice went up a notch with frustration.

"How would *you* answer somebody who sneaked up on you and took *your* gun?"

"Who is the woman?" Tom's out-of-blue question threw Jasper.

"What woman? Oh! *My* woman." Jasper thought fast. What lies could he remember? "Her name is Alice. Francesco is married to her sister. They got a farm up in Kansas. My brother-in-law came looking for me and Alice after her sister got worried."

Jesse lowered the weapon and motioned for Garrity to get to his feet, but didn't return the lawman's gun.

Garrity's gaze remained riveted on Jasper. *Hurry the hell up*, it said.

"And the other carcass?" Frank James asked.

The James brothers had a strong dislike for Pinkertons.

"That was a friend of Charley's. He figured out the marshal was taking bribes." Jasper kept his answers short, with as a little detail as possible, yet enough to be believed given his earlier conversation with the Starrs. "Me and Francesco plan to get rid of the bodies."

Technically, this was true. They would get rid of them when they turned the corpses over to federal authorities, who would then lock him away to await trial for the marshal's murder.

Another idea came to him. He could remain here and distract these rascals, make sure Garrity got away with the bodies, then disappear. Buy himself more time to go look for that journal. Where would that leave Brigit? Facing a murder charge when she told the truth about shooting Stokes. And a search could take weeks or months. Jasper resisted the temptation to veer from his chosen path.

"You could weigh the bodies down with stones and sink them in the river," Jesse motioned in the general direction of a nearby body of water. He spoke with authority on the matter.

"Thanks for the suggestion. We have a spot in mind."

"We'll be off then." Those were the first words out of Garrity's mouth.

Jesse turned a wary eye on him. "You don't sound like a Mexican, *Francesco*."

It was an Italian name but never mind.

"Muy bueno," Garrity replied.

Jesse turned to his brother. "What did he say?"

"It's good. Something like that."

"What's good?"

Garrity held out his hand. *"Por favor."*

"He wants his gun," Jasper didn't need to know Spanish to translate.

Jesse placed the revolver in the sheriff's palm. "You remind me of somebody. I think I saw your picture in a newspaper. Can't recall exactly when."

A year ago, Garrity's face had been in papers across the country, after he'd discovered upwards of a dozen bodies buried in a field not far from Parsons. The murder investigation had been in the news for months.

"He gets that a lot. I think it's the mustache." Jasper clapped the former Labette County sheriff on the back. "Why don't you get a head start, brother. Leave me a horse. I've got some catching up to do."

Garrity's frown drew into a double line.

"Go on," Jasper urged. Garrity had better get the hell away before someone else made the connection.

After the slow-moving lawman had sauntered out of the cave, Jasper turned to the others. He had to make sure they wouldn't be in any condition to remember—or follow. "I like that fella, but he doesn't drink. His wife has him on a short rein. How about a sip of that whiskey?"

Jesse's mood improved at the suggestion. "Whiskey sounds good."

"Sounds good to me, too," his brother agreed. "We'll come back here and celebrate together. After we rob the train.

CHAPTER 21

*I*n the distance, the diamond-stack locomotive blew its sooty breath into the fading light. Smoke stretched into a long, dark tail over the top of the cars. Beyond the train, the sky provided a pink and gold canvas for the pretty picture, which Brigit would've liked to have enjoyed with Jasper. But there was no sign of him or Frank in front of the trading post.

She swung down off the white horse and began to unpack the bedding and saddle bags. "I don't see their horses."

Gideon was slower to dismount. "Nope. Don't appear they got here yet."

The agreed-upon plan was to catch the last train together. She intended to make an extra stop on the way to Fort Smith to look for Charley's mother and ask her about the journal. If *Na* didn't have it, she'd know where her son was most likely to have hidden it.

Brigit couldn't wait to talk to Jasper and give him cause for hope, talk him out of his plan to confess to something he didn't do. The journal would be the evidence they needed to shore up her argument that the marshal had gone on a killing spree to prevent being incriminated in illegal activity.

She scanned the wide plain behind her before peering down the tracks that curved to the south. The oncoming train was getting closer. Maybe ten minutes away, not much more.

Brigit released her nervousness with a deep breath. Wearing ruts in the dirt wouldn't bring them here any faster. "Let's go inside. I want to talk to Mr. Wiley about the horse he accused us of stealing. If they want it back, I'll exchange it for the dress I gave them."

"If it's all the same to you, I'll wait out here. Let me know if you need me." Gideon settled onto the split-log bench next to the door, leaned against the wall, and tipped his hat over his eyes.

Apparently, he believed she could take care of it or he didn't wish to get involved, or maybe he just wanted a nap.

Brigit pushed open the door into the store, jangling a bell. An added touch since the last time she'd been here.

The grizzled old trader, who stood behind the counter, took one look at her and his eyes widened with alarm. Perhaps he thought she was a ghost, considering he'd intended for them to be shot.

She lifted the floppy hat and smoothed her hair back. "Good afternoon, Mr. Wiley. I see you remember me."

"Yes ma'am, I do."

"I understand you want your horse back?"

"Well, sure. I, ah, figured you might bring it back when you were done."

"Is that why you sent two bounty hunters after us?" Brigit stopped in front of the counter and tucked her thumb over the gun belt, making her point. She would not put up with his nonsense.

The shopkeeper's Adam's apple bobbed. "Did you meet them?"

"One of them is outside. We're traveling together."

"Uh-huh." Wiley's beady eyes darted toward the door.

"The other will be here soon. With my *husband*. You remember him?"

"Sure do." The skinny proprietor smoothed his hand over the loose coat, which had looked much better on Jasper. "He traded this for a blanket and a real nice tunic."

"Mm-hm. And we traded my ensemble for the horse. I am

returning the horse. As you've made it clear the arrangement was only temporary, I'll take my clothes now."

"No!" His wife appeared from behind a stack of crates strategically located at a spot where one could see the door. Perhaps the bell had tipped her off. She gave her husband a baleful look and he shrugged.

Had he not consulted her before reporting the supposed theft?

"You trade. No return." The Choctaw woman held her head high. The lovely skirt and jacket had been expertly altered to fit her shorter, fuller figure.

Brigit heaved a regretful sigh. "Yes, I see that."

"You keep the horse."

What good was an extra horse if one couldn't afford to pay freight to transport it? For that matter, what would Jasper do with his beloved Bandit? She needed cash, not an extra mouth to feed.

"I'll sell you the white horse," Brigit offered the storekeeper.

He shook his head. "We trade in goods."

Being difficult, was he?

"You trade on your good reputation. If word got out that you had accused a customer, or worse, took a lady's belongings under pretenses, how long do you think the railroad would let you remain on their property?"

Wiley's lips thinned.

His wife used an elbow to prompt a response.

"How much do you need?" he asked.

A *good* horse might cost two hundred dollars. She wouldn't get that much for the nag.

"One hundred dollars."

"I'll give you fifty. It's not worth more than that."

The noise of the arriving train filled the trading post. She had no time to negotiate a better price. Wiley counted the greenbacks into her palm.

The door jangled and Jasper strode inside, looking windblown and anxious. "Brigit!"

"Jasper!" Her heart danced with excitement as she rushed to meet him. "Where's Frank?"

"Getting the bodies loaded and the horses. Gideon's helping him. I told him I'd find you."

She pressed the cash into Jasper's palm. "This is what I got for that white horse. It'll pay for Bandit's transportation if you want to send him home."

Jasper looked down at the money and then back up with gratitude in his eyes. He gave her a quick kiss on the cheek before he leaned to one side to speak around her. "I left a black gelding in your corral. The owner will show up soon, I suspect. You can turn the horse over to him."

Avarice appeared in the trader's expression. "Oh, I'll be sure to do that."

Jasper put his arm around Brigit's waist, turning her toward the door.

"Wiley will do no such thing," she warned him.

"Oh, I think he will," Jasper replied with confidence.

"Who is the owner?" Wiley called out.

"Big Cherokee, white hair, you might've heard of him. Tom Starr."

Brigit thought she heard Wiley yell something, but the train's whistle drowned it out.

JASPER KEPT his worries to himself while he helped Brigit into the car where they'd loaded three horses. He threw their gear and bedding into an empty stall. "We'll ride in here."

Brigit gave a questioning look. "What about Frank and Gideon?"

"Didn't he tell you when you talked to him?"

"He didn't say a great deal."

"Never does. They're keeping watch for some men who might want to kill me."

She gave a half-hearted laugh. "That's not funny."

"It wasn't a joke."

After being invited to a robbery, Jasper had excused himself to pee, then had scrambled to join his companion. The fast-thinking sheriff had found the outlaw's mounts in that pen in the woods and turned them loose. All except for a black one with the Starr brand. *Francesco* was no fool. They wouldn't have stood a chance of outrunning the rascals if they were riding double. As it was, leading a horse loaded with two corpses had slowed them down.

Jasper took a look outside. "Frank and Gideon are pretty far down the tracks. Next to that empty car where they loaded the bodies."

A distant cloud of dust indicated oncoming riders.

Damn. They'd caught the horses.

Jasper pulled the service revolver, courtesy of Ellis Starr, who'd likely kill him with it if given the opportunity.

"What else do you see?" Brigit asked.

"Stay back."

She got right up next to him. And she had that little pistol in her hand. A fat lot of good that would do her.

The train signaled. Seconds later, the train lurched into motion.

Frank swung into the car with the bodies and Gideon followed. If they'd been seen, and they probably had, any gunfire would be directed at that car—and returned from two well-armed lawmen. The sheriff hadn't been tardy. He'd deliberately remained down there to divert the outlaws' attention. He'd done it to protect Brigit.

"Who are those riders?" she asked.

"Some old friends."

"*Friends* want to kill you?"

"It's...complicated."

The train picked up speed, leaving the dust cloud behind. The Starrs and James brothers would not catch up. Not today, anyway.

Jasper pulled the door closed and breathed a sigh of relief. He dropped down onto clean straw and motioned for Brigit to join him. "We're safe."

She studied him for a long moment. "You and Frank appear to be getting along."

Had she said that because Garrity trusted him with her? The two of them had come to an understanding. Frank took him at his word that he'd willingly go back to jail, rather than let Brigit shoulder the blame for the marshal's death. It hadn't hurt that he'd saved Garrity's life.

Jasper draped his arm around Brigit's shoulders. "He's not a bad sort. Seems up for an adventure."

"Being with you is always an adventure."

He dropped a kiss on her nose. "Glad I can add some excitement to your dull life."

In a sense, he had come full circle since the fateful day they'd met inside a railroad car that looked very much like this one. At present, he wasn't chained, but he was still a prisoner, headed for a reckoning. His life hadn't counted for much until he'd met Brigit. He wished he could come up with the words to thank her for what she'd done for him and tell her how much she meant to him.

She put her arm around his neck and sought his mouth, which sent his blood racing and made his head swim.

Maybe he didn't need words. Kissing seemed to work pretty well.

When she slid her hand beneath the deerskin tunic and stroked his skin, his pulse took off like a runaway engine. He couldn't stop it, even if he wanted to.

A tug on her arm brought her onto his lap. He pushed the skirt to her hips while she worked open the buttons on his trousers. She seemed plenty eager and he was frantic to be inside her.

They came together. Gasping. Groaning.

Brigit rode him with the same focused determination she gave to everything she did, without hesitance or shame. God, he loved her courage and her fiery spirit. He loved every inch of her, from the soft hair on her head, which he kissed, to the soles of her feet, which he would kiss if he could reach them.

The rumbling wheels matched the pace of their lovemaking. As the train roared and released steam, sweat poured down his temples. His climax hit hard, fast, and uncontrollable. Almost at the same instant, she clung to him, shuddered and cried out, then began weeping.

The sound of her distress put a vise on his heart. He touched her cheek tenderly. "Did I hurt you?"

"No. No, I'm...overwhelmed," she whispered.

That was a good word for it. He couldn't think of a better one.

Somewhere along the way, he'd gotten her shirt off. He slid his hands down her bare back, over each rounded bone along her spine before he drew his fingertips up and over her smooth, slightly damp skin. He was desperate to gorge his senses on her while he had the chance.

Brigit nuzzled his neck. She didn't move from where she sat on his lap, which was fine with him. He was in no hurry either. Before they reached the halfway point to the next stop, he would be hard again. Later, after they reached Fort Smith, he'd have to let her go. The thought cooled his ardor.

Jasper trailed kisses over her cheek. She deserved better than a hasty coupling in the straw. Except, he couldn't promise her anything, not even tomorrow. A profession of love could fuel false hope. Worse, it might spur her to double down on her confession. Regret collected in his throat, too thick to swallow.

After another moment, she slid away. She didn't meet his eyes as she pulled on the discarded shirt and buttoned it. "Frank mentioned you ran into some trouble."

"*Some trouble*? Yeah, that's one way to put it." Jasper buttoned his trousers.

"He said you saved his life."

"I'd say he saved both of us," Jasper replied, honestly. Things had a way of spiraling out of control when *he* tried to play the hero. He had little more luck with the villainous role.

His Cherokee grandmother had once told him he'd been born with a dual spirit. One was good and the other bad, and they would fight for control for years until one of them won. He'd asked her which would triumph. She'd told him it was up to him.

Even if the good spirit eventually came out on top, it was too late. He knew it. Brigit knew it too if she was honest with herself.

She combed her fingers through her hair to rid it of the straw that had somehow gotten stuck in the loose strands. The blouse hung loose on her slender form. She sat on the discarded skirt and tucked her legs beneath her. Her brown eyes, which had earlier warmed with tenderness, now snapped with intelligence. She quirked her lips into a wry smile that somehow reached inside his chest.

Was she aware of the power she had over him? If not, he had to make sure she remained uninformed, to keep her safe, but this didn't mean he couldn't encourage her budding confidence in herself as a woman. "You're beautiful, you know that?"

She made a face. "No, I don't *know* that, nor am I sure I believe it. I look much better in the dress you bought for me."

"You look much better naked."

Her laughter lifted his spirits.

"So do you, by the way."

She enjoyed flirting as much as he did and it wouldn't harm either of them to do it.

He leaned his head against the side of the stall and eyed her suggestively. "Is that a proposition?"

"Perhaps." She seemed to want to say something more.

His heart beat faster. Part of him didn't want her to declare her love, another part of him hoped she would.

"We have to convince Frank to let us off the train at Tahlequah."

Where had that come from? Was she thinking about trying to free him again?

"Well, I did save his life. But I don't think he'll agree. If you drug him, that'll make family relations awkward."

She slapped his arm, not hard. "I'm not suggesting we incapacitate Frank. But you once mentioned Charley's mother lives near Tahlequah. You called her *Na.*"

"It means *Aunt.* A lot of people call her that."

The change of subject wasn't unwelcome, but it left him with a vague sense of disappointment. Not in her. In himself. He should've thought about how to break the news of Charley's death to his mother.

"We can get word to her, send his things—"

"No, we have to talk to her." Brigit rested back on her legs and clasped her hands together. Oddly enough, she appeared to be on the verge of announcing good news. "Charley turned the journal over to his mother. I feel certain of it."

Jasper gave the heartfelt declaration a moment of consideration before dismissing it. "Charley wouldn't involve his mother in anything dangerous. He stayed away, lived in a cave, to make sure she would be safe."

Brigit nodded. "And I'll bet everyone knows that, which explains why Stokes wouldn't have bothered to go look for it there. But what if Charley managed to sneak home without anyone finding out and told her to hide it and not mention it to anyone? He had to know how important it was, and how few people could be trusted with what was in it."

She had a point, and a good one, as was often the case. Unfortunately, it introduced another danger.

"I can't risk taking you to see *Na*. You know those outlaws I mentioned? I told them I killed the marshal, and that I was looking for something that got stolen from him. Word will get out fast. The cockroaches will crawl out from under rocks to come after me. To find what I know or to kill me to keep it quiet."

His gloomy assessment cast a cloud over Brigit's bright, hopeful expression. She rubbed her hands together in her lap as if they'd gotten cold. "We have to get to that journal before anyone else does. Who can help us?"

Getting outside help wasn't a bad idea, as long she didn't cross paths with the wrong people. He could think of only one person he'd trust.

"Jake Colston. The People know him as *Wa-ya*. He's a lawyer in Tahlequah. He lives near the masonic opera house with his wife, Kate. He can get you in touch with *Na*."

"What about you?"

"I'll be the distraction for anyone who might be coming after us. Frank Garrity can go ahead with his plan to turn me over to the federal authorities in Fort Smith. Last I heard, they were holding over a hundred men in jail. They won't get to my case for a couple of weeks, at least."

Unless the judge moved it up on account of a murder charge.

She chewed on her lip, which meant she wasn't quite ready to jump on board with his suggestion. "You can't keep telling everyone you shot the marshal."

Yes, he could, and he fully intended to do so to keep her from confessing. Rather than argue, he reached out for her. "I'll keep my mouth shut until my lawyer gets there."

If she found the journal, the information it contained might help him or it might not. Regardless, this detour would keep her away long enough for him to sign a confession before she found out about it. He wouldn't have to open his mouth to do that.

Brigit snuggled up next to him. He lifted the hand she'd rested on his chest and examined each slender finger before bringing them to his lips one by one. "You have the prettiest hands."

"Why are you talking about my hands?" She angled her head to look at him and gave him one of her adorable wry smiles. "Are you well?"

"There's nothing wrong with me. I just want you to know what I'm thinking."

"I'd rather hear about what you're feeling."

He stroked the base of her thumb. "Your soft skin."

"Not that kind of *feeling*, I mean the ones in here." She placed her hand over the center of his chest. "You do have them?"

"Do I?"

Right about now would be a good time to give her sweet words and reassurances, except that wasn't what she'd asked for. She wanted to know what was going on inside that place beneath her palm. Hell if he knew. It was in an uproar.

She breathed out a soft laugh. "Oh goodness, pick one and tell me about it."

One? His heart hammered out a word. "Afraid, I guess."

Her features twisted with anguish. "What are you afraid of? Dying? Don't be, because I won't let—"

He put his finger to her lips. "Hush. I'm not afraid to die. You asked me about my feelings. That's what I'm afraid of. And I can't find the right words to tell you about the rest of them. All I can do is show you."

"Show me what?"

He pushed her down onto the straw, laced his fingers with hers, and held her arms over her head while he gave her a demonstration.

CHAPTER 22

*W*hen the whistle sounded announcing the next stop, Brigit sat up. She'd been stretched out next to Jasper with her head resting on his shoulder. "Get up! We've reached Tahlequah. We need to find Frank and Gideon and explain the new plan."

"I'm sure they'll find us," Jasper murmured, sitting up more slowly.

She retrieved the skirt from beneath her and pulled on the man-sized shirt. When she found her brother-in-law, she didn't want to appear disheveled.

"Let me help you with that." Jasper smoothed his hands over the front of the shirt and palmed her breasts.

Brigit grasped his wrists with a laugh. "*That* is not helping."

"It's not?"

She located pieces of straw in her hair. "If you want to help, make sure I don't look like I've been sleeping in a rail car."

"You haven't been sleeping."

"That's worse, Jasper. You realize that, right?"

He buttoned his trousers and grabbed the deerskin shirt. Then he kissed her again.

She wrapped her arms around his neck and returned his kiss with her whole heart. Soon enough, reality would intrude, which made these moments when she could openly love him all the more special.

In this railcar that smelled of straw and manure, she and Jasper had spent precious, private moments. Outside was a world that wouldn't be welcoming to a detective who'd fallen in love with an outlaw, or a woman who'd given herself to a man who was in no position to marry her or even watch out for her. Jasper had resisted loving her because he knew this as well as she did. Regardless, she loved him, and she wasn't about to leave him thinking otherwise.

The train slowed. Lights mounted at the depot shone through the slates along the side of the rail car and flashed across Jasper's face. His mood, like hers, had become reflective. "I'm having second thoughts about this plan of yours. We don't know who might've followed us. Or who else is looking for that journal."

"That's why I have to go after it. You won't change my mind."

He heaved a heavy sigh. "Ask for directions to the opera house. Jake and Kate live across the street. Anyone around there can point it out. It's a genteel area."

She tightened the woven sash around her waist. "Do you think I'll stand out?"

"The gun belt could draw attention."

"Or keep people away."

"That, too."

Jasper took hold of her arms. "Be careful."

"I will." Her heart beat faster. "I'll take Bandit, and make sure your horse gets home."

"Jake can take care of it. Tell him... Tell him I should've listened to him a long time ago."

"What does that mean?"

"It means he's smarter than me, which is a good thing for you."

As the train clanked to a stop, the horses moved restlessly in the stalls. The sound of freight cars being opened came closer. One of the workers rolled open the door to their car.

"We have a horse to unload," she told him.

Brigit met Frank as he strode toward them with a puzzled frown. Gideon came right along behind him. They had to be wondering why she and Jasper were getting off the train.

She quickly explained her plan to go find Charley's mother. "Jasper will continue with you to Fort Smith. He thinks the marshal's associates will be looking for him, and his arrest will create a distraction, which will give me more time to look for the journal."

"He's right about that." Frank still appeared hesitant.

Jasper had already gotten Bandit saddled up and led the horse down a ramp to the platform.

"I'll go with her," Gideon volunteered. "I know my way around this town."

"If you find anything, send word," Frank instructed him.

Brigit hugged her brother-in-law's neck. "Thank you. For everything."

Frank adjusted his coat, appearing ill at ease with her gratitude. "Stay with Gideon. Don't get any more ideas."

That was like asking her not to breathe.

She gave Jasper a tight hug and a quick kiss. "After Frank turns you over to the federal authorities, don't confess to something you didn't do. Wait for me."

"I'll be waiting." He hadn't agreed to all of her requests.

Their parting left her with the same feeling he'd confessed earlier. *Fear.*

After the train pulled out, Brigit mounted Bandit and followed Gideon, who knew the way to the Opera House. The town of Tahlequah had been burned and ransacked by both sides during the war. Residents had been rebuilt over the ten years since, and a new brick capitol building faced the square. She and Gideon were headed west of the town's center, on the lookout for a multi-story landmark that had survived the destruction.

A tickle at the back of her neck warned of someone following. A glance around at darkened buildings and homes revealed nothing. But Gideon must've felt it too, for he urged his horse into a faster walk.

She spotted the forty-foot opera house with its lights blazing on the lower level. This building was a community center for drama and debate. Based on the horses and carriages out front, an event was in progress inside. On the street behind it, the two-story home with a pitched tin roof matched the description Jasper had given her. A warm glow came from behind lace curtains hanging in the windows on either side of the door.

"That must be it."

Gideon brought his horse to a halt. "You go on and check. I'll stay out here and keep watch. Make sure no one followed us."

She dismounted and tied Bandit to the hitching post out front. With some trepidation, she approached the front door and then knocked.

A woman answered. Even in low light, the bright red color of her hair was unmistakable. She had to be Kate Colston. Her eyes widened and she gasped. "Good heavens!"

Brigit took a step back. Did Kate recognize her? They'd never met. Perhaps the shocked reaction was due to her appearance. "Mrs. Colston—"

"Call me Kate."

"Kate, I apologize for disturbing you. I am Henry Stevens' sister—"

"Of course you are. Your sister is here."

Surprise rendered Brigit mute. She had two sisters and couldn't guess. "Which one?"

"The one who looks just like you." Kate peered around Brigit's shoulder. "Is that Jasper with you?"

"No. He's..." Brigit wasn't sure how much to reveal to someone she didn't know. "With Frank Garrity. The man outside is a friend. Gideon Branch. He's watching the house in case we were followed."

Kate moved to one side and motioned. "Come in, quickly!"

Brigit stepped inside with some trepidation. "Why is Hannah here?"

"Henry sent her a message to meet him at our house. When I heard your knock, I thought it might be him."

Now, this was too strange to be believed. Henry would have no reason to be in touch with this woman, the one who'd spurned him four years ago.

Fearing a trap, Brigit hesitated when the other women started down the dimly lit hallway. "Why would my brother be contacting you?"

Kate turned with a sympathetic smile. "Henry is organizing a search. The newspapers ran a story about a murder in Denison and linked a woman calling herself Miss Stevens with a man thought to be Jasper Byrne. It claimed the two of you had fled into the Territory together."

The breath left Brigit's lungs. While this explained her brother's extraordinary measures, things were spinning out of control. "I came here to seek help with locating Charley's mother, your husband's aunt. Jasper calls her *Na*. I must find her."

"Then you shall. Follow me."

Brigit trailed her hostess down the hallway to the back of the house and into the kitchen. A fire gleamed through the wood stove's grate. Seated around a table with a lit candle at the center were two women and a tall, somber man.

Hannah ran into Brigit's embrace. "Thank God! We've been so worried."

Kate made an introduction. "Brigit, may I present my husband, Jake Colston."

He had the same golden skin and black hair that set Jasper apart. Otherwise, the two men were dissimilar. Jake stood taller, had strong, native features, and he was clean-cut and dressed like a lawyer. His tie lay on the table next to a book. "Miss Stevens. It's my pleasure to meet you, at last."

At last? He'd been expecting her?

"Brigit wants to meet *Na*," Kate said to him.

Jake helped an older woman seated next to him get up from her chair. The top of her head didn't even reach his shoulder. "This is my aunt, Mrs. Sparrowhawk. We call her *Na*.

The woman's lined face indicated advanced age, but her hair, which was pulled back into a heavy bun at the base of her neck, had the same lustrous color as her nephew's. Her eyes were bright and sharp. "You are the one Charley told me about."

A chill raised bumps on Brigit's skin. When and where had Charley told his mother about her? She'd never met *Na*'s son. How had she come to be here, at her nephew's house? Did she know... "I'm so sorry. Charley is—"

"Yes, I know." Pain flickered across his mother's face. "*Tsa-li* came to me in a vision. He had entrusted me with something. He said Raven needs it. Then he showed me a woman and told me this is the one I should give it to. I came here to see if Jake could help me find her."

"When she first saw me, she thought I was you," Hannah said.

Charley's mother had seen a ghost who showed her a vision? Unbelievable. But how else could she have known?

"Do you have what Charley gave you? The marshal's journal?" Brigit asked.

"It's here." Hannah whirled around and picked it up. "We've been looking over it. You won't believe what's in it."

"Oh, I'd believe..." Brigit's heart thudded as she took the leather-bound notebook. "Marshal Stokes killed three men in his frantic efforts to find it."

Oddly enough, the four people in the kitchen didn't seem surprised.

"The marshal isn't the only one who would go to great lengths to keep this information from coming to light," Hannah said in a low tone as if someone might be listening at a window. "Those who paid him or received payments are listed, as well as the amounts. He kept meticulous records. He must have intended to use this as blackmail."

"You need to be careful about who sees it," Jake added.

"Of course, I know that." She'd been on the run from lawmen and outlaws, and well understood the need to be careful, but she would let nothing stand in the way of getting this information to the only person who could free Jasper.

"I'll take the marshal's journal to the federal court in Fort Smith.

Jasper is about to be charged with killing Stokes, who tried to hang him to get it back. If I can present the journal as evidence to the judge, he'll see it was the marshal who had the motivation to murder people. Not Jasper."

"That might work," Jake conceded. "If the judge's name wasn't listed."

CHAPTER 23

Fort Smith, Arkansas

$\mathcal{H}$*ell on the border* was what prisoners called their lodgings in the basement of the federal courthouse in Fort Smith. The building had previously housed army officers. The basement, at one time a dining hall, was now used to house prisoners, most of them brought in by deputy U.S. marshals who policed the district, which included neighboring Indian Territory.

Close to fifty men—white, black, Indian, or a mixture—milled about the hot, dim room. Square, barred windows on each side opened into guard's quarters. No breeze blew through and damn little light got in either. A shared bucked of drinking water had been tucked into one of the old fireplaces. A twin fireplace housed the chamber pot, rarely emptied. Every so often, one of the guards or inmates would wet down the flagstone floor in an attempt to eliminate the awful smell, but it only made the air steamier and more unbearable.

Jasper crouched in one corner, trying to ignore the stench and the other inmates. When Garrity had left him in the custody of federal authorities, the former sheriff had said *see you later* without specifying time or place. Perhaps he meant in front of the gallows.

By the time Brigit found the missing journal—if she did find it— she might be too late.

Regardless, Jasper had accomplished what he'd intended to do— prevent her from confessing to killing the marshal before he could. As promised, he would keep his mouth shut until his lawyer arrived. He could as easily *sign* a confession. But until his case was called, all he could do was bide his time and wait.

Next to him, a soldier lounged against the rough stone wall, snoring away his sentence for drunkenness on duty. A peddler who'd picked the wrong pockets had positioned himself near the door, keeping a worried eye on a brawny railroad worker who'd used a spike to kill another pickpocket. One man, a Creek farmer, had attempted to engage in a conversation about how he'd acted within his rights when he vandalized a railroad track that cut through his cornfield. Empathy was all Jasper could offer.

Two more prisoners had been brought in over the past hour. A barrel-chested track layer with a bushy beard and a surly attitude. His smaller companion darted beady-eyed glances in Jasper's direction like a nervous rat. After conversing together in low tones, the big one turned around and leveled a hateful stare at Jasper. "What are you lookin' at?"

Jasper chose to remain silent. Responding to provocation seemed unwise. Besides, he didn't give bullies the satisfaction of a reaction.

"I asked you a question," the man shouted.

"Do you know who that is?" Rat-face pointed. "That's Jasper Byrne. I recognize him."

Every muscle in Jasper's body tensed. He had never laid eyes on these two.

The bearded one flexed a ham-sized fist. "I thought I smelled a yellow dog. I hear you sneaked up on a friend of mine. Shot him in the back of the head."

Had Garrity been loose-lipped? Didn't seem right. Nor did this unlikely claim of friendship with the marshal. These two troublemakers had been recruited out of some back alley with the lure of easy money by someone with access to confidential information.

"Who paid you?" Jasper asked. Someone who wanted to silence him.

"Paid us?" The smaller man rounded his eyes with false innocence. "Nobody paid us."

"We just don't like cowards." The bearded man reached down and pulled a bone-handled skinning knife out of his boot.

Guards routinely searched prisoners for weapons. If they hadn't found this one, they hadn't looked for it.

The other inmates backed away from the knife-wielding bully. One of them muttered a prayer.

Jasper slowly came to his feet. Big, angry men were a lot like big, angry bulls. To survive being gored required steady nerves and—

The bull lunged.

Jasper twisted to one side, grabbed the attacker's arm, along with the back of his shirt, and used the oaf's momentum to heave him forward, headfirst into the stone wall.

He flopped to the ground, unconscious.

Before the others could react, Jasper snatched the knife off the floor. He went into a preparatory crouch and waited for the second man to come after him.

"Guards! He's got a knife!" The other assassin scurried away, hollering his head off, while the rest of the inmates remained motionless, their attention riveted on the knife in Jasper's hand. If more than two of them ganged on him, he wouldn't make it out of here alive.

He'd skin that rat first.

"Guards!" the man screeched through the barred window.

From inside the guardroom came the sound of activity. Moments later, the wooden door beneath the courthouse steps opened and two armed guards stepped into the small boxed entry space between freedom and another door, this one forged from iron bars.

Jasper dropped the knife, but not before the guards saw him with it. They unlocked the cell door and drew their guns. The other inmates scattered. Jasper knew better than to resist when the guards tossed him onto the flagstones and locked cuffs on his wrists.

"That bull over there came at me with a knife," Jasper motioned with his head in the direction of the unconscious attacker. "His friend —the one who was hollering—might be armed, too."

"Shut up." One of the guards said. The two of them dragged Jasper across the damp floor. They pulled him to his feet and jerked his arms over his head, then chained the cuffs to an iron ring mounted on one of the sturdy uprights.

After that, they retrieved the unconscious man and dragged him out with them. Flecks of blood dotted the flagstones. The bull would have one hell of a headache when he woke up.

Jasper took no satisfaction from what he considered a simple act of self-defense. He doubted the guards would report it that way. They'd probably been bribed, too. And Garrity? Doubt wrestled with a desperate desire to believe in the integrity of the former lawman.

The first night Jasper had spent in the Parsons jail, he'd confided the truth about a railroad executive's scheme to hire train robbers. The confession hadn't gotten him anywhere. Garrity, the sheriff at the time, had sworn he'd done everything in his power to gain justice. It just wasn't enough. After the legal system failed both of them, Garrity had turned in his badge. Had he become embittered? Cynical? For all Jasper knew, Frank could've instructed Gideon to steal the journal from Brigit and bring it to him so he could get rid of it.

Jasper jerked at the fetters holding his arms above his head. Pain shot through his wrists and shoulders. Whatever was going on, locked up, he couldn't help Brigit.

The rat-faced man remained near the iron door. "You're a dead man, Byrne," he taunted from his position of safety.

Jasper released a dry laugh. "We all die. It's how we do it that matters."

His tormenter seemed to grow braver and moved a little closer. "You'll die squirming at the end of a rope...unless someone gets rid of you sooner."

Jasper maintained an indifferent expression. He could kick, but if the rat was armed, kicks wouldn't help for long.

Before the smaller man had moved more than a few feet, the Creek farmer positioned himself in front of Jasper. He crossed his arms, making his point without a word. A moment later, another one of the Indian prisoners joined him. Soon, there were four of them, standing on each side of the upright support where Jasper was chained. Whether they'd done it as a show of solidarity or because they didn't appreciate unfair odds, their interference was timely and welcomed. How long they'd stand guard was hard to say. Whether anyone else would interfere was also difficult to predict. Jasper reckoned he wouldn't last much longer than a day or two if those guards forgot about him.

Had Brigit found the journal? Had she made it to town? If she had, she would've stormed the courthouse. He smiled at the image of Saint Brigit, riding to the rescue. She'd refuse to give up her heroic, if vain, attempts to save him.

"We're partners, remember?"

He'd never had a partner before, had never trusted anyone enough to let them close. Not even the few men who thought they were his trusted friends. Brigit had demanded to be accepted on equal terms and had offered him the same. She hadn't looked down on him with haughty superiority or with the kind of terror a monster might evoke—the primary reactions he received from most women in her world. A world she would return to after all this was over.

Jasper had known from the moment she'd opened that coffin to release him, that he would not be free for long. Certainly not long enough to marry or raise a family. Now, it looked like he wouldn't even live long enough to offer her the love he'd stored up in his heart. If he'd opened up and told her how he felt about her, how she meant everything to him, she might've gotten the idea they could have a future together. He knew better than to hold onto that dream.

What would she do after he was gone? Hopefully, she wouldn't grieve too much and would eventually find someone else. Someone honest and smart, like her. An honorable man who'd love and respect and treasure her, as she deserved.

Jasper tried to rustle up magnanimous sentiments toward his unknown successor—and failed. He'd go to his grave miserably jealous of a man he'd never know.

Hours later, the heavy clink of a key turning in a lock came from behind Jasper. From where he stood, chained to the support, he couldn't see who had entered, but he tried not to get too excited. It was probably just one of the guards who'd returned to find out whether the other prisoners had killed the man they'd left helpless.

"For God's sake, why is he chained up? Take him down from there."

Garrity?

Jasper twisted in a rush of excitement, trying to see the man whose voice he recognized. Was Brigit with him? Couldn't see her...or hear her.

If she were here, she'd be the one raising hell.

He sagged with disappointment. It was still early. She'd barely had time to reach *Na's* house, much less make it back to the railway station.

Footsteps sounded.

"We put him here after he started a fight," a guard said.

"He didn't start it," declared one of the four prisoners protecting Jasper.

"Get out of the way." The guard blocked Jasper's view while reaching up to release him.

Jasper's lifeless arms dropped with his wrists still cuffed. If it would've done any good, he would've filed an objection. As it was, he couldn't manage a simple *thank you* to those men who'd saved his skin. It took all his concentration to stay on his feet, even leaning against the post for support. His mouth felt so dry he could manage only a single word. "Water."

"You heard him." Garrity's authoritative tone sent the guards scrambling.

A tin cup was passed. The lawman held it while Jasper gulped the tepid water. It was a kindness he hadn't expected and it damn near moved him to tears.

"Good of you to drop by, Francesco." Jasper hoped his wry tone covered the roughness in his voice.

"No es nada," Frank replied. Hard to tell whether he was joking. "Let's find a place to sit, brother."

"Relatives get ten minutes," the guard informed them. He left them in the enclosed area between the cell door and the wooden door leading outside. The space was used for lawyers to meet with their clients. It was also used for family visits.

Jasper sat down on the bench and gave a disbelieving laugh. "Did you tell them we're related?"

Garrity dipped the empty cup into a water bucket next to the bench before he sat down. "Only by marriage. I wouldn't claim you otherwise." He held out the cup. "Can you manage?"

"Think so. I can feel my arms now." Jasper cradled the cup in his tingling hands. He drained it before resting his head against the wall. He still didn't know if he could trust Garrity, but he was finding it hard not to like him. *"Francesco.* It's not a Mexican name. It's Italian."

Garrity huffed like he was put out. "How the hell would you know that?"

"One of my relatives was Italian."

"I thought you were Cherokee."

"I am."

"And Irish."

"That too. My grandmother on my father's side, her Pa was Italian. His name was—"

"Francesco."

"You got it."

Garrity appeared impressed. "Do you know how to speak Italian?"

"Not a lick. I do know a little Spanish. *Bring me whiskey. Spank my bottom.* Things like that."

"Useful in a brothel," the sheriff said under his breath.

A few of the inmates watched with curiosity. Most of them had lost interest quickly. Even the rat had slunk away to where Jasper couldn't see him.

"Any word from Brigit?" Jasper spoke low and tried not to sound desperate.

"Not yet." Garrity's typically nonreactive features showed an astonishing range of emotions: anger, frustration, worry. Nothing encouraging. "The judge has called your case. First thing tomorrow."

"Ah. I wondered why you were here. Came to pass on the good news." Jasper rolled his aching shoulders. He flexed his fingers to help the feeling return faster and to give him something to think about other than the fact that he'd run out of time. Something like panic tightened his chest. He released a shaky breath. "I'll be ready."

"Don't confess to something you didn't do." Garrity's severe tone had softened. Maybe because he was trying to talk quietly.

Still holding the empty cup, Jasper rested his cuffed wrists on his lap and wondered what to make of the remark. It was the perfect chance to encourage his self-destructive streak and take advantage of his fear for Brigit's safety, but that wasn't what Garrity was doing. "Did Brigit tell you to say that?"

"She didn't need to. I know what happened. It wasn't hard to figure out."

The lawman had been careful to investigate the scene and gather information, but he hadn't objected to letting an outlaw take credit for the kill. Until now.

Jasper eyed the upright lawman. "Why are you telling me this?"

It took longer than usual for the slow-talking sheriff to answer. "I've been doing some more thinking since I left you here. Truth is important."

His conscience bothered him?

Jasper shook his head. "Here's the *truth.* I'm not letting her take the fall for this."

"Wouldn't expect you to," Garrity shot back, without hesitating.

Even a duty-bound lawman couldn't deny it made more sense than *the truth.*

"Then you know what I have to do." Jasper waited for confirmation.

"I know you *think* that's what you have to do. But I'm asking you to wait a little longer. Tell the judge you won't enter a plea until after your lawyer arrives to advise you."

Jasper couldn't make sense of it. Either he'd misread the lawman or Garrity had got religion. Nothing else would explain such a sudden change of heart. "Have you been at a tent revival?"

"Has all the blood from your brain pooled in your feet?" Garrity snatched the cup away. After refilling it, he returned it to Jasper. "Have some water. It might help you think more clearly."

Being tortured didn't facilitate clear thinking.

Jasper cupped the cool tin in his palms. He took a sip while he considered what Garrity had asked and whether he should grant the request. "No jury will believe me. No judge will free me. A lawyer won't change that."

Met with silence, he looked up.

Garrity's expression appeared less angry. His face was lined with weariness. "Do you recall I told you I was going to do some investigating around town?"

Jasper nodded. "I thought that was lawman-speak for checking out the local saloons."

"I don't imbibe."

At one time, Garrity had regularly *imbibed.* But if he wasn't drunk, saved, or crazy, maybe he'd come back for another reason.

"Have you learned something new?" Jasper asked.

"A few things. And I'm still working on my statement for the hearing." Garrity pulled a fob from his vest pocket and opened his watch.

Their ten minutes was up or he was tired of talking. Either way, Jasper had only one more question. "Will it make any difference?"

"It won't if you sign a confession tomorrow."

CHAPTER 24

*I*n an upstairs bedroom, Brigit peeked out from behind the curtain. Across the street, behind the Opera House, which should've been empty at this early hour, two men loitered. The same ones who'd been there past closing last night.

"Are they still there?" asked Hannah.

"I'm afraid so." Brigit stepped away from the window. Her anxiety was already high. Now, it crashed against her in tidal waves.

"Who do you think put the dogs on your trail?"

"It could be those outlaws Jasper tricked. More likely, it's someone on the marshal's list. He was doing a brisk business in bribery and extortion."

Brigit tugged the cuffs of a Union-blue jacket. If this ruse worked, it would allow her to escape without being followed. She smoothed the knee-length skirt, which fit like a tunic over a pair of wool trousers. The outfit was unconventional and unique to Kate.

Hannah stood in front of a full-length mirror, admiring herself in the oversized shirt and skirt. "This reminds me of a kilt, only longer." She adjusted the gun belt to rest above her hips. "I think that's right. How do I look?"

"More dangerous than I did when I wore it."

"You're just saying that to flatter me." Hannah combed her fingers through her hair, which had been cut at a similar length. Both of them were well-practiced in being each other or even the same person.

Brigit lifted the riding hat off the dresser. The tulle netting would partially conceal her face. The beet juice and honey mixture had tinted her brown hair to a reddish hue. It wasn't as bright as Kate's, but it was close enough. "How I wish I hadn't lost that red wig."

"How did you?"

"In a fight. Technically, Jasper was fighting. I tried to help."

Her twin's shocked expression turned to horror.

"It's not as bad as it sounds." Brigit checked her Derringer pistol to make certain it was loaded. "Jasper is in far more danger now than he was then."

Hannah tied the woven sash around her waist. "And what about you?"

Brigit lifted the short skirt and tucked her pistol into a nifty pocket sewn into the trousers. Kate would've made a great detective if she weren't so busy with her suffrage work. "If someone sent those men outside to kill me, they've had ample opportunity. They must be waiting for something or watching to see where I go."

"After I get to Parsons, I could set a trap for them," Hannah offered. "Your friend Mr. Branch could help me spring it. He strikes me as a capable bounty hunter."

"He is. But all you need to do is lead them away so I can escape. Just keep them busy. Find out who they are, but don't set any bait. Not until you hear from me." Brigit paced in front of the window. "Please, be careful."

Hannah's laugh had a hollow ring. "You're talking to the *cautious* one. I do wish you'd reconsider. Wait for reinforcements. I can send a message to Mr. Pinkerton—

"No. We can't wait that long. Jasper will be in the grave before you can rally the troops."

"We'll do it your way then." Hannah sat on the edge of the bed and slipped on the moccasins.

Brigit tucked a notebook into one of Kate's tapestry bags. "I'll take this duplicate with all the entries copied over. Kate will pass the original journal to Henry and tell him to contact federal investigators. Show them the evidence."

Hannah cocked her head with a look of bemusement. "I don't think Henry is coming here expecting to be *given* an assignment. He'll want to go with you to Fort Smith."

Brigit waved her hand, dismissing their older brother's tendency to take control. "It doesn't matter what Henry wants. Jake is skilled in the law, clever, diplomatic—

"Less bossy."

"Our sister-in-law Lucy has smoothed Henry's rough edges. Oh, and I've thought of a way she can help, once we get Jasper out of jail and ensure the real criminals are locked up. We can talk about it later."

"You are marvelous at devising plans," Hannah said, with no hint of sarcasm.

Brigit sank onto the bed as her confidence withered. The fear she'd kept at bay overtook her. "If I'm so marvelous, Jasper wouldn't be in jail right now. He wouldn't feel compelled to sacrifice himself to save me."

Her sister drew her into an embrace, rocking her as one would a child who needed comforting. "It's not the plan that's the problem, dear sister. It's the fact that we can't get people to follow orders."

Leave it to Hannah to ease the tension with a quip, albeit one that held a grain of truth.

Brigit used a handkerchief to dry her tears before they dripped on the outfit. "Jasper doesn't follow orders. He goes along sometimes, but he won't cooperate if he thinks I'll be hurt."

"He sounds like a man I'd like very much."

"You would like him. He's..." Brigit tried to find the best words to describe Jasper. "Brave. Clever. Beautiful."

"So are you." Hannah took Brigit's hand and turned it, palm up. "Do you remember the old woman who told our fortunes?"

"How old were we, thirteen?" Brigit recalled the event with crystal clarity. How hopeless and frightened she'd felt afterward.

Her sister lightly traced her fingertip over a crease. "This lifeline, see how it's broken? She said only one thing could repair it."

True love.

Brigit yanked her hand away before Hannah finished. "Stop it. We're wasting time on silly prophecies told by a charlatan. You need to leave now so that Jake and I can catch the train after those men are gone."

"Yes, you're right." Hannah hugged Brigit and kissed her cheek. "Go with God."

"And God go with you," Brigit replied, repeating the blessing her mother and father had passed on to them so many years ago, at a time when she'd believed those words.

She stood at the window and watched as Hannah fastened the saddle bag behind Bandit's saddle. Her twin rode off behind Gideon, pretending to be unaware of the spies hiding on the far side of the Opera House. A moment later, the two men followed.

Brigit rested her hand over her heart. It palpitated so wildly it made her dizzy. The odd sensation had happened with some frequency after she'd been raped, but had lessened after she'd learned to focus her mind and cap her emotions. All this talk of fortune-tellers and visions and ghosts had put her on edge.

A knock came at the door.

"Time to leave," Kate announced. "Jake has brought the buggy around. I don't see anyone out there who looks suspicious. I think your ruse succeeded."

At least one thing had worked out the way it was supposed to.

Brigit gathered her bag. She had the most powerful—and dangerous—weapon she could wield. Incriminating evidence.

Kate helped her arrange the net around the hat brim.

"Where is *Na*?" Brigit asked. "I wanted to say goodbye."

"She's putting Samuel down for his nap."

The toddler had been in bed the night before.

"I wish I'd had more time to see him," Brigit said wistfully.

"You will. When you return for a visit. With Jasper."

God willing.

"Some people may speak to you in Cherokee," Kate added, in what came across as an afterthought. "Pretend you've lost your voice."

Or her mind.

Brigit's resolution bowed beneath the weight of recrimination. "I shouldn't have involved you and Jake this deeply."

Kate took Brigit by the shoulders. "Remember, *Wa-ya* is the name given to Jake. It means *wolf.* My brave wolf will help you through this."

Brigit hugged her new friend. "Oh, Kate, I can never thank you enough. Give Henry my love when he gets here. And tell him he has a very important part to play. Maybe the most important."

"Henry won't let you down either."

"I know he won't."

Her family—including this one by extension—had circled the wagons. They would be there for her and Jasper. And one day, he would become part of this family, if she had anything to say about it.

Outside, Jake assisted her into the buggy, holding her hand, kissing it, smiling, treating her as if she were his wife. He put on a good show. "You have what we need for my petition to the judge?" he asked her.

"Yes. In my satchel."

If this scheme worked, Jasper would be released into Jake's custody. Once they'd fled to Indian Territory, Jasper would be safe while she and Hannah worked with authorities to locate and arrest the wrongdoers.

The plan hinged on so many things going right.

Nothing she'd planned had ever gone off without a hitch.

CHAPTER 25

The cell door clanked, jolting Jasper into full wakefulness. His legs wouldn't work at first, and he had to use the wall for support to stand. He'd be less likely to fall asleep on his feet.

He didn't dare let down his guard for a single minute. Not with the other prisoners who had helped him or with Frank. Not even with Brigit, if she happened to show up. He had to be prepared to do whatever was necessary to ensure she'd be safe.

"Byrne. The judge is ready to see you," one of the guards announced. He waited by the cell door.

"What time is it?" Jasper asked.

"Time to get upstairs."

Frank Garrity had said he'd return. Maybe he hadn't found any useful information or he'd changed his mind? Or Brigit hadn't shown up and he'd gone after her. It could be any or all of those reasons.

The guard cuffed Jasper's hands in front of him before escorting him outside. He blinked in the bright daylight, then stumbled when the guard pushed him toward the stairs that led up to the first level. At the door, he was met by the bailiff, who escorted him inside the courtroom.

A big Stars and Stripes hung behind the judge's perch. The man sitting at the raised desk had no hair on top of his head, yet had plenty over his lip, perhaps as proof he could grow some.

In front of the judge's bench, another man, this one wearing spectacles, hunched over a table with a notebook and ink pen. Another fellow in a black suit occupied a table that faced the empty chairs where a jury would be seated.

Only three other people were in the room.

Jasper approached them from behind, and he could tell one of them was a woman. She wore a riding hat with netting wrapped around the brim. Was she trying to hide her features? His pounding heart told him the woman had to be Brigit.

"Mr. Byrne, approach the bench," the judge said. "Along with your attorney."

The two men and the woman turned. One of them was Jake Colston, and he was dressed like a lawyer in a crisp black suit. He tucked the woman's hand over his arm in a gesture that conveyed possession.

Only the lower part of her face was visible, but Jasper knew the shape. He'd memorized the feel of her skin against his lips. He'd never seen her wear those trousers or the odd, knee-length dress.

Brigit had come to court dressed like a suffragette...like Kate. She was pretending to be Jake's wife. Her intentions weren't clear, but if she'd decided not to reveal her true identity, it must mean she didn't intend to confess.

Jasper breathed a little easier.

Frank Garrity appeared to have gotten a haircut and a shave for the occasion. He barely acknowledged Jasper. He hadn't mentioned that Jake would be here instead of Mr. Moore, the attorney who'd originally taken the robbery case. It was a curious development, though not concerning. Jake was one of the best lawyers in the Territory.

When Jasper got close enough, he acknowledged the fake Kate with a polite, "Ma'am."

She nodded, just as politely. "Mr. Byrne. I hope you don't mind that I came along with my husband to these proceedings. We have important business in town."

Her voice had a flat, nasal quality. She even sounded like Kate.

"No, I don't mind." Jasper rubbed his hand over his mouth so no one would notice he'd smiled. What did she mean by *important business*? Had she found the journal? They must have *something* planned.

"Let's make this quick," the judge said. "You've been accused of murder, Mr. Byrne. How do you intend to plead?"

"May I say something first, your honor?" Jake held up his hand and lifted two fingers. "Two things."

"Which are?"

"We have an eyewitness who swears Mr. Byrne didn't fire the shot that killed the marshal."

Jasper's blood froze. *Oh, no. They wouldn't.* Not with Brigit in the room, disguised or not.

The judge narrowed his eyes suspiciously. "Who fired the gun?"

"Mr. Garrity has a statement," Jake said before Jasper could give his answer.

The lawman shot Jasper a look that was easy to interpret. *Don't interrupt.*

That depended on what he said.

"I brought along some notes." Garrity withdrew a folded paper from his coat pocket, along with his spectacles, which he put on. "This past week, I got deputized, along with my partner Gideon Branch, to go after the fugitive Jasper Byrne, as well as the woman who aided him, a reporter named Alice Robb. We tracked them into Choctaw Territory to the *San Bois* mountains."

Jasper shifted his gaze to Brigit, who didn't turn her head to look at him. She appeared cool and calm, but when she wet her lips, he knew better.

"When we caught up with the two fugitives, we found Marshal Stokes dead from a gunshot wound to the back of the head." Frank's laborious account continued. "Jasper Byrne had fresh rope burns on his neck and wrists, and there was other evidence that Stokes had tried to hang him. He told us the marshal was looking for a particular item that had been taken from him and he'd threatened to kill Mr. Byrne to get it back. Mr. Byrne didn't have it."

The judge's brows drew into a frown. "What was it?"

Frank glanced up. "I'll get to that in a moment." He returned to reading his paper. "We also found a shallow grave, which had been disturbed, along with a body in a state of decomposition that suggested he'd been buried for a while. I'd say at least three weeks. He's been identified as Lester Kinkaid, a missing Pinkerton agent. Marshal Stokes admitted to Byrne that he'd shot—"

"That's hearsay," the prosecutor hollered as he came to his feet.

Jasper wiped his hand over his face. Every useful detail in the story would be considered *hearsay*. He hoped this wasn't the plan.

"The woman, Alice Robb, confessed to shooting Marshal Stokes to save Mr. Byrne, who at the time was hanging from a tree." Frank looked over the spectacles at the judge. "By his neck."

"We know what *hanging* means," the judge said with irritation in his voice.

"I'll make it quick."

"Please do."

Did Frank plan to blame Alice Robb? That bucket would spring leaks as soon as the prosecutor started punching holes in it.

"What about the woman named in a Denison newspaper article?" the prosecutor said. "Brigit Stevens. The story said she was traveling with a man in disguise, who turned out to be Mr. Byrne."

"Ain't that hearsay?" Frank Garrity scratched his head.

He played the hayseed better than a hayseed.

"Answer the question," the judge ordered.

The lanky lawman heaved a sigh, then cast a look at the prosecutor that said he was too dumb to be in his job. "It's the same woman, your honor. Alice Robb dressed up and *pretended* to be Miss Stevens. None of the witnesses had ever met the *real* Brigit Stevens. You can't believe the sister of the famous railroad builder, Henry Stevens, would get tangled up with trash like Jasper Byrne."

Jasper pressed his lips together. He couldn't risk a retort, and

Garrity, damn him, knew this. No wonder he hadn't wanted to spill the beans on this plan. He didn't have extra evidence. He was bluffing with a damn risky hand. All of it was true, yet he'd woven together the facts to deliberately mislead the judge. This had to be Brigit's idea and she'd somehow talked both Frank and Jake into it.

"Why would a reporter pose as Miss Stevens?" the prosecutor pressed.

Frank shook his head. *You idiot*, the gesture implied. "So she could more easily gain information from a friend of Henry Stevens. Reporters do things like that. Miss Robb was still chasing a story. That's why she helped Byrne in the first place. Are we having *her* trial here?"

"Finish your statement," the judge ordered.

Frank read from his notes. "After we'd captured Mr. Byrne and Miss Robb, I left immediately to bring Byrne back to jail. My deputy kept Miss Robb with him, having gained her cooperation to search for the item that belonged to the marshal, which had come into the possession of the Pinkerton agent, Mr. Kinkaid."

"What item?" the judge demanded.

"Produce Miss Robb!" the prosecutor hollered.

"She escaped," Frank said bluntly. "But we found what we were looking for. Mr. Colston can answer the rest of your questions. If you don't mind, I'll take my leave."

Jasper had no idea what to think when the sheriff sallied out the door. Had Brigit found the journal or not? Was this still part of the act or was Frank done and headed home for supper?

The judge leaned on his arms. "What do you have to present, Mr. Colston?"

Jake produced a leather-bound book out of a case he'd brought with him.

Jasper's breath caught. *Could it be?*

"This journal, your honor, belonged to Marshal Stokes." Jake opened the notebook, perused it, as if looking for something specific, then spread the pages in front of the judge and pointed. "May I bring your attention to this entry. I believe it will suffice to satisfy your curiosity and call into question a murder charge against my client."

The judge looked at the open notebook. His bald head looked shiny under the glow of gas lights hanging from the ceiling. He appeared to have broken out in a sweat.

What did that little book say? Would it convince the judge to lighten the charge?

Jasper craned his neck, trying in vain to see.

"What's in that book?" The prosecutor approached the bench.

"Sufficient information to persuade His Honor to set a reasonable bond for my client, and to release Jasper Byrne into my custody until this case can be further investigated." Jake drew back the side of his coat and put his hands on his hips, revealing a holstered revolver.

It was a clear sign and Jasper knew it.

Be ready to bolt.

What was *Wa-ya* thinking? Any attempt to escape would put Brigit in the crossfire.

She smoothed her short skirt and he spotted a shape beneath it. The crazy woman had a gun under there!

Of course, she did. She had guns hidden all over her person.

"The bond is set at a hundred dollars." Down came the gavel, almost striking Jake's hand when he reached for the journal.

The judge snatched away the notebook. "I need to review this evidence."

"Keep it," Jake said. "I'll take our man."

Jasper stared in disbelief. Had they had just conducted a trade?

Jake laid crisp greenbacks on the table in front of the fellow who'd been writing. "There's one hundred dollars."

The little man shook his head. "I'm not the one you pay."

"But you don't mind taking care of this, do you?" Jake patted the fellow's shoulder. "My wife and I are in a hurry to get to an appointment."

"No! Wait! You can't leave..." the prosecutor stammered.

The judge shot him a quelling look.

"Time to go," Brigit announced.

Jasper held out his hands to the bailiff, who also took his cue from the judge and unlocked the cuffs. The moment he was free, Brigit directed him toward the door.

Jake followed behind them.

"What's Garrity up to?" Jasper whispered. "Did you plan all this?"

"Somewhat. On the fly," she whispered. "We ran into Frank outside a few minutes before the hearing. That statement was his idea. Very smart."

The whole thing was smart and crazy, and they'd done it for him, which made the least sense of all. He hadn't expected a rescue, and could hardly believe the judge would just let him walk out the door.

He threw a worried glance over his shoulder, but Brigit dragged him outside before he could ascertain whether they were being followed.

At the bottom of the stairs, Brigit pointed to three horses hitched to the rail. "Those are ours."

Strong-looking mounts. Jake must've paid dearly at the livery. And he'd spent a hundred to cover the bond. The debts were piling up.

"Thanks." Jasper couldn't think of what else to say. Thank you wasn't nearly enough. Frank Garrity had risked his reputation. Jake had risked his career. And Brigit risked getting caught. She would put herself smack dab in the middle of a gunfight. He dearly wished he could throttle her. Spank her. Kiss her.

Jake swung up on a big bay. "We'll ride to the river."

"Then what? Swim?"

Brigit went for the smaller spotted pony and mounted astride in her feminine breeches. "Frank will meet you and me and ferry us across. Jake will take our mounts and ride off in a different direction."

Her idea? Had to be. It sounded dangerous.

Jasper touched his heels to the black mare, putting himself between Brigit and whoever might decide to follow them.

They rode across the former parade grounds. As soon as they reached the busy street, Brigit turned toward the river.

A shot resounded.

The ping of a bullet striking something metal spooked Jasper's mount. He forced the horse to make a hard circle so it couldn't bolt. Coming around, he saw Brigit turn in her saddle with a look of alarm.

It was the worse thing she could do. Stop.

"Go on!" Jasper waved at her. "I'll catch up."

The next bullet struck a water trough.

Jasper couldn't tell where the shot had come from, possibly behind a wagon or inside one of the buildings facing the street.

Brigit passed the leaky trough, riding toward him. In the wrong direction.

"No! Go back!"

Another shot rang out.

She jerked to one side and then toppled off the pony.

Everything slowed—even Jasper's breathing—before it sped up. He drove his heels into the horse and rode up next to her, leaping to the ground.

Brigit staggered to her feet with her arm cradled at her side and her face screwed into a pained expression. The pony had run off, riderless. Other people in the street were scattering for cover. In all the mayhem, the shooter wouldn't have a clear shot.

"Get on my horse!" Jasper hoisted her upward. She groaned as she threw her leg over the saddle. He mounted behind her and then wrapped his arm around her waist. His heart jerked when his palm grew slick with the warm blood soaking her jacket.

He kicked the mare into a canter, dodging confused riders and drivers. A fast-moving target would be harder to hit. "Lean back. I've got you."

It wasn't far to the river, but each pounding step produced a new moan and a gush of wet heat in his hand.

Sweet Jesus.

She'd bleed to death before he could get her to safety.

CHAPTER 26

"Wake up! Open your blasted eyes and look at me."

Jasper was issuing orders again.

Brigit turned her head toward his voice and blinked to clear the blurriness from her vision. Her darling sat beside the bed, holding her hand in both of his pressed against his forehead.

She flexed her fingers to capture a lock of his dark hair. He jerked up straight, his pained frown lifting into an expression of astonishment, as though he hadn't believed she would follow his commands.

She'd follow him anywhere. He ought to know that by now.

Over his shoulder, she spotted a familiar window and curtain and the walls of a bedroom she'd been in earlier. Why had they come back here, to the Colston's house?

Memories flashed in broken pieces. She had to think hard to fit them together. They'd planned to meet Frank at the river and had boarded a ferry...and then what? She recalled another man whose face she didn't recognize. Jasper had bellowed then, too. He'd threatened to kill the sawbones if the surgeon didn't save her.

Jasper squeezed her fingers. "Brigit?"

Had she drifted off again? She forced her eyelids up.

Heavens. Poor Jasper looked terrible. Dark circles beneath his eyes made them appear sunken. His whiskers were wet. With tears? She couldn't remember ever seeing him cry.

The doctor had said something about a dangerous loss of blood.

"Am I dying?"

"You will *not* die. Trust me."

Brigit smiled at his firm tone. He thought he issue a command and even Death would obey. "I do trust you. Even if I don't always follow your orders."

"Here's an order you need to follow." He released her hand to reach for a cup on the table next to the bed. "*Na* says you've got to drink this tea."

Jasper slipped one hand beneath her head. He held the cup as she took a mouthful of bitter liquid and forced it down.

"Ugh. Do you always mind her?"

"*Everyone* minds her."

Brigit recalled a tiny Cherokee woman she'd met, who was hardly intimidating. Perhaps she couldn't remember everything that had happened because she'd fainted when the doctor had performed the emergency surgery without ether. "How long have I been here?"

"Almost week. For most of it, you've been out of your head." Jasper adjusted her pillow, which made her more comfortable. "We thought you'd come around, but you just kept sleeping. Sometimes it looked like you weren't breathing."

"It hurts to breathe," she admitted.

"I'll bet it does. That sawbones said one of your ribs deflected the bullet. You're lucky it didn't go through your lung."

She took another painful breath. "Who shot me?"

"If I knew, he'd be dead." Jasper stroked her hair away from her face with a gentleness that seemed in stark contrast with what he'd just said about killing someone.

A terrible thought occurred and she gripped Jasper's hand. "Was anyone else hurt?"

Jasper lifted her fingers to his lips. "Everyone else is fine. Hannah is in the kitchen—for the time being. We've had a few tussles about who gets to stay in here with you. She said she'd call in reinforcements."

"And Frank?"

"He's gone home."

"Good. Claire is expecting. She needs him more than I do." Brigit settled her head into the soft feather pillow. "I hope you thanked him for his help."

"I did. Except for that crazy story about Alice Robb. It made the papers. There's been speculation that she was the one in Fort Smith who got shot."

Brigit couldn't see how the mistaken identity would be too much of a problem, but she wasn't thinking clearly. "Have you heard from Henry?"

"He's out with the federal investigators. Exterminating cockroaches." Jasper stroked her forefinger to the tip and kissed it. "You've got a ferocious family."

And an attentive beau.

"Stop kissing my finger and give me a proper kiss."

He leaned over and touched his lips to hers. "How's that?"

"It'll hold me until I'm up to something with more fire." Weariness closed her eyes, although she kept their fingers laced. "Talking is tiring."

"You rest. I'm not going anywhere."

"Promise?"

"I'll swear it if you want."

"We can talk about vows later."

～

JASPER DRAGGED himself to the kitchen after Hannah pushed him out of the bedroom. She'd told him she would alert him when Brigit woke up again.

Before today, he'd feared she wouldn't make it. It had seemed as if her spirit had wandered off into that shadowy land between life and death. He'd been there once. Lost, afraid, searching everywhere for his mother, his grandfather, his father, anyone who would come for him.

He'd kept a vigil at Brigit's side. Held her hand, swearing he would not let go. Now that he was sure she would recover, he had to find the courage to break his promise.

Brigit wouldn't have caught that bullet, if not for him. She wouldn't be fighting for her life if he weren't in it. As much as he wanted to, he could not hold onto her when it wasn't in her best interest. As soon as she was well, he had to send her home. Wherever that was. With her family. Somewhere she would be safe. Not looking over her shoulder all the time or getting in the way of bullets meant for him.

Kate set a bowl of soup on the table in front of him. "Aren't you hungry?"

It smelled good and he needed something to eat, but he didn't have an appetite. "Thank you."

"I didn't make the soup. *Na* did."

"It's not just the soup I'm thanking you for. I owe you for what you and Jake did."

Kate patted his shoulder. "You owe us nothing. We're family."

He wasn't related to her at all and to Jake only indirectly. "How do you figure that?"

Na put a platter of corncakes next to a pitcher of molasses. "Clan is family. You know that. You just choose to ignore it."

He had his reasons. The primary one being, that he didn't want to subject his mother's relations to his bad luck, which rubbed off like soot from a train. Charley had the right idea. Outlaws—even reformed ones—needed to keep their loved ones at a distance if they wanted them to live.

Jake bounced his year-old son on his knee. The baby's unrestrained laughter made Jasper smile. This was the kind of life he'd imagined he would have one day, back when he was a boy. Before violence and war had crushed his family and burnt his dreams to ashes.

He and Jake might've been on the same destructive path had his friend not changed course. Jake had warned him. Brigit had offered him a second chance. But by the time she'd entered his life, it was already too late.

"What do I do now?" The question was out before Jasper realized he'd said it aloud.

"Something you don't do well," Jake answered. "You wait. I've filed a motion to have your case moved to the Cherokee courts, arguing that you're a citizen and any crime you might have committed was on Indian land."

Jasper didn't hold out much hope. "The judge won't be in a mood to grant you any favors once he realizes you gave him a *copy* of that journal and not the original."

"Our sleight of hand may help our cause. The judge can't make that list disappear. In the meantime, stay close to home."

Home? Jasper pondered the meaning of the word. He lived in a cabin on the land he'd grown up on, but he wouldn't call it home. It hadn't been for a long time.

The toddler squirmed until his father set him on the floor then he took a few wobbly steps toward Jasper, who returned him to his father before he did something stupid...like cry.

"Jake, we need more wood," Kate called from where she stood at the stove.

"I'll take care of it." Jasper sprang to his feet. It gave him something to do to take his mind off things he didn't want to think about.

"Sit down and eat." Jake stood with the baby in his arms.

Jasper was out the door before his friend could stop him. He found a stack of logs beside the house and picked up an ax.

A moment later, Jake came around the corner with his sleeves rolled up. "Are you always so hard-headed?"

"Only when I want to cut wood." Jasper balanced a log on the chopping block. He brought the ax down, splitting the log in half.

Jake picked up the pieces.

"I can handle this on my own," Jasper grumbled.

"Nobody doubts that. What I wonder is whether you can handle *not* being on your own."

"What's that supposed to mean?" Jasper braced his feet and balanced a second log. He brought the ax down with a thwack.

"Exactly what I said." Jake collected an armful of split wood. "You can come inside if you want to have a regular conversation. If you'd rather split logs, be my guest."

It took Jasper six logs to work off his irritation, and another half-dozen to wear through his resistance. He rested his hands on his knees, breathing heavily.

What was there to talk about? Talking wouldn't change anything. It wouldn't give him a life with Brigit, which was what he wanted. He wanted it so badly he would sell his soul for the chance. But that was the problem. He'd already bartered his soul away, and the Devil wasn't giving it back. Praying wouldn't do any good, either. God had given up on him a long time ago.

Brigit hadn't. She was too stubborn.

"Jasper?"

His breath caught in a half-second before he realized the speaker was only a mirror image. Hannah's smile didn't have that wry curve on one side.

"Is Brigit awake?" he asked.

"She is. *Na* is with her, feeding her soup."

"I told her I'd be there." Jasper brushed the shavings off his trousers and started back to the house.

Hannah got in his way. "Hold on, cowboy."

Jasper released a dry laugh. "I do not—and have never—herded cows for a living."

"Maybe you ought to consider it. It's time you changed careers. You'd certainly fit in with a more pungent crowd."

Hannah was way too much like her sister, except not in the nice ways. He hadn't exactly been focused on cleanliness while Brigit lay near death.

He held up his hands. "All right. I'll get a bath. After I check on her."

Hannah held her ground. "As I said, she's eating now. And a bath is an excellent idea after we have a few words together. Alone."

Well, that sounded ominous, although she hadn't brought a gun along. Not one he could see. And while Hannah hadn't come out and accused him of anything up to this point, he'd seen her eyeing him with concern, and, at times, downright confusion.

"If you want to flay me for getting your sister shot, I'm way ahead of you."

Hannah crossed her arms over her chest, a gesture that suggested defensiveness, oddly enough. "No. I wanted to thank you for being Brigit's protector these past two and half weeks."

Jasper stood there, flummoxed. *Thank* him? That's why Hannah had come out here? He hadn't imagined she would have a good opinion of him after he brought Brigit back half-dead. He shifted his stance, uncomfortable with accepting gratitude. "Nice of you to say. All things considered, she might not want to hire me again."

The twin didn't blink at his half-hearted joke. "Based on what she told me, I thought she trusted you."

He drove his fingers through his hair, not wanting to admit the truth. He had coveted the things he knew better than to take from her, and then he'd taken them, knowing it would destroy her. "Brigit does trust me, which makes what happened worse. I couldn't get to her before that bullet did."

"My understanding is that she rode back to help you and put herself in danger. You had no control over that. She exercised poor judgment." Hannah's cool assessment of what had been a chaotic situation annoyed him.

"Her judgment's not the problem. She's clever and capable and makes smart decisions when it comes to her detective work. I wouldn't be standing here otherwise. But..." Jasper heaved a sigh. "I allow, she takes some risky bets with her life."

"Which is why she needs someone to look out for her."

And he had tried, and damn near failed. The next time, she might not get so lucky. He took a deep breath and forced himself to abdicate the role. "It's a good thing she has you. You might have to tie her to the bed while she recuperates."

Hannah surprised him when she shook her head. "I have work to do. This criminal investigation has spilled over into a wholesale scandal. Powerful people will be looking for scapegoats. Brigit knows it's time for me to step in and do what I do best. Mop up."

Jasper paced in front of the woodpile. He hadn't imagined Brigit's twin would refuse. "What about your other sister or brother?"

"We don't want word to get out that a certain Miss Stevens is being tended by her family for a gunshot wound. Not after the newspapers reported what Frank told the judge. That the actress, Alice Robb, pulled the trigger. Reporters are inquiring about the woman in Fort Smith who was gunned down."

Kate had remained in seclusion, attempting to support the ruse that she'd been injured. But this area of town was busy. Even a trip to the outhouse would be noticed.

"What about Na's house?" Jasper asked.

"She's a well-known healer. Too many people seeking medicine come and go from there. We don't want anyone to make a connection between her and an unrelated white woman who's been shot. Gossip will spread," Hannah said bluntly.

Jasper swore. "Garrity shouldn't have risked her life with that story."

"It was the only way he could maintain his integrity and save you from being wrongfully convicted. I think it's rather brilliant."

"Except for the part where your sister could end up charged with murder."

The twin's countenance lost some of its high color. "Any such case brought against her would be flimsy, at best. One of the men named in the journal has already come forward with new information about the marshal's criminal activities. But we need time to sort this out. And Brigit needs peace and quiet to recuperate."

The band of fear squeezing Jasper's chest eased a little. It sounded like things were moving in the right direction. Brigit should've been safe with her family, but he could see that wasn't the case. Not until she could rejoin them without arousing suspicion.

He set the ax against the house, pulled a bandana out of his back pocket, and wiped his face. Who could he trust to keep her safe? Brigit trusted him. "I'll take her with me back to my cabin. It's in a remote area and I know how to guard it. My sister Sally can look after Brigit until she's well enough to go home."

Even if he couldn't hold onto Brigit forever, he could keep his most important promise. "I'll protect her."

CHAPTER 27

A *week later at Jasper's cabin*

Sometime in the night, Brigit awoke with Jasper stretched out beside her, his arm flung across her chest as if to defend her. In a recurring nightmare, a devil sent to drag her to hell looked like Stokes, except with her dead guardian's features. Her screams had awakened Jasper and the poor man had dragged himself out of his bedroll to soothe her. Just as he had the night before and the night before that.

Brigit turned to snuggle closer. It hurt less to move. She wasn't as cold anymore. She would never be cold as long as Jasper was there to warm her.

When she next opened her eyes, she was alone in bed.

Daylight drenched the cabin. Something smelled so delicious it stirred a rumble in her empty stomach. She rolled over and met an inquisitive gaze. The little girl wore a simple homespun dress not quite as brown as her eyes. Over the past week, Brigit had seen Jasper's niece playing in the cabin, but the child hadn't spoken to her.

"Rachel, let Miss Stevens be. She's sleeping." Sally called out from where she was seated next to the fireplace on the other side of the room.

The child flashed a shy smile before she spun and dashed out the door.

Brigit peeled off the covers. She slid her legs over the side of the bed, using her hands to steady herself while she waited for the dizziness to pass. "Where is Jasper?"

"Not far. He'll return soon," Sally replied.

Jasper certainly had the right to come and go as he pleased, but he had assured Brigit that he would be close by, should she need him. She had never needed anyone more than she needed Jasper. It was a little frightening to realize just how much.

"Be careful. Don't try to stand on your own." Sally set a skillet on the table. She wiped her hands on her apron as she crossed the room. "You'll be weak after being in bed for so long."

How long? Brigit made a face. "I can't recall when I last had a bath. I suppose that explains why Jasper fled."

Sally smiled politely. "He wanted to get some chores done. Why don't I bring you a plate of eggs? The boys finished their breakfast before you woke up, but I made more."

"The boys?" Brigit didn't think she would've missed the addition of more children.

"Tom and Candy. You remember them, don't you? Maybe you haven't noticed them because they've been sleeping in the barn, and they're on guard most of the time. Jasper told them to keep watch for strangers. Especially reporters."

Brigit rubbed her forehead. She could understand Jasper's concern about vengeful enemies, in particular, those listed in that journal, but he'd never mentioned a fear of newspapermen. "Why is he worried about reporters?

"If they find out you're here, they'll put it in the papers."

Ah. Now she remembered what he'd said about the rumors regarding the woman who was shot. If it wasn't safe for her to be here, why had he agreed to take her?

Brigit reached for a shawl someone had laid over the bed and pulled it around her shoulders. "I'm a liability for all of you."

"No more than Jasper is," Sally countered. "Besides, he knows this place and how to defend it. You're safer with him than with anyone else."

Brigit didn't need the reassurance of Jasper's protection. Even when they'd been facing imminent danger, she'd felt safe when he was near.

She pushed her hair away from her face and watched the door. He might be worried about her safety, but she was more concerned about his. "I recall the judge released Jasper on bond. Has anything else been decided?"

"If it has, we haven't gotten word yet." Sally went to the table and spooned up a plate of eggs, returning to offer it to Brigit. "Can you manage?"

"I believe so, thank you."

Brigit ate while Sally tidied up the kitchen. After she'd finished cleaning the dishes, she climbed the ladder to the loft where she and her daughter had been sleeping. Shortly, she returned with a stack of clothing—an oversized shirt, wrap-around skirt, and woven sash. "Your sister said these are for you."

Hannah perhaps meant it as a joke, but more likely she'd returned the comfortable clothing because of its practical—and sentimental—value to her twin.

Brigit reached for the articles Sally laid on the bed beside her. Jasper's sister must've washed them. She'd also done the cooking and chores, all while caring for a sick woman and dealing with her grief. "Did Jasper tell you about J.D.?"

Sally's expression grew somber. "He told me."

"I am sorry for your loss."

The younger woman quickly gazed in the direction of the front door, blinked, and wiped a tear. "It pains me to know he died in such a horrible way. But as for my loss..." she sighed. "I lost J.D. a long time ago. He was one of those men who couldn't find his way home."

Unlike Jasper.

Sally hadn't spoken the words aloud, but it was clear that was what she meant. Her brother had turned his life around. Jasper had found his way home, and those he loved were waiting here for him.

His sister had to wonder why he'd taken on an additional burden. If so, she didn't act as if she resented the imposition.

"I appreciate everything you've done for me, Sally."

"I'm happy to help." Sally placed a pair of moccasins beside the bed. "Considering what you've done for my brother, it's the least I can do."

"You might want to postpone your thanks until we hear what the courts have decided."

Sally's lips curved in a mysterious half-smile. "Is that what you thought I meant?"

What else could she mean? Unless it had something to do with Jasper forming an attachment. It might be Sally's way of saying she approved of her future sister-in-law. That sort of thinking might be a tad premature, considering how much remained to be resolved. At present, there was the small matter of bathing and getting dressed.

Brigit picked up the shirt and considered how far she could push herself. She hated to ask for more help. The washbasin wasn't far. Across the room. It was out in the open and no privacy would be afforded. She would make it work.

Jasper strode through the door with his niece fast on his heels. "I hear someone might be ready for a bath. The tub is on the porch, already filled. I strung up sheets to give you privacy."

"I'll add hot water to warm it." Sally went to the fireplace and retrieved a kettle.

Brigit watched the flurry of activity with astonishment. Had they read her mind? "That's so kind. Thank you."

The little girl edged closer and held out a bumpy cake of soap.

"Did your uncle recruit you to keep an eye on me and alert him when I woke up so he could prepare a bath?"

Rachel nodded. "He said you need it."

Jasper choked on a laugh. "I meant you'd appreciate it."

"Yes, and I'm sure everyone else will appreciate it, too." So, they hadn't read her mind, they'd smelled her. *How embarrassing.* More evidence that she was a burden. That would soon change. She would endeavor to get well and go to work on Jasper's behalf.

Jasper reached out his hand. "Do you want to walk or let me carry you?"

Brigit shifted forward to her test her weight. "I think I can—"

"Wrong answer." He swept her up in his arms.

Her face grew warm with all the attention focused on her. "Honestly, I can walk."

"Honestly, I'd rather carry you," he said in a low voice near her ear.

She put her arm around his neck rather than object and make a spectacle. In truth, she loved being held and would gladly remain in his arms for as long as he wished to hold her.

"Don't forget your clothes." Sally brought her the items.

Jasper carried Brigit to the porch. He ducked in between sheets tied to a crossbeam beneath the low-slung roof. The tin tub was barely large enough for her to squat down. But what did that matter? He'd hauled fresh water from the creek to provide her with a rare luxury, and she loved him all the more for his consideration.

She held onto his arm after he'd set her on her feet, still a little unsteady, but the dizziness had gone. "I can manage from here."

He kept his hold on her. "Are you sure?"

"Yes," she said firmly. She had burdened him enough. "I need to do this myself."

He left her clothes next to the towel. Only after he'd slipped between the curtains did she raise her hands to undo the tie at the neck of the nightgown.

After unwrapping the bandage, she studied the wound on her left side. Jasper had removed the stitches and it had scabbed over. Her ribs felt sore. They might take a little longer to heal. She could get around on her own in the meantime.

Hannah could help her put out this fire surrounding her identity. Making Alice Robb disappear wouldn't be as difficult as securing Jasper's permanent freedom, but no obstacle was insurmountable if one had a sound plan.

Brigit moved slowly as she stepped into the tub and lowered herself into the water. After she'd soaped her hands, she began to wash her hair. It would've been smarter to remain outside the tub and bend over it to soap and rinse her hair, but she didn't think she could do so without pain.

"Come with me, Rachel. We have work to do in the garden." Sally's voice came from the other side of the sheets, followed by her daughter's rapid footsteps.

"Do we have to go now?" the little girl whined.

"Yes. Now. And then we need to check the fish traps. Brigit, is there anything you need?"

A larger tub. Running water.

"No, thank you. I'll be fine."

JASPER APPROACHED the sheet concealing the bathtub and the woman in it. Sloshing sounds came from the other side, followed by a soft curse. He swallowed a laugh. Amusing as it was, he shouldn't have left Brigit alone, despite her claim to be able to manage.

"Can I be of assistance?" He tightened his grip on the bucket and waited for Brigit's answer. She might assume he only wanted to see her naked. He'd confess to always wanting that. But lust wasn't what motivated him this time. He wanted to do nice things for her. Shower her with affection. Indulge her—while he could.

"I could use some help rinsing my hair."

"Thought you might." Jasper stepped inside the makeshift curtain. "I've brought extra water and a pitcher."

"Thank you." Brigit crossed her arms over her chest in an endearing show of modesty. At the same time, she smiled with obvious relief.

He'd seen her uncovered, flushed, pale, bleeding, and there was no part of her he hadn't touched. Yet, her vulnerability touched him in a way no one else had, and it evoked a deep tenderness he never knew he possessed.

Jasper rolled up his sleeves and knelt next to the tub. He dipped the pitcher into the bucket to fill it with fresh water.

"I am a bit weak," she admitted. "And it's painful to lift my arm."

"They dug a bullet out of your side. When you lift your arm, it stretches the wound."

She twisted to examine the puckered skin under her arm below her left breast where a rib had deflected the slug that would've killed her, had it penetrated her chest cavity. A scenario that had been the stuff of his nightmares.

"I'm not usually such a baby about these things," she murmured.

"Have you been shot before?"

"No."

"You aren't being a baby. You're the strongest woman I've ever met. I've been in awe of you ever since you drugged the marshal and stole me off that train. I'm still in awe."

She gave a soft laugh, a sound between pleasure and disbelief. The blush that followed made her skin glow. "I certainly haven't been at my best lately."

"That's why you need to listen to me and do exactly as I say." Jasper cupped her chin and tilted her head. "Close your eyes," he instructed her.

He gave her a light kiss before he poured a pitcher of warm water over her hair. Using his fingers, he worked out the soap, rinsing her hair repeatedly, until it squeaked with cleanliness.

Who knew washing hair could be so arousing?

She seemed to be enjoying it too. Her lips were parted and her breathing had quickened. He loved that she couldn't hide her desire.

"Can I open my eyes now?"

"No. Not yet." He shifted her head against his shoulder. "Imagine I'm your servant."

Her lips twitched. "I never had servants."

"You have an imagination, right? Relax. Let me bathe you." Jasper plunged his arms into the water and took the soap she had clutched in her hand. After sliding it up her arm, he worked the slippery lather over her breasts. When his fingers brushed the hardened tips, she gasped.

He continued the slow, sensuous bathing, moving down her belly with circular motions, his hands ending up between her legs. Her breathing became more labored, with an occasional "ah" when he stroked just the right spot.

His sweet Brigit held nothing back. She gave herself to him, body and soul, damn the consequences. She was braver than him when it came to love.

After she'd found her release, he cradled her while her breathing slowed. He continued to hold her, despite the discomfort in his trousers, and, surprisingly, pain in his chest. It might have something to do with leaning against the side of a tub. Or the ache came from inside. Now, he understood what that phrase meant, to love someone so much it hurt.

Brigit shifted to her side and rested her head on his shoulder. He threaded his fingers through her hair, gently combing out the wet tangles. She released a contented sigh. "That was the loveliest bath I've ever had. Would you like for me to serve you?"

"We'd need a bigger tub."

"Or no tub at all. A bed would do..." She ran her hand along his forearm and over the wet sleeve. His muscles tensed at her touch. "If you remove your clothes, I'll—"

"You're not ready for that yet." He disentangled himself from her arms, picked up the towel, and held it in front of a telltale bulge. "I'll help you to dry off. We'll get you dressed and see how you manage walking."

Brigit stood, in all her naked glory. "I don't need to walk to ride you."

Jasper choked back a laugh. She'd transformed into a hoyden. His personal hoyden. "You might reinjure yourself."

"It would be worth it," she murmured.

He helped her out of the tub and wrapped her in the towel. Couldn't resist dropping kisses on her neck and shoulders. She tried to reciprocate, but he turned her around and knelt to dry her hips and legs.

This moment was about giving, not taking, which he'd been doing for most of his life.

She took the towel and tucked a corner under her arm. "Why are you allowed to kiss me, but I can't return the favor?"

"I didn't do this to curry favor. I did it because..." Because he couldn't help himself? Partly. "I wanted to give you a gift."

"Thank you." She put her arms around him in a hug. "Could I have another?"

"Not now."

He helped her dress. It was like wrapping a tempting morsel in fabric. Drawing her close, he brought the sash around her waist, being careful to avoid the injury.

"We can find a proper time and place later," she said against his shoulder.

"Nothing proper about it," he whispered in her ear. "But I look forward to a long goodbye."

CHAPTER 28

oodbye? Was Jasper joking?

His half-smile might've implied a jest, but the sadness in his eyes said otherwise.

Brigit placed her hands on his shoulders, to hold onto him more than needing support. "If I'm not dying, why do you think we'll be saying goodbye?"

"Well, at some point, it'll be safe enough for you to return home with your sister. I have to wait here until my case goes to court." His hands drifted to her waist before he released her and stepped away.

Moments ago, he'd given her the sweetest gift possible. And then...goodbye?

She couldn't panic. Not yet.

Maybe he only meant their parting would be for a short time. He'd taken a risk to bring her here, given that story about Alice Robb becoming headlines.

"If you're worried that we'll be found out, don't be. Hannah will set things up so it will be easier for me to return to Parsons without being questioned. After things calm down, I'll come back for you."

Even his smile became sad. "You've got this all figured out, don't you?"

"It seems fairly straightforward."

"Yeah. It does to me, too." Jasper heaved a sigh, though his frustration seemed reserved for him rather than her. "You know I'll likely end up in prison for robbery. You don't want to sit around here waiting for me, wasting your life. I don't want that for you, either."

Incredible. After what he'd done for her and he thought she couldn't exercise a little patience?

"Wasting my life? Is that what you call faithfulness? Besides, there's every chance they'll move your case to the Indian courts in front of a more sympathetic jury. You don't know how things will turn out. Let's wait and see."

He reached out and tucked a lock of her hair behind her hair with the tenderest touch. "I appreciate your optimism. But let me tell you how things turn out for women who fall in love with outlaws. They end up dead or they suffer. If they're lucky, they get away. But none of them escape without getting hurt. That's not the kind of life I want for you."

"You're not an outlaw. Not anymore."

"Yes, I am. No matter what I do, no one is going to let me or you forget that. Men like me destroy women like you. It's inevitable."

"It is *not* inevitable." The frantic pounding in her chest made breathing difficult. "You don't have to be a prisoner of your past, no more than your friend Jake. Do you think he destroyed Kate?"

"Their situation is different."

"Not that different. *We* can make a new life, together. Where there's a will, there's a way." She caught her breath. "I don't know who said that, but I believe it. You have to believe it, too."

He drew her into her arms and folded her against his chest. "I won't risk your life again, Brigit. You mean too much to me."

Why wasn't he listening?

"You mean the world to me, too, and I'm afraid for you. But I won't let fear stop me from loving you or being with you." She tightened her hold around his waist. "Oh, Jasper, please. Be strong enough to love me."

He took her arms and gently set her away from him. "Your sister told me she'd come after you as soon as you're well enough to travel and it's safe to do so. I'll let her know about your recovery."

The finality in his voice chilled Brigit's heart. If her pleas hadn't swayed him, arguments wouldn't either. Seduction wasn't out of the question, but he might expect that, and she wouldn't entrap him. What she needed was a plan. By engaging her mind, she wouldn't have to think about her heart and how he was breaking it.

"I'll go, then. It will relieve you from the burden of having to protect me here. Besides, I have things to do while Jake works on your case."

Jasper narrowed his eyes. "You'll stay out of trouble."

"That's impossible. If you want to keep me out of trouble, you'll have to come and do it yourself."

～

JASPER RECEIVED an answer to his letter a week later when Hannah arrived. Even knowing that sending Brigit away was the right thing to do, he almost didn't let her go. He wouldn't have, if not for the two Pinkerton agents accompanying Hannah. Extra protection, she called them.

She shared the good news about a flurry of arrests that had been made, including a witness to J.D.'s murder and the two men hired to kill Jasper while he was in jail. They had no word on when—or where—his future would be decided. This wasn't good news, but it did reaffirm his decision.

While Sally and Rachel showed their visitors a litter of newborn kittens in the barn, Jasper took Brigit aside on the porch to say goodbye. She'd traded her Choctaw finery for a stylish traveling suit, had put up her hair, and pinned on a straw hat at a jaunty angle. It made him wistful for the days when they'd pretended to be a fashionable married couple.

Did she intend to remind him? He wouldn't put it past her. She could be sneaky. Like that threat to make trouble. Hell, he could tie her to the bed and it wouldn't stop her. She'd get free and do as she damn well pleased.

He took her hands. One last touch. "Miss Stevens, you look good enough to eat."

She gave him a saucy smile. "Do you intend to partake, Mr. Byrne?"

Why the hell had he started flirting again? He'd already caused too much damage to her heart. "I'd better say goodbye before I get into trouble."

"Until we meet again."

He shook his head. They wouldn't meet again, but he couldn't manage to say it without losing his composure.

"Are you ready, Brigit?" Hannah stood beside the rented buggy.

Her bodyguards were dressed up in suits like Easterners. Maybe they meant to pose as suitors so that Brigit could return home without being under a cloud of suspicion.

Her smile wavered. "Write to me."

Writing might encourage her. No, a clean break was best.

He rubbed his chest. It hurt like hell.

"I'll be waiting," she said.

CHAPTER 29

*L*ess than an hour after Brigit had left, Jasper considered starting after them. He fought his weakness with work, chopping an enormous amount of wood that would take him six months to use.

Over the next week, he cut hay, replaced shingles on the roof, and built a new railing around the porch. Damn, he'd never been so industrious. It didn't banish his longing or nagging regret.

On the tenth day of his self-imposed exile, he'd finished a post hole and stopped to wipe the sweat from his eyes.

A man on horseback burst out of the woods into the clearing, riding at a fast clip.

Jasper reached for his gun before he recognized the visitor. *Jake.* No wonder Tom had let him pass. And coming at that speed had to mean he had news. What kind of news? Fast meant good, right. If it was bad, he'd be riding slower, less eager to deliver it.

Leaving his tools behind, Jasper broke into a dead run. By the time he reached the house, Jake had already stepped onto the porch and taken a seat in a rocking chair.

Sally handed their visitor a lemonade. She gave Jasper her

disappointed look. She'd been giving him that ever since she'd found out he decided to send Brigit away.

Still breathing heavily, Jasper plopped into the adjacent rocker. "Any news?"

Jake removed his hat. "Glad to see you, too. Have you heard from Miss Stevens?"

Now, why would Jake start with that question?

"She left a couple of weeks ago with her sister."

"Sorry to hear that."

"So am I," Sally called from inside the cabin. "And he hasn't gone to check the mail!"

"Enough of that," Jasper hollered. He shifted his attention to his friend, ready to get down to business and already dreading it. "Good news or bad news?"

"You can read about it or I can give you a summary." Jake handed over a folded newspaper.

Jasper stared at *The Cherokee Advocate.* Sure, he could read it, but he didn't want to. If it was bad news, he'd rather hear it firsthand so he could brace himself for the worst. "Give me the blasted summary."

Jake stopped rocking. "You are grouchier than a bear fresh out of hibernation."

"Don't start on me," Jasper grumbled, as he opened the paper. He stopped at a headline.

Falsely accused citizen cleared after Federal investigation

The article was written in Cherokee and English, and he could read both, but he couldn't believe it was *him* they were writing about, except his name was in the first paragraph. "What the hell is this?"

"Ah, you want the summary. Federal authorities have determined that Marshal Stokes was guilty of murder, as well as multiple other crimes, including bribery. You refused to cooperate with him, so he set you up and tried to kill you. The intrepid reporter Miss Robb, having fallen in love with you, protecting you. No one is quite certain what happened to her, though there is some speculation she was killed by one of the marshal's cronies. A barkeeper in Muskogee claims to have found her scalp."

"Very funny." Jasper read the article for himself.

He leaned back in his chair, stunned. If there hadn't been a byline, he would've thought Brigit had written it as a joke, tossing in a few grains of truth for authenticity. Mostly it read like something from a dime novel. "Who came up with this story?"

"I forget, you haven't been around politicians." Jake the lawyer made it sound like some important part of Jasper's education had been missed.

"What about the robbery charge?"

"The MK&T withdrew their complaint. Lacking evidence, the case was dismissed. There's no need for a trial. And no need for you to take the stand and tell everything you know."

That last bit explained it.

Jasper released a pent-up breath. He understood backroom bargaining. "They want to buy my silence. Is that it?"

"They want to make sure a few select names listed in the journal don't make it into the newspapers. Grant's administration doesn't need another scandal."

"What names? The judge?"

"He's been transferred somewhere he can't make trouble. It's hard to get rid of political appointees, so they just move them around like pawns on a chessboard."

"What about Bond?"

"Charged with two counts of bribery."

"That's all?"

Jake took a long swig of lemonade before he answered. "Mr. Bond has agreed to cooperate with a broader investigation into the railroad's finances."

"So, he gets a slap on the wrist?" Jasper gave a disgusted huff. "Who made this deal? You?"

"Federal prosecutors."

"Figures."

Jake set the empty glass on the porch. "The authorities have rounded up a gang of cattle rustlers. A big operation involving outlaws, several businesses, and a few politicians. Pinkerton is taking the credit for busting it open."

Because of Brigit's hard work. They couldn't put her name in the papers or it would end her undercover career. Too bad she couldn't get the credit she deserved.

Jasper rested his hands on his knees and released a long sigh. He sat there another moment before it sank in. He was a free man. No trial. No jail time. No consequences. "I didn't expect mercy."

"Oh, I wouldn't call it mercy," Jake replied. "A lucky break, maybe."

"I've never been lucky."

"Is that so?" Jake turned in his chair, dropping his friendly expression. "I'd say you're a lucky man. Or you might be a damn fool. Hard to tell at this point."

The remark roused Jasper out of his stupor. Fate hadn't kicked him into the dirt again. He had a chance to start over. Partly on account of the hard work his friend, the lawyer, had put in. He wouldn't discount that. But mostly because of what Brigit had done. She'd taken a washed-up train robber and had redeemed him.

Jasper rubbed his stinging eyes. "Do you think Brigit knows they let me off the hook?"

"I suspect everyone does. It's been in all the newspapers. The stories are pretty much the same. I picked up a few as souvenirs." Jake reached into a satchel next to the chair and removed another paper, which he held out. "This one's from Denison."

"Keep it," Jasper said. "I don't need a souvenir."

He only wanted one thing, which he'd given up. If Brigit knew he was free and hadn't come after him, she might've decided he wasn't worth the effort.

Jasper raked his fingers through his hair with a shaky sigh. "She might not want me. I wounded her and sent her away."

"Miss Stevens seems the forgiving type," Jake mused.

Did he deserve her forgiveness? Jasper knew the answer to that. *No.* No more than he deserved to be free.

He shifted to the edge of the chair. Could she be happy here with him? He couldn't see her settling down in the middle of nowhere as the wife of a poor farmer. Deriving joy from planting and harvesting corn, beans, and squash. Going out to find the nests and collect eggs. Milking the cow in the predawn, stoking the fire, preparing dinners. Sally did all that and had a good attitude about it. She loved this farm. But Brigit loved her detective work and craved adventure.

"What do I have to offer her, Jake? I'm poor as Job's turkey. I'm no good at farming. I don't possess skills most employers would deem useful."

"That's true."

Jasper gave his *friend* a sharp look. "You don't have to agree so readily."

For some reason, Jake found the retort funny. "Have you forgotten? I grew up with less than you have. You'll recall we were both outlaws together once."

The comparison was still weak.

"You were never a good outlaw. Didn't stick with it long enough."

"No. Being infamous wasn't my aim. But I'd chosen a path, like yours, that should've ended at the gallows." Jake's expression lost all trace of humor. "Kate Parsons came along and offered me a chance for a better life. If I was willing to take the risk."

"That she might not love you?"

"No, that she would, and I wouldn't deserve it."

"There's the difference. You earned your position."

"I didn't earn Redbird's love," Jake said. "She gave it to me when I had nothing and deserved nothing. It was up to me to accept it."

Jasper sat there stunned at how simple it sounded when put that way. Could it be?

What were the last words Brigit had said?

I'll be waiting.

CHAPTER 30

*B*rigit folded an old *Wanted* poster that featured a grainy photograph of an angry youth posing with an assortment of guns to reinforce his fierce, mostly fictional, reputation. She slid it into a newspaper with a more current article about the outlaw's unexpected turnabout and his well-deserved release. They could've been two different men, based on the descriptions, but she knew better. She also knew which was the real one and which was the fake. If only Jasper would acknowledge the difference.

With a sigh, she placed the paper inside her satchel and closed it.

She gazed around the empty bedroom she'd shared with Hannah. The personal articles they'd brought with them three months ago had been tucked away into two trunks and two suitcases, which were already downstairs. The mattress was stripped of linens, dresser and wardrobe emptied, tables cleared of the few items they'd put out, mostly old family pictures. The bedroom looked as deserted and forlorn as she felt.

Their apartment over the photography studio had been comfortable, though it wasn't home. A brownstone in Chicago was their permanent residence. Still, she felt like she was leaving home behind because it wasn't a building. Home was a person. Without him, she felt adrift.

"Brigit? Do you need help?" Her sister called up the stairs. "The wagon is here to take us to the station...and a strong man is willing to assist us."

A strong man. Brigit's heart thudded hard. Could it be?

She grabbed her satchel and hurried down the stairs toward what she hoped would be her future happiness. The man who met her at the bottom wasn't Jasper.

"Henry!"

Her big brother gathered her into his arms and hugged her. Warm, not too tight, then a quick release. It gave her time to replace her disappointment with excitement.

"It's so good to see you. Where's Lucy?"

"At the station with little Ginny and the rest of our clan. They're waiting to bid you adieu." Henry's eyes, the same brown as hers, pulled slightly downward in sadness. But then he perked up. Their shifting moods seemed to be linked. "You appear much improved from the last time I saw you at the Colston's house."

He'd been there?

"How is it I don't remember seeing you?"

Henry's lips, framed inside a neat beard, twisted into a wry smile. "I'm forgettable?"

Her tall, handsome brother, with his commanding looks and presence, was hardly *forgettable*. "That must've been when I was in a stupor."

He took her hands and held them out from her side while he made a quick examination. "You are healthy and full of life now. That's a lovely gown."

"Thank you." Brigit stepped back and tugged at her jacket, somewhat self-conscious about her thinner frame. The identical traveling suit, with its gold and brown stripes, looked better on Hannah. "I should fill it out, at some point."

"First, you must eat more," Hannah informed her. "I've ordered legal steak for our dinner on the train." She exchanged a glance with their brother.

An inside joke between them? That would be a first.

"Rather than *illegal* steak? I assume that is in some reference to the cattle rustling operation."

"Our brother unraveled the financial web created to facilitate the purchase and movement of stolen cattle. His diligent efforts have given the investigators what they needed to strengthen their case against Mr. Bond and his associates." Hannah paused, dramatically. "Henry is too bashful to tell you."

Brigit laughed.

Henry only smiled. "Mr. Bond won't be able to slither away this time."

Jasper would be pleased to know. She would write him. Although thus far, he hadn't answered her letters, not even after she'd received word the charges against him were dismissed.

Her heart urged her to go after the man she wanted, but a wiser voice bade her wait. They would find no happiness together unless Jasper let go of the past and his guilt, and faced his fears as bravely as he'd faced their enemies.

Brigit took her brother's arm and smiled up at him, proudly. "You'd make a good Pinkerton, brother."

Poor Henry looked alarmed. "Oh, no. I'm much more suited to building and operating railroads, as Lucy will tell you."

"Perhaps we'll find someone better suited to the job," Hannah added, with a slightly mysterious air.

Brigit's spirits sagged. Her sister was trying to lighten them, but the reminder of conversations they'd had about the possibilities for Jasper's future made the day gloomier. What future could there be if he wouldn't show up to claim it?

She held onto her hat to prevent it from being taken away when she stepped out into the brisk Kansas wind. She longed to be in her unrestrained clothing, with her hair loose, wearing moccasins. That would certainly shock the office if she returned in what had become her favorite garb.

Henry helped her into the wagon, then Hannah, who put an arm around her in a gentle hug. "Dearest, he's an idiot. Not worth your tears."

Was she crying? Brigit wiped the evidence from her cheek. "Henry isn't an idiot."

"You know who I'm talking about."

"Neither is Jasper."

"That remains to be seen."

Henry clucked at the mules and started toward the impressive railroad station that anchored the end of a wide street. Her brother had laid out, designed, and overseen the building of the Katy headquarters, as well as the railroad. Then the accusations had started—fraud, theft, even murder. He'd been innocent of wrongdoing, but the scandal had destroyed his career. He had worked hard and bravely to build a new life for himself and for the woman he loved him madly.

Jasper could do the same. Brigit didn't doubt his strength or courage. It was his love for her she'd started wondering about.

The skies were blue, the air fresh, a beautiful summer day. People were out on the sidewalks, gathered in groups. Probably still gossiping about the cattle-rustling ring and a certain outlaw's courageous role in bringing down a dirty marshal. These fickle farmers had changed their tune after reading newspaper accounts about the case.

Her sister-in-law Lucy waited at the doorway to the railway station. After an affectionate greeting, she handed over her baby, the spitting image of her golden-haired mother. Brigit snuggled the sweet little girl before giving her to Hannah.

"Take a look at this." Lucy's eagerness fairly bubbled out of her when she handed Brigit a local newspaper. "When you have some free time on the train ride, read the latest installment of *Lace and Steele*. I took your suggestion about a new direction, and I think it's perfect. Bran the outlaw, transformed into a hero. My editor thinks Bran could have his own series."

Brigit swallowed the lump in her throat before responding with a dry reply. "Jasper would be appalled. He prefers to see himself as an outlaw."

Lucy gazed at her with puzzlement. "You don't believe that, do you?"

"No, I don't believe that. Jasper does."

Hannah returned their niece, somewhat reluctantly it appeared, then slipped her arm around Brigit's waist. "Come along. Let's find the rest of the family." She whispered the next remark. "You are beginning to sound cynical."

"I'll endeavor to be hopeful and full of optimism."

"*If* that rascal shows up, I may throw him under the train," Hannah said, under her voice.

Frank and Claire waited on the platform, along with their three boys. There were hugs all around, and kisses, except for Billy, who stood off to one side and acted as if he didn't need either. Like most boys his age.

Billy removed his engineer's hat before offering her his hand. The wind blew strands of red-blonde hair into his eyes. "Aunt Hannah, I've been thinking I might become a detective like you. That is if the railroad doesn't hire me when I'm eighteen."

"The Pinkerton agency would welcome a sharp young man." Hannah took his hand, shook it, then bent down and placed a quick kiss on his cheek.

The boy blushed to the tips of his ears.

Gideon Branch had been standing off to one side near the ticket window. He waited until the family had finished their goodbyes before he approached.

He held out his hand to Brigit. "Miss, I wanted to wish you well."

Passengers around them slid sideways glances that conveyed disapproval and judgment. As a dark-skinned man, Gideon encountered this kind of relentless prejudice all the time. Yet, he'd succeeded despite it. And so would Jasper. With or without her.

Brigit reached for her friend's hand and shook it. "Thank you, Mr. Branch. I hear you've been named U.S. Deputy Marshal for the Indian Territory. You are the best man for the job."

"I appreciate that high praise. Especially coming from you." Gideon tipped his hat. "Keep yourself safe."

"And you also." Brigit continued to scan the platform. She'd given Jasper details about her departure—if he'd read her last letter.

The small flame of hope she'd kept alive flickered.

Discouraged, she boarded the train to take her seat, not feeling up to conversing. One way she and Hannah were different. Her twin was more outgoing and would continue talking until the last whistle.

While Brigit looked out the window, a man stopped at the empty seat next to her. He didn't say a word, only flicked back his coat as he sat down with his hat still on his head, showing no manners whatsoever. His holstered gun pressed against her hip.

As she turned to tell him the seat was taken, he shifted the wide brim upward and gave her a wry smile. Her breath caught in her throat.

"Jasper," she managed in a wispy voice.

As he removed the hat, he smoothed his dark hair, which he hadn't cut. His face was unshaven and lined with fatigue. He wore a layer of dust over his clothing, which would indicate he'd ridden into town, jumped off his horse, and dashed for the train.

She clutched her hands in her lap to restrain herself from touching him. No longer would she throw herself at the aggravating man. This time, it was his move. "Did you follow a herd on the way into town?"

His amused gaze met her serious one. "Only a small one. I'm practicing to become a cowboy. Your sister suggested it."

She eyed the scarf tied around his neck above the open shirt collar, which revealed a tantalizing slice of brown skin glistening with sweat. "You wouldn't make a good cowboy."

"That's what I told her."

"You are a heartless cad for making me think you weren't coming to see me off."

His teasing smile faded. "That may be true, the part about being a heartless cad, but I haven't come to see you off. I've come to fetch you before you get away from me. In case you're wondering, I love you."

Emotions ricocheted inside her chest: relief, happiness, anger, so many, she couldn't sort them out and gave up trying.

"It took long enough for you to get around to saying it," she managed, without her voice cracking.

He used his thumb to tenderly wipe a tear from her cheek. "Forgive me?"

"What for?" She leaned in for a kiss.

He held the back of her neck while he kissed her with heart-pounding passion, extinguishing every doubt she had about his love for her. By the time he let go, they had the attention of everyone in the car.

Jasper shifted off the seat. He went down on one knee in the aisle and his dark green eyes filled with what she'd longed to see in them. Hope. "You once said you intended to arrange a second chance for me. Is that offer still good?"

"It is," she gasped, breathless from his soul-stirring kiss.

"Will you marry me, Miss Stevens?"

"Say yes!" a woman shouted.

The departure whistle sounded.

Brigit scooted off the bench and embraced him. "Yes, you rascal. Only you would wait until the last possible moment to ask."

He lifted her for a big hug to the delight of the passengers, who applauded. After he'd set her on her feet, he swept off his hat and made a grand bow.

Someone tossed a coin and it landed in his hat.

"Thank you." He turned to a plump gentleman in the seat across from them and held out his hat. "Maybe you'd like to turn out your pockets. For the poor."

The passengers laughed, even the staid gentleman. "Certainly." The good-natured fellow dropped a handful of coins into Jasper's dusty hat.

"I'll contribute," shouted a woman. She couldn't get to her bag fast enough.

Jasper, the charmer, held Brigit's hand while he walked up to the front of the car, accepting more coins in his hat and thanking the passengers graciously. He was in fine form in his Robin Hood role, which he played to the hilt.

When he reached the door, he checked inside the hat and gave the donors his most winning smile. "The poor thank you!" he announced, then spoke an aside to Brigit. "Do you think they know that means us?"

He was joking, but just in case. "Jasper, we *will* give this money to charity."

They exited the car and met her sister on the steps. Family and friends were gathered on the platform behind her.

"What are you doing?" Hannah demanded of Jasper.

"Stealing your sister off this train." His tone sounded menacing.

Hannah didn't back down. "Why should she marry you?"

Brigit decided she would like to hear that answer too.

"My wealth," Jasper jangled the coins in the hat. "And my natural charm, winning personality...oh, and I happen to love her."

"That's good enough for me," Brigit said. "I love him too. Now, will you let us by?"

The train sent out a last burst of steam before it shuddered and began to move.

Hannah held onto the rail and stepped up instead of down. "I have a better idea. Mr. Pinkerton needs another detective. One who has experience with railroad thievery. He was impressed with Mr. Byrne's contributions to the Kinkaid case. Why not bring Jasper to Chicago with us? See if he's got what it takes."

Brigit had considered this, of course, but had planned to bring it up later, when Jasper would have time to think about it. Would he up and leave the land of his mother's people and trade the familiar for the unknown?

Her relatives walked alongside the slow-moving train toward the end of the platform. They might be watching to see whether Jasper would leap off the train. She scanned their faces: Henry's anxious, Lucy looking pleased, Claire worried, and Frank... Who could tell what he was thinking? He waved and walked off toward Gideon, who had a smile on his face.

301

Brigit hugged Jasper's arm. "Well, what do you say? Can you stick to investigating crimes instead of committing them?"

"Hm, that's a tough one." He reached around her waist, gazing out over the passing landscape as if to catch one last glimpse of the western skies. "Where there's a will, there's a way. Isn't that what you told me?" He leaned down to kiss her and whispered. "Guess you'll have to trust me."

∾

JASPER AND BRIGIT'S *story concludes* Steam! Romance & Rails, *but it isn't the end. You can read more stories that branch off from this series like interconnected railroad lines. See the list here.*

MORE FROM E.E. BURKE

*Keep reading **Steam! Romance and Rails** for more dark deceits, daring heroes, and scorching love stories.*
Her Bodyguard
Redbird
A Dangerous Passion
Fugitive Hearts
Lawless Hearts

Find out what happens to a train-load of women who sign up with the railroad to become brides.
The Bride Train Series
Valentine's Rose
Patrick's Charm
Tempting Prudence
Seducing Susannah

Two storekeepers compete for more than business when a mail-order bride arrives in the same town where the Steam! series began. You might recognize some of the residents.
Victoria Bride of Kansas

Santa's Mail Order Bride
Also on Audible

Enjoy more Western romance in the Rockies
Jolie, A Valentine's Day Bride
The Drum (Twelve Days of Christmas Mail-Order Brides)

Set off on romantic adventures in two original novels inspired by the works of Mark Twain
Tom Sawyer Returns
Taming Huck Finn

RESEARCH NOTES

As in other Steam! novels, real historical events form the basis for a suspenseful plotline in *Lawless Hearts*.

In 1871, President Ulysses S. Grant appointed William Story as district judge for the federal district court for Western Arkansas, which included what was then Indian Territory (modern-day Oklahoma). Both the size of the region—over seventy-four thousand square miles—and the presence of Native American courts, whose jurisdiction extended only to tribe members, complicated federal law enforcement efforts and led to lax oversight. This resulted in criminals from surrounding states fleeing into the Territory to take advantage of the situation.

To make matters worse, greed and corruption turned the rule of law into something that could be bought and sold. Ultimately, the judge and several Deputy U.S. Marshals were implicated in a system of graft, including bribery and kickbacks. Judge Story resigned before impeachment proceedings were started.

During this same period, the railroads were beset with a parade of self-serving owners and managers, some of whom were downright scoundrels. Add to this a growing problem with cattle rustling, as the shipping of beef became big business, and you have a recipe for trouble...and an exciting story.

I also took inspiration from the history of the Pinkerton Agency and the country's first female detective, Kate Warne. According to Pinkerton's records, she convinced the progressive founder that women could be "most useful in worming out secrets in many places which would be impossible for a male detective." She often went undercover, wore disguises, changed her accent at will, and became a huge asset to the agency. Because of her success, Alan Pinkerton hired other females and he appointed Warne as their supervisor, a position she held until her untimely death in 1868.

I hope you have enjoyed the *Steam! Romance and Rails* series, and the journey back into an exciting era in America's history. Although that time is far behind us, it left an indelible mark that helped shape our country into who and what we are today.

E.E. Burke

ABOUT THE AUTHOR

E.E. Burke is a bestselling author of historical fiction and romances that combine her unique blend of wit and warmth. Her books have been nominated for numerous national and regional awards, including Booksellers' Best, National Readers' Choice, and Kindle Best Book. She was also a finalist in the RWA's prestigious Golden Heart® contest. Over the years, she's been a disc jockey, a journalist, and an advertising executive, before finally getting around to living the dream--writing stories readers can get lost in.

Find out more about her books at her website: www.eeburke.com.